Extraordinary acclaim for

Case
Histories

"Addictive. . . . Atkinson writes such fluid, sparkling prose that an ingenious plot almost seems too much to ask, but we get it anyway. If Lorrie Moore decided to write a genre-busting detective novel it might resemble *Case Histories*."   — Laura Miller, Salon.com

"Atkinson is very good indeed. . . . *Case Histories* is essentially a balancing act, with evil and ignorance stacked opposite truth and healing. In this aspect the book is more satisfying than many detective novels — not just because it is so well written, but in its defiant refusal to let the dark side win. . . . Everyone who picks it up will feel compelled to follow it through to the last page."
                                                    — *Guardian*

"Like Donna Tartt in *The Little Friend,* Atkinson here combines a compelling narrative drive with sophisticated psychological portraits and telling detail. . . . Playful humor, an impressive technique, and an offbeat detective with a penchant for weeping are the most obvious pleasures of a page-turner that succeeds in being both brainy and thoroughly entertaining."   — *Booklist* (starred review)

"The lifelike characters in *Case Histories* are what make it such a compelling hybrid; part complex family drama, part mystery. . . . Plot-driven as *Case Histories* is, it works because Ms. Atkinson sets up her surprises so well."   — Janet Maslin, *New York Times*

"Thrilling. . . . Atkinson has many strengths as a writer. She is an erudite and witty prose stylist. Her plotting is deft and rich."
                            — Sharon Dilworth, *Pittsburgh Post-Gazette*

"An amazing performance. . . . A family chronicle and thriller all at once. . . . This is a novel that looks at murder and the profound loss that accompanies it with an unusually clear eye."
— Roberta Silman, *Boston Globe*

"A compelling page-turner that explores the fine line between love and obsession, grief and recovery, guilt and redemption. . . . This ingeniously crafted modern-day suspense narrative combines elements of a traditional detective novel with riveting psychological character studies. . . . *Case Histories* propels the reader forward with a rare intensity and compassion." — Joni Rendon, *Bookpage*

"This dark novel is also delightful, fascinating, and bitingly funny to read. Atkinson has brought to life a marvelously diverse cast of unforgettable characters." — Jennifer Reese, *Entertainment Weekly*

"Atkinson is delightfully wicked. . . . This is a rich, exciting, gorgeously written novel — quite possibly the best of the year."
— Kit Reed, *Hartford Courant*

"Although solutions and surprises abound, in *Case Histories* Atkinson is less interested in detailing the steps of an investigation than in exploring the rough and tumble that happens along the way. Her humor — and she is a very funny writer — is the sort that comes from being able to see the way happiness and sadness can emerge from the same situation. Her reach is certainly long enough to touch cruelty and grief, but it also extends far in the opposite direction — all the way to joy."
— Jacqueline Carey, *New York Times Book Review*

"Hard to put down. . . . *Case Histories* gleams with the quiet confidence of a literary star on the rise."
— Elisabeth Egan, *Chicago Sun-Times*

"Atkinson is a master plot juggler. Here, handling half a dozen story lines, she writes about such minefield topics as child molestation, incest, and mental illness with compassion and gentle humor. . . . Is it too much to hope that we haven't seen the last of this singular sleuth?" — Vick Boughton, *People*

"The pleasures of this novel are many. . . . *Case Histories* stands out as a wistful, heartbreaking novel about real disasters. Ultimately, it's a novel with a deep understanding of the fragility of existence and the will to survive." — Timothy Peters, *San Francisco Chronicle*

"Rich . . . abundantly inclusive, smartly rendered, somehow plaintive yet rollicking. . . . The case histories of *Case Histories* include not only disappearances and murders, but all the old English detective novels Kate Atkinson has ever read and enjoyed. And just as the Whitbread Award–winning writer has inventively conjured up Borges, Mary Poppins, and Ovid in previous books, she begins to conjure up all manner of elements from the detective genre in a mix of (mainly understated) send-up and admiration." — John Glassie, *The Believer*

"Atkinson's mysteries are as satisfying as anything dreamed up by Raymond Chandler." — Joanna Smith Rakoff, *Time Out New York*

"If *Case Histories* were a typical crime novel, it would be an entertaining adventure resting solely on some bizarre plot twists. But Atkinson draws her characters to some depth, and in revealing their flaws and motivations achieves a richer, more satisfying result. . . . One knows that happy endings will be elusive but still hopes the characters will find salvation. This most human of needs, driven by a search for answers and illuminated by lively writing, elevate *Case Histories* above a potboiler crime novel and renders it a small work of art." — Robin Vidimos, *Denver Post*

Case Histories

A

Novel

KATE ATKINSON

BACK BAY BOOKS

Little, Brown and Company

New York Boston

For Anne McIntyre

Back Bay Books / Little, Brown and Company
Hachette Book Group
1290 Avenue of the Americas, New York, NY 10104
littlebrown.com

Originally published in the U.S. in hardcover by
Little, Brown and Company, November 2004
First Back Bay paperback edition, October 2005

Back Bay Books is an imprint of Little, Brown and Company, a division of
Hachette Book Group, Inc. The Back Bay Books name and logo are trademarks of
Hachette Book Group, Inc.

The publisher is not responsible for websites (or their content)
that are not owned by the publisher.

The characters and events in this book are fictitious.
Any similarity to real persons, living or dead, is
coincidental and not intended by the author.

Originally published in Great Britain by Doubleday

The interview with Kate Atkinson reprinted in the reading group guide at the back of this
book originally appeared in Publishers Weekly on October 25, 2004. Copyright © 2004 by
Reed Business Information, a division of Reed Elsevier Inc. All rights reserved.

Library of Congress Cataloging-in-Publication Data
Atkinson, Kate.
    Case histories : a novel / by Kate Atkinson. — 1st American Ed.
        p.   cm.
    ISBN 9780316740401 (hc) / 9780316010702 (pb)
    1. Fate and fatalism — Fiction.   2. Loss (Psychology) — Fiction.   I. Title.
PR6051.T56C37 2004
823'.914 — dc22   2004002379

Printing 35, 2024

LSC–C

Book design by JoAnne Metsch

Printed in the United States of America

Ye shall know the truth, and the truth

shall make you free.

JOHN 8:32

Case Histories

CASE HISTORY NO. 1 1970

Family Plot

How lucky were they? A heat wave in the middle of the school holidays, exactly where it belonged. Every morning the sun was up long before they were, making a mockery of the flimsy summer curtains that hung limply at their bedroom windows, a sun already hot and sticky with promise before Olivia even opened her eyes. Olivia, as reliable as a rooster, always the first to wake, so that no one in the house had bothered with an alarm clock since she was born three years ago.

Olivia, the youngest and therefore the one currently sleeping in the small back bedroom with the nursery-rhyme wallpaper, a room that all of them had occupied and been ousted from in turn. Olivia, as cute as a button they were all agreed, even Julia, who had taken a long time to get over being displaced as the baby of the family, a position she had occupied for five satisfying years before Olivia came along.

Rosemary, their mother, said that she wished Olivia could stay at this age forever because she was so *lovable*. They had never heard her use that word to describe any of them. They had not even realized that such a word existed in her vocabulary, which was usually restricted to tedious commands: *come here, go away, be quiet,* and — most frequent of all — *stop that.* Sometimes she would walk into a room or appear in the garden, glare at them, and say, *Whatever it is you're doing, don't,* and then simply walk away again, leaving them feeling aggrieved and badly done by, even when caught red-handed in the middle of some piece of mischief — devised by Sylvia usually.

Their capacity for wrongdoing, especially under Sylvia's reckless leadership, was apparently limitless. The eldest three were (everyone agreed) "a handful," too close together in age to be distinguishable to their mother so that they had evolved into a collective child to which she found it hard to attribute individual details and which she addressed at random — *Julia-Sylvia-Amelia-whoever you are* — said in an exasperated tone as if it were their fault there were so many of them. Olivia was usually excluded from this weary litany; Rosemary never seemed to get her mixed up with the rest of them.

They had supposed Olivia would be the last of the four to occupy the small back bedroom and that one day the nursery-rhyme wallpaper would finally be scraped off (by their harassed mother because their father said hiring a professional decorator was a waste of money) and be replaced by something more grown-up — flowers or perhaps ponies, although anything would be better than the Elastoplast pink adorning the room that Julia and Amelia shared, a color that had looked so promising to the two of them on the paint chart and proved so alarming on the walls and which their mother said she didn't have the time or money (or *energy*) to repaint.

Now it transpired that Olivia was going to be undertaking the same rite of passage as her older sisters, leaving behind the — rather badly aligned — Humpty Dumptys and Little Miss Muffets to make way for an *afterthought* whose advent had been announced, in a rather offhand way, by Rosemary the previous day as she dished out on the lawn a makeshift lunch of corned beef sandwiches and orange squash.

"Wasn't Olivia the afterthought?" Sylvia said to no one in particular, and Rosemary frowned at her eldest daughter as if she had just noticed her for the first time. Sylvia, thirteen and until recently an enthusiastic child (many people would have said overenthusiastic), promised to be a mordant cynic in her teenage years. Gawky, bespectacled Sylvia, her teeth recently caged in ugly orthodontic braces, had greasy hair, a hooting laugh, and the long, thin fingers and toes of an alien from outer space. Well-meaning people called her an "ugly duckling" (said to her face, as if it were a compliment, which was certainly not how it was taken by Sylvia), imagining a future Sylvia casting off her braces, acquiring contact lenses and a bosom, and blossoming into a swan. Rosemary did not see the swan in Sylvia, especially when she had a shred of corned beef stuck in her braces. Sylvia had recently developed an unhealthy obsession with religion, claiming that God had spoken to her (as if God would choose Sylvia). Rosemary wondered if it was a normal phase that adolescent girls went through, if God was merely an alternative to pop stars or ponies. Rosemary decided it was best to ignore Sylvia's tête-à-têtes with the Almighty. And at least conversations with God were free, whereas the upkeep on a pony would have cost a fortune.

And the peculiar fainting fits that their GP said were on account of Sylvia "outgrowing her strength" — a medically dubious explanation if ever there was one (in Rosemary's opinion). Rosemary decided to ignore the fainting fits as well. They were probably just Sylvia's way of getting attention.

Rosemary married their father, Victor, when she was eighteen years old — only five years older than Sylvia was now. The idea that Sylvia might be grown-up enough in five years' time to marry anyone struck Rosemary as ridiculous and reinforced her belief that her own parents should have stepped in and stopped her from marrying Victor, should have pointed out that she was a mere child and he was a thirty-six-year-old man. She often found herself wanting to remonstrate with her mother and father about their lack of parental care, but her mother had succumbed to stomach cancer not long after Amelia was born, and her father had remarried and moved to Ipswich, where he spent most of his days in the bookies and all of his evenings in the pub.

If, in five years' time, Sylvia brought home a thirty-six-year-old, cradle-snatching fiancé (particularly if he claimed to be a great mathematician), then Rosemary would probably cut his heart out with the carving knife. This idea was so agreeable that the *afterthought*'s annunciation was temporarily forgotten and Rosemary allowed them all to run out to the ice-cream van when it declared its own melodic arrival in the street.

The Sylvia-Amelia-Julia trio knew that there was no such thing as an *afterthought,* and the "fetus," as Sylvia insisted on calling it (she was keen on science subjects), that was making their mother so irritable and lethargic was probably their father's last-ditch attempt to acquire a son. He was not a father who doted on daughters, he showed no real fondness for any of them, only Sylvia occasionally winning his respect because she was "good at maths." Victor was a mathematician and lived a rarefied life of the mind, where his family was allowed no trespass. This was made easy by the fact that he spent hardly any time with them. He was either in the department or his rooms in college, and when he was home he shut himself in his study, occasionally with his students but usually on his own. Their father had never taken them to the open-air pool on Jesus Green, played rousing games of Snap or Donkey, never tossed them in the air and caught them or pushed them on a swing, had never taken them punting on the river or walking on the Fens or on educational trips to the Fitzwilliam. He seemed more like an absence than a presence: everything he was — and was not — was represented by the sacrosanct space of his study.

They would have been surprised to know that the study had once been a bright parlor with a view of the back garden, a room where previous occupants of the house had enjoyed pleasant breakfasts, where women had whiled away the afternoons with sewing and romantic novels, and where, in the evenings, the family had gathered to play cribbage or Scrabble while listening to a radio play. All these activities had been envisaged by a newly married Rosemary when the house was first bought — in 1956, at a price way beyond their budget — but Victor immediately claimed the room as his own and somehow managed to transform it into a sunless place, crammed with heavy bookshelves and ugly oak filing cabinets and reeking of the untipped Capstans that he smoked. The loss of the room was as nothing to the loss of the way of life that Rosemary had planned to fill it with.

What he actually did in there was a mystery to all of them. Something so important, apparently, that his home life was trifling in comparison. Their mother said he was *a great mathematician,* at work on a piece of research that would one day make him *famous,* yet on the rare occasions when the study door was left open and they caught a glimpse of their father at work, all he seemed to be doing was sitting at his desk, scowling into empty space.

He was not to be disturbed when he was working, especially not by shrieking, screaming, savage little girls. The complete inability of those same savage little girls to abstain from the shrieking and the screaming (not to mention the yelling, the blubbering, and the strange howling like a pack of wolves that Victor had never managed to fathom) made for a fragile relationship between father and daughters.

Rosemary's chastisements may have washed over them like water, but the sight of Victor lumbering out of his study, roused like a bear from hibernation, was strangely terrifying, and although they spent their lives challenging all that was outlawed by their mother, they never once thought of exploring the forbidden interior of the study. The only time they were ushered into the gloomy depths of Victor's den was when they needed help with their maths homework. This wasn't so bad for Sylvia, who had a fighting chance of understanding the greasy pencil marks with which an impatient Victor covered endless pages of ruled paper, but as far as Julia and Amelia were concerned Victor's signs and symbols were as mysterious as ancient hieroglyphs. If they thought of the study at all, which they tried not to, they thought of it as a torture chamber. Victor blamed Rosemary for their innumeracy — it was clearly their mother's deficient female brain that they had inherited.

Victor's own mother, Ellen, had lent a sweet and balmy presence to his early infancy before being taken off to a lunatic asylum in 1924. Victor was only four at the time and it was judged better for him not to visit his mother in such disturbing quarters, with the result that he grew up imagining her as a raving madwoman of the Victorian variety — long white nightdress and wild hair, roaming the corridors of the asylum at night, prattling nonsense like a child — and it was only much later in his life that he discovered that his mother had not "gone insane" (the family's term for it) but had suffered a severe postpartum depression after giving birth to a stillborn baby and neither raved nor prattled but lived sadly and solitarily in a room decorated with photographs of Victor, until she died of tuberculosis when Victor was ten.

Oswald, Victor's father, had packed his son off to boarding school by then, and when Oswald himself died, accidentally falling into the freezing waters of the Southern Ocean, Victor received the news calmly and returned to the particularly difficult mathematical puzzle he had been working on.

Before the war, Victor's father had been that most arcane and useless of English creatures, a polar explorer, and Victor was rather glad that he would no longer have to live up to the heroic image of Oswald Land and could become great in his own, less valiant, field.

Victor met Rosemary when he had to go to the emergency room at Addenbrooke's, where she was a student nurse. He had tripped down some steps and fallen awkwardly on his wrist, but he told Rosemary that he'd been on his bike when he was "cut up" by a car on the Newmarket Road. "Cut up" sounded good to his ears, it was a phrase from a masculine world he'd never managed to inhabit successfully (the world of his father) and "the Newmarket Road" implied (untruthfully) that he didn't spend his whole life cloistered in the limited area between St. John's and the maths department.

If it hadn't been for this chance hospital encounter, accidental in all senses, Victor might never have courted a girl. He already felt well on his way to middle age, and his social life was still limited to the chess club. Victor didn't really feel the need for another person in his life, in fact he found the concept of "sharing" a life bizarre. He had mathematics, which filled up his time almost completely, so he wasn't entirely sure what he wanted with a wife. Women seemed to him to be in possession of all kinds of undesirable properties, chiefly madness, but also a multiplicity of physical drawbacks — blood, sex, children — which were unsettling and *other*. Yet something in him yearned to be surrounded by the kind of activity and warmth so missing in his own childhood, which was how, before he even knew what had happened, like opening the door to the wrong room, he was taking tea in a cottage in rural Norfolk while Rosemary shyly displayed a (rather cheap) diamond-chip engagement ring to her parents.

Apart from her father's whiskery bedtime benedictions, Victor was the first man Rosemary had ever been kissed by (albeit awkwardly, lunging at her like an elephant seal). Rosemary's father, a railway signalman, and her mother, a housewife, were startled when she brought Victor home to meet them. They were awed by his undoubted intellectual credentials (the black-rimmed spectacles, the shabby sports jacket, the air of permanent distraction) and the possibility that he might even be a bona fide genius (a possibility not exactly refuted by Victor), not to mention the fact that he had chosen their daughter — a quiet and easily influenced girl, hitherto overlooked by almost everyone — to be his helpmeet.

The fact that he was twice Rosemary's age didn't seem to worry them at all, although later, when the happy couple had departed, Rosemary's father, a manly type of man, did point out to his wife that Victor was not "a great physical specimen." Rosemary's mother's only reservation, however, was that although Victor was a doctor, he seemed to have trouble giving her any advice about the stomach pains that she was a martyr to. Cornered at a tea table covered in a Maltese lace cloth and loaded with macaroons, Devon scones, and seedcake, Victor finally confirmed, "Indigestion, I expect, Mrs. Vane," a misdiagnosis that she accepted with relief.

Olivia opened her eyes and stared contentedly at the nursery-rhyme wallpaper. Jack and Jill toiled endlessly up the hill, Jill carrying a wooden bucket for the well she was destined never to reach, while elsewhere on the same hillside Little Bo-Peep was searching for her lost sheep. Olivia wasn't too worried about the fate of the flock because she could see a pretty lamb with a blue ribbon round its neck, hiding behind a hedge. Olivia didn't really understand the *afterthought,* but she would have welcomed a baby. She liked babies and animals better than anything. She could feel the weight of Rascal, the family terrier, near her feet. It was *absolutely forbidden* for Rascal to sleep in the bedrooms, but every night one or other of them smuggled him into their room, although by morning he had usually found his own way to Olivia.

Olivia shook Blue Mouse gently to wake him up. Blue Mouse was a limp and lanky animal made from toweling. He was Olivia's oracle and she consulted him at all times on all subjects.

A bright slice of sunlight moved slowly across the wall, and when it reached the lamb hiding behind the hedge, Olivia climbed out of bed and pushed her feet obediently into her small slippers, pink with rabbit faces and rabbit ears, and much coveted by Julia. None of the others bothered with their slippers, and now it was so hot that Rosemary couldn't even get them to wear shoes, but Olivia was a biddable child.

Rosemary, lying in her own bed, awake, but with limbs that she could barely move, as if the marrow in her bones had turned to lead piping, was at that very moment trying to devise a plan that would stop the other three from corrupting Olivia's good behavior. The new baby was making Rosemary feel sick, and she thought how wonderful it would be if Victor suddenly woke from his snore-laden sleep and said to her, "Can I get you something, dear?" and she would say, "Oh, yes, please, I would like some tea — no milk — and a slice of toast, lightly buttered, thank you, Victor." And pigs would fly.

If only she weren't so fertile. She couldn't take the pill because it gave her high blood pressure, she had tried a coil but it dislodged itself, and Victor saw using condoms as some kind of assault on his manhood. She was just his broodmare. The only good thing about being pregnant was that she didn't have to endure sex with Victor. She told him it was bad for the baby and he believed her because he knew nothing — nothing about babies or women or children, nothing about *life*. She had been a virgin when she married him and had returned from their one-week honeymoon in Wales in a state of shock. She should have walked away right there and then, of course, but Victor had already begun to drain her. Sometimes it felt as if he were *feeding* on her.

If she had had the energy she would have got up and crept through to the spare bedroom, the "guest" bedroom, and lain down on the hard single bed with its daisy-fresh white sheets anchored fast by tight hospital corners. The guest bedroom was like an air pocket in the house, its atmosphere not breathed by anyone else, its carpet not worn by careless feet. It didn't matter how many babies she had, she could go on dropping them like a cow, year after year (although she would kill herself if she did), but not one of them would ever occupy the pristine space of the guest bedroom. It was clean, it was untouched, it was hers. The attic would be even better. She could have it floored and painted white and put in a trapdoor, then she could climb up there, pull up the trapdoor like a drawbridge, and no one would be able to find her. Rosemary imagined her family wandering from room to room, calling her name, and laughed. Victor grunted in his sleep. But then she thought of Olivia, roaming the house, unable to find her, and she felt fear, like a blow to her chest. She would have to take Olivia up to the attic with her.

Victor himself was in that kind place between waking and sleeping, a place untainted by the sour feelings of his everyday life, where he lived in a houseful of women who felt like strangers.

Olivia, thumb plugged snugly into her mouth and Blue Mouse clenched in the crook of her elbow, padded across the hallway to Julia and Amelia's bedroom and clambered in beside Julia. Julia was dreaming furiously. Her savage hair, plastered to her head, was wet with sweat and her lips moved constantly, muttering gibberish as she battled with some unseen monster. Julia was a heavy sleeper: she talked and walked in her sleep, she wrestled the bedclothes and woke up dramatically, staring wild-eyed at some fancy that had gone before she could remember it. Sometimes her sleep was so operatic that she brought on an asthma attack and woke in a state of mortal terror. Julia could be a very annoying person, Amelia and Sylvia agreed. She had a bewilderingly mercurial personality — punching and kicking one minute, a sham of cooing and kissing the next. When she was smaller Julia had been subject to the most profligate tantrums, and even now a day rarely went by without Julia having a hysterical fit over something or other and flouncing out of a room. It was Olivia who usually tagged after her and tried to console her when no one else cared. Olivia seemed to understand that all Julia wanted was some attention (although she did seem to want an awful lot of it).

Olivia tugged at the sleeve of Julia's nightdress to wake her, a process that always took some time. Amelia, in the next bed, was already awake but kept her eyes closed to savor the last drop of sleep. And besides, if she pretended to be asleep she knew that Olivia would climb into bed with her, hanging on to one of her limbs like a monkey, her sun-browned skin hot and dry against hers, the spongy body of Blue Mouse squashed between them.

Until Olivia was born, Amelia had shared a room with Sylvia, which although it held many drawbacks was definitely preferable to sharing with Julia. Amelia felt stranded, vague and insubstantial, between the acutely defined polar opposites of Sylvia and Julia. It didn't matter how many *afterthoughts* there were — she sensed she would always be lost somewhere in the middle. Amelia was a more thoughtful, bookish girl than Sylvia. Sylvia preferred excitement to order (which was why, Victor said, she could never be a great mathematician, merely adequate). Sylvia was nuts, of course. She'd told Amelia that God (not to mention Joan of Arc) had spoken to her. In the unlikely event of God speaking to anyone, Sylvia did not seem the obvious choice.

Sylvia loved secrets and even if she didn't have any secrets she made sure that you thought she did. Amelia had no secrets, Amelia knew nothing. When she grew up she planned to know everything and to keep it all a secret.

Would the arrival of the *afterthought* mean that their mother would juggle them around again in another arbitrary permutation? Who would Olivia move in with? They used to fight over who had the dog in bed with them; now they argued over Olivia's affections. There were five bedrooms in all, but one was always kept as a *guest bedroom* even though none of them could remember a guest ever staying in the house. Now their mother had begun talking about *doing out* the attic. Amelia liked the idea of having a room in the attic, away from everyone else. She imagined a spiral staircase and walls painted white, and there would be a white sofa and a white carpet, and gauzy white curtains would hang at the window. When she grew up and married she planned to have a single child, a single perfect child (who would be exactly like Olivia), and live in a white house. When she tried to imagine the husband who would live with her in this white house, all she could conjure up was a blur, a shadow of a man who passed her on stairs and in hallways, and murmured polite greetings.

By the time Olivia had roused them all it was nearly half past seven. They got their own breakfast, except for Olivia, who was hoisted onto a cushion and served cereal and milk by Amelia and fingers of toast by Julia. Olivia was theirs, their very own pet lamb, because their mother was worn out by the *afterthought* and their father was a great mathematician.

Julia, stuffing herself with food (Rosemary swore that Julia had a Labrador hiding *inside her*), managed to slice herself with the bread knife but was dissuaded from wailing and waking their parents by Sylvia clamping her hand over her mouth, like a surgical mask. At least one incident a day involving blood was the norm — they were the most *accident-prone* children in the world, according to their mother, who suffered endless trips to Addenbrooke's with them — Amelia cartwheeling her way to a broken arm, a scalded foot for Sylvia (trying to fill a hot water bottle), a split lip for Julia (jumping off the garage roof), Julia, again, walking through a glass door — watched by Amelia and Sylvia in dumbfounded disbelief (how could she not *see* it?), and Sylvia's strange fainting episodes, of course — vertical to horizontal with no warning, her skin drained of blood, her lips dry — a rehearsal for death, betrayed only by a slight vibration of the eyelid.

The only one who was immune to this communal clumsiness was Olivia, who in her whole three years had sustained nothing much worse than a few bruises. As for the others, their mother said she may as well have finished her nurse training, what with the amount of time she spent at the hospital.

Most thrilling of all, of course, was the day that Julia cut off her finger (Julia did seem strangely attracted to sharp objects). Julia, five years old at the time, wandered into the kitchen unnoticed by their mother, and the first Rosemary knew about the amputated finger was when she turned round from aggressively chopping carrots and noticed a shocked Julia holding her hand aloft in mute astonishment, exhibiting her wound like a martyred child saint. Rosemary threw a tea towel over the bloody hand, scooped up Julia, and ran to a neighbor, who drove them in a screech of overexcited brakes to the hospital, leaving Sylvia and Amelia with the problem of what to do with the tiny, pale finger, abandoned on the kitchen linoleum.

(An ever-resourceful Sylvia thrust the finger into a bag of frozen peas and Sylvia and Amelia caught a bus to the hospital, Sylvia clutching the defrosting peas all the way as if Julia's life depended on them.)

Their first plan for the day was to walk along the river to Grantchester. They had gone on this expedition at least twice a week since the holidays began, giving Olivia a piggyback when she grew tired. It was an adventure that took them most of the day because there were so many distractions to explore — on the riverbank, in the fields, even in other people's back gardens. Rosemary's only admonition was *don't go in the river,* but they invariably set off with their swimming costumes concealed under their dresses and shorts and hardly a trip went by without them stripping off and plunging into the river. They felt grateful to the *afterthought* for transforming their normally prudent mother into such a careless guardian. No other child of their acquaintance was enjoying such a hazardous existence that summer.

On one or two occasions Rosemary had given them money to buy afternoon tea at the Orchard Tea Rooms (where they were not the most welcome of guests), but mostly they took a hastily put together picnic that was usually eaten before they were even past Newnham. But not today, today the sun had traveled even closer to Cambridge and had them trapped in the garden. They tried to be energetic, playing a halfhearted game of hide-and-seek, but no one found a good hiding place, even Sylvia settled for nothing more creative than the nest of dry timothy grass behind the black currant bushes at the bottom of the garden — Sylvia, who had once stayed hidden and undiscovered for a record three hours (stretched like a sloth along a high, smooth branch of the beech tree in Mrs. Rain's garden opposite), only found after she fell asleep and plummeted from the tree, acquiring a greenstick fracture to her arm when she hit the ground. Their mother had a tremendous argument with Mrs. Rain, who wanted to have Sylvia arrested for trespassing (*Stupid woman*). They were always sneaking into Mrs. Rain's garden, stealing the sour apples from her orchard, and playing tricks on her because she was a witch and therefore deserved to be maltreated by them.

After an apathetic lunch of tuna salad they began a game of rounders, but Amelia tripped and had a nosebleed and then Sylvia and Julia had a fight that ended in Sylvia slapping Julia and after that they contented themselves with making daisy chains to plait into Olivia's hair and to collar Rascal with. Soon even this was too much effort and Julia crawled into the shade under the hydrangea bushes and fell asleep, curled up with the dog, while Sylvia took Olivia and Blue Mouse into the tent and read to them. The tent, an ancient thing that had been left in the shed by the previous owners of the house, had been pitched on the lawn since the beginning of the good weather, and they vied for space with one another inside its mildewed canvas walls, where it was even hotter and more airless than in the garden. Within minutes, Sylvia and Olivia had fallen asleep, the book forgotten.

Amelia, dreamy and languid with heat, lay on her back on the scorched grass and fired earth of the lawn, staring up at the endless, cloudless blue, pierced only by the giant hollyhocks that grew like weeds in the garden. She watched the reckless, skydiving swallows and listened to the pleasing buzz and hum of the insect world. A ladybird crawled across the freckled skin of her arm. A hot-air balloon drifted lazily overhead and she wished she could be bothered to wake Sylvia and tell her about it.

Rosemary's blood was running sluggishly in her veins. She drank a glass of tap water at the kitchen sink and looked out the window at the garden. A hot-air balloon was crossing the sky, moving like a bird caught on a thermal. Her children all seemed to be asleep. This unwonted tranquility made her feel an unexpected twinge of affection for the baby inside her. If they would all sleep all the time she wouldn't mind being their mother. Except for Olivia, she wouldn't want Olivia to sleep all the time.

When Victor proposed to her fourteen years ago, Rosemary had no idea what being the wife of a college lecturer would entail, but she had imagined it would involve wearing what her mother called "day dresses" and going to garden parties on the Backs and strolling elegantly across the plush green of the courts while people murmured, "That's the famous Victor Land's wife. He would be nothing without her, you know."

And, of course, the life of a lecturer's wife had turned out to be nothing like she had imagined. There were no garden parties on the Backs, and there was certainly no elegant strolling across the college courts, where the grass was afforded the kind of veneration usually associated with religious artifacts. Not long after she was first married she had been invited to join Victor in the Master's garden, where it soon grew apparent that Victor's colleagues were of the opinion that he had married (horribly) beneath him ("A nurse," someone whispered, in a way that made it seem like a profession only slightly more respectable than a streetwalker). But one thing was true — Victor would be nothing without her, but he was also nothing with her. At that very moment he was toiling in the cool dark of his study, the heavy chenille curtains closed against the summer, lost in his work, work that never came to fruition, never changed the world or made his name. He was not great in his field, merely good. This gave her a certain satisfaction.

Great mathematical discoveries were made before the age of thirty, she now knew, courtesy of one of Victor's colleagues. Rosemary herself was only thirty-two. She couldn't believe how young that sounded and how old it felt.

She supposed Victor had married her because he thought she was domesticated — her mother's loaded tea tables probably misled him, but Rosemary had never made so much as a plain scone when she lived at home, and since she was a nurse he probably presumed she would be a nurturing and caring person — and she might have presumed that herself in those days, but now she didn't feel capable of nurturing a kitten, let alone four, soon to be five, children, to say nothing of a great mathematician.

Furthermore, she suspected the great work was a fake. She had seen the papers on his desk when she dusted in that hole, and his reckonings looked not dissimilar to her father's intense calculations of racing form and betting odds. Victor didn't strike her as a gambler. Her father had been a gambler, to her mother's despair. She remembered going with him to Newmarket once when she was a child. He had lifted her onto his shoulders and they had stood by the winning post. She had been terrified by the noise as the horses thundered down the homestretch and the crowd at the stand side grew frenzied, as though the world might be about to end rather than a 30/1 outsider winning by a short head. Rosemary couldn't imagine Victor anywhere as spirited as a racecourse, nor could she see him in the smoky commonalty of a betting shop.

Julia emerged from beneath the hydrangeas looking querulous with heat. How was Rosemary ever going to turn them back into English schoolchildren when the new term began? Their open-air life had transformed them into gypsies, their skin brown and scratched, their sun-scorched hair thick and tangled, and they seemed to be permanently filthy, no matter how many baths they took. A drowsy Olivia stood at the opening of the tent and Rosemary's heart gave a little twitch. Olivia's face was grubby and her bleached plaits were askew and looked as if they had dead flowers entwined in them. She was whispering a secret into Blue Mouse's ear. Olivia was her only beautiful child. Julia, with her dark curls and snub nose, was pretty but her character wasn't, Sylvia — poor Sylvia, what could you say? And Amelia was somehow . . . bland, but Olivia, Olivia was spun from light. It seemed impossible that she was Victor's child, although, unfortunately, there was no doubting the fact. Olivia was the only one she loved, although God knows she tried her best with the others. Everything was from duty, nothing from love. Duty killed you in the end.

It was very wrong, it was as if the love she should have had for the others had been siphoned off and given to Olivia instead, so that she loved her youngest child with a ferocity that didn't always seem natural. Sometimes she wanted to eat Olivia, to bite into a tender forearm or a soft calf muscle, even to devour her whole like a snake and take her back inside her where she would be safe. She was a terrible mother, there was no doubt about it, but she didn't even have the strength to feel guilty. Olivia caught sight of her and waved.

Their appetites were listless at teatime and they picked at the unseasonable lamb hot pot that Rosemary had spent too much time making. Victor emerged, blinking in the daylight like a cave dweller, and ate everything in front of him and then asked for more, and Rosemary wondered what he would look like when he was dead. She watched him eating, the fork traveling up and down to his lips with robotic rhythm, his huge hands, like paddles, wrapped around the cutlery. He had farmer's hands, it was one of the things she had first noticed about him. A mathematician should have slender, elegant hands. She should have known from his hands. She felt sick and crampy. Maybe she would lose the baby. What a relief that would be.

Rosemary rose from the table abruptly and announced *bedtime*. Normally there would be protests but Julia's breathing was labored and her eyes were red from too much sun and grass — she had all kinds of summer allergies — and Sylvia seemed to be in the grip of some form of sunstroke, she was sick and weepy and said her head hurt, although that didn't stop her from being hysterical when Rosemary told her to go to bed early.

Almost every night that summer the eldest three had asked if they could sleep outside in the tent, and every night Rosemary said no on the principle that it was bad enough they looked like gypsies without living like them, and it didn't matter if gypsies lived in caravans — as Sylvia was at pains to point out — Rosemary was trying her best to retain good government in this family, against all the odds and without any help from a husband, for whom the quotidian demands of meals and housework and child care were meaningless and who had only married her in order to have someone who would look after him and it made her feel worse when Amelia said, "Are you alright, Mummy?" because Amelia was the most neglected of all of them. Which is why Rosemary sighed, took two paracetamol and a sleeping tablet — which was probably a lethal cocktail for the baby inside her — and said to her most forgotten child, *If you want you can sleep in the tent with Olivia tonight.*

The dewy grass and canvas smell of the tent was a thrilling thing to wake up to — better certainly than Julia's breath, which always seemed to grow sour in the night. Olivia's own indefinable scent was just detectable. Amelia kept her eyes closed against the light. The sun already felt high in the sky and she waited for Olivia to wake and climb under the old eiderdown that was making do as a sleeping bag, but it was Rascal rather than Olivia who finally roused her by licking her face.

There was no sign of Olivia, only an empty shell of covers as if she'd been winkled out of them, and Amelia felt disappointed that Olivia had got up without waking her. She walked barefoot across the dew-wet grass, Rascal trotting at her heels, and tried the back door of the house, which turned out to be locked — apparently her mother hadn't thought to give Amelia a key. What kind of a parent locks her own children out of their home?

It was quiet and felt very early but Amelia had no idea what time it was. She wondered if Olivia had got into the house some-how because there was no sign of her in the garden. She called her name and was startled by the tremor in her voice. She hadn't real-ized she was worried until she heard it. She knocked on the back door for a long time but there was no answer, so she ran along the path at the side of the house — the little wicket gate was open, giving Amelia more cause for alarm — and into the street, shout-ing, "Olivia!" more forcefully now. Rascal, sensing entertainment, began to bark.

The street was empty apart from a man getting into his car. He gave Amelia a curious look. She was barefoot and dressed in Sylvia's hand-me-down pajamas and supposed she did look odd but she hardly cared. She ran to the front door and rang the bell, keeping her finger on the buzzer until her father, of all people, yanked the door open. He had obviously been roused from sleep — his face looked as rumpled as his pajamas, his mad-professor hair sticking out at all angles from his head as he stared fiercely at her as if he had no idea who she was. When he recognized her as one of his own he was even more puzzled.

"Olivia," she said, and this time her voice came out as a whisper.

In the afternoon, a bolt of lightning cracked the flat skies above Cambridge, signaling the end of the heat wave. By that time, the tent in the back garden had become the center of a circle that had grown wider and wider as the day progressed, pulling more and more people inside it — first the Lands themselves, roaming the streets, scrambling through undergrowth and hedges, yelling Olivia's name until they were hoarse. By then the police had joined the search and neighbors were checking gardens and sheds and cellars. The circle rippled outward to include the police divers fishing the river and the complete strangers who volunteered to comb meadow and fen. Police helicopters flew low over outlying villages and countryside as far as the county borders, truck drivers were alerted to keep an eye out on the motorway, and the army was brought in to search the fens, but none of them — from Amelia screaming herself sick in the back garden to the Territorial Army recruits on their hands and knees in the rain on Midsummer Common — could find a single trace of Olivia, not a hair or a flake of skin, not a pink rabbit slipper nor a blue mouse.

2

CASE HISTORY NO. 2 1994

Just a Normal Day

Theo had begun to try and walk more. He was now officially "morbidly obese," according to his new, unsympathetic GP. Theo knew that the new, unsympathetic GP — a young woman with a very short haircut and a gym bag thrown carelessly in the corner of the doctor's office — was using the term to try and frighten him. Theo hadn't considered himself "morbidly obese" until now. He had thought of himself as cheerfully overweight, a rotund Santa Claus kind of figure, and he would have ignored the GP's advice, but when he got home and told his daughter, Laura, about the conversation in the doctor's office she had been horrified and had immediately drawn up a plan of exercise and diet for him, which was why he was now eating chaff with skim milk for breakfast and walking the two miles to his Parkside office every morning.

Theo's wife, Valerie, had died from a postoperative blood clot in the brain at the absurd age of thirty-four, so long ago now it was sometimes hard to believe he had ever had a wife or a marriage. She had only gone into the hospital to have her appendix removed, and, when he looked back on it now, he realized that he should probably have sued the hospital or the health authority for negligence, but he had been so caught up in the day-to-day care of

2 4   K A T E   A T K I N S O N

their two daughters — Jennifer was seven and Laura was only two when Valerie died — that he had hardly had time even to mourn his poor wife, let alone seek retribution. If it hadn't been for the fact that both girls looked like her — more and more now that they were older — he would have found it hard to conjure up anything but a vague memory of his wife.

Marriage and motherhood had made Valerie more solemn than the student whom Theo had carefully courted. Theo wondered if those people who were destined to die young had some kind of premonition of the shortness of the hours and that gave their life an intensity, a seriousness like a shadow. Valerie and Theo had been fond of each other, rather than passionate, and Theo didn't know if the marriage would have lasted if she'd lived.

Jennifer and Laura had never been troublesome girls, and they'd made it easy for Theo to be a good parent. Jennifer was a medical student in London now. She was a sober, driven girl with not much time for frivolity and jokes, but that didn't mean she didn't feel compassion, and Theo couldn't imagine her sitting in a GP's office one day telling some fat bloke she'd never met before that he was morbidly obese and he should get off his arse a bit more. That wasn't really what the new GP had said to Theo, but she might as well have.

Like her sister, Laura was one of those organized, capable girls who achieved what she set out to do with the minimum of fuss, but, unlike Jennifer, Laura had a carefree character. That didn't mean she wasn't an achiever — she had all her scuba-diving certificates and planned to be a master diver by the time she was twenty. She was taking her driving test next month and she was expected to get As in all her exams. She had a place waiting for her at Aberdeen to study marine biology.

She had got a job for the summer working in a pub on King Street and Theo worried about her coming home at night, imagined some maniac knocking her off her bike on Christ's Pieces and doing unthinkable things to her. He was hugely relieved that she had decided to go straight to university in October and not go backpacking across Thailand or South America or wherever, the way all her friends seemed to be doing. The world was a place freighted with danger. "You don't worry about Jenny," Laura said, and it was a fact. He didn't worry about Jennifer, and he pretended (to himself, to Laura) it was because Jennifer's life was invisible to him in London, but the truth was that he simply didn't love her as much as he loved Laura.

Every time Laura left the house he worried about her, every time she leaped on her bike, put on her wet suit, stepped on a train. He worried when she went out in a high wind that a piece of falling masonry might drop on her head, he worried that she would take a student flat with an unserviced water heater and die of carbon-monoxide poisoning. He worried that her tetanus shots weren't up to date, that she would walk through a public building that was pumping Legionnaires' disease through the air-conditioning, that she would go to the hospital for a routine operation and never come out again, that she would be stung by a bee and die from anaphylactic shock (because she'd never been stung by a bee, so how did he know she wasn't allergic). Of course he never said any of these things to Laura — they would have seemed ridiculous to her. Even if he expressed the mildest trepidation about something ("Careful making that left turn, you've got a blind spot" or "Turn the light off at the switch before you change the bulb"), Laura would laugh at him, would have said he was an old woman and couldn't even change a lightbulb without foreseeing a disastrous chain of events unfolding. But Theo knew that the journey that began with a tiny screw not being threaded properly ended with the cargo door blowing off in midair.

"Why worry, Dad?" was Laura's constant amused reaction to his qualms. "Why not?" was Theo's unvoiced response. And after one too many early morning vigils waiting for her to come home from work in the pub (although he always pretended to be asleep), Theo had suggested casually that they needed a temp in his office and why didn't she come and help them out and to his astonishment she'd thought about it for a minute and then said, "Okay," and smiled her lovely smile (hours of patient, expensive orthodontic work when she was younger), and Theo thought, "Thank you, God," because although Theo didn't believe in God he often talked to him.

And for her very first day at work at Holroyd, Wyre, and Stanton (Theo was the "Wyre"), Theo wasn't going to be there, which upset him a lot more than it did Laura, of course. He was in court in Peterborough, a tedious dispute over a land boundary that should have gone to a local solicitor but the client was an old one of Theo's who had moved recently. Laura was dressed in a black skirt and a white blouse and had tied her brown hair back and he thought how neat she looked, how pretty.

"Walk to the station, promise, Dad?" Laura said sternly as Theo got up from the table, and Theo said, "If I must," but knew he wouldn't make the train if he did and thought he could pretend to walk and then take a taxi. He finished his low-calorie, high-fiber cattle-feed cereal and drained his cup of black coffee, thinking about cream and sugar and a Danish pastry, one of the ones with apricot and custard that looked like a poached egg, and thought perhaps they might sell them at the station buffet. "Don't forget your inhaler, Dad," Laura said to him, and Theo patted his jacket pocket to prove he had it. The very thought of not having his Ventolin inhaler made Theo feel panic, although he didn't know why. If he had an asthma attack on any English street probably half the people on it would be able to whip out an inhaler and offer it to him.

He said to Laura, "Cheryl will show you the ropes" — Cheryl was his secretary — "I'll be back in the office before lunch, maybe we can go out?" and she said, "That would be nice, Dad." And then she saw him off at the front door, kissing him on the cheek, saying, "I love you, Dad," and he said, "Love you too, sweetheart," and at the street corner he'd looked back and she was still waving.

Laura, who had brown eyes and pale skin and who liked Diet Pepsi and salt and vinegar crisps, who was as smart as a whip, who made scrambled eggs for him on Sunday mornings, Laura, who was still a virgin (he knew because she told him, to his embarrassment), which made him feel immensely relieved even though he knew she couldn't stay one forever, Laura, who kept a tank of saltwater tropical fish in her bedroom, whose favorite color was blue, whose favorite flower was the snowdrop, and who liked Radiohead and Nirvana and hated Mr. Blobby and had seen *Dirty Dancing* ten times. Laura, whom Theo loved with a strength that was like a cataclysm, a disaster.

Theo and David Holroyd had set up in partnership not long after Theo's marriage to Valerie. Jean Stanton joined them a couple years later. All three of them had been at university together and they wanted a "go-ahead, socially responsible" law practice, the kind that did more than its fair share of domestic and matrimonial and legal-aid work. Their good intentions had weakened over the years. Jean Stanton had discovered she liked litigation more than domestic violence and that her politics had changed from center left to Conservative with a large "C," and David Holroyd found that, as a fifth-generation East Anglian lawyer, conveyancing was his lifeblood, and so it usually fell to Theo to "keep up the ethical end of it," as David Holroyd put it. The practice had grown substantially, there were three junior partners now and two associates and they were bursting at the seams in the Parkside office, but none of them could bear the idea of moving.

The building had been a dwelling-house originally, five floors in all, from damp kitchen cellar to servants' cold attics, the rooms piled together rather haphazardly but nonetheless a decent residence for a well-to-do family. After the war it had been broken up into businesses and flats and now only fragmented and ghostly traces of the interior remained — a decorative plasterwork border of swags and urns above the desk where Cheryl worked and the egg-and-dart frieze beneath the cornice in the hall.

The drawing room, oval ended and neoclassic in its restraint, with a view of Parker's Piece from the windows, was now the boardroom for Holroyd, Wyre, and Stanton, and in winter there was always a real coal fire burning in the grate of the marble fireplace because David Holroyd was an old-fashioned sort. Theo had stood in the boardroom many times, sharing a glass of wine with his partners and associates, all of them full of the provincial bonhomie of successful professionals. And, of course, Jennifer and Laura had been in and out of that place all the time, ever since they were little, but it was still odd to think of her in there today, filing and fetching and carrying, and he knew how polite and willing she would be and felt proud because everyone in the office would be saying to one another, "Laura's a lovely girl, isn't she?" the way that people always did.

Sheep on the line. The ticket inspector did not elucidate whether it was a flock or a few stragglers. Enough of them anyway for everyone on the train to Cambridge to feel the bump and judder. The train had been stopped for ten minutes before the conductor made his way through the four carriages and informed them about the sheep, quashing speculation about cows, horses, and suicidal humans. After half an hour the train was still stationary, so Theo supposed it must be a flock rather than some solitary stray. He wanted to get back to Cambridge and take Laura out for lunch but it was "in the lap of the gods," as the conductor put it. Theo wondered why it was the lap of the gods and not the hands of the gods.

It was stifling in the train, and someone, the guard presumably, opened the doors and people began to clamber out. Theo was sure it was against railway bylaws, but there was a narrow verge and an embankment at the side of the train so it seemed quite safe, there was no way another train could plow into them in the way that theirs had into the sheep. Theo alighted cautiously, and with difficulty, pleased with himself for being so adventurous. He was curious to see what sheep looked like after a close encounter with a train. Walking along the track, he soon discovered the answer to his question — bits of sheep, like joints of meat with wool attached, had been flung about everywhere, as if they'd been torn apart in a bloody massacre by a pack of wolves. Theo was surprised how strong his stomach was for this carnage, but then he had always regarded lawyers as being rather like policemen and nurses in their ability to rise above the mess and tragedy of everyday life and deal with it in a disinterested way. Theo had a strange sense of triumph. He had traveled on a train that had almost been derailed but no harm had come. The odds surely dictated that his chances (and therefore the chances of those close to him) of being in another train accident had lessened.

The driver was standing next to his engine, looking baffled, and Theo asked him if he was "okay," and he said, by way of answer, "I saw just the one and I thought, Well, I probably don't need to brake for that, and then" — he made a dramatic gesture with his arms as if trying to reenact a flock of disintegrating sheep — "and then the world went white."

Theo was so taken by this image that it occupied his mind for the rest of the journey, which recommenced once they had transferred to another train. He imagined describing the scene to Laura, imagined her reaction — horrified and yet darkly amused. When he finally got off the train he took a cab halfway but then got out and walked. It would make him even later but Laura would be pleased.

Theo rested for a minute on the pavement before tackling the steep stairs up to the first-floor office of Holroyd, Wyre, and Stanton. The GP was right, Laura was right, he had to lose some weight.

The front door was propped open with a cast-iron doorstop. Every time Theo entered the building he admired this door to the office, it was painted a glossy dark green, and the handsome brass furniture — letter box, keyhole, lion-headed door knocker — were the original fittings. The brass plaque on the door, polished every morning by the office cleaner, announced, HOLROYD, WYRE, AND STANTON — SOLICITORS AND ATTORNEYS-AT-LAW. Theo took a deep breath and set off up the stairs.

The inner door that led into the reception area was also — unusually — open, and as soon as Theo walked in it was obvious that something was terribly wrong. Jean Stanton's secretary was cowering on the floor, a trail of vomit on her clothes. The receptionist, Moira, was on the phone, dictating the address of the firm with a kind of hysterical patience. She had blood in her hair and on her face and Theo thought she was injured but when he went toward her to help her she waved him away with her hand and he thought she was dismissing him until he realized she was trying to send him in the direction of the boardroom.

Afterward, again and again, Theo pieced together the events that preceded this moment.

Laura had just finished photocopying a land registry form when a man came into reception, a man so nondescript that afterward not one single person in Holroyd, Wyre, and Stanton could give a half-decent description of his features, and the only thing they could remember about him was that he was wearing a yellow golfing sweater.

The man seemed confused and disoriented, and when Moira, the receptionist, said, "Can I help you, sir?" he said, "Mr. Wyre, where is he?" in a high, strained voice, and Moira, alarmed by the man's manner, said, "I'm afraid he's late back from court, do you have an appointment? Can *I* help with anything?" but the man took off down the corridor, running in an odd way, like a child, and charged into the boardroom where the partners were having a lunchtime meeting, although not Theo, who was still on his way back from the station (although he had forgotten about the meeting).

Laura had been sent out earlier to buy sandwiches for the meeting — prawn cocktail, cheese and coleslaw, roast beef, tuna and sweet corn, and a chicken and salad (no mayonnaise) for her father because he really needed to think more about his weight and she had thought affectionately what a dope he was because he'd forgotten his meeting when he'd suggested lunch to her this morning. The sandwiches and coffee and notebooks were all laid out on the mahogany boardroom table (oval to match the shape of the room) but no one had sat down at the table yet. David Holroyd was standing in front of the fireplace, telling one of the junior partners about the "bloody fantastic" holiday he'd just returned from, when the stranger rushed into the room and from somewhere, probably from beneath the yellow golfing sweater he was wearing, but no one was sure, pulled out a bowie knife and sliced through the dark worsted of David Holroyd's Austin Reed suit, the white poplin of his Charles Tyrwhitt shirt, the tropical tan on the skin of his left arm, and, finally, the artery in the arm. And Laura, who liked apricot yogurt and drank tea but not coffee and who had size six feet and who loved horses, who preferred plain chocolate to milk chocolate and had spent five years learning classical guitar but never played anymore and who was still sad that their pet dog, Poppy, had been run over the previous summer, Laura, who was Theo's child and his best friend, dropped the land registry form and ran into the boardroom after the man — perhaps because she had a Red Cross certificate or because she had taken a self-defense course at sixth-form college, or perhaps it was from simple curiosity or instinct, it was impossible to know what she was thinking as she ran into the boardroom where the man, this complete stranger, had spun on the balls of his feet with the agility and grace of a dancer, his hand still moving in the same arc that had cut through David Holroyd's arm and which now scythed through Laura's neck, carving through her carotid artery, sending a great plume of her precious, beautiful blood across the room.

In a dream, in slow underwater motion, Theo moved down the corridor and into the boardroom. He noticed coffee cups and sandwiches on the mahogany table and realized he had forgotten about the meeting. There was blood spattered across the cream walls and David Holroyd was slumped like a bloody sack near the marble fireplace, while nearer to the door, his own child lay on the floor, frothy blood bubbling gently from the gash in her throat. Theo was aware of someone sobbing uncontrollably, and someone else saying, "Why doesn't the ambulance get here?"

Theo dropped to his knees next to Laura. Cheryl, his secretary, was kneeling over her, incongruous in skirt and bra. She had removed her blouse and had tried to staunch the blood from Laura's wound. She was still holding the blouse, now a wet bloody rag, and her bare skin was slick with blood. It had run in rivulets down her cleavage — the word "bloodbath" came into Theo's mind. There was blood everywhere. Theo was kneeling in a pool of it, the carpet was soggy with it. Laura's blood. Which was his blood also. Her white blouse was now dyed crimson. He could smell the blood — copper and salt and the rankness of a butcher's shop. Theo wondered if there was a way of slitting open his own veins and arteries and siphoning off his blood and giving it to his daughter. And all the time Theo was praying, "Please, God, let her be alright," like a terrible unstoppable mantra and he felt that if he could keep on saying those words he could prevent this thing from happening.

Laura's eyes were half open and Theo wasn't sure whether she was dead or not. He remembered last year, comforting Poppy at the side of the road after she'd been knocked down by a car outside the house. The dog was small, a terrier, and he had held it in his arms while it died and had seen the same dull look in its eyes as it moved into an unreachable, inescapable place. He pressed his hand against Laura's wound but there wasn't really any blood to stem anymore so now instead he held her hand, a hand that was soft and warm, and he bent close to her face and murmured in her ear, "Everything's all right, Laura," and then he cradled her head in his lap and stroked her blood-matted hair, and his secretary, Cheryl, wept and said, "God loves you, Laura."

At the moment he stopped praying, at the moment he knew she was dead, Theo understood it would never cease to happen. Every moment Laura would be standing by the photocopier, negotiating the complexities of the land registry form, wondering when her father would be back or whether she could take a lunch break because she was starving. Maybe regretting taking this job because it was actually quite boring but she'd done it to please her father, because she liked to make him happy, because she loved him. Laura, who slept curled up in a ball, who liked hot buttered toast and all the Indiana Jones movies but not *Star Wars,* whose first word was "dog," who liked the rain but not the wind, who planned to have three children, Laura, who would be forever standing by the photocopier in the office in Parkside waiting for the stranger and his knife, waiting for the world to go white.

CASE HISTORY NO. 3 1979

Everything from Duty,
Nothing from Love

Michelle had been setting her alarm five minutes earlier every day. This morning it had gone off at twenty past five. To-morrow it would be quarter past. She could see that she would have to call a halt eventually or she would be getting up before she went to bed. But not yet. She was only one step ahead of the baby, who woke up with the birds and the dawn, and the birds and the dawn were coming earlier every day at this time of year.

She needed more time, there simply wasn't enough of it. This was the only way she could think of making it. Not making it ex-actly, if you could make it from scratch — brand-new time — that would be fantastic. Michelle tried to think of ways you might manufacture something so abstract, but all she could think of were examples from her own small-scale domestic economy — knitting and sewing and baking. Imagine if you could knit time. Christ, her needles would be clacking day and night. And what an advantage she would have over her friends, none of whom knew how to knit (or bake or sew), but then none of them had saddled themselves at the age of eighteen with a husband and a baby and a bloody cot-tage in the middle of nowhere, surrounded on all sides by nothing but horizon, so that it felt as if the sky were a huge stone that was pressing you into the ground. No, not saddled. She loved them. She really did.

And anyway, where would she ever find the time to make time? There *was* no time. That was the whole point. What if she stopped going to bed altogether? She could shut herself away like someone in a fairy tale, in a room at the top of a tower and spin time like gold. She could stay awake until there was so much time, lying in golden hanks at her feet, that it would last her the rest of her life and she would never run out again. The idea of living in a tower, cut off from everyone and everything, sounded like heaven to Michelle.

The baby was a parcel delivered to the wrong address, with no way of sending it back or getting it redelivered. ("Call her by her name," Keith said to her all the time. "Call her Tanya, not 'it.'") Michelle had only just left her own (unsatisfactory) childhood behind, so how was she supposed to be in charge of someone else's? She knew the term was "bonding," it was in a baby book she had (*How to Have a Happy Baby.* Hah!). She hadn't "bonded" with the baby, instead she was shackled by it.

All the people who had told her that having a termination and finishing her A Levels was the sensible thing for her to do had been right after all. And if she could put the clock back — which would be another way of getting some time — then that's exactly what she would do. She would be a student somewhere now if she hadn't had the baby, she'd be drinking like a fish and taking drugs and handing in mediocre essays on the 1832 Reform Act or *The Tenant of Wildfell Hall* instead of sprinkling coriander seeds on a tray of compost while listening to the baby cry wherever it was she had left it when she couldn't stand the noise anymore. The bedroom, probably, so that even now the baby was edging its fat caterpillar body toward the edge of the bed or chewing on an electrical cord or suffocating itself with a pillow.

Michelle put the tray of seeds on the kitchen windowsill, where she would be able to watch them push their way into the light.

From the window she could see the beginnings of her vegetable garden, neat drills of turned soil and geometric shapes marked out with pea sticks and string. Keith didn't understand why she had started a vegetable garden. "We're living on a bloody *farm*," he said, stretching his arms out expansively so he looked like a scare-crow — they were in a field at the time — "the place is full of vegetables. We're allowed to take whatever we want." No, actually, the place was full of *potatoes,* which was different. And swede and kale — cattle food, peasant food. Michelle wanted courgettes and spinach and beetroot. And coriander. And she wanted flowers, beautiful scented flowers, roses and honeysuckle and lilies — pure white lilies, the kind you would give to a bride or a corpse.

The field in which they were conducting this argument was empty of everything except for hummocky, uneven grass, over which Michelle was striding furiously, bumping the pushchair along in front of her so that the baby bounced around inside like a crash-test dummy. Anger was making her walk so fast that Keith, despite his long legs, was having to trot to keep up with her.

"What's wrong with potatoes?" he asked, and Michelle said, ex-cept that she was shouting now, "It's March, there aren't any bloody potatoes, there isn't anything, there's nothing, nothing but mud, mud everywhere and rain, it's like the bloody Somme!" and he said, "Don't be such a stupid bloody drama queen!" And she thought how ridiculous his country accent sounded, like a yokel in a television comedy, a bloody potato-eating peasant. Michelle had got rid of her accent, listening to how middle-class people spoke on the television, how her teachers spoke at school, until she sounded so flat that she could have been from anywhere. She started walking even faster until she was almost jogging.

"And anyway," he shouted after her, "maybe I don't want to eat bloody coriander!" She came to an abrupt halt, whiplashing the baby in the pushchair. She turned round and said, "Well, maybe *I* do," and glared at him for the longest time, wishing she had the woodcutting ax with her, the ax that would split his skull like a melon or a pumpkin cleaved in two. No, not a melon, melons were sweet and exotic, not pedestrian enough for his head, and pumpkins were vegetables that belonged in fairy tales. A turnip. Turnips were brutal, yokel vegetables. And he would drop like a headless scarecrow, right here in the field, and sink into the soil and never be seen again, and she could give the baby to her mother and ruin another life.

Or perhaps — nightmare idea — he would grow and divide and multiply out of sight, in the soil, and come the summer he would suddenly shoot up, a hundred Keiths, a thousand Keiths, nodding and swaying like sunflowers in the field.

A woodcutting ax — how absurd was that? Everyone else had central heating or at least heating that came from somewhere that they didn't have to think about, they didn't have to go out in all weather and saw and chop wood to make a fire, they didn't have to wait for hours for the fire to heat a back boiler just so they could have hot water.

They didn't even have coal because the wood was free, from the estate. Woodcutting axes were things you had in fairy tales. Maybe that's what had happened to her, maybe she'd got stuck in some evil fairy tale, and until she'd picked every potato in the field or chopped down all the trees in the wood, she wouldn't be free. Unless she learned to spin time. Or her head exploded. So much toil and drudgery, it was like being a serf in the Middle Ages. It was *feudal*.

"Let me take the pushchair," Keith said. "You're going to give Tanya brain damage, carrying on like that." Michelle felt suddenly spent of all her fury, she was too tired all the time to sustain anything, even anger. They walked side by side now, at a slower pace, so that the baby finally fell asleep — which had been the purpose of the walk, a whole lifetime ago.

After a while, Keith put his arm round her shoulder and rubbed the top of her head with his chin and said, "I do love you, baby, you know that, don't you?" and it would have been quite a nice moment if it hadn't been raining and the bug-baby hadn't started crying again.

Michelle had been brought up in a chaotic house in Fen Ditton, one of the dreary satellite villages that the poor of Cambridge were banished to. Her father was a drinker and "a waste of space," according to Michelle's mother, but nonetheless she had stayed with him because she didn't want to be on her own, which Michelle and her sister were agreed was pathetic. Their mother drank too but at least she didn't get violent. Michelle's sister, Shirley, was fifteen and still at home and Michelle wished she could come and live with them but they didn't have the room. She missed Shirley, she really did. Shirley wanted to be a doctor, she was very clever, everyone said she was going "to make something of herself." They used to say that about Michelle, before Keith, before the bug was born. Now it seemed she had managed to make nothing of herself.

The cottage was tiny. Their bedroom was squashed into the eaves and the baby's bedroom was more like a cupboard, although it spent hardly any time in its room, in its cot, where it should be sleeping peacefully instead of always wanting to be picked up and lugged around. She hadn't read a book since the baby was born. She had tried, a novel propped awkwardly on a pillow while she breast-fed, but the baby wouldn't suck properly if it thought her attention was elsewhere. And then she had to give up the breast-feeding (thank goodness) because her milk ran out ("You have to try and relax and enjoy the baby," the midwife said, but what *exactly* was there to enjoy?), and maneuvering a bottle and a book and a baby would have needed three pairs of hands. Which would be another way of getting more time.

Michelle had spent a long time decorating the baby's room when she was pregnant. She'd painted the walls egg-yolk yellow and stenciled a frieze of ducklings and lambs and sewn cheerful yellow-and-white gingham curtains for the tiny window so that the whole place had been like a box of sunshine. Michelle had always done things properly. From an early age she'd been neat and tidy, and her mother used to laugh and say, "I don't know where she gets it from, not from me" (and how true that was). She'd been the same at school: her workbooks were never smudged, her illustrations and maps were always finely drawn, everything underlined and tabulated and indexed and she'd worked so hard and so methodically that even when the quality of her work hadn't been up to scratch her teachers gave her good marks. And she was supposed to go to university, to break free, and instead she'd been *diverted,* by someone with an HNC from agricultural college who worked on an estate farm and didn't have two beans to rub together.

She started going out with Keith Fletcher when she was sixteen and he was twenty-one and nearly everyone she knew had been jealous because he was older and had a motorbike and was just this incredibly sexy, handsome guy, with an earring and black hair and that foxy smile so that she used to think of him as a gypsy, which seemed very romantic but of course an earring and a foxy smile didn't make you into a gypsy. Didn't make you into anything in particular. And now he didn't even have the motorbike because he'd got rid of it and bought an old van instead.

And way back then, when all Michelle had to worry about was whether she could get an essay in on time or whether she had a decent pair of tights, back in that other time when she was young, she had thought that a country cottage was also romantic, and when she'd first seen the cottage she thought it was the quaintest, prettiest thing ever because it was so small and so old, more than two hundred years old, built of brick with patterns of flint bedded around the lintels and sills and it had once been — yes — the forester's cottage, and the estate had given it to them to live in when they got married. It was a "tied" cottage and Michelle thought that was funny (but not in a way that made her laugh) because it wasn't the cottage that was tied — it was Michelle.

She'd had a glimpse of a possible future — the pretty cottage, the garden full of flowers and vegetables, bread in the oven, a bowl of strawberries on the table, the happy baby hitched on her hip while she threw corn to the chickens. It would be like a Hardy novel, before it all goes wrong.

When she married, already six months' pregnant, she left school and quit her out-of-school-hours job in a café, and Keith said, "It's okay. After the baby comes you can still go to college and everything," although they both knew it would no longer be a good university but some crappy polytechnic in some crappy town (probably Cambridge, God help her), where she would end up doing an HND in business studies or hotel management, but nonetheless Michelle thought, "Yes, I will do that, of course I will," but in the meantime if she was going to be a wife and mother she was going to do it properly, which is why she spent all her days cleaning and scrubbing and baking and cooking, and assiduously reading housekeeping books, continually amazed at just how many skills and crafts could go into making "a lovely home" — the patchwork quilts you could sew, the curtains you could ruffle, the cucumbers you could pickle, the rhubarb you could make into jam, the icing-sugar decorations you could create for your Christmas cake — which you were supposed to make in September at the latest (for heaven's sake) — and at the same time remember to plant your indoor bulbs so they would also be ready for "the festive season," and it just went on and on, every month a list of tasks that would have defeated Hercules and that was without the everyday preparation of meals, which was doubly difficult now that the baby was weaned.

When her mother saw her pureeing cooked carrot and baking egg custards for the baby, she said, "For Christ's sake, Michelle, just give her a jar of Heinz baby food," but if she bought her jars of food she would eat them out of house and home, she was so greedy, fattening herself up like a pupa. She was *always* hungry, you could never give her enough. And anyway jars were cheating, you had to do things *properly,* although even Shirley, who was usually on her side, said, "Michelle, you don't have to put so much effort into everything." But she did because she was driven by something, only she didn't know what it was but she was sure that if one day she could get everything finished then she'd be free of whatever it was that was driving her. "You'll never get everything perfect, Michelle," Shirley said. "That's impossible." But it wasn't. Given enough time you could make anything perfect.

She thought they should get some chickens of their own and perhaps a goat to milk, because maybe something was missing — maybe it would just take one fat white wyandotte to make the idyll possible. Or a Sicilian buttercup. Really, chickens had the prettiest names — the Brahma and the marsh daisy and the faverolles. She had a book from the library. She'd stolen the book because she hardly ever got the chance to get into town to go to the library. She didn't believe in stealing, but she didn't believe in being ignorant like a peasant, either. Or perhaps a goat — a LaMancha or a Bionda dell'Adamello. The goat book was stolen too. Country life had turned her into a common thief. Goats had ridiculous names — the West African dwarf and the Tennessee fainting goat. Or perhaps it would take a perfect strawberry patch, a wigwam of runner beans or a row of marrows and then, suddenly, like finding a magic key, it would all work. She hadn't mentioned the marsh daisy or the West African dwarf to Keith, because although he was country born and bred, he'd rather go to a supermarket any day than raise livestock. And anyway, he wasn't really speaking to her because every time he reached for her in bed she pushed him away and rolled over with her cold back to him and thought, "So this is what it's like to fall out of love with someone."

Sometimes Michelle tried to remember what it was like before the baby came, when it had just been the two of them and they could lie in bed all day and have feverish, exhausting sex and then eat toast and jam and watch television on the tiny black-and-white

set that they used to have at the foot of the bed until Michelle
knocked it over because Keith was watching the snooker (on a
black-and-white set, what was the point of that?) and the baby was
screaming and she *just couldn't do it anymore.*

She did love them, she really did. She just couldn't feel it.

They weren't bonded together, like molecules, molecules that
couldn't bond together into stable elements and instead bounced
around like bingo balls. She should have studied science, not spent
all her time with her head in novels. Novels gave you a completely
false idea about life, they told lies and they implied there were endings when in reality there were no endings, everything just went
on and on and on.

And then she started getting up even earlier because if she wanted
to get out of this mess she was going to have to study for her A
Levels. If she got up at four in the morning — when everything
was miraculously peaceful, even the birds and the baby — then she
could prepare the evening meal, tidy the kitchen, and get a wash
on, and then, if she was lucky, she could get her old schoolbooks
out and take up her education again where she had left off. Because you couldn't make time, she'd been deluded about that.
Time was a thief, he stole your life away from you and the only
way you could get it back was to outwit him and snatch it right
back.

It was just a normal day (normal for Michelle, anyway). It was a
Saturday, and Michelle had been up since half past three and was
feeling particularly satisfied with her strategy. A dish of lasagna,
neatly cling filmed, was sitting in the fridge, waiting to be heated up
later, and she had made a chocolate cake — Shirley's favorite, because her sister often took the bus and came to visit on a Saturday.
She had read three chapters of Mowat's *Britain Between the Wars* and

CASE HISTORIES ~ 43

had made notes for an essay on *King Lear*. The baby was fed, washed, and dressed in the nice blue-and-white-striped OshKosh dungarees that Shirley had bought. Michelle washed the windows while the baby amused itself in the playpen. The sky was blue and the breeze was fresh and Michelle could see green shoots appearing in the vegetable plot, even the coriander had germinated.

After a while she glanced at the baby and saw that it was asleep, curled up like a bug on the floor of the playpen, and Michelle thought she could use the opportunity to get on with her geography, and at that moment Keith lumbered into the house with a pile of logs he'd just chopped and he dropped the logs onto the hearth with a great clatter, making the baby wake up with a start. Automatically, like a switch thrown, the baby began to scream and Michelle began to scream as well, just standing there in the middle of the room, with her arms by her side, screaming, until Keith slapped her on the face, hard, so that her cheek felt as if it had been branded.

Her throat was very sore from the screaming and she felt weak, as if she were going to drop to the floor, and what should have happened at that moment — because, let's face it, they had been here before (although not the slapping) — was that she would burst into tears and Keith would put his arms round her and say, "It's okay, baby, it's okay," and she would sob until she felt better and they would cuddle the baby between them until it felt better too.

Then they could have made a fire with the logs, because it was still chilly in the evenings, and heat up the lasagna and settle down to watch some rubbish on the new color television they'd bought to replace the old black-and-white one. They would have gone to bed with full stomachs and had sex to make up and slept well so that they would be ready for another day of the same old, but what actually happened was that Keith made a move to put his arms round her and she spat at him, which was something new as well, and then she ran outside and got the ax from where it was stuck in a log beside the sawhorse, and then she ran back inside with it.

* * *

It was very cold, because of course the fire had never been lit. Michelle was sitting on the floor. The baby was asleep again. She looked exhausted, the way she did when she was left to cry herself to sleep, and every so often she gave a tiny little hiccup of grief. Michelle felt as if she had a stone inside her, something hard and unyielding that was making her feel sick. She hadn't known it was possible to feel this bad. She looked at Keith and felt sorry for him. When you chopped logs with the ax and they split open they smelled beautiful, like Christmas. But when you split someone's head open it smelled like an abattoir and quite overpowered the scent of the wild lilacs you'd cut and brought into the house only this morning, which was already in another life.

If she could have had one wish — if her fairy godmother (noticeably absent from her life so far) were to suddenly appear in the cold living room of the cottage and offer to grant her whatever she wanted, Michelle knew exactly what she would ask for. She would ask to go back to the beginning of her life and start all over again.

She wondered if she should get up from the floor and clean up a bit but she felt so tired that she thought she might just stay there and wait until the police came. She had all the time in the world now.

4

Jackson

Jackson switched on the radio and listened to the reassuring voice of Jenni Murray on *Woman's Hour.* He lit a new cigarette from the stub of the old one because he had run out of matches, and faced with a choice between chain-smoking or abstinence, he'd taken the former option because it felt like there was enough abstinence in his life already. If he got the cigarette lighter on the dashboard fixed he wouldn't have to smoke his way through the packet, but there were a lot of other things that needed fixing on the car and the cigarette lighter wasn't high on the list. Jackson drove a black Alfa Romeo 156 that he'd bought secondhand four years ago for £13,000 and that was now probably worth less than the Emmelle Freedom mountain bike he had just given his daughter for her eighth birthday (on the proviso that she didn't cycle on the road until she was at least forty).

When he'd come home with the Alfa Romeo, his wife took one dismissive look at it and said, "You bought a policeman's car then." Four years ago Josie was driving her own Polo and was still married to Jackson, now she was living with a bearded English lecturer and driving his Volvo V70 with a CHILD ON BOARD sign in the rear window, testifying both to the permanence of their relation-

ship and to the smug git's need to show the world that he was pro-
tecting another man's child. Jackson hated those signs.

He was a born-again smoker, only starting up again six months
ago. Jackson hadn't touched a cigarette for fifteen years and now it
was as if he'd never been off them. And for no reason. "Just like
that," he said, doing an unenthusiastic Tommy Cooper impression
to his reflection in the rearview mirror. Of course it wasn't "just
like that." Nothing ever was.

She'd better hurry up. Her front door remained determinedly
closed. It was made of cheap varnished wood, with a mock-
Georgian fanlight, and was the spit of every other door on the estate
in Cherry Hinton. Jackson could have kicked it in without breaking a sweat. She was late. Her flight was at one and she should
have been on her way to the airport by now. Jackson cracked the
car window to let in some air and let out some smoke. She was
always late.

Coffee was no good for punctuating the tedium, unless he was
prepared to piss into a bottle, which he wasn't. Now that he was
divorced he was free to use words like "piss" and "shit" — elements
of his vocabulary almost eliminated by Josie. She was a primary-
school teacher and spent much of her working day modifying the
behavior of five-year-old boys. When they were married she would
come home and do the same to Jackson ("For God's sake, Jackson,
use the proper words. It's a *penis*") during their evenings together,
cooking pasta and yawning their way through crap on television.
She wanted their daughter, Marlee, to grow up "using the correct
anatomical language for genitalia." Jackson would rather Marlee
grew up without knowing genitalia even existed, let alone informing him that she had been "made" when he "put his penis in
Mummy's vagina," an oddly clinical description for an urgent,
sweatily precipitate event that had taken place in a field somewhere
off the A1066 between Thetford and Diss, an acrobatic coupling
in his old F Reg BMW (320i, two-door, definitely a policeman's

car, much missed, RIP). That was in the days when a sudden desperate need to have sex was commonplace between them, and the only thing that had made this particular incidence memorable had been Josie's uncharacteristically Russian roulette attitude toward birth control.

Later she blamed the consequence (Marlee) on his own unpreparedness, but Jackson thought Marlee was a winning result and anyway what did Josie expect if she started fondling his — and let's be anatomically correct here — penis while all he was trying to do was get to Diss, although for what reason was now lost to time. Jackson himself was conceived during the course of a guesthouse holiday in Ayrshire, a fact that his father had always found inexplicably amusing.

He shouldn't have thought about coffee because now there was a dull ache in his bladder. When *Woman's Hour* finished he put Allison Moorer's *Alabama Song* on the CD player, an album that he found comfortingly melancholic. *Bonjour Tristesse*. Jackson was going to French classes with a view to the day when he could sell up and move abroad and do whatever people did when they retired early. Golf? Did the French play golf? Jackson couldn't think of the names of any French golfers, so that was a good sign because Jackson hated golf. Maybe he could just play *boules* and smoke himself to death. The French were good at smoking.

Jackson had never felt at home in Cambridge, never felt at home in the south of England if it came to that. He had come here more or less by accident, following a girlfriend and staying for a wife. For years, he had thought about moving back north, but he knew he never would. There was nothing there for him, just bad memories and a past he could never undo, and what was the point anyway when France was laid out on the other side of the channel like an exotic patchwork of sunflowers and grapevines and little cafés where he could sit all afternoon drinking local wine and bitter espressos and smoking Gitanes, where everyone would say, *Bonjour, Jackson,* except they would pronounce it "zhaksong," and he would be happy. Which was exactly the opposite of how he felt now.

Of course, at the rate he was going it wouldn't be early retirement, just retirement. Jackson could remember when he was a kid and retired men were the old guys who tottered between the allotment and the corner of the pub. They had seemed like *really* old guys but maybe they weren't much older than he was now. Jackson was forty-five but felt much, much older. He was at that dangerous age when men suddenly notice that they're going to die eventually, inevitably, and there isn't a damn thing they can do about it, but that doesn't stop them from trying, whether it's shagging anything that moves or listening to early Bruce Springsteen and buying a top-of-the-range motorbike (a BMW K 1200 LT usually, thus considerably upping their chances of meeting death even earlier than anticipated). Then there were the guys who found themselves in the rut of routine alcoholic tedium — the lost and lonesome highway of your average beta male (his father's way). And then there was Jackson's own chosen path that led to the everyday Zen of a French house with its white stucco walls, geraniums in pots on the windowsills, a blue door, the paint peeling because who gives a damn about house maintenance in rural France?

He had parked in the shade but the sun had moved higher in the sky now and the temperature in the car was becoming uncomfortable. She was called Nicola Spencer and she was twenty-nine years old and lived in a neat ghetto of brick-built houses. The houses and the streets all looked the same to Jackson, and if he lost his bearings for a moment he ended up in a Bermuda Triangle of identical open-plan front lawns. Jackson had an almost unreasonable prejudice against housing estates. This prejudice was not unrelated to his ex-wife and his ex-marriage. It was Josie who had wanted a house on a new estate, Josie who had been one of the first people to sign up to live in Cambourne, the purpose-built Disneylike "community" outside Cambridge with its cricket pitch on the "traditional" village green, its "Roman-themed play area." It was Josie who had moved them into the house when the street was still a building site and insisted that they furnish it with practical modern designs, who had rejected Victoriana as cluttered, who had thought an excess of carpets and curtains was "suffocating," and yet now she was inhabiting Ye Olde Curiosity Shop with David Lastingham — a Victorian terrace crammed with antique furniture that he'd inherited from his parents, every available surface swathed and draped and curtained. ("You're sure he's not gay then?" Jackson had asked Josie, just to rile her — the guy had professional manicures, for heaven's sake — and she laughed and said, "He's not insecure with his masculinity, Jackson.")

Jackson could feel the ache in his jaw starting up again. He was currently seeing more of his dentist than he had of his wife in the last year of their marriage. His dentist was called Sharon and was what his father used to refer to as "stacked." She was thirty-six and drove a BMW Z3, which was a bit of a hairdresser's car in Jackson's opinion, but nonetheless he found her very attractive. Unfortunately, there was no possibility of having a relationship with someone who had to put on a mask, protective glasses, and gloves to touch you. (Or one who peered into your mouth and murmured, "Smoking, Jackson?")

He opened an out-of-date copy of *Le Nouvel Observateur* and tried to read it because his French teacher said they should immerse themselves in French culture, even if they didn't understand it. Jackson could only pick out the odd word that meant anything and he could see subjunctives scattergunned all over the place — if ever there was an unnecessary tense it was the French subjunctive. His eyes drifted drowsily over the page. A lot of his life these days consisted of simply waiting, something he would have been useless at twenty years ago but which he now found almost agreeable. Doing nothing was much more productive than people thought; Jackson often had his most profound insights when he appeared to be entirely idle. He didn't get bored, he just went into a nothing kind of place. He thought sometimes that he would like to enter a monastery, that he would be good at being an ascetic, an anchorite, a Zen monk.

Jackson had arrested a jeweler once, an old guy who'd been fencing stolen property, and when Jackson came looking for him in his workshop he'd found him sitting in an ancient armchair, smoking his pipe and contemplating a piece of rock on his workbench. Without saying anything, he took the rock and placed it in Jackson's palm, as if it were a gift — Jackson was reminded of his biology teacher from school who would hand you something — a bird's egg, a leaf — and make you explain it to him rather than the other way round. The rock was a dark ironstone that looked like petrified tree-bark, and sandwiched in the center of it was a seam of milky opal, like a hazy summer sky at dawn. A notoriously tricky stone to work, the old man informed Jackson. He had been looking at it for two weeks now, he said, another two weeks and he might be ready to start cutting it, and Jackson said that in another two weeks he would be in a remand prison somewhere, but the guy had a great lawyer and made bail and got away with a suspended sentence.

A year later Jackson received a parcel addressed to him at the police station. Inside there was no note, just a box, and in a nest lined with midnight-blue velvet was an opal pendant, a little plaque of sky. Jackson knew he was being given a lesson by the old man, but it had taken him many years to understand it. He was keeping the pendant for Marlee's eighteenth birthday.

Nicola's husband, Steve Spencer, was convinced his wife "had taken a lover" — that's how he put it, so it sounded delicate and rather courtly to Jackson's ears, whereas most of the suspicious spouses who came to him tended to voice their mistrust in cruder terms. Steve was the nervy, paranoid type and he couldn't understand how he'd managed to net someone like Nicola, because she was "so gorgeous." Jackson had known "gorgeous" in his time and it wasn't the Nicola Spencers of the world, although he thought that if he was married to Steve Spencer he might be tempted to "take a lover." Steve was a pharmacist in a chain of drugstores and seemed to have no hobbies or interests other than Nicola. She was "the only woman in the world" for him. Jackson had never believed that there was one person in the world that you were destined for. And if there was, knowing his luck, she'd be working in a rice field in the middle of China or be a convicted killer on the run.

When she wasn't at work, Nicola Spencer went to the gym, to Sainsbury's (and once, for no apparent reason, to Tesco's), to her mother's, to the homes of a friend called Louise and a friend called Vanessa. Vanessa was part of a married couple — Vanessa and Mike — who were also friends of "Steve and Nicola." Louise and Vanessa, as far as Jackson could tell, didn't know each other. Nicola also went regularly to the garage, for petrol obviously, and in the garage shop she sometimes bought milk and nearly always bought chocolate and a copy of *Hello* or *Heat*. She had also been to a garden center, where she bought a tray of bedding plants that she had put straight into the garden and had then failed to water, judging by the look of them when Jackson climbed up on the garden fence to have a snoop at what went on chez Spencer, or, more accurately, *au jardin* Spencer.

In the last four weeks Nicola had also been to a DIY superstore, where she bought a screwdriver and a Stanley knife, to Habitat, where she bought a table lamp, to Top Shop for a white T-shirt, to Next for a white blouse, to Boots (twice for cosmetics and toiletries and once with a prescription for Ponstan), to Robert Sayle's for two blue hand towels, and to a fish stall on the market, where she bought (expensive) monkfish for a meal — for the aforesaid Vanessa and Mike — which Steve Spencer later reported to have been "a disaster." Nicola was apparently not a great cook. She also led a bloody boring life, unless something fantastically interesting happened to her when she was pushing a trolley up and down the economy aisles of her airline. Is that what had happened to Josie when she "took" David Lastingham? Was she just so bored with Jackson that she couldn't bear it anymore? She met him at a party, a party that Jackson hadn't gone to because he was working, and the pair of them had "tried to control their feelings" but they obviously hadn't tried hard enough because within six months they were taking each other at every available clandestine opportunity and now David Lastingham got to put his penis in Mummy's vagina whenever he felt like it.

Josie had filed for divorce as soon as it was possible. Irretrievable breakdown — as if it were all his fault and she wasn't shagging some poncy guy with a goatee. ("David," Marlee said, not as grudgingly as Jackson would have liked. "He's alright, he buys me chocolate, he makes nice pasta." It was a six-lane motorway from that girl's stomach to her heart. "I cook nice pasta," Jackson said and heard how childish that sounded and didn't care. Jackson had got someone he knew to look up David Lastingham on the pedophile register. Just in case.)

Jackson smoked the last cigarette. Nicola hadn't done anything the least suspicious on Jackson's watch, so if she was having an affair then she must be literally playing away from home — all those stopovers in midrange hotels, warm evenings, and cheap alcohol provided the perfect conditions for fostering bad behavior. Jackson had tried to explain to Steve that he was going to have to pay for Jackson to fly with Nicola if he really wanted to find out if anything was going on, but Steve wasn't keen to fund what he seemed to think would be a free holiday abroad for Jackson. Jackson thought he might just go anyway and then do some creative accounting when it came to the bill, a return trip to almost anywhere in Europe could easily disappear into the catchall heading of "Sundries." Maybe he would wait until she was on a flight to France and tag along. Jackson didn't want a holiday, he wanted a new life. And he wanted to be finished with Nicola Spencer and her own dull life.

When Jackson set up as a private investigator two years ago he had no expectation of it being a glamorous profession. He'd already been a member of the Cambridgeshire Constabulary for twelve years and before that he was in the military police, so he had no illusions about the ways of the world. Investigating other people's tragedies and cock-ups and misfortunes was all he knew. He was used to being a voyeur, the outsider looking in, and nothing, but nothing, that anyone did surprised him anymore. Yet despite everything he'd seen and done, inside Jackson there remained a belief — a small, battered and bruised belief — that his job was to help people be good rather than punishing them for being bad.

He left the police and set up the investigation agency after his marriage disappeared in front of his eyes. "What about your pension?" Josie said to him. "What about it?" Jackson said, a cavalier attitude he was beginning to regret.

For the most part, the work he undertook now was either irksome or dull — process serving, background checking and bad debts, and hunting down the odd rogue tradesman that the police would never get round to ("I gave him £300 up front for materials and I never saw him again." Surprise, surprise). Not to forget missing cats.

On cue, Jackson's mobile rang, a tinny rendition of "Carmen Burana," a ring tone reserved exclusively for Binky Rain ("Binky" — what kind of a name *was* that? Really?). Binky Rain was the first client Jackson had acquired when he set up as a private investigator and he supposed he would never be rid of her until he retired and even then he could imagine her following him to France, a string of stray cats behind her, pied piper–like. She was a catwoman, the mad, old-bat variety that kept an open door for every feline slacker in Cambridge.

Binky was over ninety and was the widow of "a Peterhouse fellow," a philosophy don (despite living in Cambridge for fourteen years, Jackson still thought of the mafia when he heard that word). "Doctor Rain" — Julian — had long gone to rest in the great Senior Common Room in the sky. Binky herself had been brought up in colonial Africa and treated Jackson like a servant, which was how she treated everyone. She lived in a bungalow in Newnham on the way to Grantchester Meadows in what must have once been a perfectly normal between-the-wars redbrick, but years of neglect had transformed it into an overgrown Gothic horror. The place was crawling with cats, hundreds of the damn things. Jackson got the heebie-jeebies just thinking about the smell — cat urine, tomcat spray, saucers of tinned food on every surface, the cheap stuff that was made from the parts of animals that even the burger chains shunned. Binky Rain had no money, no friends, and no family and her neighbors avoided her, and yet she effortlessly maintained the facade of aristocratic hauteur, like a refugee from some ancien régime, living out her life in tatters. Binky Rain was exactly the kind of person whose body lay undiscovered in her house for weeks, except that her cats would probably have eaten her by the time she was found.

Her complaint, the reason she had originally engaged Jackson's services, was that someone was stealing her cats. Jackson couldn't work out whether cats really did go missing or whether she just thought they went missing. She had this thing about black cats in particular. "Someone's taking them," she said in her clipped little voice, her accent as anachronistic as everything else about her, a remnant, a leftover from another time, another place, long turned into history. The first cat to go missing was a black cat ("bleck ket") called Mrs. Chippy — named after the cat on board Shackleton's ship *Endurance*. Her brother-in-law had been a stalwart of the Scott Polar Research Institute on Lensfield Road and had spent a winter camped on the ice of the Ross Shelf, making Binky an expert on antarctic exploration, apparently. Scott was "a fool," Shackleton "a womanizer," and Peary "an American," which seemed to be enough of a condemnation in itself. The way Binky talked about polar expeditions ("Horses! Only an idiot would take horses!") belied the fact that the most challenging journey she had undertaken was the voyage from Cape Town to Southampton in first class on the *Dunnottar Castle* in 1938.

Jackson let his voice mail pick up Binky's message and then listened back to her imperial tones commanding him to visit her as soon as possible on "a matter of some urgency" to do with "Frisky."

Binky Rain had never paid Jackson in the two years he had known her, but he supposed this was fair as, for his part, he had never found a single missing cat in those two years. He saw his visits to her more as a social service: no one else ever visited the poor old cow and Jackson had a tolerance for her idiosyncrasies that surprised even himself. She was an old Nazi boot but you had to admire her spirit. Why did she think people were taking her cats? Jackson thought it would be vivisection — the usual paranoid belief of cat lovers, but no, according to Binky they took them to make gloves out of them. (Bleck gloves, obviously.)

Jackson was just debating with himself whether to give up on tardy Nicola and obey Binky's summons when the front door flew open. Jackson slid down in the driver's seat and pretended to be concentrating on *Le Nouvel Observateur*. He could see from fifty yards away that Nicola was in a bad mood, although that was more or less her default setting. She looked hot, already tightly buttoned into the airline's ugly uniform. The uniform didn't show off her figure, and the heels she was wearing — like the Queen's shoes — made her ankles look thick. The only time Jackson saw Nicola without makeup was when she was running. *Au naturel*. She ran like someone training for a marathon. Jackson was a runner — he ran three miles every morning, up at six, out on the street, back for coffee, before most people were up. That was what army training did for you. Army, the police, and a hefty dose of Scottish Presbyterian genes. ("Always running, Jackson," Josie said. "If you run forever you come back to where you started from — that's the curvature of space for you, did you know that?")

Nicola looked much better in her running clothes. In her uniform she looked frumpy but when she ran around the maze of streets where she lived, she looked athletic and strong. For running, she wore tracksuit bottoms and an old Blue Jays T-shirt that she must have picked up in Toronto, although she hadn't flown across the Atlantic during the time that Jackson had been watching her. She had been to Milan three times, Rome twice, and once each to Madrid, Düsseldorf, Perpignan, Naples, and Faro.

Nicola got in her car, a little girly Ford Ka, and took off like a rocket for Stansted. Jackson wasn't exactly a slow driver but Nicola went at terrifying speeds. When this was over he was considering alerting someone in traffic. Jackson had done a stint in traffic before plainclothes and there were times when he would have liked to pull Nicola over and arrest her.

His phone rang again as the traffic slowed in a holding pattern around Stansted. This time it was his secretary, Deborah, who snapped, "Where are you?" as if he was supposed to be somewhere else.

"I'm fine, thank you. How are you?"

"Someone phoned. You may as well go and see them while you're out and about." Deborah said "out and about" as if Jackson were getting drunk or picking up women.

"Do you want to enlighten me further?" he asked.

"No," Deborah said. "Something about finding something."

Once Nicola arrived at the airport her movements followed their usual routine. She parked her car and went inside the terminal, and Jackson watched her until she disappeared from view. After that he went to the toilets, had a double espresso from a paper cup that did nothing to cool down the heat of the day, purchased cigarettes, read the headlines in a newspaper that he didn't buy, and then drove away again.

By the time Nicola's plane to Prague was climbing steeply away from the flat countryside below, Jackson was walking up the path of a large house on Owlstone Road, frighteningly close to where Binky Rain lived. The door was answered by a woman stranded somewhere in her forties who squinted at Jackson over the top of a pair of half-moon spectacles. Academic, he thought to himself.

"Mrs. Land?" Jackson said.

"Miss Land," she said. "Amelia Land. Thank you for coming."

Amelia Land made a terrible cup of coffee. Jackson could already feel its corrosive effect on his stomach. She was wandering around the neglected kitchen, searching for biscuits, even though Jackson had told her twice that he didn't want one, thank you. Finally, she retrieved a packet of damp digestives from the depths of a cupboard and Jackson ate one just to keep her happy. The biscuit was like soft, stale sand in his mouth, but Amelia Land seemed satisfied that her duty as a hostess had been done.

She seemed very distracted, even mildly deranged, but, living in Cambridge, Jackson had got used to university types, although she said she lived in "Oxford, not Cambridge. It's a *completely* different place," and Jackson had thought, "Yeah, right," but said nothing.

Amelia Land kept babbling on about blue mice, and when he'd said gently to her, "Start at the beginning, Miss Land," she'd carried on with the blue-mice theme and said that *was* the beginning, and "Please call me Amelia." Jackson sighed inwardly, he sensed this tale was going to take a lot of coaxing.

The sister appeared, disappeared, and then reappeared, holding in her hand what looked like an old doll. You would never have taken them for relatives, one tall and heavy, her hair graying and falling out of a kind of topknot, the other short and curvy and — Jackson knew this type too — flirting with anything male and still breathing. The sister wore bright red lipstick and was dressed in what looked like secondhand clothes, layers of mismatched eccentric garments, her wild hair piled haphazardly on her head and fixed with a pencil. They were both dressed for cold weather rather than the sweltering day outside. Jackson could see why — he had shivered as he crossed the threshold, leaving the sunshine behind for the wintry gloom of the interior.

"Our father died two days ago," Julia said, as if it were an everyday nuisance. Jackson looked at the doll on the table. It was made of some kind of grubby toweling material and had long thin legs and arms and the head of a mouse. And it was blue. Understanding finally dawned. He nodded at it. "A blue mouse," he said to Amelia.

"No, *the* Blue Mouse," she said, as if that distinction were vital. Amelia Land might as well have had "unloved" tattooed on her forehead. She was dressed in a way that suggested she'd stopped shopping for new clothes twenty years ago and that when she had shopped for clothes it had been exclusively in Laura Ashley. The way she was dressed reminded him of old photographs of fishwives — clumpy shoes and woolen tights and a cord dirndl skirt and around her shoulders some kind of shawl that she was hugging to herself as if she were freezing, which wasn't a surprise because this place was *Baltic,* Jackson thought. It was as if the house had its own climate.

"Our father died," Amelia said brusquely, "two days ago."

"Yes," Jackson said carefully. "Your sister just said that. I'm sorry for your loss," he added, rather perfunctorily because he could see that neither of them seemed particularly sorry.

Amelia frowned and said, "What I mean is . . ." She looked at her sister for help. That was the trouble with academic types, Jackson thought, never able to say what they mean and half the time never meaning what they say.

"Let me hazard a guess," he said helpfully. "Your father died —" They both nodded vigorously as if relieved that Jackson had grasped this point. "Your father died," he continued, "and you started clearing out the old family home —" he hesitated because they looked less sure of this, "This is the old family home?" he checked.

"Well, yes," Julia said. "It's just" — she shrugged — "that sounds so *warm,* you know. 'Old family home.'"

"Well," Jackson said, "how about we remove any emotional significance from those three words and just treat them as two adjectives and a noun. Old. Family. Home. True or false?"

"True," Julia admitted reluctantly.

"Of course, strictly speaking," Amelia said, staring out the kitchen window as if she were talking to someone in the garden, "'family' isn't an adjective. 'Familial' would be the adjective."

"No, it wouldn't," Julia said.

Jackson decided the best thing would be to carry on as if neither of them had spoken. "Not close to the old guy then?" he said to Julia.

"No, we weren't," Amelia said, turning round and giving him her full attention. "And we found this in a locked drawer in his study." The blue mouse again. The Blue Mouse.

"And the significance of the 'Blue Mouse'?" Jackson prompted.

He hoped they hadn't just discovered their old man was some kind of soft-toy fetishist.

"Did you ever hear of Olivia Land?" Julia asked.

"Rings a bell," Jackson said. A very small bell. "A relative?"

"She was our sister," Amelia said. "She disappeared thirty-four years ago. She was taken."

Taken? Oh, not alien abduction, that would really make his day. Julia took out a packet of cigarettes and offered him one. She made offering a cigarette seem like an invitation to sex. He could feel the sister's disapproval from where he sat but whether it was of the nicotine or the sex, he wasn't sure. Both probably. He declined the cigarette, he would never have smoked in front of a client anyway, but he inhaled deeply when Julia lit up.

"She was kidnapped," Julia said, "from a tent in the garden."

"A tent?"

"It was summer," Amelia said sharply. "Children sleep outside in tents in the summer."

"So they do," Jackson said mildly. Somehow he had the feeling that Amelia Land had been the one in the tent with the sister.

"She was only three," Julia said. "She was never found."

"You really don't know the case?" Amelia said. "It was very big."

"I'm not from this area," Jackson said and thought of all the girls who must have disappeared over the last thirty-four years. But, of course, as far as the Land sisters were concerned, there was only one. He felt suddenly too sad and too old.

"It was very hot," Amelia said. "A heat wave."

"Like now?"

"Yes. Aren't you going to take notes?"

"Would it make you happier if I did?" he asked.

"No," Amelia snapped.

They had obviously reached some kind of conversational impasse. Jackson looked at the Blue Mouse. It had "clue" written all over it. Jackson attempted to join the dots. "So, let's see," he ventured. "This is Olivia's and she had it with her when she was abducted? And the first time it's been seen since is when it turns up after your father's death? And you didn't call the police?"

They both frowned. It was funny because although they looked quite different they shared exactly the same facial expressions. Jackson supposed that was what was meant by "fleeting resemblance."

"What wonderful powers of deduction you have, Mr. Brodie," Julia said, and it was hard to tell whether she was being ironic or trying to flatter him. She had one of those husky voices that sounded as if she were permanently coming down with a cold. Men seemed to find that sexy in a woman, which Jackson thought was odd because it made women sound less like women and more like men. Maybe it was a gay thing.

"The police didn't find her *then*," Amelia said, ignoring Julia, "and they're not going to be interested *now*. And, anyway, maybe it's not a matter for the police."

"But it's a matter for me?"

"Mr. Brodie," Julia said, very sweetly, too sweetly. They were like good cop, bad cop. "Mr. Brodie, we just want to know why Victor had Olivia's Blue Mouse."

"Victor?"

"Daddy. It just seems . . ."

"Wrong?" Jackson supplied.

Jackson rented a house now, a long way from the Cambourne ghetto. It was a cottage really, in a row of similar small cottages, on a road that must once have been in the countryside, farm cottages, probably. Whatever farm they had been a part of had long since been built over by streets of Victorian working-class terraces. Nowadays even houses that were back-to-backs with their front doors opening straight onto the street went for a fortune in the area. The poor moved out to the likes of Milton and Cherry Hinton, but now even the council estates there had been colonized by middle-class university types (and the Nicola Spencers of the world), which must really piss the poor people off. The poor might always be with us, but Jackson was puzzled as to where they actually lived these days.

When Josie left for nonconnubial bliss with David Lastingham, Jackson considered staying on and living in the marital Lego house. This thought had occupied him for roughly ten minutes before he rang the estate agent and put it on the market. After they had split the proceeds of the sale, there wasn't enough money left for Jackson to buy a new place, so he had chosen to rent this house instead. It was the last in the terrace, on the run-down side, and the walls between it and the house next door were so thin that you could hear every fart and cat mewl from the neighbor's. The furnishings that came with it were cheap and it had an impersonal atmosphere, like a disappointing holiday home, that Jackson found strangely restful.

When he moved out of the house he had shared with his wife and daughter, Jackson went round to every room in the house to check that nothing had been left behind, apart from their lives, of course. When he walked into the bathroom he realized that he could still smell Josie's perfume — *L'Air du Temps* — a scent she had worn long before he had ever met her. Now she wore the Joy by Patou that David Lastingham bought her, a scent so old-fashioned that it made her seem like a different woman, which she was, of course. The Josie he had known had rejected all the wifely attributes of her mother's generation. She was a lousy cook and didn't even possess a sewing basket, but she did all the DIY in their little box house. She said to him once that when women learned that wall anchors weren't the mysterious objects they thought they were, they would rule the world. Jackson had been under the impression that they already did and made the mistake of voicing this opinion, which resulted in a statistical lecture about global gender politics — "Two-thirds of the world's work is done by women, Jackson, yet they only own one-tenth of the world's property — do you see any problem with that?" (Yes, he did.) Now, of course, she had turned into retro woman, a kind of Stepford wife, who baked bread and was going to knitting classes. Knitting! What kind of a joke was that?

When he moved into the rented house he bought a bottle of *L'Air du Temps* and sprayed the tiny bathroom with it, but it wasn't the same.

Amelia and Julia had given him a photograph, a small, square, faded color photograph from another time. It was a close-up of Olivia, grinning for the camera, all her regular little teeth on show. There were freckles on her snub nose and her hair was looped up in short plaits, tied with green-and-white gingham ribbons, although all the colors in the photograph had acquired a yellow tint with age. She was wearing a dress that matched the ribbons, the smocking on the dress partly concealed by the blue mouse that she was clutching to her chest. Jackson could tell she was making the blue mouse pose for the camera — he could almost hear her telling it to smile, but its features, appliquéd in black wool, carried the same air of gravity then that they did now, except that time had robbed the blue mouse of half an eye and a nostril.

It was the same photograph that the papers had used. Jackson had looked up the microfiche files on his way home. There were pages and pages about the search for Olivia Land, the story ran for weeks, and Amelia was right — the big story before Olivia had been the heat wave. Jackson tried to remember thirty-four years ago. He would have been eleven years old. Had it been hot? He had no idea. He couldn't remember eleven. The important thing about it was that it wasn't twelve. All the years before he was twelve shone with an unblemished and immaculate light. After twelve it was dark.

He listened to the messages on his answering machine. One from his daughter, Marlee, complaining that her mother wouldn't let her go to an open-air concert on Parker's Piece "and would Jackson talk to her, please, please?" (Marlee was eight, no way was she going to an open-air concert.) Another "Frisky" message from Binky Rain and one from his secretary, Deborah Arnold, berating him for not coming back into the office. She was ringing from home — he could hear two of her loutish teenagers talking in the background over the blare of MTV. Deborah had to shout in order to inform him that there was "a Theo Wyre" trying to get in touch with him and she didn't know what it was about except that he "seemed to have lost something." The name "Theo Wyre" sounded startlingly familiar but he couldn't place it. Old age, he supposed.

Jackson fetched a Tiger Beer from the fridge, pulled off his boots (Magnum Stealths, the only boot as far as Jackson was concerned), lay down on the uncomfortable couch, and reached over to his CD player (the good thing about living in a tiny house was that he could touch almost everything in the room without getting up) and put on Trisha Yearwood's 1995 *Thinkin' About You* album, now unavailable for some reason. Trisha might be mainstream, but that didn't mean she wasn't good. She understood pain. He opened *An Introduction to French Grammar* and tried to focus on the correct use of the past using *être* (although when he lived in France there would be no past and no future, only present), but it was difficult to concentrate because the gum above his rogue tooth was throbbing.

Jackson sighed and retrieved the blue mouse from the mantelpiece and placed it against his shoulder and patted its small, soft back, in much the same way he had once comforted Marlee when she was small. The blue mouse felt cold, as if it had been in a dark place for a long time. Not for a moment did Jackson think that he could find that little girl with the gingham ribbons in her plaits.

Jackson closed his eyes and opened them again immediately because he'd suddenly remembered who Theo Wyre was. Jackson groaned. He didn't want to remember Theo Wyre. He didn't want anything to do with Theo Wyre.

Trisha was singing "On a Bus to St. Cloud." Sometimes it seemed to him as if the entire world consisted of one accounting sheet — lost on the left-hand side, found on the right. Unfortunately the two never balanced. Amelia and Julia Land had found something, Theo Wyre had lost something. How easy life would be if it could be one and the same thing.

5

Amelia

Victor died as he wished, in his own bed, in his own home, of nothing much more than old age. He was eighty-four and for as long as they could remember had been adamant that he wanted to be buried rather than cremated. Thirty-four years ago, when their baby sister Annabelle died, Victor had bought a "family plot" for three people in the local cemetery. Amelia and Julia hadn't really considered the arithmetic of this until Victor himself died, by which time the plot was two-thirds full — their mother having joined Annabelle with gratuitous haste — leaving just enough room for Victor but excluding his remaining children.

Julia said it demonstrated typically inconsiderate behavior on Victor's part, but Amelia said their father had probably deliberately planned it this way in case it turned out that there was an eternal afterlife and he might be forced to spend it with them. Amelia didn't really think this was likely — Victor was a staunch atheist and it wasn't in his stubborn, abrasive character to suddenly start hedging his bets at the end — it was just that proposing a contradictory viewpoint to Julia's came automatically to her. Julia was as tenacious (and as yappy) as a terrier when it came to disputes, so that they both constantly found themselves arguing the case for opinions that neither of them really cared about one way or the other, like a pair of bickering, jaded courtroom lawyers. Some days it felt as if they had returned to their turbulent childhood selves and any moment now would resort to the covert pinching, hair pulling, and name-calling of those earlier years.

They had been summoned. "Like attending the deathbed of a king," Julia said resentfully, and Amelia said, "You're thinking of *King Lear*," and Julia said, "What if I am?" and Amelia said, "You can only relate to life if you've seen it on the stage," and Julia said, "I never even mentioned fucking *Lear*," and so they were arguing before the train had even pulled out of King's Cross. Victor died a few hours after they arrived. "Thank fuck," Julia said, as they had been suspicious that Victor was trying to finesse them back into the family home to look after him. They both resented the word "home" — it was decades since either of them had lived there, yet they couldn't stop using the word.

Amelia said, "Sorry," but Julia was staring out the train window at suburban London passing by and didn't speak again until they were traveling through the full summer fields of East Anglia, when she said, "Lear wasn't dying, he was abdicating power," and Amelia said, "Same thing sometimes," and was glad they'd made peace.

They sat on either side of him, waiting for him to die. Victor was beached on his bed in what had once been the marital bedroom, a room that was still decorated in the overblown female style that their mother had once favored. Was Rosemary getting ready at this very moment to welcome Victor into the clammy soil of the family plot? Amelia imagined her parents clasping each other's bodies in a cold embrace and felt sorry for their poor mother, who probably thought she had escaped Victor forever.

And anyway, Amelia pointed out to Julia, picking up the argument despite her best intentions, neither of them wanted to be close to their father in life, so why would they want to be close to him in death? Julia said that wasn't the point. It was "the principle of the thing," and Amelia said, "When did you start having principles?" and so the conversation went downhill again, long before they had got round to discussing the more difficult topic of the funeral service itself, for which Victor had left no guidelines.

When had they decided to stop calling him "Daddy" and start calling him "Victor"? Julia sometimes called him "Daddy," especially when she was trying to cajole him into a pleasanter mood, but Amelia liked the distance that "Victor" gave. It made him more human somehow.

Victor's chin was bristled with white, and this new beard, coupled with the weight he had lost, made him unfamiliar. Only his hands seemed not to have shrunk — still huge, like bony shovels, brutish against his sticklike wrists. He suddenly mumbled something neither of them could make out and Julia cast a look of panic across the bed at Amelia. Julia had expected him to be dying but she hadn't expected him not to be himself. "Do you want anything, Daddy?" she said loudly to him and he shook his head as if trying to dislodge a cloud of flies but it was impossible to say whether or not he had heard them.

Victor's GP had told them on the phone that district nurses were coming in three times a day. "Popping in" was the phrase he had used, which made everything seem convivial and informal, but neither Amelia nor Julia had expected those adjectives would be applicable to Victor's death, as they certainly hadn't been applicable to his life. They thought the nurses would stay, but the minute Amelia and Julia arrived, one of them said, "We'll be off now then," and the other shouted to Victor over her shoulder, "They're here!" in a cheerful way as if Victor had been waiting anxiously for his daughters, which he wasn't, of course, and the only one pleased to see them was Sammy, Victor's old golden retriever, who made a gallant attempt to greet them, his arthritic hips moving stiffly as his claws clacked across the polished boards of the hallway.

Victor had a massive stroke, the GP said on the phone. A month ago, a different GP had told them that there was nothing wrong with Victor except for old age and that he had "the heart of an ox." "The heart of an ox" had seemed a muddled axiom to Amelia: wasn't it "heart of a lion" and "strong as an ox"? What was an ox? Just a cow? There were so many facts that Amelia no longer felt certain about (or perhaps she had never known them). She would soon be nearer fifty than forty, and she was sure that every day she could feel more neural pathways disappearing — fusing and arcing and dying — leaving her unable to retrieve information. Right up until the end, Victor's mind had been as methodical as an efficient library, whereas Amelia felt that hers was more like the cupboard under the stair where ancient hockey sticks were shoved in beside broken Hoovers and boxes of old Christmas decorations, and the one thing you knew was in there — a five-amp fuse, a tin of tan shoe polish, a Phillips screwdriver — would almost certainly be the one thing you couldn't lay your hands on.

Victor's mind might have remained organized but his house hadn't. After they left home it had steadily deteriorated until it was now almost squalid, like one of those houses where environmental health officers had to be brought in to clean up after some unfortunate had lain dead and unnoticed for weeks, lying in a pool of their own putrefaction.

Everywhere you looked there were books, all of them mildewed and foxed, none of them inviting you to read them. Victor had long since given up maths, it was years since he had kept up with research or shown any interest in journals or publications. When they were children Rosemary had told them that Victor was a "great" mathematician (or perhaps it was Victor himself who had told them that), but whatever his reputation it had long since faded and he had been nothing more than a plodding member of the department. His speciality had been probability and risk, which Amelia didn't understand at all (he was always trying to demonstrate probability to her by tossing coins), but it struck her as ironic that a man who studied risk for a living had never taken one in his life.

"Milly? Are you alright?"

"What *is* an ox?"

"A cow. A bullock." Julia shrugged. "I don't know. Why?"

They had eaten ox heart as children. Rosemary, never having so much as boiled an egg before her marriage, had learned to cook the kind of stalwart, old-fashioned food that Victor favored as being both nutritious and cheap. Boarding-school food, the kind he was brought up on. The very thought of all those liver-and-bacon casseroles and steak-and-kidney puddings made Amelia feel sick. She could still see a bloody heart sitting on the kitchen counter, dark and glistening, and swagged with threads of fat, looking as if it had only just stopped beating, while her mother, huge knife in hand, contemplated it with an enigmatic expression on her face.

"Oxtail soup, I remember that," Julia said, making a disgusted face. "Was it really made from a *tail*?"

Rosemary had slipped out of her own life very easily. She had shown no tenacity for it at all when she discovered that the baby girl she was carrying when Olivia disappeared had a twin, not Victor's longed-for son, but a tumorous changeling that grew and swelled inside her unchallenged. By the time anyone realized it signaled a life ending rather than a life beginning, it was too late. Annabelle lived for only a few hours and her cancerous counterpart was removed, but Rosemary was dead within six months.

Victor seemed to be snoring — a deep, wheezing noise as if his windpipe were narrowing and collapsing. This was followed at regular intervals by a dreadful gasping when his reflexes kicked in and he found another breath. Amelia and Julia stared at each other in alarm. "Is that a death rattle?" Julia whispered, and Amelia said, "Shush," because it seemed impolite to talk about the mechanics of death in front of the dying. "He can't hear," Julia said, and Amelia said, "That's not the point."

This noise subsided after a while and Victor gave all the signs of being peacefully asleep. Amelia made them both tea, scrubbing out the stains from the mugs first, and they drank the tea standing by the window, looking down into the darkness of the garden.

"What about the funeral service?" Julia whispered. "He won't want anything Christian, will he?" Apart from a few feeble attempts on Rosemary's part to send them to Sunday school, they had been brought up without religion. As a mathematician, Victor considered it his duty to inculcate skepticism in his daughters, especially as he thought they were frivolous girls — apart from Sylvia, of course, who had always traded on being a bit of a maths nerd. After she left their lives, "nerd" was turned into "prodigy" by Victor and later still into "child genius" so that the longer she was gone the more clever she became, whereas, as far as Victor was concerned, Amelia and Julia grew more brainless the older they got. There was a time when Amelia might have argued with him, although it would more likely have been Julia who would have put up a spirited defense of "the arts" because Amelia found it difficult to counter Victor's hectoring style. Now she wasn't so sure, wasn't he right? Didn't they, after all, know nothing?

"And so what do you think?" Julia said. "He has left the house to us, hasn't he? Do you think he's left us any money? Christ, I hope he has." Victor had never discussed his will with them, never discussed money with them. He gave the impression of having none, but then he had always been miserly. Julia started airing her grievances about the family plot again, and Amelia said, "It would be quicker to cremate him, you know. I think it takes longer to get a burial certificate."

"But we'd probably be cursed for life," Julia said, "like women in Greek tragedy who don't observe the correct rituals for their dead father, the king," and Amelia said, "We're not characters in a play,

Julia. This isn't *Euripides,*" and Julia said, "No, really, Milly, it's bad enough that we don't love him," and Amelia said, "Whatever," and frowned when she heard herself sounding like one of her students.

Julia announced she was going to have a nap and she cradled her head in her arms on the grubby bedspread so that she looked as if she were making some kind of strange homage to her dying father. Victor's big hands rested on top of the coverlet, folded piously in a way that suggested he was prepared for death. It would have taken only the slightest effort for him to raise one of those hands and rest it on Julia's head, to give her a final benediction. Had he ever touched them in a kind way? A kiss, a hug? A tender caress on the cheek? If he had, Amelia couldn't recall it. "Wake me if anything happens," Julia mumbled. "If he dies or something." Julia was still a heavyweight sleeper, and she was as dead to the world as Victor within minutes. Amelia looked at the dark curls on her sister's head and felt a rush of affection for her that was more like a pang of grief.

Julia hadn't had much work recently. She used to work all the time, provincial theater, archly modern plays in tiny London studios and bit parts in television — underclass victims in *The Bill* and terminal patients in *Casualty* (she'd died twice in ten years), but now she never even seemed to be called to auditions. She had done some kind of corporate training video last year but it was for an oil company subsidiary and Amelia had been annoyed with her for doing it, saying that she "should have considered the politics of it," and Julia had said that it was easy to have "the luxury of politics when you had enough food to eat," and Amelia said, "That's a ridiculous exaggeration. When did you ever starve?" but now she was sorry because Julia had been happy when she told her about the job and she'd spoiled it for her.

Amelia had seen almost all of Julia's work, and although she always told her how "wonderful" she was, because that was theatrical protocol, she often found herself thinking that Julia wasn't really very special at all when she was onstage. The best thing she'd seen her in was a pantomime in Bristol, a generic kind of piece, probably *Cinderella,* where Julia had been cast as a dog — a black poodle with a lion cut and a French accent. Julia's shape, short and busty, had somehow been perfectly suited to the costume and she had caught a certain kind of Parisian arrogance that the audience loved. She hadn't needed a wig — her own untamed hair had been piled up in a topknot with a bow in it. Amelia had never thought of Julia as a poodle before then — she always imagined her as a Jack Russell. It seemed suddenly very sad to Amelia that the best role of Julia's career was as a dog. And that she didn't need a wig to play a poodle.

Was he dead? He looked very much like he did when he was asleep — lying on his back with his eyes closed and his beaky mouth open — but there was no sign of the rise and fall of his troubled breathing and his skin was an odd putty color that suddenly brought back the memory of a dead Rosemary in a hospital bed, so unexpected that Amelia couldn't move for a moment. She must have fallen asleep as well. The bad daughters of the king who couldn't even sustain a deathbed vigil.

Sammy got up awkwardly from the rug by the side of the bed and hobbled over to Amelia, thrusting his dry nose into her hand inquiringly. "Poor old boy," Amelia said to the dog. She gently shook Julia awake and told her Victor was dead. "How do you know he's dead?" Julia asked, foggy with sleep. She had a livid red mark on her cheek where her watch had dug into her.

"Because he's not breathing," Amelia said.

An almost festive air had been created between them by Victor's departure, and although it was only six o'clock in the morning, Julia, as if following some prescribed postmortem procedure, poured them a large brandy each. Amelia thought she would be sick if she drank it and surprised herself by enjoying it. Later, they walked, quite drunk at eight in the morning, to the local Spar to buy provisions, filling their basket with things that Amelia would never normally have bought — bacon, sausages, floury white rolls, chocolate, and gin — giggling like the little girls they had forgotten they ever were.

Back at the house they made bacon-and-egg rolls, Julia eating three for the one that Amelia had. Julia lit up a cigarette the moment she had finished eating. "For God's sake," Amelia said, waving the smoke away from her face, "you have some kind of oral fixation, you do know that, don't you?" Julia smoked in a theatrical fashion, making a performance of it, as she did of everything. She used to practice in the mirror when she was a teenager (as Amelia remembered it, a lot of Julia's younger life had been practiced in the mirror). The way Julia was holding her hand up to the morning light revealed the ghostly silver thread of the scar where her little finger had been sewn back onto her hand.

Why had they had so many accidents when they were young? Were they trying to get Rosemary (or indeed anyone) to notice them, to single them out from the melee of *Amelia-Julia-Sylvia?* Even now, Julia and Amelia were clumsy, always covered in bruises from bumping into furniture or tripping over carpets. Last year alone, Amelia had dropped a heavy pan on her foot and trapped her hand in a car door while Julia had sustained a whiplash in a taxi and sprained her ankle falling off a stepladder. Amelia didn't think there was much point in seeking attention once you were over forty, especially if there was no one to give it. "Do you remember the way Sylvia used to faint?" she asked Julia.

"No. Sort of."

Every time she remembered Victor was dead, Amelia felt giddy. It was as if someone had lifted a great stone off her body and now she might be about to rise up, like a kite, like a balloon. Victor's corpse was still tucked up in bed upstairs, and although they knew they should do something, phone someone, react in an urgent way to death, they were overcome with a kind of indolence.

In fact it wasn't until the next day that they journeyed to the Poor Clares' convent and, after an interminable wait, spoke to "Sister Mary Luke" — the ridiculous name that, even after nearly thirty years, neither of them could get used to. When they told her that Victor was dead, Sylvia looked astonished and said, "Daddy? Dead?" And just for once her saintly composure slipped and she burst out laughing.

As a nun in an enclosed order, Sylvia was so excluded from normal life that it never occurred to them to consult with her about the funeral. By then they had already decided what to do with him anyway. After the undertaker had eventually removed Victor's body, Julia had produced the gin and they proceeded to get horribly drunk. Amelia couldn't remember when she had been so drunk, possibly never. The afternoon gin, sitting on top of the morning brandy, made them almost hysterical, and somewhere in the midst of this alcoholic orgy they tossed a coin to determine Victor's final fate.

Julia, histrionic as usual, was cross-legged and clutching onto her crotch, saying, "Oh God, stop it, I'm going to wet myself!" and Amelia had to run outside and be sick on the lawn. The damp night air almost brought her back to sobriety but by then it was nearly dawn and Amelia had claimed heads but the coin had come down tails (which was a one-in-two probability, thank you, Daddy) and Julia declared that "the old fucker was going to be burned."

Amelia was awake early, too early. She wouldn't have minded if she'd been at home — her real home, in Oxford — but she didn't want to rattle around on her own in this place and Julia wouldn't be up for ages — Amelia sometimes wondered if her sister's genes hadn't been spliced with a cat's. Julia scoffed at the "provincial hours" that Amelia kept — Julia hadn't been in her bed before two in the morning since they arrived, emerging bleary-eyed at midday, begging hoarsely for coffee ("Sweetie, please,") as if she had been on some great nighttime quest that had tested her nerves and spirit, rather than having spent the time slumped on the sofa with a bottle of red wine, watching long-forgotten films on cable.

It had amazed them when they discovered that Victor — who neither of them could remember ever having watched television — not only owned a huge wide-screen set but also subscribed to cable — and to everything, not just sport and films but all of the X-rated channels. Amelia had been shocked, not so much by the "adult" content of these (although it was disgusting enough) but by the idea of their own father sitting there, night after night, in his old armchair watching *Red Hot Girls* and God knows what other filth. She was relieved that Julia — usually so airily tolerant of the shortcomings of the male sex — was as horrified as she was. One of the first things they did was to get rid of the armchair.

Amelia only watched the news and documentaries on television, occasionally the *Antiques Roadshow* on a Sunday, and was astonished at the absolute crud on offer twenty-four hours a day. Did this supply some sort of narrative in people's lives? Did they honestly think that this kind of balderdash was a high point of evolution? "Oh, lighten up, Milly," Julia (predictably) said. "What does it matter what people do? At the end of the day we're all dead."

"Well, obviously," Amelia said.

As soon as they cleared the house of Victor and his worldly goods they would be able to put it on the market and be done with it. Or at least, get it ready to put on the market, as Victor's solicitor had muttered "probate" with a kind of Dickensian gloom. Nonetheless, the will was entirely straightforward, everything divided down the middle, with nothing going to Sylvia because (apparently) she had expressly asked for nothing. "Like Cordelia," Julia said, and

Amelia said, "Not really," but, surprisingly, they had left it at that. They were fighting less since Victor's death three days ago. A new air of camaraderie had been fostered between them as they raked through Victor's clothes (fit only for garbage) and dumped pitted old aluminium cooking pans and maths books that disintegrated at their touch. Everything in the house seemed unsavory somehow, and in the kitchen and bathroom Amelia wore rubber gloves and cleaned constantly with antibacterial spray. "He didn't have the plague," Julia said, but without conviction because she had already boiled all the sheets and towels that they were using.

Even though it was July and hot, Victor's house had its own damp, chilly climate that seemed unconnected to the outside world. Every evening since their arrival they had lit a fire and sat in front of the sitting-room hearth with the same kind of devotion that prehistoric people must have afforded flames, except that prehistoric people didn't have Victor's extensive cable package to entertain themselves with. During the daytime it was startling to wander out into the weed-choked garden to get some fresh air and discover a hot, white Mediterranean sun beating down on them.

Amelia was sleeping in Sylvia's old room, the one Sylvia had slept in until she discovered her absurd, inexplicable vocation. She had already converted to Catholicism, of course, which drove Victor to apoplexy, but when she gave up her place at Girton, where she was due to start a maths degree, to enter the convent, it seemed as if Victor might actually kill her. Julia and Amelia, still at school, thought that renouncing the world and entering an enclosed order was an unnecessarily dramatic way of getting away from Victor. (Were they really going to cremate him tomorrow, burn him into ashes? How extraordinary that you could be given the license to do that to another human being. Just get rid of them, as if they were rubbish.)

And, of course, Sylvia didn't have to deal with any of the aftermath of their father's death. What a fantastic form of avoidance being a bride of Christ was. Julia enjoyed telling people that her sister was a nun because they were always so astonished ("*Your* sister?"), but Amelia felt embarrassed by it. God spoke to Sylvia on a regular basis but she was always coy about the content of these conversations, just smiling her holy smile (enigmatic and infuriating). Anyone would think God was an intimate acquaintance, someone with whom Sylvia discussed existential philosophy over bottles of cheap wine in the snug of a quaint riverside pub. God and Sylvia had been on speaking terms for almost as long as Amelia could remember. Did she really think he spoke to her? She was delusional, surely? At the very least a hysteric. Hearing voices, like Joan of Arc. In fact, it was Joan of Arc she used to speak to, wasn't it? Even before Rosemary died or Olivia disappeared. Had anyone ever entertained the possibility that Sylvia was schizophrenic? If God spoke to Amelia she would presume she had gone insane. Someone should have paid attention to Sylvia's oddness, they really should have.

Sammy, sprawled full length at the foot of Amelia's too-small single bed, began to whimper in his sleep. His tail thumped excitedly on the eiderdown, and his paws made ghostly scrabbling motions as if he were chasing the rabbits of his younger days. Amelia would have left him to this happy dream but then the thought struck her that, rather than chasing something, perhaps he himself was being chased, and that the noises he was making were the sounds of fear rather than excitement (how could two things so opposite seem so similar?), so she hauled herself into a sitting position and stroked his flank until he was soothed back into a calmer sleep. His body felt hollow with age. Sammy was the only living creature that Amelia could remember Victor treating as an equal.

She supposed she would have to take Sammy back to Oxford with her. Julia would say she wanted Sammy, but she would never manage with a dog in London. Amelia had a garden in Oxford, she owned the upper half of a small semidetached Edwardian villa, just the right size for one person, and shared a garden with her down-stairs neighbor, a quiet geometrician at New College called Philip who seemed to have a complete lack of sexual interest in either gender but who had a dog (albeit a noisy Pekingese) and was handy at fixing things and therefore constituted the perfect neighbor. ("Or serial killer," Julia said.) He wasn't a gardener, to Amelia's re-lief, and allowed her to get on with as much mulching and digging and planting as she liked. Amelia believed in gardening in the same way that Sylvia believed in God. Like Sylvia, she had been con-verted. She didn't know she was a gardener until she was thirty, when she had planted a Queen of Denmark rose one November and the following June had watched as blossom after blossom burst forth. It was a revelation — you plant something, it grows. "Well, duh," Julia said (like a moronic teenager) when Amelia attempted to explain this miracle.

She had been in Cambridge only a few days and yet her other life, her real life, already seemed a world away and she had to oc-casionally remind herself that it existed. Part of her wanted to stay here forever and blunder on into an argumentative old age with Julia. Together, perhaps they could keep all the dread and loneli-ness of life at bay. And she could get to grips with Victor's garden — there were years of neglect to make up for. She would have liked to lie there for hours, planning out beds (delphiniums, campanula, coreopsis, veronica) and redesigning the lawn (A water feature? Something Japanese perhaps?), but she climbed reluctantly out of bed, followed loyally by Sammy, and went down to the cold kitchen, where she filled the kettle and then slammed it on the hob to show how annoyed she was that Julia was still asleep.

Amelia was in the dining room, boxing up an endless parade of crockery and ornaments. Julia was in the study where she was sup-posed to be. She had been in there since they started clearing out Victor's goods and chattels, and said (melodramatic as ever) that she thought she might be under a spell that condemned her to be trapped in there forever. Victor's dank, airless lair had remained a black hole throughout the years and was now piled high with all kinds of dusty papers, files, and folders. It was like a bonfire waiting for a match. They had pulled the curtains down, and Julia said, "Let there be light!" and Amelia said, "It's quite a nice room really."

Julia was so badly affected by the dust in the house that, as well as all the medication she took (she treated it like sweets), she had started to wear a face mask and goggles that she'd bought in a do-it-yourself place. You could still hear her chesty cough from half a mile away.

Amelia was surprised that when midday came around Julia hadn't sought her out to suggest lunch. When she went looking for her she found her leaning against Victor's desk, a troubled look on her face. "What?" Amelia said, and Julia indicated one of the drawers to Victor's desk. "I broke the lock," she said.

"Well, it doesn't matter," Amelia said. "We have to go through everything. And technically it all belongs to us now."

"No, I didn't mean that. I found something," Julia said, opening the drawer and removing an object, handling it delicately like an archaeologist removing an artifact that might disintegrate in the air. She handed it to Amelia. For a moment Amelia was puzzled and then suddenly she was stepping into space, as if she'd walked through a door that opened onto nothing. And as she fell all she could think of was Olivia's Blue Mouse, clutched in her hand.

"You like him."

"No, I don't." They were making supper together, Amelia poaching eggs, Julia warming baked beans in a saucepan. They were both at the frontier of their culinary capabilities.

"Yes, you do," Julia said. "That's why you were so antagonistic toward him."

"I'm antagonistic toward everyone." Amelia could feel herself blushing and concentrated on the bread in the toaster as if it needed psychic assistance to pop up. "You like him too," she muttered.

"I do. There's something very attractive about Mr. Brodie. He has his own teeth, he isn't even going bald yet," she said. "I bags him," and Amelia said, "Why you?" and Julia said, "Why not? And anyway, you already have a boyfriend. You have Henry."

Amelia thought the word "boyfriend" sounded ridiculous when it was applied to a forty-five-year-old woman. When it was applied to herself.

It was a shame Julia hadn't encountered Jackson Brodie when she was wearing her goggles and face mask. He wouldn't have found her so attractive then. Because he *had* found her attractive, there was no doubt about it. Of course some men were into things like that, masks and bondage and God only knows what else (Rubber! Why?).

"Oh, you're such a prude, Milly," Julia said. "You should try something adventurous with Henry. Spice things up between you. It took you long enough to find a boyfriend, it would be a shame to lose him because you can't get out of the missionary position."

Amelia buttered the toast and laid it on plates. Julia tipped the beans on top. Amelia had begun to enjoy sharing domestic tasks with Julia, basic though they were. She'd lived on her own since her second year at university, that was a long time, more than two decades. Solitary life hadn't been a choice, no one had ever wanted to live with her. She mustn't get used to being with Julia. She mustn't get used to waking up in a house where someone knew her, inside out.

"Handcuffs," Julia continued airily, as if she were discussing seasonal accessories, "a little bit of leather or a whip."

"Henry's not a horse," Amelia said irritably. Were accessories still seasonal? They were when their mother was around. Rosemary had worn white shoes and carried a white handbag in the

summer. A little straw hat. Zip-up suede boots for winter and —
was she imagining this? — a woolen tammy. If only she'd taken
more notice of Rosemary when she was alive.

"There's nothing wrong with a little light bondage," Julia said,
"I imagine Henry would like it. Men love anything filthy." She said
the word "filthy" with relish. Amelia had once, completely unin-
tentionally, accompanied Julia into a sex shop in Soho. Upmarket,
aimed at women only, as if it were a proud emblem of the triumph
of feminism, when in fact it was just full of pornographic smut.
Amelia had followed Julia inside under the misapprehension that it
sold bath products and was stunned when Julia picked up an object
that looked like a pink horse's tail and declared admiringly, "Oh,
look, a butt plug — how cute!" Sometimes Amelia wondered if
women hadn't been better off darning and sewing and baking
bread. Not that she could do any of those things herself.

"Are accessories still seasonal?"

"Yes, of course," Julia said decisively, and then, less certain,
"aren't they? You know, you're very lucky to have a steady boyfriend, Milly," and Amelia said, "Why, because I'm so unattractive?" and Julia said, "Don't be a silly-Milly." "Silly-Milly" was
what Sylvia called her when they were young. Sylvia always made
fun of people. She could be very cruel.

"At your age," Julia said (would she just *shut up?*), "women are
usually either on their own or stuck in tedious marriages." Amelia
slipped the poached eggs on top of the beans.

"Our age," Amelia corrected her. "And you're being patroniz-
ing, 'Steady boyfriend' and 'Julia' aren't words that have ever occurred in the same sentence. If it's not a good thing for you, why
is it a good thing for me?" There was something about eating eggs
that seemed wrong — swallowing something, annihilating something that contained new life. Banishing it into the inner darkness.

Julia put on a great show of being hurt. "No, really, what I mean
is your Henry seems just the ticket, you're lucky to have found

someone who suits you. If I found someone who suited me I would settle down, believe me."

"I don't." Amelia looked at the eggs — like sickly, jaundiced eyes — and thought of her own eggs, a handful left, old and shrivelled like musty dried fruit where once they must have been bursting toward the light —

"Come on, Milly, the food's getting cold. Milly?"

Amelia fled the room, running awkwardly up the stairs before throwing up in the bathroom toilet. They had scrubbed and bleached the toilet but it still bore the stains of years of careless use by Victor, and the very thought of him in here made her start to retch all over again.

"Milly, are you alright?" Julia's voice drifted up the stairs.

Amelia came out of the bathroom. She paused on the threshold of Olivia's room. It was the same as it had always been — the bed, stripped of all bedding, the small wardrobe and chest of drawers, all empty of clothing. All of the past seemed concentrated in this one little room. There was a ghost living in this house, Amelia thought, but it wasn't Olivia. It was her own self. The Amelia she would have been — should have been — if her family hadn't imploded.

And then suddenly, standing there in Olivia's decrepit bedroom, Amelia had what she could only term an epiphany — she thought this must be how people who received mystical visions felt, those who, like Sylvia, thought they heard the voice of God or felt grace falling on them (although she knew it was actually evidence of an unstable temporal lobe). Amelia simply *knew,* and the knowledge was like a warm wave that passed through her body — Olivia was coming back. She might be coming back as no more than a shadow of grease and ash, but she was coming back. And someone had to be here to welcome her.

"Milly?"

6

Theo

Every year he walked to the office in Parkside and then walked the two miles home again. The same pilgrimage for ten years now. A four-mile round-trip, each year a little more tiring because he was carrying more weight, but there was nothing any doctor could say that could scare Theo now.

When he arrived in Parkside he was out of breath and stood around on the pavement for a while before attempting the stairs. He rested with his hands on his thighs, inhaling and exhaling in slow determined breaths, like an athlete who had just run a hard race. Passersby gave him covert (and not so covert) looks indicating varying degrees of distaste, as if they were trying to imagine what terrible flaw in a person's character could allow him to become so fat.

He had been inside the building only three times in the last ten years. The other times he had simply made a lurking kind of obeisance on the pavement.

David Holroyd didn't die. He was still alive when the paramedics arrived and was taken to the hospital, where he was sewn up and where the blood of several strangers was pumped into him. Now he worked three days a week and the rest of the time he tended to the garden in his cottage in rural Norfolk.

The boardroom had been repainted and a new carpet laid over the indelible stain of Laura's blood, but no one who had been there that day was comfortable with the idea of going back, and within the year Holroyd, Wyre, and Stanton moved to an ugly sixties office building near the Grafton Centre, reincarnated as simply "Holroyd and Stanton" because Theo gave up his partnership after Laura's death and never returned to work. He had enough in stocks and bonds and savings to finance his rather frugal life. The money he received from the criminal injuries compensation scheme was donated to the dogs' home where they had obtained Poppy.

The front door, once a handsome bottle green, was now painted white and no one had polished the brass for a long time. There was no security on the door — no locks or entry phone or surveillance camera. Anyone could still walk in unchallenged.

The brass plaque on the door that had once read, HOLROYD, WYRE, AND STANTON — SOLICITORS AND ATTORNEYS AT LAW had been replaced by a plastic one that announced, BLISS — BEAUTY THERAPY. Before Bliss it was the mysterious "Hellier plc," which came and went between the third and fourth anniversaries. After Hellier plc disappeared, the offices had lain empty for a long time before "JM Business Consultants" moved in. Theo went up there, on the sixth anniversary, on the pretense of asking about IT training, but the girl on reception frowned and said, "That's not what we do," although she didn't elucidate what it was that they did do, which looked to Theo to be not very much at all, unless it was acting as a collection depot for the large cardboard boxes that were stacked everywhere. He'd only wanted to have a look, see the place — the spot — but as well as the boxes blocking the hallway there were flimsy partition screens everywhere and he didn't want to make a fuss and frighten the girl.

The stairs took it out of him and he had to rest at the top before going through the new glass door that was etched with the word

"Bliss" in a swooping, romantic script, like a promise, as if he might be about to enter Elysium or the Land of Cockayne.

The receptionist, dressed in a clinical white uniform, was called "Milanda," according to her name badge, which sounded to Theo more like a brand of low-cholesterol margarine than a name. She regarded Theo with horror and he was tempted to reassure her that fat wasn't infectious, but instead he said that he would like to surprise his wife for her birthday, with "a bit of pampering." It was a lie but it wasn't a lie that harmed anyone. He wished now that he *had* given Valerie more "pampering," but it was much too late for that now.

Once Milanda had managed to get over her initial fright at the size of him, she suggested a "Half-Day Spa" package — pedicure, manicure, and a "seaweed wrap" — and Theo said that sounded "just the ticket," but could he leaf through the brochure and see what else there was? And Milanda said, "Of course," with a fixed smile on her face because you could see she was worried that Theo would be a very bad advertisement for a beauty salon, sitting there in reception on the (possibly too flimsy) cane-work sofa next to the fiberglass fountain whose waters competed with the "soothing sounds" of the *Meditation* CD — an odd mix of panpipes, whale song, and crashing surf.

The offices had been completely refitted since his last abortive visit, the walls were lilac now and the doors painted in a palette of purples and pinks and blues. The whole shape of the place had been changed by interior plasterboard walls, creating open spaces as well as smaller rooms — "therapy suites," according to the signs on the doors.

Was the boardroom still there, untouched, or had it been transformed into — what? A steam room, a sauna? Or divided into cubicle-size rooms for "Thai massage" or "Brazilian waxing"? (The brochure offered extraordinary services.) A woman arrived for an appointment and Milanda escorted her into one of the therapy suites. Theo stood up — casually, as if stretching his legs — and made a pretense of sauntering down the hallway.

The door to the boardroom (painted a kind of cyanotic blue) was ajar and when Theo gave it a little nudge it swung open helpfully, giving him a view of the whole room. Theo had never made it this far before and had no idea how the room might have evolved over the past decade, but he was surprised when he found it empty of furniture and fittings, the floorboards dusty and scratched, the paint-work chipped. It had always been the beating heart of the office but now it was being used as a storeroom, stacked with boxes of oils and creams, a massage table folded and propped against one wall, a laun-dry basket overflowing with used white towels. The marble fireplace was still there. There were even ashes lying cold in the grate.

The spot itself, the place where his daughter had been slaugh-tered, was beneath some kind of trolley. The trolley looked like something that belonged on a hospital ward, but in the place of medicines, it was laden with dozens of bottles of nail varnish in different colors. In St. Petersburg, once, Theo had visited the Church of Our Savior on the Spilled Blood, built over the place where Alexander II was assassinated. It was a fantastic edifice of mosaic and gold, of spires and enameled onion domes, yet he had found the interior a soulless space, echoing with the cold. Now he realized that the atmosphere didn't really matter, what mattered was that it existed, and its existence meant that no one could ever forget what had happened there. The place where Laura fell was marked by a trolley of nail varnish. What kind of a shrine was that? Surely a spring should have bubbled up, or a tree blossomed, on the sacred spot where his daughter's blood was spilled?

Exsanguinated. A strange, dramatic word that seemed to belong in a revenge tragedy, but no revenge had ever been possible for Theo. KNIFE-WIELDING MANIAC MURDERS LOCAL GIRL! the local headlines said. The nationals too. For a few days it had been news and then everyone seemed to forget. Not the police, of course.

They had really cared, Theo had never doubted that for a minute. He still saw Alison, his family liaison officer, occasionally, even now, and the police had followed up every possible lead, there had been no client confidentiality left at Holroyd, Wyre, and Stanton once the police had raked through every file and item of correspondence. The media talked about it being a random crime, the work of a psychopath, but the man — the knife-wielding maniac — had entered the office looking for Theo, for "Mr. Wyre." Theo had done something, precipitated something, he had made someone, someone in a yellow golfing sweater, so crazy that the man wanted to kill him. Had that bloodlust been assuaged, had the man in the yellow golfing sweater found some primitive satisfaction in slaying Theo's child? His own blood.

The trolley was on wheels and Theo had been about to move it when one of the concealed doors in the curve of the oval wall was opened suddenly by a trim woman dressed in the same white uniform as Milanda. She frowned at Theo, but before she could protest at his presence he said, "Sorry, wrong room!" and backed out the door, performing a ridiculous kind of salaam in an attempt to calm her fears.

"I'll get back to you," he said breezily to Milanda, waving the brochure still clutched in his hand. He made for the stairs as rapidly as his bulk would allow, although the best he could manage was a kind of rolling waddle. He imagined Milanda at his back, rugby tackling him on Parker's Piece. Theo's heart was knocking uncomfortably inside his chest and he took refuge in a café on Mill Road, where he ordered a modest latte and a scone but nonetheless was subject to the disapproval of the waitress, who made it clear that she thought someone so overweight shouldn't be eating at all.

Time did not heal — it merely rubbed at the wound, slowly and relentlessly. The world had moved on and forgotten and there was only Theo left to keep Laura's flame alive. Jennifer lived in Canada now and although they talked on the phone and e-mailed each other, they rarely talked about Laura. Jennifer had never liked the pain of remembering what had happened, but for Theo it was the pain that kept Laura alive in his memory. He was afraid that if it ever began to heal she would disappear.

Afterward, after it happened ten years ago, Theo didn't want to speak to anyone, didn't want to speak, didn't want to acknowledge the existence of a world that went on without Laura in it, but when he got home from the hospital, he forced himself to phone Jennifer. When she answered the phone and heard his voice she said, "What?" in that impatient way she had, as if he only phoned her to annoy her. And then she grew even more impatient because he couldn't speak at all and it was only after the most extraordinary act of will that he was able to say, "Jenny, a bad thing has happened, a very bad thing," and all she said was "Laura," in a flat voice.

Theo would have committed suicide, perhaps not that day, not until after the funeral, after he had put all his affairs in order, but he couldn't kill himself because then Jennifer would know (although she must always have known, surely?) that he loved Laura more than her. Because if it had been Jennifer who had died and not Laura, Theo knew he wouldn't have even thought about killing himself.

Even now, Theo hoped that one day the stranger who had come looking for him and who had found his child instead would return. Theo imagined opening his front door to the man in the yellow golfing sweater and opening his arms wide to embrace the knife, embracing the death that would reunite him with Laura. He had buried her, not cremated her. He needed a grave to go to (all the time) somewhere where she felt tangible, within arm's reach, just six feet away. There had been times when the grief had been so bad that he had thought about digging her up, exhuming her poor rotting body, just so he could cradle her one last time, reassure her that he was still here, still thinking about her, even if no one else was.

Theo paid for his coffee, leaving a tip that was bigger than the bill. The worse the service, the more Theo tended to tip. He supposed it was a character weakness. He thought of himself as a person made almost entirely out of weaknesses rather than strengths. He had to fight his way upstream against a tide of tourists, all enraptured by the colleges, the tangible fabric of history — scholarship and architecture and beauty. When Theo had first come to Cambridge as a student he thought it was the most beautiful place on Earth. He had been brought up in a prosaic suburb in Manchester, so Cambridge had seemed like the architecture of transcendence. When he first glimpsed inside the courts of the colleges it had been like seeing visions of paradise. He hadn't known anything so beautiful existed, yet now he hadn't even looked at a college for ten years. He walked past the gorgeous frontages of Queens' and Corpus Christi and Clare and King's and saw nothing but stone and mortar and, eventually, dust.

"Closure," that was what they called it. It sounded so Californian. He had avoided the word, avoided the act, but he knew he couldn't go to his grave not knowing who the man in the yellow golfing sweater was. He checked his watch. He didn't want to be late.

Theo read a copy of *Reader's Digest* while he waited. Waiting rooms seemed to be the only place you ever saw *Reader's Digest* these days. The woman on reception said Mr. Brodie was "tied up at the moment" but would be able to see him in ten minutes if he'd like to wait. "I'm his assistant, Deborah," she added, "but you can call me Mrs. Arnold." Theo couldn't tell whether or not she was trying to be funny. He remembered how at Holroyd, Wyre, and Stanton that used to be a standing joke among the staff — he'd heard them on the phone saying to clients, "I'm sorry, Mr. Holroyd is all tied up in his office just now," in that singsong secretary voice they all used and then when they came off the line they always burst into laughter. Mr. Brodie's secretary didn't look as if she were deriving any amusement from the idea of her boss in some bondage scenario beyond the closed door of his office. Instead she was taking her aggression out on her computer keyboard in a way that suggested that, like Cheryl, his own secretary, she had been trained on upright typewriters, built like tanks. He still saw Cheryl sometimes — she was retired now but Theo had visited her in her overheated bungalow and had (rather awkwardly) drunk tea and eaten her All-Bran tea loaf.

Cheryl was the last person that Laura had ever spoken to — "Would you like more than one copy of this form?" — a prosaic note to end a life on.

Deborah Arnold paused in her attempt to destroy her keyboard and offered him a coffee, which he declined. He was beginning to suspect that Mr. Brodie, far from being tied up in his office, wasn't even in there at all.

If the police had never found the man who killed Laura then it seemed absurd to think that some backstreet private eye could, but Theo thought that the merest chance of that happening was better than no chance at all. And if he did find the man perhaps he wouldn't open his arms and embrace his death; perhaps instead it would be Theo who would be the maniac wielding the knife.

A man hurried into the office and Deborah Arnold said, "There you are at last," without looking up from the keyboard. "Sorry," the man — Theo presumed this was Jackson Brodie — said to Theo, "I had to go to the dentist." Deborah gave a bark of laughter as if this were a risible excuse. The man shook Theo's hand and said, "Jackson, Jackson Brodie, please come in and have a seat," and ushered him toward the inner office. As Jackson closed the door, Deborah's sarcastic tones could be heard singing out, "Mr. Brodie will see you now."

"I'm sorry," Jackson said to Theo. "She's delusional. She thinks she's a woman."

7

Caroline

The church was called St. Anne's. Caroline had no idea who St. Anne was. She had been brought up without religion, had never even been to a proper church service, not one in a regular church anyway, not even for her wedding to Jonathan, which had taken place in a registry office because Jonathan's first wife was alive and well, although, thankfully, living in Argentina with a horse breeder. The church was on a back road, small and very old with a squat Saxon tower and a graveyard that had closed its gates to business years ago and was now overgrown, in a picturesque way, with wildflowers and briar. She couldn't identify any of the flowers and thought maybe she would get a book, order it online from Amazon, because of course they lived miles away from any bookshop.

The church was midway between their own small village and another even smaller one, so Caroline supposed that at some time in the medieval past the church had decided to economize and make the two villages share a priest. And of course in those days no one thought anything about walking long distances. Country children used to walk five miles to school in the morning and five miles home at night without complaining. Or perhaps they did complain but no one ever recorded their comments for posterity. That was how history worked, wasn't it? If it wasn't written down it never existed. You might leave behind jewelry and pottery, ornamental tombs, you might leave behind your own bones to be dug up at a later age, but none of those artifacts could express how you *felt*. The dead under her feet in St. Anne's old graveyard were tongueless and dumb. She couldn't imagine James and Hannah walking any distance to school. They seemed to have no idea what feet were for.

Caroline had driven past the church several times, but it had never struck her until now that she could actually go inside. She knew the vicar, of course, or at least, she had known him: he died last year and his replacement hadn't arrived yet. The new incumbent wouldn't have just the two churches to look after: there were four or five denuded parishes under his care nowadays (or perhaps it would be a woman?) because no one went to church anymore, not even Jonathan's mother.

It had nothing to do with religion — Caroline was just sheltering from the rain. She'd taken the dogs for a walk, the church was about a mile from their own house (which was an estate, really), and the dogs had got into the graveyard and were now moving like Hoovers across the ground, their noses down, their tails up, their small dog brains consumed with the idea of uncharted territory and a thousand new scents. Caroline could only smell the one scent — the sour, melancholy smell of greenery.

The dogs had already urinated on several gravestones and Caroline hoped no one was spying on her. Watching, not spying. "God, you're so paranoid, Caro," Jonathan said. "That's what comes from being a townie." The dogs were Labradors and they belonged to Jonathan. That's what he brought to the marriage, two dogs and two children. James and Hannah, Meg and Bruce. Meg and Bruce were the dogs. The dogs and the children behaved well for Jonathan, less well for Caroline, although the dogs were better than the children. When it had started to rain she tied the dogs up on the porch (it would be good if she could do that with the children). She hadn't realized that "Caro" was a diminutive of Caroline until she met Jonathan. It sounded very Regency, like in all those old-fashioned historical novels she used to read when she was younger. Much younger. Of course, he came from the kind of background — county — where people were called "Caroline." And Lucy, and Amanda and Jemima, so he should know.

She suspected there might be a special ecclesiastical word for "porch," but if there was she didn't know it, although she knew there were all kinds of particular terms for the bones of the church, its carcass and ribs, like medieval poetry — apse, chancel, nave, transept, clerestory, sacristy, misericord — although she wasn't too sure what any of them meant, except for "misericord," because it was one of those words that once you'd come across it you always remembered it.

The misericords in St. Anne's were ancient, made of oak, not the oak of the church door, which was gray and bleached like old driftwood, as if it had been at sea for a long time, the misericords were the color of peat or wet tea leaves. If you looked at them closely you realized they were carved with weird, pagan creatures, more like hobgoblins than men, half hidden among trees and leaves — here acanthus and there what looked like a palm tree. This must be the "green man," only there were lots of them on the ends of the pews — all different — so green *men* would have been more appropriate. She didn't know they had green men in Yorkshire as well. As well as where she had lived before. In another life, one she could hardly remember sometimes. And at other times remember only too well.

She loved that word, "misericord," because it sounded so wretched and yet it wasn't. It meant tenderhearted, from the Latin for heart, "*cor*," from which you also get "core" and "cordial" but not "cardiac," which came via the Latin from the Greek for heart — "*kardia*" (although they must surely be related at some ancient, ur-level). They had done neither Latin nor Greek at Caroline's school, but later, after she had left school, when she had had a lot of time on her hands, she had patiently worked her way through primers and elementary Classics textbooks so that she could at least understand the etymology of words, to follow them back down their limbs and trunks until she reached their roots. Her own name contained *"cor"* if you moved the letters around. Caro. Cora. Cor. Like the crows, like the crows that feed on the dead. If you knelt on the hard floor, which in this church meant you couldn't avoid kneeling on the cold stone slab of someone's tomb (but they were probably glad of the company), and looked one of the green men in the eye, you could see the primordial gleam of madness in there and the —

"Are you all right?"

"Yes," Caroline said. "I think so." The man offered his hand because her knees were stiff from kneeling on the floor, on the dead. The man's hand was soft and rather cold for someone who was patently alive.

"My name's John Burton," he said (cordially).

"You're very young," Caroline said. "Or is that a sign I'm getting old — when vicars and policemen begin to look young?" and the vicar (John Burton) laughed and said, "My mother always says it's when bishops start looking young that you have to worry," and Caroline wondered what it was like to inhabit so easily a world where your mother made jokes about bishops, where people were called Caro.

"You'll be the new vicar then," Caroline said. He was wearing his cassock (was that what it was called?) so it was hardly a wild guess, and he looked down at his vestments and gave a rueful grin and said, "You've got me bang to rights, guv," only he sounded faintly ludicrous because he said the words in his rather effete, upper-crust voice. Jonathan had retained (or acquired) a rough limestone edge to his voice that made him seem no-nonsense and forceful. "Very Heathcliffe," her friend Gillian had said sarcastically, because, of course, he was moneyed and (very) expensively educated and his mother spoke like the Queen.

"I know who you are too," John Burton said, and Caroline said,

"Do you?" and thought, "Are we flirting? Surely not," and John Burton — the Reverend John Burton — said, "Yes, of course I do. You're the head teacher at the primary school," and Caroline thought, "Damn," because she really preferred it when no one knew who she was. No one at all.

Getting married again hadn't been part of the plan. The plan had been to bury herself in a town somewhere and do good works, like an eighteenth-century Quaker or some Victorian gentlewoman driven by philanthropy. She'd even thought about going abroad — India or Africa — like a missionary, working on a literacy project with women or outcastes, because being an outcast was something she understood.

She came north, expecting it to be gritty and industrial, but she knew that it was the novels she had read that had formed this picture in her head, and, of course, instead of being like *North and South* or *Saturday Night and Sunday Morning,* it was gritty and *post*-industrial and so much more difficult than she'd imagined. She'd spent her probationary year in Liverpool, then she did another couple years in Oldham and finally settled in Manchester. She was a "superteacher," although they didn't call it that, trained to be the savior of socially excluded kids, fast-tracking through inner-city Gehennas so that one day she was destined to be head of some imploding school that she would have to try and rescue from disaster, like the captain of a sinking ship. And that was fine and good because she was atoning, but instead of joining a convent, an order of penitents (an idea she'd been tempted by), she'd become a teacher, which was probably more useful than shutting yourself away, praying every four hours, night and day, although, of course, you couldn't be sure — it might be that cloistered women praying night and day was the only thing that was preventing some cataclysmal disaster — a meteor or global nuclear meltdown.

So, her life had been moving forward according to this plan. She lived in a small flat, one bedroom, walls painted white, scented candles, everything kept simple (very like a secular anchorite in fact) and socialized minimally with the other staff. There were a couple of middle-aged divorcées that she sometimes went to the cinema with or with whom she shared a bottle of wine, someplace where it was quiet enough to talk. The conversation generally bemoaned the lack of suitable men — "all the good ones married or gay" — the usual stuff, and when they poked around in her own life she said, "One bad marriage is enough" in a way that suggested it had been too bad to talk about. She was taking a break from relationships, she said, only she didn't say how long that break had been. Twenty-two years since she'd been with a man! The middle-aged divorcées would be astonished if they knew that. But then, celibacy was a part of being an anchorite, wasn't it? Or was it anchoress? The Reverend Burton would know ("Call me John, for God's sake." He laughed). Of course, she'd had sex with women in that time, so you couldn't really call it celibacy.

He was a funny chap, John Burton. Sandy, gingery hair, quite small and fine boned, nothing like Jonathan. He had a sweetness about him, a kind of essential goodness that was lovely. He had been an inner-city penitent too, but it had broken him in some way, and so now he was interred in the country like a convalescent. Jonathan wasn't the kind of man who would ever have a breakdown. Jonathan had incredibly good manners (from his mother, from Ampleforth College, although the Weavers weren't Catholics, far from it), which was one of the things that attracted her to him, but underneath he was flinty and indestructible, which was also what attracted her. ("Adamantine" — that would be a very good word for him. From the Greek, but the origin somewhat obscure.)

Gillian, a friend from teacher training college, had invited her to stay on her parents' farm for the August bank-holiday weekend. They had paired up at college because they were older than most of the other students. They weren't close friends — although Gillian thought they were closer than they actually were — but Gillian was easy company, funny, cynical, yet unchallenging, so, after debating long and hard with herself (as she did about everything), Caroline finally accepted the invitation. "A weekend in the country," she said to herself, "What harm can there be in that? Really?"

And it was lovely, really lovely. Gillian's parents were jolly types and Gillian's mother wanted to feed them all the time, which was fine by both of them. Gillian's mother told them how admirable it was that they were such independent "girls" with careers and mortgages and choices when what she really meant was that Gillian — an only child — was well into her thirties now and wasn't she ever going to produce a grandchild?

The guest bedroom was clean and comfortable and Caroline slept better than she had for years, probably because it was so peaceful. The only sounds were the sheep bleating and the cocks crowing, the never-ending birdsong, the acceptable noise of the occasional tractor. The air smelled sweet and it made her realize what a long time it had been since she had breathed really good clean air. The vista from her bedroom window was of rolling green dales, seamed and braided with gray stone walls that ran on forever, into infinity, and she thought it was the most beautiful view she'd ever had in her life (although she'd had some rotten views), so that she was in love with the landscape before she fell in love with Jonathan, who in some ways was just a kind of extension and embodiment of the countryside.

And it was hot, much hotter than she'd expected Yorkshire to be, not that she'd known what to expect of Yorkshire, not having been there before. ("What, never visited God's own county?" Jonathan said in mock horror. "I've been hardly anywhere," she replied truthfully.)

On Saturday afternoon Gillian took Caroline to an agricultural fair, a small one, local to the dale, "not like the Great Yorkshire Show or anything — more of a fete," Gillian explained. It was being held in a field a couple miles away, on the outskirts of a village that Gillian told her she would love because it was "all picture-postcard quaint," and Caroline smiled and said nothing because, yes, it was all beautiful and might be Yorkshire (which seemed to be more of a state of mind than a place) but it was still the *country*. But, of course, Gillian was right, the village was like a Platonic ideal of a village — a packhorse bridge, a beck, skirted with yellow flag irises, that threaded its way among the gray stone houses, the old red telephone box, the little postbox in the wall, the village green with its fat white sheep grazing unfettered. ("Yorkshire sheep," Jonathan said. "They're bigger," and months later she regurgitated this fact to a colleague at school who fell about with laughter so that she felt like an idiot. By then she had a ruby-and-diamond ring on her finger, a ring that had once belonged to Jonathan's father's mother. It wasn't until afterward that his own mother, Rowena, told her that she'd refused that ring and insisted on new diamonds instead — from Garrards — because she didn't want a "hand-me-down.")

Caroline, needless to say, had never been to an agricultural fair in her life and was charmed by everything. Yes, that was what had happened to her. She had been charmed, bewitched, glamorized somehow — by the combed sheep and ruffled cows and the squeaky-clean pigs, by the marquees with their displays of prizewinning jams and sponge cakes, the crocheted shawls and knitted matinee jackets, the exhibitions of marrows and potatoes and leeks and roses, by the WI serving cream teas in a warm tent that smelled of grass, by the vicar — a big man with the rosy skin of a drinker — who opened the fair and told funny jokes (nothing like his successor, John Burton). There was an ice-cream van and a children's gymkhana and a small perfect antique merry-go-round. It was unreal. It was ridiculous. At any moment Caroline expected a steam train to pull up and the cast of bloody *Heartbeat* to alight on the platform. But instead it was Jonathan Weaver, who didn't alight but *strode*. "He got those thighs from show jumping," Gillian whispered. "Amateur, but he could have gone far, as they say." Oh no, now it was like a Jilly Cooper novel.

"Untitled aristocracy," Gillian said. "You know, ancient family, farmed-the-land-since-Domesday kind of thing, only they're dilettantes, not real farmers — she said bitterly."

"Why not?"

"They've always had other income, lots of it — London leases, land, the slave trade, wherever people get their money from, so they play at farming — a show herd of Red Devons, and their sheep are like something Marie Antoinette would have shepherded — and this is sheep country, let's not forget, where a sheep's a sheep, and all the farm cottages are modernized and central heated and they're rebuilding the original kitchen garden with National Trust money, no less."

Caroline didn't really understand this farmer's daughter's diatribe so she just said, "Right," and then Gillian laughed and said, "But, by Christ, I'd shag the daylights out of him any day."

She remembered standing in front of a display for BEST STRAWBERRY JAM, the jars — topped with gingham mobcaps and labeled in a way that was reminiscent of *The Country Diary of an Edwardian Lady* — were garnered with rosettes and little "commended" cards and she was thinking that you should be able to taste the prizewinning jam, not just look at it, when suddenly he was standing beside her and introducing himself and then there was a kind of blackout here because the next thing she remembered was sitting up high in the passenger seat of his Range Rover, being driven to his house. He'd said something polite about "coming up to the house for some tea" but it must have been lust, pure and raw, and dammed up for too long, which had impelled her — abandoning Gillian, who was furious with her (quite rightly) for going off in such a public manner with someone she'd only just met.

They drove on a long straight road that ran through parkland

and it was only after five minutes or so that she realized that he owned this road, and the parkland, and everything — he owned *landscape,* for God's sake. And although it was lust that had got her this far she had genuinely thought that his invitation to tea would involve an elegant, light drawing room, on the walls of which would hang paintings of horses and dogs. There would be large sofas that would be upholstered in a pale lemon damask silk and there would be a grand piano on which were displayed family photographs in heavy silver frames (this image was largely based on a childhood school visit to a stately home). She could see herself perched nervously on the edge of one of the lemon damask sofas while Jonathan's mother presided over the tea tray — pretty, antique china — as she interrogated her politely about her "fascinating" urban life.

In reality, Jonathan's mother was still at the fair, graciously presenting rosettes to the pony club, and neither Jonathan nor Caroline got anywhere near the drawing room (which would turn out to be nothing like she'd imagined it) because they went round the back of the house where he took her into some kind of scullery, and they were hardly in the door before he pulled her pants down around her ankles and made her bend over the old wooden draining-board while he shoved himself roughly inside her, and as she hung on to the (handy) taps of the Belfast sink, she thought *sweet Jesus Christ, now this is what you call "fucking,"* and now look at her — driving a Land Rover "Discovery" and buying clothes from Country Casuals in Harrogate and sitting opposite him at the breakfast table (mahogany, Chippendale) with his two brattish children. Could someone please tell her how the hell that had happened?

"Well," John Burton said, "I suppose I should be going." They had been sitting on a pew, side by side, quite companionably, but not speaking to each other. That was the thing about a church, you could be quiet and no one questioned why. The rain had almost stopped, although you could still smell it — green and summery — through the open door. "The rain's easing off," he said, and Caroline said, "Yes, I think it is." He stood up and escorted her outside. The dogs had been asleep and now made a great performance of welcoming Caroline's reappearance, although she knew they couldn't care less really.

"Good-bye, then," John Burton said and shook her hand again. She felt a little flutter, something long dormant coming back to life. He climbed on his bike and cycled off, turning once to wave, an action that made him wobble ridiculously. She stood and watched him moving away from her, ignoring the overexcited dogs. She was in love. Just like that. How totally, utterly insane.

8

Jackson

Victor's last rites took minimalism to a new level of austerity. Jackson, Julia, and Amelia were the only people present, unless you counted Victor himself, quietly decomposing in a cheap veneered oak coffin that remained starkly unadorned by any farewell flowers. Jackson had expected, if nothing else, a sense of occasion. He had imagined that Victor's funeral would take place in the chapel of St. John's, his old college, where he would be lauded by his ex-colleagues in a tedious high Anglican service punctuated by hymns sung badly to the accompaniment of a pained-sounding organ.

Amelia and Julia were sitting in the front pew of the crematorium chapel. Jackson had managed to resist their invitation to sit between them, in the place of Victor's nonexistent son. Jackson leaned forward and whispered to Julia, "Why is there no one else here?" Nominally, he was there in a professional role: he wanted to know who would turn up at Victor's funeral, and he supposed in the event nobody was as interesting as somebody.

"No one is here because we didn't tell anyone," Amelia said as if it were the most reasonable thing in the world.

Amelia was not dressed in black for her father's funeral, not a hint of it, quite the opposite in fact as she was sporting ribbed woolen tights in a bright scarlet that was quite alarming. Jackson wondered if there were a symbolic significance to this — there was probably some ancient Cambridge custom that dictated a bluestocking replaced her legwear with red on the death of her father. There seemed to be ancient Cambridge customs for most things (sorry, *Oxford*). Why would anyone wear woolen tights in the middle of summer? The crematorium chapel was chilled by the air-conditioning, but outside it was hot. Julia was just as bad, rejecting the black of bereavement and muffling herself from head to toe in a vintage coat in grass-green velvet (were they cold-blooded, like reptiles?). Her mad hair looked as if it had been groomed by a troupe of circus dogs. Jackson, in his black funeral suit and severe black tie, was the only one who appeared to be mourning Victor.

Amelia's brazen legs reminded him of the legs of a bird he'd seen recently in a *National Geographic* in his dentist's waiting room.

Julia twisted round to face Jackson. "I always think on these occasions," she said, "well, not so much these occasions" — she indicated the coffin in an offhand way — "as, you know, family stuff, birthdays, Christmas, that Olivia might turn up."

"That's ridiculous," Amelia said.

"I know." They both lapsed into sadness but then Julia rallied herself and said, "You look very handsome in a suit, Mr. Brodie." Amelia gave Julia a disparaging look. Julia's eyes were watering and she sounded choked up but she declared it was hay fever rather than grief "in case you get the wrong idea." She swallowed a Becotide and offered one to Jackson, which he refused. Jackson had never had an allergy in his life (except to people, perhaps). He considered his constitution to be robustly northern. He'd watched a documentary recently on the Discovery Channel that showed how northerners still had hardy Viking DNA and southerners had something else, something softer, Saxon or French.

"The decor in here is so dreary," Julia whispered loudly, and Amelia tutted as if she were at the theater and Julia were an annoying stranger. "What?" Julia said to her crossly. "He's not going to leap out of his coffin and object, is he?" A brief spasm of horror gripped Amelia's features at this idea, but at least the notion of a resurrected Victor shut them both up, even if only momentarily. Even a tedious Anglican service would have been preferable to the squabbling Land sisters.

On his way to Victor's funeral, Jackson had paid a visit to the old offices of Holroyd, Wyre, and Stanton, now a beauty parlor called Bliss. "Beauty Therapists" — that's how they styled themselves, which made Jackson think of psychiatry rather than facials and manicures. Healing people with beauty. How would you do that? Music? Poetry? Landscape? Sex? What did he turn to when he needed healing? "From Boulder to Birmingham," Emmylou Harris. His daughter's face. That was corny, but it was true.

There was a room in Theo's house. Theo had invited him to his house to show him the room. Jackson could not have lived with a room like that in his house. An upstairs bedroom that looked like a police incident room — photographs and maps pinned to the wall, flowcharts and whiteboards, timetables of events. Two metal filing cabinets, bursting with files, boxes on the floor containing yet more files. Anything that could possibly have been relevant to his daughter's death was in that room. And a good number of those things Theo shouldn't have been in possession of — the scene-of-crime photographs, for example, not tacked up on the wall (for which small mercy Jackson gave thanks) but that Theo produced from the filing cabinet. Ghastly pictures of his daughter's body that Theo handled with a kind of professional detachment, as if they were holiday snaps that might interest Jackson. He knew it wasn't like that, that time had somehow inured Theo to every horror, but Jackson was shocked nonetheless. "I've got a few contacts," Theo said, without expounding. He'd been a lawyer, and lawyers, in Jackson's experience, always had contacts.

Theo had spent the last ten years of his life doing nothing but investigating his daughter's death. Was that the right thing to do or was it the crazy thing to do? The room was like something a psychopath might have kept, not any psychopath Jackson had ever come across, of course, but the psychopaths who inhabited crime novels and television programs. Jackson thought they should make more television drama about car crime committed by fourteen-year-old boys high on glue and cider and boredom — it would be a lot more realistic, just not very interesting.

Looking at Victor's coffin made Jackson wonder about Laura Wyre's funeral. Hundreds of people had attended, according to the press reports. Theo had hardly any memory of it, even though he had all the press clippings. When Jackson asked Theo about his daughter's funeral his eyes had flickered from side to side as if his brain were disassociating from the memory. Weren't there stages of bereavement you were supposed to go through — shock, denial, guilt, anger, depression — and then acceptance, when you were supposed to come out the other end and be okay, move on. Jackson had received grief counseling once. His school had arranged for someone to come in, from the "West Yorkshire Adolescent Psychiatric Unit," an overblown title to place on the hunched shoulders of the short, red-haired psychologist whose breath smelled of raw onions and who consulted with Jackson in the makeshift cupboard that passed for a sickroom at his school. The red-haired, bearded psychologist told Jackson that he had to move on, to get on with his own life, but Jackson was twelve years old and had nowhere left to move on from and nowhere obvious to go.

Jackson wondered how many times people had suggested to Theo that he had to get on with his life. Theo Wyre was stuck somewhere near the beginning of the bereavement process, at a place he'd made all his own, where if he fought hard enough he might be able to bring his daughter back. It wasn't going to happen — Jackson knew that the dead never came back. Ever.

The yellow golfing sweater. That was the thing, the thing that should have led them to the murderer. None of Theo's clients had expressed any interest in golf (was golf the "royal game" or was that tennis?). This indifference to the game stemmed from the fact that most of Theo's clients were women — his caseload was almost entirely matrimonial and domestic. (So why was he in Peterborough on a boundary dispute the day his daughter died?) It was a depressing business going through his files, containing as they did an endless parade of women who were being battered, abused, and defeated, not to mention the string of ones who were just plain unhappy, who couldn't stand the sight of the poor schmuck they were married to. It was an education (although one Jackson had already been subject to) because Theo was extraordinarily good at documenting the banal details of failure, the litany of tiny flaws and cracks that were nothing to an outsider but looked like canyons when you were on the inside — "He buys me carnations, carnations are crap, every woman knows that so why doesn't he?" "He never thinks to run a bit of Toilet Duck round the bowl, even though I leave it out where he can't miss it and I've asked him, I've asked him a hundred times." "If he ever does any ironing it's 'Look at me, I'm ironing, look how well I'm doing it, I iron much better than you, I'm the best, I do it properly.'" "He'd get me my breakfast in bed if I asked him to, but *I don't want to have to ask.*" Did men know how much they got on women's nerves? Theo Wyre certainly did.

Jackson had always been good, never left the toilet seat up and all that clichéd stuff, and anyway he'd been outnumbered, two women to one man. Boys took a long time to become men but daughters were women from the kickoff. Jackson had hoped they would have another baby, he would have liked another girl, he'd have liked five or six of them, to be honest. Boys were all too familiar but girls, girls were extraordinary. Josie had shown no interest at all in having another baby, and on the one occasion Jackson had suggested it, she gave him a hard look and said, "You have it then."

Did anyone wear a golfing sweater who wasn't interested in golf? And if it came to that what made it a golfing sweater as opposed to merely a sweater? Jackson had searched through the police photographs until he found the one of a yellow sweater that the eyewitnesses were agreed was "very like" the one worn by Laura Wyre's killer. As eyewitnesses went, they were rubbish. Jackson peered closely at the logo on the sweater, a small appliqué of a golfer swinging a club. Would you wear that if you weren't a golfer? You might buy it in a secondhand shop and not care because it was a good sweater ("60 percent lambswool, 40 percent cashmere") and you could afford it.

Yellow for danger, like those tiny poisonous yellow frogs. That homeless girl this morning on St. Andrews Street, her hair was the color of poisonous frogs. He'd almost tripped over her on the way to Bliss. She had a dog with her, a whippety sort of thing.

"Can you help me?" the homeless girl said to him, and he squatted on his haunches so that he wasn't towering over her and said, "What do you want me to do?" and she'd stared off into the middle distance somewhere and said, "I don't know." She had bad skin, she looked like a druggie, a lost girl. He'd been late so he'd left the girl with the frog-yellow hair and thought, On the way back I'll ask her name.

And the spouses of all those disgruntled women in Theo's filing cabinet — did any of them play golf? The police had investigated every single one of them and found two who were golfers, both with cast-iron alibis. They had scoured the exes for grudges over divorces and affairs, over custody disputes, alimony and child support, and couldn't find a single likely suspect. They interviewed everyone, took alibis from everyone, they had even taken DNA and fingerprints, although there were no fingerprints at the scene and no DNA because the man had touched nothing, he hadn't even opened the door to the office — the lower door had been propped open and the receptionist (Moira Tyler) reported that he had pushed the inner door open with his elbow. And that was it, straight through to the boardroom at the back, slash, slash, and out again. No messing, no shouting, no name-calling, no anger vented. Like a contract killer rather than a crime of passion. *Crime passionnel.* He'd taken the knife away with him and it had never been found.

Jackson had scrutinized the exes who'd had restraining orders taken out against them. Nada. *Rien.* Everyone had been interviewed, everyone had alibis that held up. And as for the killer being someone from Theo's personal life, well, Theo didn't seem to have a personal life, outside of his daughters, outside of Laura. He hardly ever mentioned the other one, Jennifer. (Why not?)

Julia seemed to be asleep. Amelia, slumped in her seat, stared glumly at the carpet. She had terrible deportment. Jackson had been assuming that someone was going to acknowledge a death had occurred, that a vicar would appear from somewhere and say a few impersonal words before launching Victor into the unknown, and so he was astonished when Victor's coffin suddenly slid quietly away and disappeared behind the curtains with as much ceremony as if it had been a suitcase on a baggage carousel. "That's *it?*" Jackson said to Julia.

"What did you want?" Amelia asked, standing up and stalking out of the chapel on her red bird legs. Julia took Jackson's arm and squeezed it and they walked out of the crematorium chapel together as if they'd just been married. "It's not illegal," she said brightly. "We checked."

It was hot, not funeral weather at all, and Julia, who had begun to sneeze the moment they were outside, said cheerfully, "Not as hot as where Daddy is at the moment." Jackson put on his Oakleys and Julia said, "*Oo-la-la,* how serious you look, Mr. Brodie, like a Secret Service agent," and Amelia had made a noise like a rooting pig. She was standing on the path, waiting for them. "That's it?" Jackson repeated, disentangling himself from Julia's grip.

"No, of course it's not," Amelia said. "Now we have tea and cake."

* * *

"If you were a dog, what do you think you would be?" Julia stuffed a large piece of cake into her mouth. "I don't know." Jackson shrugged. "A Labrador maybe?" and they had both, in unison, shouted, "No!" incredulously, as if he were insane even to contemplate being a Labrador. "You are *so* not a Labrador, Jackson," Julia said, "Labradors are *pedestrian*."

"Chocolate Labs aren't so bad," Amelia said. "It's the yellow ones that are . . . tedious."

"Chocolate Labradors." Julia laughed. "I always think you should be able to eat them."

"I think Mr. Brodie is an English pointer," Amelia said decisively.

"Really?" Julia said. "Golly. I wouldn't have thought of that one." Jackson hadn't realized that people still said "golly." They were very *loud,* the Land sisters. Embarrassingly loud. He wished they would be less demonstrative. Of course, madness was endemic in Cambridge, so they didn't stick out so much. He would have hated to have been sitting with them in a café in his native northern town, where no one had ever said "golly" since the beginning of time. They both seemed remarkably skittish today, a mood apparently not unrelated to having just cremated their father.

Julia embarked on a second cup of tea. It was too hot for tea; Jackson longed for an ice-cold beer. Julia's white teacup bore the imprint of her mouth in lipstick and Jackson experienced a sudden memory of his sister. She had worn a less strident color, a pastel pink, and on every cup and glass she ever drank from she left behind the ghostly transfer of her lips. The thought of Niamh made his heart feel heavy in his chest, literally, not metaphorically.

"I don't think so," Julia said, after having mulled over the dog question (did they ever agree about anything?). "No, not a pointer. And certainly not an English one. Perhaps an Old Danish pointer. That's 'Old' with a capital 'O,' Mr. Brodie, in case you think I'm referring to your age. Or perhaps a Large French one. Ditto with the 'L' there, Mr. Brodie. But you know, Milly, I think Mr. Brodie is a German shepherd. You can just tell he would drag you out of a burning building or a river in flood. He would *save* you!" She turned to Jackson and gave him the benefit of a brilliant theatrical smile. "Wouldn't you?"

"Would I?" Jackson said.

Amelia stood up abruptly and announced, "That was lovely but we can't spend all day enjoying ourselves," and Julia roused herself and said, "Yes, come on, Milly, chop-chop, we have shopping to do. Mystery shopping," she added, and Amelia groaned and said, "I hate mystery shopping."

Jackson took out his wallet to pay the bill. He had been keeping the photograph of Olivia in his wallet and every time he opened it to prize out one of his almost-exhausted credit cards, he saw her face, grinning at him. Not really grinning at him, of course, but at whoever was behind the camera.

"Mummy," Julia said. "Daddy never took photographs." All three of them stared sadly at the photograph.

"Julia and I are the only ones left," Amelia said. "We're the only two people left in the whole world who remember Olivia. We can't go to our grave not knowing what happened to her."

"Why now, after all this time?" Jackson asked.

"It's not 'after all this time,'" Amelia bristled. "We never *forgot* about Olivia. It's just that finding Blue Mouse, I don't know, it's as if it *found us*."

"Three of us," Julia corrected Amelia. "Sylvia remembers Olivia."

"Sylvia?" Jackson puzzled.

"Our eldest sister," Amelia said dismissively. Jackson waited, letting his silence ask the question for him. Eventually, Julia answered, "She's a nun."

"And when exactly were you going to tell me about her?" Jackson asked, trying not to sound as annoyed as he felt.

"We're telling you now," Julia said as if she were the embodiment of reason. "Don't be a crosspatch, Mr. Brodie. You're a much nicer person than you pretend to be, you know."

"No, I'm not," Jackson said.

"Yes, you are," Julia said. (Why didn't they just *go*, for God's sake?) Suddenly, to Jackson's surprise, Julia stood on tiptoe and kissed him on the cheek. "Thank you," she said, "for coming to the funeral and everything."

Jackson started to worry about being late. On the way back to the car park he had to fight his way against a herd of foreign-language students, all entirely oblivious to the existence of anyone else on the planet except other adolescents. Cambridge in summer, invaded by a combination of tourists and foreign teenagers, all of whom were put on earth to *loiter*, was Jackson's idea of hell. The language students all seemed to be dressed in combats, in khaki and camouflage, as if there were a war going on and they were the troops (God help us if that were the case). And the bikes, why did people think bikes were a good thing? Why were cyclists so smug? Why did cyclists ride on pavements when there were perfectly good cycle lanes? And who thought it was a good idea to rent bicycles to Italian adolescent language students? If hell did exist, which Jackson was sure it did, it would be governed by a committee of fifteen-year-old Italian boys on bikes.

And as for the tourists . . . enthralled by the colleges, by history, they didn't want to see what was behind all that, the money and power. The vast tracts of land they owned, not just in Cambridge, they owned most of Cambridge anyway. The colleges still yielded influence over licenses and leases and God knows what else. Someone had once told him that they used to say that you could walk the length of England and never leave land owned by Trinity. And all those beautiful gardens they had that you had to pay to go into. All that wealth and privilege in the hands of a few while the streets were full of the dispossessed, the beggars, the jakies, the mad. Cambridge seemed to have a particularly high incidence of insanity.

Still — and it was a close call — Jackson preferred the summer population to the yahs and hooray Henrys of term time. Was it just the envy of the underclass? Was it his father's voice in his head that he could hear? Jackson worried that he was turning into a grumpy old man. Perhaps being a grumpy old man wasn't necessarily a bad thing. Having a permanent toothache didn't help, of course. ("Endodontic treatment," Sharon had murmured seductively in his ear during his last appointment.)

Jackson double-parked outside the house. The windows had wooden venetian blinds rolled up so that he could see inside the living room — floor-to-ceiling bookshelves, potted palms, big couches — shabby but arty, academics, probably. The street was choked with oversize SUVs, the middle-class mother's vehicle of choice, the rear windows all sporting the obligatory CHILD ON BOARD and BABY ON BOARD signs. Jackson lit up a cigarette and put on Lucinda Williams's *Sweet Old World* as an antidote. There were balloons tied to the gatepost signaling its status as a house *en fête*. The sound of little girls' hysterical screams rose up from the garden at the back and filled the air like the call of some terrifying prehistoric bird. The SUVs were empty, the drivers all inside, but Jackson decided to stay in the car. He didn't feel up to facing the inquisitive female warmth that always seemed to greet him whenever he walked into the midst of a pack of mothers.

He leafed through some of the many papers and files he had brought with him from Theo's house. The room — the "incident room" as he now thought of it — wasn't Laura's bedroom, that was at the back of the house, overlooking the garden. Jackson had half expected it to be preserved as it had been the day that Laura left it for the last time — he'd been in those kinds of shrines before, sadder and more faded by the year, but to his surprise Laura's bedroom showed no sign of her. It was decorated in neutral colors in the style of a hotel and was nothing more than a guest bedroom. "Not that I have guests," Theo said, with that sad, drooping smile he had. He was like one of those big melancholic dogs, a Newfoundland or a Saint Bernard. Oh no, he was thinking like Julia. What kind of a dog was he? He'd said "Labrador" because it was the first dog that came into his mind. Jackson didn't know dogs, he'd never had one, not even as a kid. His father had hated dogs.

Jackson remembered what Laura Wyre's room looked like ten years ago. There'd been a patchwork quilt, a tank of tropical fish, a pile of teddy bears on the bed. Books everywhere, clothes on the floor, cosmetics, photographs. It was as untidy as you might expect an eighteen-year-old's bedroom to be. That wasn't the impression of Laura that Theo gave now. In death, she had become incapable of untidiness, of flaws. Laura had become a saint in Theo's memory, a holy girl. Jackson supposed that was natural.

Ten years ago there had been a framed photograph on the wall of her bedroom — a picture of Laura with a dog. She was pretty and had a lovely smile. She looked like a nice girl, not a saint, but a nice girl. Jackson thought of Olivia, safe in the wallet in his pocket, grinning, unseen in the darkness. "Enclosed." That's what Amelia had said about Sylvia when he asked her if she'd been invited to the funeral. ("Not even Sylvia?") "Of course we *told* her," Amelia said, "but she can't come, she's not allowed out. She's *enclosed*."

Was Olivia enclosed somewhere, under a floor, in the earth? No more than a tiny pile of leveret-thin bones waiting to be found.

Jackson had been in Laura's bedroom by chance. He was working on another case at the time, a girl called Kerry-Anne Brockley who had disappeared from the Chesterton area of town. Kerry-Anne was sixteen years old, unemployed and certainly no virgin. She had been killed on her way home from a night out with friends — raped, strangled, and dumped in a field outside town.

She had been walking home from a nightclub at two in the morning, wearing a lot of makeup and very few clothes, and there were some unspoken assumptions that she had somehow invited what had happened to her. Not on Jackson's team. If he'd thought that any of his officers thought that, he would have hung them out to dry.

They still didn't have a suspect in custody but Jackson was returning home for his first night's sleep in days, cadging a lift in the back of a squad car with a family liaison officer (a woman called Alison who Jackson should have married instead of Josie). Alison was returning some photographs of Laura to Theo. Photographs, always photographs. All those poignant images of girls that had gone. The Kerry-Annes and the Olivias and the Lauras, all of them precious, all of them lost forever. All of them holy girls. Sacrifices to some unknown, evil deity. Please God, never Marlee.

Theo Wyre had answered the door, a man hollowed out by grief. His face, Jackson had thought at the time, was the color of Wensleydale cheese. He offered them tea and Jackson thought — neither for the first nor the last time — how strange it was that people just kept on going, even when their world no longer existed. Theo had even produced cake from somewhere, saying, "Cherry and almond, I made it the day before she died. It keeps well." He shook his head sadly as if he couldn't believe that the cake still existed but his daughter didn't. Needless to say, neither of them ate it. Jackson said, "Do you mind if I have a look at Laura's bedroom, Mr. Wyre?" because he knew that as far as Theo Wyre was concerned he was just another detective, not someone who wasn't on this case. It wasn't much more than curiosity on Jackson's part, there was nothing to suggest that Laura Wyre's murder was linked to "his" murder, Kerry-Anne Brockley. And it was just a bedroom, an untidy bedroom that a girl was never going to enter again, never fling down her bag on the floor and kick off her shoes, never lie on the bed and read a book or listen to her stereo, never sleep the restless, innocent sleep of the living.

That was two years before Marlee was born and Jackson didn't know then what he knew now — what it was like to love a child, how you would give your own life in a heartbeat to save theirs, how they were more precious than the most precious thing. He no longer missed Josie as much as he thought he would, but he missed Marlee nearly all the time. That was why he didn't want to take on Theo Wyre. Theo terrified him, it made the death of his own child a possibility, it forced him to imagine it, to substitute Marlee for Laura Wyre. But what could he do? He could hardly say no to the poor guy, the size of a blimp, wheezing and puffing on his inhaler, nothing left but a memory — the shape of a space where a twenty-eight-year-old woman should have been.

Theo had a body; Amelia and Julia needed one. Olivia was a different kind of space than Laura, an incorporeal mystery, a question without an answer. A puzzle that could tease you until you went mad. He would never find Olivia, never find out what happened to her, he knew that and he would just have to find the right time to tell them that. He was never going to be able to bill them either, was he? Sorry, your baby sister's dead and gone forever and that will be £500 for services rendered. ("You're too soft to be in business," Deborah Arnold said to him every month when she did the accounting. "Too soft or too stupid.")

If it was Marlee and he had to decide — dead or missing forever — which would he choose? No, he couldn't go there, couldn't bear to imagine it, couldn't tempt fate by trying to. Either scenario depicted the worst thing that could possibly happen. What did you do when the worst thing that could happen to you had already happened — how did you live your life then? You had to hand it to Theo Wyre, just carrying on living required a kind of strength and courage that most people didn't have.

The front door opened and all the little party girls and their party mothers hit the street at top volume. Jackson hastily stuffed photographs of Laura Wyre's crime scene beneath the front passenger seat. He was about to get out of the car and go inside when Marlee ran out. Jesus, she was dressed like a hooker. What did Josie think, letting her go out looking like a pedophile's dream? She even had lipstick on. He thought of JonBenét Ramsey. Another lost girl. When he was in Bliss earlier, a girl had come in, a friend of the receptionist (Milanda — had she made her name up?), and made an appointment for a "Brazilian," and Milanda said, "Yeah?" and the girl said, "My boyfriend wants me to get one. He wants to pretend he's making love with a young girl," and Milanda said, "Yeah?" as if that were a good reason.

Jackson knew the statistics, knew how many known pedophiles would be hanging out in any one area, knew how they'd be clustered, thickly, like flies, around playgrounds, schools, swimming pools (and houses that were signposted with balloons). "Claire's Accessories" — that's where Jackson would go if he were a pedophile. What if reincarnation existed, what if you came back as a pedophile? But then what would you have had to do in the first place to deserve that? What did the holy girls come back as? Flocks of doves, groves of trees?

"Hiya, sweetheart. Good party?" (Were you just going to run out into the street, not knowing if anyone was waiting for you?) Where were you going? Did you know I was here?

"Yep."

"Did you remember to say 'thank you'?"

"Yep. I said, 'Thank you very much for having me.'"

"You're fibbing," Jackson said.

"No, I'm not."

"Yes, you are. Basic interrogation fact: people look up to the left when they're remembering and up to the right when they're inventing. You looked up to the right." Shut up, Jackson. She wasn't even listening.

"My bad," she said indifferently.

"Your bad?" What language was that? She looked exhausted,

she was black under the eyes. What did they do at these parties? She was drenched with sweat.

"We were dancing," she said, "to Christina Aguilera. She's wicked." She did a little move to indicate dancing, and it was so sexual that it turned Jackson's heart over. She was eight years old for fuck's sake.

"That's nice, sweetheart." She smelled of sugar and sweat. He remembered the first time he held her, when the whole of her head fit into the palm of his hand and Josie said "be careful" (as if he wouldn't be) and he had vowed to himself that nothing bad would ever happen to her, that he would keep her safe. A solemn promise, an oath. Did Theo Wyre make that same vow when Laura was first placed in his arms? Almost certainly. (And what about Victor Land?) But Jackson couldn't make Marlee safe, he couldn't make anyone safe. The only time you were safe was when you were dead. Theo was the world's greatest worrier, but the one thing he didn't worry about anymore was whether or not his daughter was safe.

"You've got lipstick all over you," Marlee said to him. Jackson examined himself in the rearview mirror and discovered the vivid imprint of Julia's crimson mouth on his cheek. He rubbed at it aggressively but the color remained like a spot of heat on his face.

"She was such a little scrap of a thing," Binky Rain was saying, although Jackson wasn't really listening. He had caved in to a flurry of "Carmen Buranas" and said to Marlee, "Do you want to go and visit an old lady on the way home?" sweetening this not-very-inviting invitation with the promise of cats so that now she was rolling around in the weed-filled jungle of Binky's garden with an assortment of reluctant felines.

"And she's your child?" Binky, looking doubtfully at Marlee. "I don't think of you as having a child."

"No?" he said absently. He was thinking about Olivia Land, she was just a scrap of a thing too. Would she have wandered off? Amelia and Julia said no, that she was very "obedient." Obedient enough to leave the tent in the middle of the night and go with someone who told her to? Go where? Jackson had tried to sweet-talk his old pal Wendy in police records to show him the evidence from Olivia's case, but even if she'd been willing it wouldn't have done any good because it was all missing. "Sorry, Jackson, it's gone AWOL," Wendy said. "It happens. Thirty-four years is a long time."

"Not that long," Jackson said. Although Olivia's case had never been officially closed, there was hardly anyone left alive who had worked it. Before the days of sophisticated DNA testing and police profiling, before computers for God's sake. If she were abducted now there would be a better chance of finding her. Maybe. All the senior detectives who had worked the case were dead and the only person Jackson could find any trace of was a female PC called Marian Foster who seemed to have done most of the interviews with the Land girls. She had just retired as a superintendent from a northern force that was too close to Jackson's old home for him to feel excited about the prospect of a visit. Of course, nowadays the parents would be the first people you thought about, especially the father. How aggressively had the police gone after Victor when they interviewed him? If it had been Jackson's case, Victor Land would have been his prime suspect.

Out of earshot of Marlee, Jackson asked Binky, "Do you remember the disappearance of Olivia Land? Little girl abducted from around here thirty-four years ago?"

"Frisky," Binky said, sticking to her own agenda. "She's hardly more than a kitten."

"The Land family," Jackson persisted. "Did you know them? He was a maths lecturer at St. John's. They had four little girls." You didn't forget the disappearance of a child in a neighboring street, did you?

"Oh, *those* girls," Binky said. "They were *wild* children, completely undisciplined. In my opinion, children should be neither seen nor heard. Really, families like that deserve what happens to them." Jackson thought of several responses to this remark, but in the end he kept them all to himself. "And, of course," Binky continued, "he was the son of Oswald Land, the so-called polar hero, and I can assure you that *he* was a complete charlatan."

"Do you remember seeing anyone who didn't belong, a stranger?"

"No. The police were such a nuisance, going from house to house, asking questions. They even searched *my* garden, can you believe. I gave them short shrift, I can tell you. She was very strange."

"Who was strange? Mrs. Land?"

"No, that eldest one, long white streak of a thing."

"Strange how?"

"Very *sly*. And you know, they used to break into my garden, shout things, and steal from my lovely apple trees. This was such a lovely orchard." Jackson looked around at the "epple" trees, now as gnarled and ancient as Binky Rain.

"Sylvia?"

"Yes, that was her name."

Jackson left Binky's by way of the back garden gate. He'd never exited that way before and was surprised to find himself in the lane that ran along behind the back of Victor's garden. He hadn't realized how close the two actually were to each other — he was standing only a few yards from where the fateful tent was pitched. Had someone climbed over the wall here, plucked Olivia from sleep? And then left the same way? How easy would it be to climb a wall with a three-year-old slung over your shoulder? Jackson could have managed it with no bother. The wall was smothered in ivy, providing plenty of hand- and footholds. But that mode of entry implied an intruder and that wouldn't explain why the dog didn't bark in the night. Rascal. And it was the kind of dog that would have barked, according to Amelia and Julia, so it must have known Olivia's captor. How many people would the dog *not* bark at?

He tugged at the ivy and discovered a gate in the wall, the spit of Binky's. He thought of *The Secret Garden,* a film he had watched on video with Marlee and that had enraptured her. No one would have had to climb anything — he or she could have just walked into the garden. Or perhaps no one walked in and then out with Olivia — perhaps someone walked out with her and then walked back in again. Victor? Rosemary Land?

Marlee was almost asleep by the time they reached David Lastingham's house. Would he ever call it David and Josie's house? (No.) The sugar high Marlee had been riding had long since turned into irritability. She was covered in grass seeds and cat fur, which would undoubtedly cause a row with Josie. Jackson suggested that she sleep at his house tonight, at least that way he could get her cleaned up, but she declined because "We're going berry picking in the morning."

"Berry picking?" Jackson said as he rang David Lastingham's doorbell. He thought of hunter-gatherers and peasants.

"So Mummy can make jam."

"Jam? Your mother?" The born-again wife, the jam-making peasant mother, came out of the kitchen, licking something off her fingers. The woman who was previously too busy to cook — the queen of Iceland — who now spent her evenings making cozy casseroles and carelessly tossing together salads for her new, reconstituted family. It was hard to believe that this was the same woman who used to give him blow jobs while he was driving, who would pin him up against any available surface and groan, "*Now,* Jackson. Hurry," who fitted her body against his in sleep, who used to wake up every morning and turn sleepily to him and say, "I still love

52 K A T E A T K I N S O N

you," as if relieved that the night hadn't stolen her feelings for him.
Until one morning, three years after Marlee was born, she woke
up and didn't say anything.

"You're late," she said to him now, "Where have you been?"

"We went to see a witch," Marlee said.

Le chat noir. Les chats noirs. Did *chats* have a gender? Was there a
chatte?

"*Bonsoir, Jackson.*" Joan Dodds greeted him with the stress on the
soir rather than the *bon*. She despised tardiness in people.

"*Bonsoir, Jackson,*" the whole class chorused as Jackson made his
sheepishly late entrance.

"*Vous êtes en retard, comme toutes les semaines,*" Joan Dodds said.
She was a retired schoolteacher who had the kind of character that
would have made her an excellent dominatrix. Jackson remembered
a time when the women in his life actually seemed to want to
make him happy. Now they all just seemed to be angry all the
time. Jackson felt rather like a small, rather naughty, boy. "*Je suis dé-
solé,*" he said. You had to wonder about the French, how they
could make a simple "sorry" sound so extreme and forlorn.

In Bliss, Jackson had shown Milanda his license and asked if he
could see the place where Laura Wyre was killed. "Morbid" was
her only comment. The boardroom, as Theo had reported, was now
used as a storeroom. The nail-varnish trolley had been moved and
was no longer acting as her cenotaph. Laura's blood was in plain
sight, a washed-out (but not washed-out enough) stain on the bare
floorboards. "Christ," Milanda said, finally roused out of her tor-
por, "I thought that was paint or something. That's disgusting."

When he was on his way out the door, Milanda said, "She's not
haunting the place. I'd know if she were here. I've got second
sight, I'd feel her if she were here."

"Really?" Jackson said — Milanda seemed like an unlikely re-
cipient of second sight — and she said, "Oh, yes, seventh daugh-

ter of a seventh daughter," and Jackson thought, *Inbred, rural,* and Milanda fixed him with her baby blue eyes — an unnatural, startling color that he realized must be contacts — and said, "You, for example," and Jackson said, "Yes?"

"Yeah," Milanda said. "Black cats are very lucky for you." And Jackson felt an unexpected disappointment because for one weird, unnerving moment he thought she was actually going to say something portentous.

9

Amelia

"*D*on't be a crosspatch, Mr. Brodie," Amelia mimicked. "What are you like, Julia?" (And she had kissed him! She had actually kissed him!) "Why not just take your clothes off in the street?"

"Oh, I do believe you're jealous, Milly!" Julia laughed with (cruel) delight. "What would Henry say if he found out?"

"Shut up, Julia." Amelia could feel herself heating up and she walked faster to get away from Julia. Julia had to run to keep up. She sounded wheezy and Amelia thought it was insane for someone with hay fever to smoke so much. Amelia had absolutely no sympathy for her.

"Do we have to go so fast? Your legs are much longer than mine."

They were on Regent Street, approaching a girl who was sitting on the ground, on an old sheet, a dog — some kind of lurcher — stretched out at her side.

Jackson hadn't given two hoots that she'd thought he was an English pointer, but he looked downright pleased to know that Julia thought he was a German shepherd. And Julia would choose that because it was *exactly* the right dog, not a Doberman, not a rottweiler, and certainly not a pointer — he was German shepherd through and through. She had lied to Jackson, well not exactly lied, but she had led him to understand that she was an Oxford don when in fact she was just a lecturer at the poly, teaching "communication skills" (as it was so laughably called) to day-release slaters and apprentice bricklayers and other assorted riffraff. She wanted to like those boys, to think they were good — perhaps a little too rumbustious but at heart decent human beings — but they weren't. They were little shits who never listened to a word she said.

Julia was immediately attracted to the homeless girl's dog, of course, which meant that one or the other of them would have to give the girl money because you could hardly make a fuss of the dog and not give something in return, could you? Julia was on her knees on the pavement, letting the dog lick her face. Amelia wished she wouldn't do that, you didn't know where that dog's tongue had been — well, you did, that's why you didn't want it washing your face.

The girl had yellow hair, an odd canary color, and her face was sallow, almost jaundiced. Amelia used to give money to beggars and *Big Issue* sellers, but these days she was more circumspect. She had once come across one of her own students begging on Oxford High Street. Amelia knew for a fact that the girl — Lisa, a day-release hairdresser — was living comfortably at home with her parents, and the dog she had with her (because they all had dogs, of course) was the family pet. Plus, it was a well-known fact that a lot of beggars actually had homes, and some of them even had cars. Was it a well-known fact? How did she know it? From the *Sun* probably. The slaters were always leaving copies of the *Sun* strewn around in their wake. What an extraordinary image that suddenly conjured up in her mind — copies of the sun broadcast carelessly around the universe like gold coins. She laughed, and the girl looked at her and asked, "Can you help me?" and Amelia said, "No."

"Oh, Milly, for heaven's sake," Julia said, abandoning her puppy talk and raking through her bag for her purse. "There but for fortune and all that." Julia came up with a five-pound note — five pounds that she actually owed to Amelia — and handed it to the girl, who took it as if she were doing Julia a favor. It hadn't been the money, the girl hadn't wanted money, not really. She had asked Amelia if she could help her and Amelia had told the truth. She couldn't help her, she couldn't help anyone. Least of all herself.

"She'll spend it on drugs," she said to Julia as they walked away from the girl.

"She can spend it on what she wants," Julia said. "In fact drugs sound like a good idea. If I was in her position I would spend money on drugs."

"She's in that position *because* of drugs."

"You don't know that. You don't know anything about her."

"I know she's sponging off people who exhaust themselves working for a living." Oh God, she was turning into a fascist in her old age. She'd be demanding the return of hanging and flogging soon, well not flogging perhaps but capital punishment — after all, why not? There were enough people in the world, surely, without keeping space for the evil bastards who tortured children and animals and macheted innocent people. "Evil bastards" — that was tabloid language from the slaters' *Suns*. She may as well cancel her subscription to the *Guardian* right now, the way she was going.

"Is 'macheted' a verb?" Amelia asked Julia.

"Don't think so."

Well, that was the end then, she was Americanizing words. Civilization would fall.

They stopped outside a burger bar. Inside it was heaving with foreign-language students, they were spilling out onto the pavement and Amelia groaned at the sight of them. She was sure the only language they improved when they were in Cambridge was obscenities or vocabulary for junk food.

In London, Julia did a lot of mystery shopping for an agency — burger bars and pizza places, high-street clothes shops and big chemists' chains. As far as Julia was concerned it almost qualified as acting and as a bonus she usually got to keep the goods or eat the food. The agency was delighted when they discovered she was in Cambridge, where they no longer had a mystery shopper.

"Right," Julia said, consulting a piece of paper. "We have to ask for one burger with fries and one chickinlickin burger with no fries, a large Coke, a banana milk shake, and a strawberry slurry."

"Which is?"

"An ice cream. More or less."

"I'm not asking for a chickinlickin burger," Amelia said. "I wouldn't ask for a chickinlickin burger to save your life."

"Yes, you would. But you don't have to. I'm going to ask for it all. And it's not to take away. It's to sit in."

"That's not even grammatical," Amelia said.

"There's nothing grammatical about this meal. Grammar isn't the issue. We're looking for attitude. We're assessing quality of service."

"Can't I just have a coffee?"

"No." Julia started sneezing again. It was always embarrassing when Julia had a sneezing fit, one after the other, explosive, uncontrollable sounds, like a cannon firing. Amelia had once heard someone say that you could tell what a woman's orgasm would be like if you heard her sneeze. (As if you would want to know.) Just recollecting this thought made her uncomfortable. In case this was common knowledge, Amelia had made a point ever since then of never sneezing in public if she could help it. "For God's sake, take more Zyrtec," she said crossly to Julia.

Amelia was acutely uncomfortable in places like this. They made her feel old and elitist and she didn't want to feel either of those things, even if they were true. Julia, on the other hand, was a chameleon, adapting immediately to whatever was in hand, shouting her order to the spotted, callow youth behind the counter (did any of them wash their hands?) in a kind of Essex accent that she probably thought was plebeian but sounded completely at odds with the way she was dressed. The coat Julia was wearing was bizarre, like something from a Beardsley drawing. Amelia hadn't really looked at it properly until now. It was such a bright color that it would be impossible to lose sight of Julia, unless she were to lie down on a hill of green summer grass, which would have rendered her invisible. When Olivia became invisible she was wearing a cotton nightdress that had belonged to each of them in turn and had once been pink but by the time it reached Olivia was a washed-out kind of no color. Amelia could see her as clear as day, climbing into the tent in the washed-out nightdress, the pink rabbit slippers, one arm clamping Blue Mouse to her chest.

Julia's coat was too big for her. It flapped open and trailed on the floor as she maneuvered the tray of food through an impassable wad of foreign students. Amelia kept saying, "Excuse me, excuse me," in a pointed way but it was no good. The only way you could get them to move was by elbowing them roughly out of the way.

When they finally got a seat Julia commenced to tear into the burger with a kind of primitive gusto. "Mm, meat," she said to Amelia.

"Are you sure?" Amelia said. She would have been sick if she'd eaten any of this food. "It's definitely meat," Julia said. "What animal it's from is another question. Or what part of the animal. We used to eat tail, after all. Oxen — what kind of a plural is that?"

"Old English. I think. There must be a whole generation of children thinking 'chicken' is spelled 'chickin.'"

"There are worse things."

"Such as?"

"Meteors."

"The possibility of a meteor colliding with the earth doesn't mean that we should embrace the Americanization of our language and culture."

"Oh, shut up, Milly, do."

Julia ate the chickinlickin burger, but the strawberry slurry defeated even her. Amelia sniffed the milk shake tentatively. It tasted completely artificial, as if it had been made in a laboratory. "This is made entirely of chemicals."

"Isn't everything?"

"Is it?"

"Come on," Julia said. "Enough of the chitchat, let's get to work." She took out a form and began to fill it in. "*Did your server greet you?* I'm sure he did."

"Why don't you wear your glasses? You can't see a thing without them."

"What did the server say?"

"You're so vain, Julia."

"I think he said, 'G'day there.' "

"I don't know, I wasn't paying attention. Julia?"

"They're all Australian. The entire British workforce is Australian."

"Julia. Julia, listen to me. When Victor went over your homework with you in his study, did he ever, you know, do anything? Did he ever interfere with you?"

"Who's doing their jobs in Australia, do you think? Come on, Milly, we have to get on with this. Now, *Did your server smile? Did he?* Gosh, I really can't remember."

She could tell Jackson thought she was foolish, a foolish *woman*. He had that masculine dourness about him that was so infuriating — the type that thought women were in thrall to their periods and chocolate and kittens (which was quite a good description of Julia) when Amelia really wasn't like that — well, perhaps the kittens. She wanted him to think better of her, she wanted him to like her. *Oo-la-la, how serious you look, Mr. Brodie, like a Secret Service agent.* Julia was so *obvious*. "Oo-la-la," for God's sake.

"Do you want tea?" she asked Julia when she floated into the kitchen, an empty glass in her hand.

"No. I'm going to have more gin," Julia said, searching through the kitchen cupboards for something to eat. Did Julia always drink this much? Did she drink on her own? Why was that worse than drinking with someone?

He liked Julia, of course. All men liked Julia which was no surprise since she offered herself on a plate to them. Julia had once told her that she loved giving a man oral sex (which was undoubtedly why she wore that red lipstick) and Amelia had a distressing vision of Julia on her knees in front of Jackson's — she wanted to say "cock" but the word wouldn't really form in her mind because it was too obscene, and "penis" always sounded so ridiculous. Amelia didn't want to be this prudish. She felt like someone who'd lost her way and ended up in the wrong generation. She would have been much more suited to a period with structure and rank and rules, where a button undone on a glove signaled licentiousness. She could have managed quite well living within those kinds of strictures. She had read too much James and Wharton. No one in Edith Wharton's world really wanted to be there but Amelia would have got along fine inside an Edith Wharton novel. In fact, she could have happily lived inside any nineteenth-century novel.

She could hear the bath running upstairs (it took forever) and she knew that Julia would take her gin up to the bathroom with her (and probably a joint as well) and lie there for hours. Amelia wondered what it felt like to be so self-indulgent. Julia tore a piece off a loaf of bread and stuffed it into her mouth. Why couldn't she use the knife and cut it? How did she manage to make eating a piece of bread look sexual? Amelia wished she hadn't had that vision of Julia giving Jackson — say it — a blow job. She'd never given anyone a blow job in her life, not that she would ever tell Julia that, as she would just start rattling on again about "Henry" and his sexual needs. Hah!

"Are you sure you don't want one?" Julia said, waving the gin bottle around, "it might help you to relax."

"I don't want to relax, thank you very much." How did this happen to her? How did she become this person she didn't want to be?

＊　＊　＊

Amelia didn't understand how being "good at literature" had warped into teaching "communication skills." She'd applied to Oxbridge when she was in the sixth form at school. She wanted to show her teachers and Victor — mainly Victor — that she was clever enough. Her teachers had been dubious and hadn't helped her to prepare in any way so that she'd muddled her way through the entrance papers with their impenetrable questions about *The Faerie Queene* and *The Dunciad* — neither of which she'd read — and their absurd plots to test ingenuity in essay writing — "Imagine you are proposing the invention of the wheel" — fancy giving that to the slaters and brickies as an assignment, they would bring sex into it somehow, of course, they brought sex into everything. Amelia didn't know whether they did that because they knew it embarrassed her (it was ridiculous to be over forty and still blushing) or because they would do it anyway.

To Amelia's surprise, Newnham had given her an interview. It took her a long time to realize that Victor had probably pulled some strings, or the college, recognizing the name, had given her an interview as a courtesy. She'd wanted to go to Newnham as long as she could remember; when they were children they used to peer through the gates into the garden. She always imagined heaven looked like that. She didn't believe in heaven, of course. She didn't believe in religion. That didn't mean that she didn't want to believe in heaven.

Before her interview she imagined walking through those self-same gardens, admiring the beautiful herbaceous border, discussing *Middlemarch* and *War and Peace* with an earnest new friend or being punted along the river by some handsome, no-good medical student, being someone that people wanted to know — "Oh, look, there's Amelia Land. Let's go and talk to her. She's so interesting" (or "such good fun," or "very pretty," or even "absolutely outrageous"), but it hadn't worked out like that at all. Her interview at

Newnham was mortifying — they were kind, concerned even, treating her like she was slightly sick, or suffering a disability, but they asked her questions about works and authors she had never heard of. Worse than Spenser and Pope, now it was *Rasselas, Prince of Abyssinia* and Ruskin's *Unto This Last*. It wasn't what Amelia thought of as literature. Literature was big books (*Middlemarch* and *War and Peace*) that you could fall in love with and lose yourself in forever. And so she'd ended up at a far-flung, mediocre redbrick with no intellectual cachet but where at least they let you write long essays about your love affair with *Middlemarch* and *War and Peace*.

Julia came back into the kitchen and poured more gin. She was getting on Amelia's nerves. "I thought you were having a bath," she said irritably.

"I am. Who rattled your cage?"

"No one."

Amelia took her tea through to the living room and turned the television on. Sammy joined her on the sofa. There was some kind of celebrity reality show on. She didn't know who any of the "celebrities" were and there didn't seem to be anything real about the predicaments they found themselves in. She didn't want to go to bed, didn't want to sleep in Sylvia's cold bedroom that caught the light from the street lamp outside and had damp creeping down the walls from the roof. Maybe she could move into the guest bedroom? To Amelia's knowledge no one had ever slept in it. Would it call down a curse on her head from their mother? If their mother was a ghost, not that Amelia believed in ghosts, she thought the guest bedroom would be where she would take up residence. She imagined her lying on the narrow bed, its white coverlet now spotted with mold, lazing away her days with magazines and boxes of chocolates, discarding the wrappers on the floor now that she was no longer in thrall to housework. And what about Olivia's room, could Amelia bear to sleep in there? Could she lie in that small bed and stare at the peeling nursery-rhyme wallpaper and not feel her heart break?

Who took Olivia? Did Victor come creeping across the grass in the night and dig her out of the tent with his big shovel hands while Amelia slept? Her own father? Why not? It happened all the time, didn't it? And did he keep Blue Mouse as some terrible souvenir? Or was there a more innocent explanation (but what?).

They had always found refuge in thinking of Olivia living a different life somewhere else, rather than being dead. For years and years the three of them had woven a story for Olivia — snatched in the night by a figure very like the Snow Queen, only kind and loving and coming from a more temperate kingdom. This empyreal creature had been desperate for a little girl of her own and had chosen Olivia because she was perfect in every way. The fictional Olivia was brought up in the most luxurious paradise their girlish imaginations could conceive of — wrapped in silks and furs, fed on cakes and sweets, surrounded by dogs and kittens and (for some reason) peacocks, bathing in golden baths and sleeping in silver beds. And although they knew Olivia was happy in her new life they believed that one day she would be allowed to return home — which was always the unquestionable consummation of this wishful narrative.

As they grew, so did Olivia, and it was only when Julia reached adolescence (her hormones releasing enough energy to power a small town) that Olivia's other, fabulous life faded away. Yet it was so strongly embedded in Amelia's consciousness that even now she found it difficult to believe that Olivia might actually be dead and not a thirty-seven-year-old woman living in an Arcadian bower somewhere.

Julia came into the living room and squashed herself onto the sofa between Amelia and Sammy, where there was clearly no room for her. "Go away," Amelia said to her. Julia produced a bar of chocolate and broke a piece off for Amelia and a piece for the dog.

"I mean, it's not *impossible* that Olivia's still alive," Julia said, as if she had been listening to Amelia's thoughts (what a horrible idea). "Perhaps she was kidnapped by someone who wanted a child, and they brought her up as their own, so she forgot about us, forgot she was Olivia, just thought she was someone else, say . . . Charlotte —"

"Charlotte?"

"Yes. And then when the kidnappers were on their deathbed they told her who she was. 'Charlotte, you are really Olivia Land. You lived on Owlstone Road in Cambridge. You have three sisters — Sylvia, Amelia, and Julia.'"

"How likely is that, Julia?"

Amelia changed the channel until she came across *Now, Voyager,* and Julia said, "Oh, leave that on."

"Your bath will overflow."

"Milly?"

"What?"

"You know what you were saying about Victor?"

"What?"

"If he ever *interfered* with me. That's such a stupid term, such a euphemism. What it means is did Daddy ever make you suck his cock or did he ever stick his fingers inside you while he jerked himself off —" Amelia couldn't bear this. She concentrated on Bette Davis looking tragic and tried to block out the obscenities Julia was spouting.

"Whichever way you look at it, it's rape," Julia concluded. "And no, since you ask, he didn't. He tried though." Amelia wanted to put her hands over her ears. She wanted to be deaf.

"He *tried?* What do you mean he tried?"

"He tried to stick his hands down my knickers once but I just screamed the place down. He was trying to explain fractions," she added as if that were somehow relevant.

That would be Julia, she would scream. Amelia would simply have let him do it. Only he didn't, he'd never tried to do anything with her. He'd never *interfered*.

"What did he do to you, Milly?" Julia asked gently, putting her hand on Amelia's forearm as if she were sick or bereaved. Amelia had caught him once with Sylvia. She had walked into the study without knocking, which was absolutely forbidden, so she must have been in one of her dreamy moods, and there had been Daddy with Sylvia and ever since she had tried to forget what she had seen. Sylvia facedown on Victor's desk like a half-crucified martyr, her skinny white buttocks exposed, and Victor *preparing* himself —

Amelia shook Julia off and said harshly, "Nothing. He never did anything, I would never have let him. Go and get your bath, Julia."

Amelia woke up with a start. It was dark and silent in the house, no ghosts walking, only the slight electrical buzz of the street lamp outside. Amelia couldn't remember if Julia had got out of the bath and had to get up to check that she hadn't drowned silently. The bath was empty, the bathroom dripping with cold condensation. There were towels thrown around everywhere. Julia was safely in her bed, her bedclothes in the usual disorder and her poodle hair still damp. Her breathing was heavy and regular, although Amelia could hear a gurgling in her chest. Julia's lungs always sounded as if they needed wringing out, like dishcloths. What would she do if Julia died before her? If she was the last one left? (Sylvia didn't count.) Sammy, asleep on Julia's bed, woke up and wagged his tail when Amelia came in the room. Amelia straightened Julia's covers and the dog slipped clumsily off the bed and followed her out of the room.

On the way back to her own room Amelia paused outside Olivia's closed door. Sammy looked at her inquiringly and she turned the doorknob and walked into the room. Moonlight shone diffusely through the filthy window. She lay down on her back on the small bed. Sammy flopped to the floor. The effort made him groan.

On the last day of her life, Olivia had woken in this bed, looked at these walls. Would she have died if she'd slept here and not in the tent? If only Amelia could go back, take Olivia's place that night, fight off whatever evil it was that had taken her. If only Amelia could have been chosen instead.

10

Theo

The girl had a tube of sweets clutched in her hand — garish-colored things that were probably made entirely of chemicals and E-numbers. She offered one to Theo and he took it out of a sense of politeness. It tasted vaguely of petrol or lighter fluid. It didn't taste as if it could do any good to growing bones and minds. Theo never bought sweets, and although he loved chocolate he didn't like buying it in shops because of the disapprobation this always attracted. Fat people weren't supposed to eat anything, but they were especially not supposed to eat confectionery, so instead he belonged to an online "tasting club," which meant that every month a chocolate company sent him a new selection to try and in return he sent back a review ("creamy and delicious, the hazelnut praline gives just the right amount of contrast") that felt oddly onerous, like doing bizarre homework. That was how he rationed his chocolate consumption, just the one box of something creamy and delicious every month.

He didn't really care about his cholesterol and his blood pressure. He would be happy to die of a stroke or a heart attack. "Strokes don't necessarily kill, Dad," Jennifer e-mailed crossly from Toronto. "They're more likely to leave you incapacitated. Is that what you want?" Perhaps she was afraid she would have to look after him, but he would never do that to her. As far as Theo was concerned the parent-child relationship was one way, you gave them all your love and they were under no obligation to pay a penny back. Of course, if they did love you then that was the icing on the cake with cherries on top. And chocolate shavings and those little silver balls that cracked your fillings. Laura used to love those. He always decorated the cakes he made. Cakes, pastry, scones — he'd learned how to make everything after Valerie died. He turned out to be a much better cook than his wife.

He hired a woman to come in and clean twice a week and a girl, a student, to pick them up from school and look after them until he got home from work. Otherwise he did everything himself — housework, child care. He went to PTA meetings, parents' evenings, took the girls to birthday parties, threw birthday parties in return. The other children's mothers treated him as an honorary woman and said he would make someone a wonderful wife, which he took as a compliment.

The girl said she was eight but she was dressed more like a teenager. But that was how it was nowadays. In the past, children used to be dressed as small adults so there was nothing new in that. When Laura was eight she wore dungarees and jeans and nice dresses for best — "frocks," Valerie would have called them, if she'd been around. White ankle socks, sandals, T-shirts, and shorts. He bought Laura her own clothes and didn't make her wear Jennifer's castoffs. A lot of people thought Theo spoiled his girls, but how could you spoil a child — by neglect, yes, but not by love. You had to give them all the love you could, even though giving that much love could cause you pain and anguish and horror and, in the end, love could destroy you. Because they left, they went to university and husbands, they went to Canada and they went to the grave.

Theo declined a second sweet. "It's polite to offer one to everyone," Deborah Arnold said to the girl. Rather reluctantly,

Theo thought, the girl slid off her seat and went over to Deborah's desk and without a word offered the tube of sweets to her. Deborah took three. There was something oddly admirable about the woman. Terrifying but admirable.

"What's your job?" the girl asked him.

"I'm retired," Theo said, wondering if she knew what that meant.

"Because you're old," she said, nodding sagely. Theo agreed with her, "Yes, because I'm old."

"My daddy's going to retire," the girl said. "He's going to live in France." Deborah Arnold laughed derisively.

"France?" Theo said. He couldn't imagine Jackson in France somehow. "Have you been to France?"

"Yes, on holiday. Some people ate thrushes."

"Oh my God," Deborah Arnold said. "Neither of you are supposed to be here," she added as if they were jointly responsible for the French dining on innocent songbirds.

"I just wanted a quick chat with Mr. Brodie — to see how things were going," Theo said apologetically. Deborah Arnold seemed extraordinarily busy — typing, filing, and copying like a woman possessed. Did Jackson Brodie really generate this much business? He seemed a little too laid-back to keep an assistant so fully occupied. She'd called herself his assistant; he'd called her his secretary.

"So, Mr. Brodie's out on a case?" Theo asked, to make conversation more than anything. Deborah gave him a pitying look over the top of her spectacles as if she couldn't believe he could be duped into thinking that Jackson actually worked. After five minutes, she said, "He's at the dentist. Again."

"Dad fancies the dentist," the girl said, popping another sweet into an already overloaded mouth. It seemed sad that such little girls knew about "fancying," knew anything at all about sex. Perhaps they didn't, perhaps they just knew the words. The girl, Marlee, did seem very precocious though, more like an eighteen-year-old than an eight-year-old. Not like his eighteen-year-old (because Laura would always be eighteen). Laura had had a freshness about her, an innocence, like a light shining from within. Jackson had never mentioned having a daughter, but then you didn't, did you? Bank managers, bus drivers, they didn't spend their time saying, "I have a daughter, by the way."

"Have you got children?" Marlee asked him.

"Yes," Theo said. "I have a daughter called Jenny. She lives in Canada. She's grown-up." Of course, he felt like he was denying Laura, expected to hear a cock crow every time he made this answer, but people didn't want to hear him say, "Yes, I have two, one alive and well and living in Toronto and one dead and in the earth."

"Grandchildren?" Marlee asked.

"No," Theo said. Jennifer and her husband, Alan — New York, Jewish, avuncular, heart surgeon — had decided not to have children and it had seemed to Theo to be indelicate to ask why. Jennifer had a career, of course. She was an orthopedic consultant, and they had a good life, a nice house in the suburbs, a place on Lake Ontario, a "cottage" as the Torontonians quaintly called their huge lakeshore houses. Theo had gone to stay one summer. The house was surrounded on three sides by trees and at night it was the quietest, darkest place he had ever been, the only illumination coming from the fireflies that danced outside his bedroom window all night long. It was a great place. They had a canoe that they took out on the lake, there were hiking trails through the ancient woods, they had a barbecue every day on their lakeside terrace — it would have been a paradise for kids. Of course, you never missed what you never had. And once you'd had it you missed it all the time. Perhaps Jennifer was being sensible. If she didn't have a child she couldn't lose it.

"Are you sad?"

"No. Yes. A little, sometimes." (A lot, all the time.)

"Have another sweet."

"Thanks."

＊　＊　＊

After ten years Theo had suddenly become impatient. Ten years of garnering evidence, of doggedly accumulating every last scrap of anything, and now he wanted to know. Jackson had removed all his client files, loading up the backseat and the boot of his car with box after box of other people's life histories — their divorces, their house purchases, their last wills and testaments. Had Jackson discerned something yet from all this information, like a soothsayer, like those clairvoyants they brought in, that Theo himself had brought in. Even the police had brought a clairvoyant in, but they hadn't briefed him properly and he had thought they were looking for a body when, of course, they already had one. The clairvoyant said the girl's body was "in a garden, within walking distance of a river," which pretty much narrowed it down to half of Cambridge, if anyone was going to go and look for her, which they weren't. How many girls were out there, unturned by the plow, unseen by the passerby? If only you could lock girls away, in towers, in dungeons, in convents, in their bedrooms, anywhere that would keep them safe.

There was a girl he passed all the time. Sometimes she was on Regent Street, she was often on Sydney Street, and he'd seen her at the Grafton Centre, sitting on an old sheet, a blanket around her shoulders. A "beggar girl." It was like something from history, from the eighteenth century. This morning she was on St. Andrews Street and Theo gave her five pounds, which was all the change he had on him.

The girl looked ill but the dog with her always looked well cared for, a nice glossy black lurcher, still young. The beggar girl had custard-yellow hair, cut raggedly short, and no one ever seemed to give her money, perhaps because she never asked for it, never made eye contact or said something cheery to make people feel good about themselves, good about her being a beggar. Or perhaps because she looked as if she might spend it all on drugs. Theo thought she would probably buy dog food before drugs.

Theo always gave her money but he felt there must be something better he could do — buy her a good meal, find her a room, ask her name, anything, before she slipped through the cracks, but he always felt too shy, too worried that any interest might be misconstrued, that she would turn on him and snarl, "Fuck off, Granddad, you old pervert."

"Does your father know you're here?" Deborah Arnold asked Marlee.

"Mum left him a message on his mobile."

"Well, I have to go out," Deborah said. "I have to catch the post" — this last remark addressed to Theo, who wondered what he was supposed to do about it. "Can you keep an eye on her?" Deborah said, nodding in the direction of Marlee, and Theo wanted to say, "But I'm an almost complete stranger. How do you know I'm not going to do something dreadful to her?" Misinterpreting his hesitation, Deborah said, "It's just for fifteen minutes, or until his nibs comes back." Marlee clambered on his knee and put her arms around his neck, and said, "Please, please, nice man, say yes," and Theo thought, Dear God, hadn't anyone told her to be cautious around strangers? Just because he looked like Father Christmas didn't make him benign, although he was, of course. But Deborah Arnold was out the door and down the stairs before Theo could protest.

"My daddy'll be back soon," Marlee reassured him. "My daddy." The very words brought a lump to his throat. Laura's second-favorite film, after *Dirty Dancing,* was *The Railway Children,* and he'd bought a copy on video a couple years before she died. They had watched it together several times and they both always cried at the end when the train stops and the steam and smoke slowly clear around the figure of Bobbie's father and Jenny Agutter (who always reminded him a little of Laura) cries out, "Daddy, my daddy," and it was odd because it was such a happy moment for Bobbie and yet it always seemed unbearably sad. Of course, he'd never watched the film since Laura's death. It would kill him to watch it. Theo never doubted for a moment that when he died he would be reunited with Laura, and, in his mind, it was just like *The Railway Children* — he would walk out of a fog and Laura would be there and she would say, "Daddy, my daddy." It wasn't that Theo believed in religion, or a God, or an afterlife. He just knew it was impossible to feel this much love and for it to end.

Marlee was bored. She had finished the sweets and they had played a game of tic-tac-toe — which she was already familiar with — and hangman, which she wasn't, so Theo taught her, but now she was getting whiny with hunger. From the first-floor window of Jackson's office they had a tantalizing view of a sandwich shop. "I'm starving," she declared melodramatically, doubling up to demonstrate her hunger pains.

Perhaps Deborah Arnold wasn't coming back. Perhaps Jackson wasn't coming back, perhaps he never got the message about his daughter. Perhaps he had reacted badly to a dental anesthetic, perhaps he had died under the anesthetic, or been run over on the way back from the dentist.

Theo supposed he could leave Marlee alone while he slipped across the street to buy them both something to eat. It would take, at the most, what — ten minutes? What harm could happen to her in ten minutes? It was an absurd question to ask himself because Theo knew exactly what could happen in ten minutes — a plane could explode over a town or fly into a building, a train could derail, a maniac in a yellow golfing sweater could run into an office, wielding a knife. Leaving her in an office — what was he thinking! Offices ranked higher than planes, mountains, or schools on Theo's list of dangerous places.

"Come on then," he said to her. "We'll pop across the road and bring a sandwich back."

"What if Daddy comes and can't find us?"

Theo felt touched by the "us." "Well, we'll put a notice on the door," he said.

"Back in ten minutes," Marlee said. "That's what Daddy puts."

Of course it wasn't as simple as that. It was three o'clock in the afternoon and the sandwich shop was about to close and had hardly any sandwiches left and the ones on offer — egg mayonnaise or roast beef and horseradish — prompted Marlee to act out a vivid pantomime of vomiting. As they came out of the sandwich shop she slipped one small, dry hand into his and he gave it a reassuring squeeze. She got suddenly excited when she spotted a burger bar across the street and almost dragged Theo into it. The letters "CJD" came into his mind but he tried to suppress them and anyway she wanted something called a "chickinlickin burger," which Theo hoped had chicken in it rather than mad cow, but then what part of the chicken and how old? And what had the chicken in turn been fed on? Mad cow probably.

He bought her a chickinlickin burger ("with fries," she begged) and a Coke. For fast food it seemed very slow and Theo wondered if anyone monitored the service in these places. Most of the people working here seemed to be children — Australian children at that.

They had been gone a lot longer than ten minutes. If Jackson was back he would be sending out search parties by now. As if the very thought of his name conjured him up, Jackson suddenly appeared out of a crowd of jostling foreign students. He looked slightly wild and grabbed hold of Marlee's arm so that she squealed in protest, "*Daddy,* mind my Coke."

"Where've you been?" Jackson shouted at her. He glared at Theo. What a cheek, when all Theo was doing was looking after the girl, which was more than her parents were doing.

"I'm babysitting," Theo said to Jackson, "not cradle snatching."

"Right," Jackson said, "Of course, I'm sorry, I was worried."

"Theo's looking after me," Marlee said, taking a huge bite out of her burger, "and he bought me fries. I like him."

When Theo returned along St. Andrews Street the girl with the custard-yellow hair was no longer there and he worried that she might never be there again. Because that was how it happened: one moment you were there, laughing, talking, breathing, and the next you were gone. Forever. And there wasn't even a shape left in the world where you'd been, neither the trace of a smile nor the whisper of a word. Just nothing.

11

Jackson

"Your soft palate looks very inflamed," Sharon murmured. "Does it hurt?"

"Nugh, nurnh."

"I suspect you're blowing out an abscess, Jackson."

Officially she was "Miss S. Anderson, BDS, LDS," and he'd never been invited to call her by her Christian name, although she was free enough with his own first name. Doctors, bank managers, complete strangers, all used first names now. It was one of Binky Rain's bugbears. "And I said to the man in the bank ["men in the benk"] — a *cashier* — 'Excuse me, young man, but I don't recall us having been introduced. As far as you're concerned, my name is *Mrs.* Rain, and I don't give a damn what yours is.'" Binky Rain made "cashier" sound like something you wouldn't want to pick up on the sole of your shoe.

He felt absurdly vulnerable, lying there in the chair, prostrate and helpless, subject to the whims of Sharon and her silent dental nurse. Both Sharon and the dental nurse had dark, enigmatic eyes, and they had a way of looking at him indifferently over their masks as if they were contemplating what they might do to him next, like sadistic belly dancers with surgical instruments.

Jackson tried not to think about this, nor about that scene in *Marathon Man,* and instead worked on conjuring up a picture of France. He could grow vegetables, he'd never grown a vegetable in his life, Josie had been the gardener, he'd carried out her orders, *Dig this, move that, mow the lawn.* In France, the vegetables would probably grow themselves anyway. All that warm fertile soil. Tomatoes, peaches. Vines, could he grow vines? Olives, lemons, figs — it sounded biblical. Imagine watching the tendrils creeping, the fruit plumping, oh God, he was getting an erection (at the idea of vegetables, what was *wrong* with him?). Panic made him swallow and gag on his own saliva. Sharon returned the chair to an upright position and said, "All right?" her head cocked to one side in an affectation of concern while he choked noisily. The silent dental nurse handed him a plastic cup of water.

"Soon be done now," Sharon lied, tilting him backward again. Jackson concentrated on something unpleasant this time. Laura Wyre's body. Felled in her tracks, like an animal, like a deer.

Mr. Wyre, where is he? It was an odd-sounding question — wouldn't it be more normal to say, "Where's Mr. Wyre?" Did the killer actually say that? What if he'd said, "Miss Wyre" or "Ms. Wyre"? Could Moira Tyler (the only person the killer spoke to) have misheard him? In the chaos of the moment — but then the moment wasn't chaotic at that point. He was just a guy in a yellow golfing sweater asking the whereabouts of one of the solicitors.

And Laura's own private life, was it as transparent as it appeared to be? A sacrificial virgin. Was she a virgin? Jackson couldn't remember reading that in the autopsy report. Theo believed she was, of course. Jackson could imagine that Marlee could be married and divorced three times and have ten children and he would still believe that she was a virgin.

The press had loved Laura's blamelessness. It was always so much better when it was a nice middle-class girl with sound habits and educational aspirations who got topped rather than some prostitute or tarty unemployed teenager (the Kerry-Anne Brockleys of this world). But who was to say that Laura Wyre didn't have secrets? An affair with a married man that she didn't want to hurt her father with, perhaps. Or had she innocently acquired a stalker, some shitty little pervert who'd become fixated on her? Maybe she was pleasant to him (sometimes that was all it took) and he'd become deluded, imagining that she was in love with him, that they had some cosmic thing going on between them. There was a word for that but Jackson couldn't remember it, some syndrome, not Munchausen. There were only four options. The guy either knew Theo personally or was a stranger to him. He either knew Laura personally or was a stranger to her. Erotomania — that was it. It sounded like a bad Dutch porn movie.

There was that survey, years ago, that found that women didn't feel threatened by a man carrying the *Guardian* or wearing a CND badge. Jackson had wondered at the time how many rapists started carrying a *Guardian* around with them. Look at Ted Bundy. Stick your arm in a plaster cast and women think you're safe. No woman was ever truly safe. It didn't matter if you were as tough as Sigourney Weaver in *Alien Resurrection* or Linda Hamilton in *Terminator 2,* because wherever you went there were men. Crazy men. The thing he liked about tough women such as Ripley and Sarah Connor (and yes, he knew they were fictional) was that it didn't matter how kick-ass they were, their motives stemmed from a kind of maternal love, a maternal love for the whole world. No, don't go there, Jackson, don't think about Sarah Connor. Think about something bad, think about the exhaust on your car that needs fixing, think about something boring. Golf.

"I've cleaned out the pus, Jackson," Sharon whispered softly, "and I'm going to put a dressing on, but we can't keep on treating the symptoms. We have to eliminate the cause. The root."

Laura's closest friends at sixth-form college had been Christina, Ayshea, Josh, Joanna, Emma, Eleanor, Hannah, and Pansy. Jackson knew this because Theo had a handy wall chart with the heading STUDENTS AT LAURA'S COLLEGE, as opposed to another chart, LAURA'S FRIENDS OUTSIDE OF COLLEGE (scuba-diving club, people from the pub she'd worked with, and so on), and yet a third chart for LAURA'S CASUAL ACQUAINTANCES (which was basically anyone whose path had ever crossed hers).

STUDENTS AT LAURA'S COLLEGE was a numbered list, the numbers indicating the closeness of the friendship — number one being her best friend and so on. Every student at the college was listed. How much time had Theo spent trying to decide if someone should be ranked 108 or 109 on the list? He hadn't even done the list on a computer but had laboriously handwritten all the names. The guy was crazy.

The friends were also color coded by sex — blue ink for the girls, red for the boys, which made it easy to see that Laura's closest friends were mostly girls. The top ten were all blue with only two exceptions — Josh and Tom. Laura Wyre had obviously been a girl's girl, one destined never to become a woman's woman. Toward the end of the list there was an almost solid phalanx of red names — great clusters of boys, most of whom Laura Wyre had probably never even noticed, let alone spoken to. The use of the red ink made the boys stand out and look more dangerous, or incorrect somehow. Jackson had a sudden image of his essays at school, spiderwebbed with the angry red-ink annotations of his teachers. It was only after he left school and joined the army that he discovered he was intelligent.

The police had interviewed all the students at Laura's college, except that unfortunately most of the top ten were missing. "Gap year," Theo had said to Jackson. He had worried that Laura would want to take a gap year, visit the dangerous corners of the world, but she would have been safer in a flea-infested, heroin-filled dosshouse in Bangkok than she was in her father's office. "Mea culpa," Theo said to Jackson with his sad, dog smile.

Throughout the whole investigation the police never really believed that Laura was anything more than an unfortunate bystander, that it was Theo who was the real target. Jackson suddenly

remembered Bob Peck in *Edge of Darkness* — they really *didn't* make
TV like that anymore, in fact it might have been the last good BBC
drama that Jackson had seen. 1984? 1985? He tried to remember
1985. Three years after the Falklands. His best mate Howell left the
army and Jackson signed on for another five years. He hadn't seen
Howell for a long time, he should get in touch. He'd gone into security, the default profession for ex-soldiers. Jackson started going out
with a girl called Carol but then she joined the CND and announced
her political views were "incompatible" with her relationship with
Jackson. Jackson pointed out that he wasn't exactly in favor of nuclear warfare himself, but she was more interested in chaining herself
to things and shouting abuse at the Thames Valley Police.

In 1985 Laura Wyre would have been nine years old and Olivia
Land was fifteen years' missing. In *Edge of Darkness,* Craven, the Bob
Peck character, had also been obsessed with his daughter — Emma,
that was her name, the same name as the number-five-ranked girl on
Theo's red-and-blue list and the only one of the top-ranking girls who
lived within easy reach of Cambridge. Christina, the number-one
best friend, was married and living in Australia, Ayshea was a teacher
in Dorset, Tom worked for the EC in Strasbourg, Josh seemed to
have disappeared off the map, Joanna was a doctor in Dublin, Eleanor
a solicitor in Newcastle, Pansy was working for a publisher in Scotland. A *hejira* of girls. Were they in flight from something? ("If you
run forever you come back to where you started from, Jackson.") He
wanted to speak to someone who knew a different Laura from the
one Theo knew. It wasn't that Theo's Laura wasn't genuine, but no
matter how close he'd been to his daughter there were going to be
things about her that he didn't know or wouldn't understand. That
was how it was supposed to be. It didn't matter how much you hated
it, they were always going to have secrets.

Emma Drake lived in Crouch End and worked for the BBC.
When he phoned her she said she'd be happy to speak to Jackson

and arranged to meet him after work, across the road from Broad-casting House, at the Langham, "For cocktails."

She was a nice girl, polite and chatty, and she drank three man-hattans, one after the other, in a way that suggested she liked to take the edge off the day as quickly as possible. She wasn't really a girl, Jackson reminded himself. She was a twenty-eight-year-old woman.

"I remember thinking that could have been me," she said, toss-ing a nut into her mouth. "I haven't eaten all day," she added apologetically. "Been locked in a studio. I suppose that was a self-ish thing to think, wasn't it?"

"Not really," Jackson said.

"I mean it couldn't, not really, I wasn't there, in that office, at that moment in time, but there's something about random vio-lence . . ."

"Was it? Random?" Jackson said. "You don't think that maybe the guy who killed Laura meant to, that she was his target, not her father?" A man in a dinner jacket sat down at a piano in the cor-ner of the room and lifted his fingers above the keys with a Liber-ace kind of flourish before beginning to play a loud, florid version of "Some Enchanted Evening." "Oh dear." Emma Drake made a face and laughed. "Maybe she'd met someone, I don't know. Every-one seemed to be traveling or working abroad. Laura was one of the few people who was going straight to university after the summer holidays. I was in Peru, I didn't hear about her death until weeks afterward. That seemed worse somehow, it was already consigned to history for everyone else."

"The tiniest scrap of something that no one thought to men-tion," Jackson persevered. He wondered if another manhattan would help or hinder, and whether he should be plying young women with alcohol and then letting them go and fend for them-selves out on the mean streets of London. Was Marlee going to do this, get a good education, go to university and end up in a crappy job with the BBC, drink too much and go home alone on the tube all the way to a rented flat in Crouch End? He suggested coffee to Emma Drake and was relieved when she agreed.

"I'm sorry, I really can't think of anything," she said, frowning at the pianist who had moved on to an Andrew Lloyd Webber medley. "I suppose there was that thing with Mr. Jessop."

"Mr. Jessop?"

"Stan." Her frown grew deeper but it didn't seem to be related to *The Phantom of the Opera.* "Her biology teacher."

"A thing? As in a relationship?" He had seen the name of Stan Jessop before, it was written on another of Theo's wall charts — TEACHERS AT LAURA'S COLLEGE. He had been interviewed by the police two days after Laura's murder and eliminated from their inquiries.

Emma Drake bit her lip and swirled the dregs of her manhattan round the glass. "I don't know, you'd have to ask Christina. She was much closer to Laura than me, she was in Mr. Jessop's class as well."

"She's on a sheep farm in the middle of the Australian outback."

"Is she?" Emma said, brightening up for a moment. "That's amazing. We all seem to have lost touch. You wouldn't think you would, would you?" Oh, you do, Jackson thought. You lose touch with everyone eventually.

The coffee arrived and Jackson thought he should have ordered a sandwich for her as well. What did girls like her eat when they finally made it home? Did girls like her eat at all?

"We all promised to meet up ten years to the day after we left school," she said. "Outside the Hobbs Pavilion, a couple of weeks ago. Of course, no one came."

"You went?"

She nodded and her eyes filled up with tears. "Stupid. I felt stupid, standing there, waiting. I never thought anyone would come, not really, but I thought I should, you know, just in case. It wasn't that no one turned up, it was that *Laura* didn't turn up. I mean I know she's dead, and I didn't expect her to appear, it was just that it brought it home to me — there was no 'ten years' time' for Laura, no future. Everything stopped for her. Just like that."

Jackson handed her a tissue (he always carried tissues, half the people he met seemed to end up in tears). "And Mr. Jessop?"

"It was a rumor, really. Laura wasn't secretive, exactly, but she was very discreet, kept herself to herself. God, I sound like my mother. I don't think about Laura. That's awful, isn't it? Awful that you end up being forgotten and when people do remember you they talk about you in clichés. I mean, I thought about her when I was standing in front of Hobbs Pavilion, because I knew there was a chance that the others might come, but there was no hope at all that Laura would turn up. But the rest of the time . . ." She chewed on her lip and Jackson wanted to stop her because she was going to make it bleed. "It's as if she didn't exist," she concluded flatly.

"You know, she wasn't a virgin," Jackson said tentatively, and Emma sighed and said, "Well, no one was. She wasn't a *saint*. She was just like everyone else, she was *normal*."

"But she didn't seem to have any boyfriends. The police didn't interview any."

"She never really went out with anyone. Slept with a few boys, that's all."

Was that normal behavior? Was that what girls did ten years ago? If so, what were they doing now? And what would they be doing in ten years' time? When Marlee was the age at which Laura Wyre ceased to exist. Jesus.

"She was really thick with Josh. They were at primary school together. I never liked him much. He was always full of himself. He was very clever."

"I can't find out where he is," Jackson said.

"He dropped out. Now he's a DJ in Amsterdam, apparently. Laura lost her virginity to him."

"Her father thought she was still a virgin," Jackson said, and Emma Drake laughed and said, "Fathers always do."

"Even when there's evidence to the contrary?"

"Especially then."

"And Mr. Jessop?" Jackson prompted.

"Oh, we all fancied him." Emma smiled at the memory. "He was really cute, far too good-looking to be a teacher. Laura and Christina were in his A-Level class. Laura was definitely his favorite, star pupil and all that. There was nothing in it, he had a wife and a baby." (As if that ever stopped anyone.) "Laura used to babysit for them. I used to go and keep her company. Laura didn't think she was good with babies, but she was okay with Nina — the Jessops' baby. Laura liked his wife, Kim. They got on well. I always thought that was funny. Kim was really common." Emma Drake's hand flew to her mouth in horror. "Oh, God, that's a dreadful thing to say. It's so snobbish. But, you know what I mean, she was really sort of blond and tarty. A Geordie. Oh dear. I should shut up."

This girl was a mine of information. And yet she'd never been interviewed. Kim Jessop had never been interviewed either. "No one mentioned anything about Mr. Jessop and Laura at the time," Jackson said.

"Well, they wouldn't. He wasn't the crazy guy who stabbed her, was he? Look — it was just a rumor, nothing more than a crush. I feel bad just talking about it."

"Having a crush on your teacher's hardly unusual. I'm sure Laura wouldn't mind us talking about it." As if she were alive, as if she were real. Laura Wyre didn't care about anything anymore.

"Oh, no, no, I don't mean *Laura* had a crush. It was Mr. Jessop who had the crush. On Laura."

Jackson put Emma Drake in a cab and gave the driver a ridiculously generous twenty-five pounds to take her back to Crouch End and see her into her flat. Then he made his own, cheaper, way to King's Cross and spent the whole journey home staring out the window at nothing.

*   *   *

"There you go, Jackson, all patched up and ready to go." Sharon pulled her mask down and smiled at him as if he were three years old. He almost expected her to give him a badge or a sticker.

"Let's make an appointment to take out the root, shall we?"

He thought she'd been speaking metaphorically when she'd talked about the root of the cause, not an actual *root*. In his head.

Out in the street he checked his phone. There was a voice message from Josie, asking him to look after Marlee for the afternoon and informing him that his daughter was waiting in the office for him. Except that she wasn't. There was no one in the office and it was unlocked. A message on the door in handwriting that he recognized but that was neither Deborah's nor Marlee's said "Back in ten minutes." He had to think for a moment before he realized it was Theo's handwriting (God knows he'd seen enough of it in the last few days). This time it was in neutral black ink. "Back in ten minutes" meant nothing when you didn't know when the ten minutes started. Jackson felt an unexpected twinge of panic. What did he really know about Theo? He seemed like a good guy, seemed completely harmless, but evil psychopaths didn't have "evil psychopath" tattooed on their foreheads. Why did he think Theo was a good guy? Because his daughter was dead? Was that a guarantee?

Jackson ran down the stairs and onto the street. Where was she? With Theo? With Deborah? On her own? With a *stranger*? He'd wanted to buy Marlee a mobile phone but Josie objected (when had she become the only one who got to make decisions about their child?). Think how useful it would be now. Jackson caught a glimpse of Theo coming out of the burger bar along the street. He was so big that you couldn't miss him. And Marlee was with him. Thank you, God. She was dressed in a tiny skirt and a crop-top.

There were pictures of little girls dressed like that all over the Internet.

Jackson pushed his way with no attempt at civility through a crowd of Spanish teenagers and grasped Marlee's arm and shouted, "Where've you been?" at her. He felt like punching Theo, although he didn't know why, as it was obvious that Marlee was fine, stuffing her face with chips. She would probably follow a stranger for a single Malteser.

"I'm babysitting," Theo said to Jackson, "not cradle snatching," and Jackson felt ashamed. "Right," he said. "Of course, I'm sorry, I was worried."

"Theo's looking after me," Marlee said, "and he bought me fries. I like him." Jesus, was it as simple as that?

"Did your mother just dump you here?" Jackson asked when they got back to the office.

"David brought me."

"So David dumped you?" What a tosser.

"Deborah was here."

"Well she's not here now. [Where the hell was she?] You left the office open, so anyone could have walked in, and you went off with a complete stranger. Do you have any idea how dangerous that could be?"

"Don't you know Theo?"

"That's not the point. You don't."

Marlee's lip began to wobble and she whispered, "It's not my fault, Daddy," and his heart lurched with guilt and contrition. "Sorry, sweetheart," he said. "You're right, it's my fault." He put his arms round her and kissed the top of her head. She smelled of lemony shampoo and burger grease. "My bad," he murmured into her hair.

"Is it alright to come in?" A woman stood uncertainly in the doorway. Jackson loosened his grip on Marlee, who'd been letting him squeeze the air out of her in a long-suffering kind of way.

"I only came to make an appointment," the woman said. Late thirties, jeans, T-shirt, thonged sandals. She looked fit (Jackson imagined kickboxing) but she had dark shadows under her eyes. A Sarah Connor type. Or that nurse from *ER* that all men knew they would treat so much better than her on-screen boyfriends did. (Jackson had started to watch a lot of television since the break up of his marriage.) There was something familiar about her. Most people who looked familiar to Jackson usually turned out to be criminals, but she didn't look like a criminal.

"Well," he said, gesturing vaguely round the office, "we can talk now if you like?"

The woman glanced over at Marlee and said, "No, I think I'll make an appointment," and Jackson knew right then that it was something he didn't want to know about.

She made an appointment for eleven o'clock on Wednesday, "because I won't be on nights then," and Jackson thought, "Nurse," which was why she looked familiar because nurses and policemen saw far too much of each other professionally. He liked nurses, and not because of any *Carry On* films or mucky postcards or porny outfits or any of the usual reasons, and not the big, practical nurses with huge backsides and no imagination (and there were a lot of them), no, he liked ones that understood suffering, the ones that suffered themselves, the ones with dark shadows under their eyes that looked like Sarah Connor. The ones that understood pain, in the way Trisha and Emmylou and Lucinda did when they sang. And maybe when they weren't singing as well, who knew?

She definitely had a certain something. A *je ne sais quoi*. Her name was Shirley, she said, and he knew, without having to ask her, what she was here for. She'd lost someone. He could see it in her eyes.

"Are we going home now?" Marlee asked with an extravagant sigh as she clambered into the back of the car. "I'm *starving*."

"No, you're not."

"Yes, I am. I'm growing," she added defensively.

"I would never have noticed."

"The car smells of cigarettes. It smells *disgusting*, Daddy. You shouldn't smoke."

"I'm not smoking now. Sit on the other side, not behind me."

"Why?"

"Why not?" (Because if for some reason the seat belt fails you'll go straight through the windscreen, which will be marginally safer than going straight into the back of me.) Marlee moved over into the left passenger seat. The Diana seat. She locked the door. "Don't lock the door, Marlee."

"Why not?"

"Just not." (So that if the car catches fire it'll be easier to get you out.)

"What did that lady want?"

"Miss Morrison?" Shirley. It was a nice name. "Are you buckled in?"

"Yeah."

"'Yes,' not 'yeah.' I don't know what Miss Morrison wanted." He did know. He could see it in her eyes. She'd lost something, someone, another entry to make on the debit side of the lost-and-found register.

The most interesting case he'd had in months had been Nicola Spencer (which just about said it all really). Otherwise it had been dull, routine stuff, and yet now, suddenly, in the space of a couple of weeks, he had acquired a cold murder case, a thirty-four-year-old unsolved abduction, and whatever fresh misery Shirley Morrison was about to lay at his feet.

He glanced at Marlee. She was writhing around in the backseat like a miniature Houdini. She ducked down out of view. "What are you doing? Is your seat belt still on?"

"Yes, I'm trying to reach this thing on the floor." Her voice was muffled with the effort.

"What thing?"

"This!" she said triumphantly, reappearing like a diver coming up for air. "It's a tin, I think." Jackson looked in the rearview mirror at the object she was holding aloft for his inspection. Oh, Christ, Victor's ashes.

"Put it back, sweetheart."

"What is it?" She was trying to open the ugly metal urn now and Jackson reached round and grabbed it off her. The car swerved and Marlee gave a scream of horror. He settled the urn in the foot well of the front passenger seat. Julia had asked him to collect it from the crematorium this morning "because you have a car, Mr. Brodie, and we don't," which Jackson didn't think was a particularly valid reason, given that he'd never known Victor. "But you were the only person at his funeral," Julia said.

"You're not going to cry, are you?" he said to the mirror.

"No" — said very angrily. Marlee could be like a force of nature when she was angry. "You nearly crashed."

"No, I didn't." He raked around in the glove compartment for sweets but all he could find were cigarettes and loose change for parking meters. He offered her the money.

"What's in the tin?" she persisted, taking the money. "Is it something bad?"

"No, it's not anything bad." Why wouldn't he tell her what was in the tin? She understood about life and death, she'd buried enough hamsters in her eight years on earth, and last year Josie had taken her to her grandmother's funeral. "Well, sweetheart," he began hesitantly, "you know when people die?"

"I'm bored."

"Let's play a game then."

"What game?"

Good question. Jackson wasn't very good at games. "I know. If you were a dog, what dog would you be?"

"Don't know." So much for that. Marlee began to grumble in earnest. "I'm hungry, Daddy. *Daddy.*"

"Yeah, okay. We'll get something to eat on the way."

"Say 'yes,' not 'yeah.' Way to what?"

"A convent."

"What's that?"

"It's a bunch of women locked up together."

"Because they're bad?"

"Because they're good. I hope."

Well, it was one way to keep women safe. Just put them in a convent. "Get thee to a nunnery." The convent smelled like every Catholic church Jackson had ever been inside — an excess of incense and Mansion House polish. People always said to him, "Once a Catholic, always a Catholic," but it wasn't true. Jackson hadn't been inside a church for years — except for funerals (weddings and christenings never seemed to figure on his social calendar) — and he had no belief in any god. His mother, Fidelma, had done her best to raise them in the church but somehow it had never stuck with Jackson. Sometimes there were fragments of memories, his mother's long-forgotten voice. *Anima Christi, sanctifica me.*

Their parents had somehow emigrated to the north of England — how and why, Jackson never knew. His father, Robert, was a miner from Fife and his mother was from County Mayo, a not entirely harmonious Celtic union. Jackson and his brother, Francis, and his sister, Niamh. Francis was named for his mother's father and Jackson himself was named for his father's mother. Not that his grandmother was called Jackson, of course — it was a maiden name (Margaret Jackson) and it was a Scottish tradition, his father informed him.

Jackson didn't know who (if anyone) Niamh was named for. His big sister, a year younger than Francis and six years older than Jackson. After Niamh's birth his mother had become a successful practitioner of the rhythm method, and Jackson had been an unexpected addition to the family, conceived in that boarding house in Ayrshire. The baby of the family.

"What are you thinking, Daddy?"

"Nothing, sweetheart." They both whispered, although Sister Michael, the fat, almost boisterous nun in whose wake they were being swept along, had a booming voice that echoed along the hallway.

Sister Michael, he knew from Amelia and Julia, was an "extern." There were six externs at the convent, negotiating with the outside world on behalf of the "interns" — the ones who never left, who spent their days, day after day, until they died, in prayer and contemplation. Sylvia was an intern.

Marlee was rapt with fascination at this new world. "Why does Sister Michael have a man's name?"

"She's named after a saint," Jackson said. "St. Michael." Why did Marks and Spencer use St. Michael as their trademark label? To make them sound less Jewish? Would Sister Michael know the answer to that? Not that he was about to ask her. Michael was the patron saint of paratroopers, Jackson knew that. Because of the wings? But then all angels had wings. (Not that Jackson believed in the existence of angels.) The corridor, which turned into another one, and then another one, was dotted with statues and pictures — St. Francis and St. Clare, naturally, and multiples of doe-eyed Christs on the cross, bleeding and broken. *Corpus Christi, salva me.*

Jesus, he'd forgotten how physically extreme this stuff was. Or "Sadomasochistic, homoerotic nonsense," in Amelia's caustic summary. Why was she so uptight all the time? He was sure it had nothing to do with Olivia. Or her father's death. He knew it was the most politically incorrect thing he could think, and, God knows, he would never have voiced it out loud, not in a million years, but, let's face it, Amelia Land needed to get laid.

"And this one is Our Lady of Krakow," Sister Michael was explaining to Marlee, indicating a small statue in a glass case. "She was rescued from Poland by a priest during the war. At times of national crisis, she can be seen to cry." Jackson thought it might have been better if the priest had rescued a few Jews instead of a plaster statue.

"She cries?" an awestruck Marlee asked.

"Yes, tears roll down her cheeks." Jackson wanted to say, "It's shite, Marlee, don't listen," but Sister Michael turned and looked at him, and, despite her plump, jolly face, she had nuns' eyes, and nuns' eyes, Jackson knew, could see right inside your head, so he nodded respectfully at the statue. *Sanguis Christi, inebria me.*

"Sister Mary Luke" was expecting them, Sister Michael said, moving on, escorting them deeper into the complex corridors of the convent, her habit flapping as she marched purposively onward. Jackson remembered how nuns had a way of moving around very fast, without ever running, as if they were on wheels. Perhaps it was part of their training. He was surprised more criminals didn't use a nun's habit as a disguise. It was perfect misdirection — no one would ever notice your face, all they would see would be the outfit. Look at all the witnesses to Laura's murder, all any of them had seen was the yellow golfing sweater.

Jackson thought that Julia had said to him that Sylvia was a "greyhound" but perhaps what she'd actually said was that she *had* a greyhound, because she did. It was sitting patiently by her side when they came face-to-face with her. She was on one side of a grille and they were on the other, an arrangement that reminded Jackson partly of the charge desk in the detention cells and partly of a harem, although he wasn't sure what part of his memory the harem bit came from. Jackson supposed that Sylvia looked like a greyhound, inasmuch as she was long and skinny, but she wasn't bonny, as his father would have said. She was toothy and bespectacled, whereas the greyhound was a sleek, brindled creature, the kind of hound you saw in medieval paintings, accompanying a noblewoman to the hunt. Jackson wasn't at all sure where he had conjured that image up from either. Perhaps it was just because there was something medieval in general about a convent. The dog stood up when they entered and gently licked Marlee's fingers through the grille.

Franciscans, Jackson reminded himself. "Like some hippie order," Julia had said. "They go around barefoot in the summer and they make their own sandals for the winter, and they keep animals as pets and they're all vegetarians." Amelia and Julia had briefed him at length about the convent. They seemed genuinely to despise Sylvia's vocation. "Don't be fooled by that holier-than-thou stuff," Julia warned him. "Underneath all that penguin crap she's still Sylvia." "It's just a form of escapism," Amelia added dismissively. "She doesn't have to pay bills, or think about where her next meal's coming from. She never has to be *alone.*" Was that why Amelia frowned so much, then, because she was alone? But hadn't Julia said something about a "Henry"? It was difficult to imagine Amelia in the arms of a man. Whoever Henry was, he wasn't doing it for Amelia. (When did he stop calling her "Miss Land" and start calling her "Amelia"?)

Amelia said that she hardly ever visited Sylvia but they kept up a fitful, dutiful correspondence, "although Sylvia doesn't exactly have much to write about — prayer, prayer, and more prayer — and then, of course, she does a lot of what is housework by any other name — they bake communion wafers, and starch and iron the priest's vestments, all that kind of stuff. And she does a lot of gardening, and *knits* things for the poor," she added disparagingly, and Julia said, "She's making the knitting up," and Amelia said, "No, I'm not," and Julia said, "Yes, you are. I have visited her, you know, quite a lot," and Amelia said, "That was when you were auditioning for a nun in *The Sound of Music*," and Julia said, "No, it was not," and Jackson said wearily, "Oh, shut up, the pair of you," and they both turned and looked at him as if they'd just seen him for the first time. "Well," he said, "really, catch yourself on," and wondered when he'd started speaking like his mother.

"Well, that was interesting," Jackson said, addressing Marlee via the rearview mirror. She looked as if she were nodding off to sleep. Sister Michael had taken her off to feed her, once she'd made the acquaintance of Sister Mary Luke's dog ("Jester" — his racing name apparently. He was a rescue dog). The other interns had fussed around Marlee as if they'd never seen a child before and she seemed more than happy with the beans on toast, angel cake, and ice cream they had rustled up for her. If they'd given her chips they would probably have had a convert for life on their hands.

"Don't mention to your mother that I took you to a convent," he said.

Actually it hadn't been that interesting. Sylvia knew he was coming, Amelia had telephoned ahead and explained that Jackson was looking into Olivia's disappearance again but didn't tell her what had prompted this. After Marlee had been taken away by Sister Michael, Jackson produced the blue mouse from where it had been squashed into his pocket ("enclosed") and showed it to Sylvia. He wanted the shock factor. He remembered Julia saying that Amelia fainted when she saw it, and Amelia, after all, was not a fainter. Sylvia looked at the blue mouse, her dry, thin lips compressed together, her small, mud-colored eyes not wavering in their gaze. After a few seconds, she said, "Blue Mouse," and reached a finger through the grille. Jackson moved the blue mouse closer to her and she touched its old, infirm body tenderly with one finger. A tear rolled silently down her cheek. But no, she hadn't seen it since the day Olivia disappeared and she couldn't even begin to imagine why it would be in among her father's possessions.

"I was never close to Daddy," she said.

*   *   *

"The angel cake was nice," Marlee said sleepily.

Jackson's phone rang. He looked at the number — Amelia and Julia — and groaned. He let his voice mail pick it up, but when he played the message back he was so alarmed at what he heard that he had to pull the car to the side of the road to listen to it again. Amelia was sobbing, a primal inchoate kind of lamentation that was grief, raw and untempered. Jackson wondered if Julia were dead.

"Breathe, Amelia, for God's sake," he said. "What is it? Is it Julia?" but all she said was, "Please, Jackson ['Jackson?' He'd never heard her call him that. It sounded way too intimate for Jackson's liking], please, Jackson, please come, I need you." And then she was cut off, or she cut herself off more likely so that he would have to go to Owlstone Road and find out what had happened (not Julia, surely?).

"What is it, Daddy?"

"Nothing, sweetheart. We're just going to take a little detour on the way home." Sometimes Jackson felt as if his whole life were a detour.

"We went to a convent!" Marlee shouted as she ran through the front door.

"A convent?" David Lastingham laughed, catching Marlee as she ran past him and lifting her high in the air and then hugging her to his body. Jackson thought, I'll wait until he puts her down and then I'll deck him, but then Josie came out of the kitchen, wearing an apron for God's sake. Jackson had never seen Josie in an apron. "A convent?" she echoed. "What were you doing in a convent?"

"They had angel cake," Marlee said.

Josie looked to Jackson for an explanation but he just shrugged and said, "As they do."

"And the dog was dead," Marlee said, suddenly crestfallen at the memory.

166 ⌐∿ KATE ATKINSON

"What dog?" Josie asked sharply. "Did you run over a dog, Jackson?" and Marlee said, "No, Mummy. The dog was old and now he's happy in heaven. With all the other dead dogs." Marlee looked as if she were going to cry again (there had already been a lot of crying) and Jackson reminded her that they had seen a live dog as well. "Jester," she remembered happily. "He was in prison with a nun, and they had a statue that cried, and Daddy's got a tin in his car with a dead man in it."

Josie gave Jackson a disgusted look. "Why do you always have to get her overexcited, Jackson?" and before he could say anything, Josie turned to David and said, "Will you take her upstairs, darling, and get her in the bath?" Jackson waited until Marlee and David — the usurper in his life, the man who now conducted his daughter's bedtime routines and fucked his wife — had gone upstairs before saying, "Do you really think that's wise?"

"Wise? What are you talking about?"

"I'm talking about some man you hardly know being left alone with your naked daughter. Our naked daughter. Oh, and by the way, do you think it's really a good idea to allow her to dress like a child prostitute?"

Swift as a snake, she punched his face. He reeled, more with astonishment than pain — it was a girly kind of jab — because not once while they were married had they ever been violent toward each other.

"What the fuck was that for?"

"For being disgusting, Jackson. That's the man I live with, the man I love. Do you honestly think that I would live with someone I didn't trust with my daughter?"

"You'd be amazed how many times I've heard that."

David Lastingham must have heard them shouting because he ran downstairs yelling at Jackson, "What are you doing to her?" which Jackson thought was rich, and Josie, helpfully, said, "He accused you of interfering with Marlee."

"*Interfering?*" Jackson sneered at her. "Is that what the middle classes call it?" but by this time David Lastingham had reached the bottom of the stairs and aimed a sloppy but enraged right hook that Jackson didn't see coming but that he certainly felt when it landed. In fact he could have sworn he actually heard his cheekbone crack. Jackson thought, That's it, now I kill him, but Marlee suddenly appeared at the top of the stairs and said, "Daddy?"

Josie spat at him, "Get out of our fucking house, Jackson, and, oh and by the way, did I tell you — we're moving to New Zealand. I was going to sit you down and do the tea-and-sympathy thing, break it to you gently, but you don't deserve that. David's been offered a job at Wellington, and he's accepted it and we're going with him. So there, Jackson, how do you like that?"

Jackson parked the Alfa in one of the lockups he rented at the top of the lane, experiencing his usual momentary guilt about the noise his exhaust made. He was thinking about Sylvia, giving up her life to be shut up in that place. She knew more than she was telling — he was sure of that. But right now he didn't want to think about Sylvia. He wanted to think about a hot bath and a cold beer. He was furious that he'd let David Lastingham land a punch. He was thinking that the day couldn't get much worse, even though he knew from experience that the day can always get worse, and to prove that thesis a dark figure slipped out from the shadows behind the garage and hit him over the head with something that felt horribly like the butt of a gun.

"Yeah, but really, you should have seen the other guy," Jackson joked weakly but Josie didn't laugh. She smelled of fruit and sunshine and he remembered that another berry-picking expedition had been planned for today. Her brown forearms were scratched as if she'd been wrestling with cats. "Gooseberry bushes," she said when he pointed them out.

"Sorry," Jackson said. "They found my donor card. It had you down as my next of kin. It was only a mild concussion, they shouldn't have bothered."

"You were lying there most of the night, Jackson. You were lucky it was so warm. Imagine if it had been winter." She said this accusingly rather than compassionately, as if it were his own fault that he'd been mugged. Actually, he really would like to see the other guy because he was pretty sure he'd done some damage back. Jackson had been lucky, his reactions had been fast and he had moved intuitively when he saw the figure coming at him, enough to deflect the blow so that it only gave him a concussion rather than smashing his skull like an egg. And he'd got one back in, nothing as considered as a good right hook or a roundhouse kick, or any of the more refined tactics and moves he'd been taught at one time or another. Instead it had been the automatic brute response of the hard man out on a drunken Saturday night, and he had nutted the guy full in the face. He could still hear the nose squelching as his forehead connected with the soft tissue. It hadn't done his concussion much good, of course, and he must have passed out at that point because the next thing he remembered was the milkman trying to rouse him sometime before dawn.

Josie drove him home. "They want someone to stay with me for twenty-four hours," he said apologetically to Josie, "in case I lapse back into unconsciousness."

"Well, you'll just have to find someone else," she said as she pulled up at the top of the lane, not even driving down it. He realized he was still waiting for sympathy that wasn't going to come. He climbed awkwardly out of the Volvo's passenger seat. All the bones in his skull seemed to have been rearranged like tectonic plates slipping and sliding against one another. Every movement reverberated around his skull. He felt seriously damaged.

Josie rolled down the window so she could speak to him. For a second he thought she was going to lean out and give him a wifely kiss farewell or offer to stay and look after him, but instead she said, "Perhaps it's time you got another next of kin, Jackson."

When he got home Jackson propped Blue Mouse on the mantelpiece. He'd known that sooner or later he would start to capitalize the damn thing. He put Victor's urn (he'd forgotten to return it to Amelia and Julia amid all the hysteria) between Blue Mouse and the only ornament that adorned the mantelpiece — a cheap pottery wishing well that had WISHING YOU WELL FROM SCARBOROUGH written on the side of it. After the split the marital property had been divided up in a way that Josie considered fair — Jackson took his "crap" (Josie's term for his country CDs and the little souvenir wishing well) and Josie took everything else. Perhaps Blue Mouse would watch over him, seeing as there was no one else who would. Jackson swallowed two of the Co-codamol that the hospital had given him (although what he wanted was morphine) and lay down on the sofa and listened to Emmylou singing "From Boulder to Birmingham," but there was too much pain going on for even Emmylou to heal.

12

Caroline

Caroline glanced at her stepchildren in the backseat of the Discovery and thanked God they didn't go to her school. They attended some small private place in the middle of nowhere where they did a lot of outdoor games and spoke French all day Wednesday. In principle, of course, there was nothing wrong with that and it would have been interesting to have applied it to the curriculum of some of the inner-city schools she used to teach in. Only two years but it seemed like a lifetime ago. Yet another lifetime. How many times could you shed your skin? Hannah and James were making faces at her in the rearview mirror, so they were either unbelievably stupid and didn't think she could see or they just didn't care. Either way they were inbred. Rowena, Jonathan's mother, talked all the time about "breeding" because she had a stable of hunters (big, frightening brutes), but sometimes she seemed to be applying the concept to her own family, and Caroline wanted to point out to her that natural selection led to a vigorous species whereas "breeding" resulted in congenital defects, in pale, blond children who spoke French on Wednesdays and whose blank Midwich Cuckoo faces suggested latent idiocy. In Caroline's professional opinion.

After the wedding, Rowena moved into the "dowager house," a small house on the estate, which she always referred to as "my little cottage" even though it had four bedrooms and two sitting rooms. She made a point of "not interfering," which meant that she interfered all the time but behind Caroline's back. She put on a good front though. At the wedding she had smiled benignly throughout like someone mainlining Valium and she had paid for the whole thing, the marquee, the string quartet, the silver-service lackeys, the cold salmon and roast venison, the vast vases of white lilies from which someone had unfortunately forgotten to remove the stamens so that the guests were continually showered with pollen. And no one mentioned that it was a registry-office wedding, or that it was a second marriage, even though the offspring of the first marriage were notable by their presence, running around like rats that had been transformed into children — dressed in white satin outfits that wouldn't have looked out of place in the doomed court of Louis XVI.

They had arrived on a plane from Buenos Aires a few days before the wedding and then never went back because "Jemima" — the first wife — had decided that they should have an English education and Jonathan concurred. And it really hadn't bothered Caroline because (and, yes, she understood the irony) she was great with children, which was why she was so good at her job. And the two didn't necessarily go hand in hand — she knew plenty of teachers who saw children as an annoying by-product of the profession rather than its raison d'être. She just hadn't expected Hannah and James to be such little bastards.

It was the au pair's day off so Caroline had volunteered to pick them up from school. The au pair was a Spanish girl called Paola, and Caroline tried to keep her spirits up with Rioja and sympathy because she seemed to be on the point of leaving all the time, and who could blame her? She was stuck in the middle of nowhere with a crap climate and two evil brats turning the screw on her all the time. They couldn't even be bothered to pronounce her name properly — "Powla," she continually corrected them, making the vowels stretch exotically like a cat yawning, and yet they still insisted on "Porla" in their posh, tight little voices. They had lived in a Spanish-speaking country for the last two years, for heaven's sake, and yet they couldn't even say, *"Buenos días,"* or if they could they wouldn't.

Their small insular school kept its children busy for longer hours than the village school. Caroline had finished work more than an hour ago but Hannah and James had all sorts of extracurricular activities tagged onto the end of their day — clarinet and cricket, piano, "voice" (as if they didn't have one), folk dancing (Jesus), and fencing — when they first mentioned the fencing she thought they meant building actual fences. She would have liked to drop them — preferably from a great height — into a class in Toxteth or Chapeltown and see what good their fencing did them then.

They drove past the village school and she could hear James making snorting noises. She'd heard him refer to the village kids as "oiks" and she'd almost slapped him. She suspected his slow male brain had confused "oik" with "oink," which was why he always snorted when he came within breathing distance of the lower orders. She wasn't sure that she could refrain from violence toward him for much longer.

It had been a coincidence that the headmistress of the school was due for retirement just after they returned from their honeymoon. It had been easy to get the post. Caroline's credentials far outstripped anything that could be asked of her in a three-classroom village school, and she felt completely at home there within days of returning from Jersey — which was where they had spent their one-week honeymoon, in The Atlantic, in a sea-view room overlooking St. Ouen's Bay, although they had viewed the sea very little as they spent most of their time in bed. "Oh, The Atlantic," Rowena said, on their return. "Such a lovely hotel. What did you do all week?" and Jonathan said, "Oh, you know, the zoo, the orchid place, walked out to la Corbière, had afternoon tea in the Secret Garden," and Rowena had such a satisfied smile on her face at this mind-numbingly bourgeois itinerary that Caroline only just stopped herself from saying, "Actually, Rowena, all we did was fuck the living daylights out of each other."

"You're going to work after your wedding then?" Rowena had said to her in the airless atmosphere of their wedding marquee, and Caroline replied, "Yes," and didn't feel a need to elaborate. The collar of Rowena's cream raw-silk suit had been defiled by a smear of burnt-orange lily pollen that Caroline hoped Rowena's dry cleaners would have great difficulty in removing.

Everyone in the village talked about what a hard job it was being headmistress of the school but it couldn't have been easier. The kids were sweet, nice country children, just one mild case of attention deficit, a couple of scabby kids, one wee shit, and statistically there should be at least one abused kid in there, but so far Caroline hadn't identified him or her. They were nearly all up to speed on reading (a miracle), they knew old-fashioned playground games, and their lives ran on an agricultural calendar so that harvest festival was a proper harvest festival and someone brought an honest-to-goodness, real-life lamb into show-and-tell in spring. There was even a maypole on the village green that the kids danced around, innocent of all phallic connotations. She loved the job and hoped that if she got divorced she'd be able to keep it because everything was so damned feudal around here that it was probably in the gift of the lord of the manor, who for all intents and purposes appeared to be Jonathan. Not that she was intending to get divorced, but it was hard to believe that this would go on forever. Nothing else did, so why should this? And you couldn't stay one step ahead all the time. It didn't matter how long you were lost. Sooner or later you would be found.

And it would be impossible to live here and not work. What would she do all day long? Jonathan made up things to do. He was always in and out of the farm office or striding around the hills, looking at fields and fences — although not doing fencing (of any kind), but he had a manager to run the farm and everything would go on just as well if he never went into the office or looked at a fence. He went out a lot with his shotgun and killed things, as if that were somehow an important part of running a farm, but in fact it was just because he loved shooting (or killing). He was a good shot and a good teacher, and Caroline discovered she had quite a talent as a markswoman — not that she shot anything living, not like Jonathan, just targets and clay pigeons and tin cans off walls. She liked the guns, she liked the heft of them in her arms, she liked that moment of fine poise just before squeezing the trigger when you knew your aim would prove to be true. It was astonishing that you could wander around the countryside (even though it was countryside you owned) brandishing lethal weapons and no one stopped you.

When he wasn't pretending to run the estate or shooting something smaller and more helpless than himself, Jonathan went out on one or other of his mother's hunters. Everyone was always saying to Caroline, "Do you ride?" and couldn't believe it when she said no. Rowena was a "wonderful horsewoman" of course (as if she were a centaur) and Jemima had spent most of her marriage on horseback from the sound of it. People seemed to find it hard to believe that Jonathan would marry someone who didn't know a forelock from a fetlock, but actually he didn't give two hoots whether or not she liked horses. That was one of the really good things about him — he was totally indifferent to anything she did. In fact he was pretty much indifferent to anything anyone did. There was a connection loose there, she was sure, an absence of social bonding. In another life he might have found himself branded a psychopath. Psychopaths were everywhere — they weren't necessarily killing and raping and practicing a trade as serial killers. Psychopathic tendencies, that's what they said Caroline had. Well not Caroline, of course, the person that she used to be. Caroline considered it a serious misdiagnosis. Now, James, he was definitely a sociopath, that's what breeding did for you.

Jemima, their mother, had visited last summer. She was a perfect little piece of English porcelain who clearly got on famously with Rowena, bonded over girths and martingales, and the Red Devons and the problem with the "upper meadow" — Caroline didn't even know they had an upper meadow, let alone a problem with it.

"So you got divorced . . . why exactly?" she asked Jonathan, holding him in a slippery, sweaty postcoital embrace while half a mile down the road Jemima was laying her delicate blond head onto the one-hundred-and-twenty-pounds-a-pop Hungarian goose-down pillows in one of the three spare bedrooms of the dowager house. "Oh, God," Jonathan groaned. "Jem was so *boring*. You have no idea, Caro," and he laughed a dirty kind of laugh and rolled her over and took her from behind — say what you like, the man had stamina — and as she half suffocated in their own pillows (slightly less expensive, but only just) she wondered if Jemima ever took it up the arse and thought probably not, but you never knew with posh girls, they were capable of all kinds of depravity that was unsuspected by oiks.

They had honeymooned in Jersey because, rather late in the day, Caroline realized that she didn't have a passport. Jonathan didn't care, he wasn't terribly interested in anywhere that wasn't North Yorkshire. She could have got a passport, she had a birth certificate — in the name of Caroline Edith Edwards. Caroline thought "Edith" was probably the name of a grandmother, because it was an old-fashioned name for someone born in 1967. "Caroline Edwards" was six years younger than Caroline, although, of course, she had never reached Caroline's age. She was dead by the time she was five years old, "taken by an angel," according to her gravestone, although her death certificate claimed it was a more prosaic leukemia that had carried her off. Caroline had visited the grave, in Swindon, and laid a little posy of flowers on it, just to say thank you to Caroline Edith Edwards for the gift of her identity, even though it was taken rather than given.

＊　　＊　　＊

When they finally arrived back at the house it was almost half past five and Hannah and James immediately started demanding something to eat. Paola was sitting at the kitchen table looking morose, but when she saw them she got up and started rooting through the freezer for minipizzas and Caroline had to tell her to sit down and do nothing because it was her day off. It wasn't as if there was anywhere for her to go. Sometimes she went out for a walk, but she was from Barcelona and had no affinity with damp, green countryside. Sometimes Caroline gave her a lift to the bus stop on her way into school, and she spent the day moping around Richmond or Harrogate, but getting back again was a problem. More often than not she just stayed in her room. A couple of times Caroline had given her money to go down to London for the weekend because she seemed to know hundreds of Spanish people down there. Caroline was terrified that she wouldn't come back. Paola was the closest thing she had to a friend, someone who was more of an outsider than she was. Gillian was long gone, doing VSO in Sri Lanka, and Caroline wished now that she had done that.

Rowena didn't see the point of having an au pair and constantly found ways of antagonizing Paola. "The children are out of the house all day," she argued with Caroline. "It's not as if you have a baby." There was an invisible question buried in this statement. Was she planning on having a baby? Rowena didn't want the bloodline of the Weavers diluted with Caroline's suspect DNA. ("What did your father *do,* exactly, dear?" Caroline Edith Edwards's father was a butcher but that would have been too much for Rowena to bear, so she said something vague about accountancy.) They didn't need a baby. They had an heir and Hannah would do as the spare. They were a complete family — two adults, two children, four corners of a square, solid, like the keep of a castle. No room for any more, no room for a baby the size of a flea currently being incubated inside Caroline's belly. Jonathan would be cock-a-hoop probably. How many times would she make the same mistake in her life? The idea was that you were allowed to make one big mistake, and then rectify it and not make it again. And, anyway, whether you rectified it or not, what did it matter, because it would follow you forever. Wherever you went, whatever you did, there was always a corner somewhere that you would turn and there you would see that little bug lying on the floor, the little bug that had cried itself into the oblivion of sleep. The little bug in its new OshKosh dungarees.

John Burton's hair was thinning, the faint outline of a monk's tonsure forming on top of his head. Caroline's heart went out to him when she noticed his little bald patch. She was continually amazed at the absurdities of passion. He was kneeling in front of the altar doing something that she supposed was religious, but when she drew closer she realized that he was sweeping the floor with a dustpan and brush. He gave an embarrassed laugh when he caught sight of her and said, "The lady who cleans the church is on holiday."

"Where?" She loved the way he said "the lady" rather than "the woman."

"Majorca."

"Do you pay her?"

"Yes, of course," he said, looking shocked.

"I thought churches were full of women doing things for the love of it, arranging flowers and polishing brasses and all that stuff."

"I think that's the past you're thinking about," he said. "Or a television program."

Caroline sat in the front pew and said, "I could do with a cigarette." He sat down next to her, the brush and dustpan still in his hand, and said, "I didn't know you smoked?" and she said, "I don't. Not really." He was wearing vicarish trousers, black and nondescript and rather cheap, a white T-shirt, and an old gray cardigan that she wanted to stroke as if it were an animal. Even when he was in mufti he looked like a vicar. She couldn't imagine him in jeans or a suit. She didn't think he had any idea about how she felt about him. If she told him she would spoil his innocence. Of course she didn't *know* him, not at all really. But what difference did it make? Maybe he wasn't the right person for her (obviously not, in fact) and let's not forget that she was married (But so what? Really?) but surely there wasn't just one person in the whole world who was meant for you? If there was then the odds against your ever bumping up against him would be overwhelming, and knowing Caroline's luck even if she did bump up against him she probably wouldn't realize who he was. And what if the person who was destined for you was a shanty dweller in Mexico City or a political prisoner in Burma or one of the million people she was unlikely ever to have a relationship with? Like a prematurely balding Anglican vicar in a rural parish in North Yorkshire.

She felt suddenly tearful. "My au pair's going to leave me," she said. Oh, how pathetic must that sound to him. On a scale of world peace and third-world poverty, how did an unhappy Spanish au pair rate? But he was kind, as she knew he would be, and he said, "I'm sorry," as if he really were, and then they sat in silence and stared at the altar and listened to the summer rain drumming on the ancient stone slates.

13

Amelia

Julia hauled a scuttle full of coal into the sitting room, escorted by a limping Sammy. "I can't believe Victor never put in central heating," she gasped, dropping the scuttle to the floor so that coal dust and tiny pieces of coal, like polished, unworked jet, spilled on the carpet. Amelia frowned at her and said, "I've just cleaned in here," and Julia said, "That's what will be written on your gravestone," and Amelia said, "Oh, really, by you?" and Julia said, "God, I'm gagging for it, aren't you?" and Amelia said, "Apropos of what exactly?"

"Two weeks of enforced celibacy since we've been here," Julia said. "it's doing my head in, it really is. I'm having to wank every night."

"Oh, for God's sake, Julia, you're so *crude*. It's disgusting." Amelia hated that word, the slaters and brickies used it all the time, the hairdressers too — the girls were just like the boys. "You wanker!" — yelling at each other across the room.

"What would you call it then?" Julia asked, and Amelia said, "I don't know — pleasuring yourself," which made Julia fall about laughing and say, "God, don't tell me you don't do it, Milly. Everyone does it, it's normal. I'm sure you do it and think about

Henry — oh, no, you don't think about Henry. I bet you think about *Jackson!*" Julia seemed particularly delighted with this idea. Amelia wanted to slap her. "You do it, don't you, Milly? You frig yourself and think about Jackson!"

"You are disgusting, Julia. *Offensively* disgusting." Amelia knew she had turned as red as her tights — donned especially in case Jackson dropped in today because he had seemed rather taken with them at Victor's funeral. She'd woken up that morning and felt a good feeling, as if the blood in her veins were warm honey, and she thought, He's going to visit this morning, and she had put on some of Julia's makeup and left her hair loose because it was more girlish and she'd made a pot of coffee and warmed up the stale croissants that Julia had bought the day before. And she'd picked some flowers from the garden (hard to find among the weeds) and put them in a vase so that Jackson would look at her and see that she was a woman. But he hadn't come, of course. She'd never had any intuition, womanly or otherwise. It had just been wishful thinking.

Julia sang out, "Milly's got a new boyfriend. Poor old Henry. Milly likes Jackson," as if she were eight years old again. Part of Julia would always be eight years old, just as part of Amelia would always be eleven years old — the age she was when the world stopped.

"How old are you, Julia?"

"Not as old as you."

"I'm leaving the room before I hit you."

Amelia splashed cold water from the kitchen tap on her cheeks. She could still hear Julia chortling away to herself in the living room. If she started up again she was going to yank her head off. Julia wouldn't let it go though, following her into the kitchen, saying, "Jesus, Milly, you're so uptight, I can't imagine what you and Henry are like in the bedroom." Neither could Amelia because, of course, Henry didn't exist. He was an invention, conjured out of nothing, born of an exasperation with Julia's constant nagging about

Amelia's celibate state and (horrors) her insistent offer to "set her up" with someone. "I *have* someone, thank you," she informed Julia irritably, after one-too-many intimate inquiries from her sister. "A colleague, in the department" — and, searching for the first male name she could think of, Amelia came up with "Henry," which was the name of her downstairs neighbor, Philip's, dog, a revolting little Pekingese whose eyes looked as if they were about to pop out of its head any minute. "If Henry was a dog, what kind of dog would he be?" Julia asked, predictably, and Amelia had, unthinkingly, answered, "Pekingese" so that Julia frowned and said, "Oh, poor Milly."

Since then, the fictional Henry had gradually acquired the accretions of a personality. He was a little on the bald and paunchy side, a beer drinker rather than a spirits man, and once, long ago, had a wife who died of cancer and whom he had nursed, devotedly, at home. Henry had no children but he had a tabby cat called Molly, who was a good mouser. Lying, Amelia discovered, was all about the details.

Henry and Amelia conducted a sedate fictitious relationship that revolved around theatergoing, art-house cinema, Italian restaurants, country pubs, and invigorating walks. They had spent two weekends away, one in the Mendips and one in North Devon, Amelia carefully researching both locations on the Internet in case Julia proved curious about the geography or the history, although, naturally, Julia only wanted to know about the food and the sex ("Oh, come on, Milly. Don't be coy"). It was important not to make Henry too interesting because then Julia might actually want to meet him, so sex was "a bit routine" but nonetheless "nice" — a word which repelled Julia. Recently, Amelia had revealed that Henry was a keen golfer, a pastime that was guaranteed to result in indifference on Julia's part.

Henry had proved such a success with Julia that Amelia had introduced him into the workplace as well. He served as a useful antidote to the looks of pity and amusement that always seemed to be her lot. She had heard the other lecturers call her "spinsterish" and she knew that a couple of people thought she was a lesbian. The idea of lesbianism made her feel slightly squeamish. Julia said she had had sex with women, dropped it into the conversation with the same casual air as if she were talking about which super-market she preferred or the latest books she'd read. Amelia had made a point of not looking surprised because that was the kind of reaction Julia loved, of course. Was there no limit to the kind of thing Julia would do? Would she do it with a dog?

"Bestiality," Julia ruminated. "Well, only if I had to."

"Had to? For a part?"

"No, of course not. To save your life, for example."

Would Amelia have sex with a dog to save Julia's life? What an appalling test.

Henry was useful at college too. As far as the inmates of the staff room were concerned, he was someone that her sister had intro-duced her to. Because Julia was an actress they all believed she must live a glamorous life, which was usually annoying for Amelia but sometimes useful. This Henry lived in Edinburgh, making him in-accessible and giving her something to do on the weekends — "Oh, just flying up to Scotland, Henry's taking me fishing," which is the kind of thing she imagined people doing in Scotland — she always thought of the Queen Mother, incongruous in mackintosh and waders, standing in the middle of a shallow brown river (somewhere on the outskirts of Brigadoon, no doubt) and casting a line for trout. Amelia had never been farther north than York, and then only to see Julia in pantomime, playing Dick Whitting-ton's cat in an interpretation that seemed to suggest that the animal was permanently on heat. Amelia envisaged that between York and the royal-infested Scottish Highlands there was a grimy waste-land of derelict cranes and abandoned mills and betrayed, yet still staunch, people. Oh and moorland, of course, vast tracts of brooding landscape under lowering skies, and across this heath strode brooding, lowering men intent on reaching their ancestral houses, where they were going to fling open doors and castigate orphaned, yet resolute, governesses. Or — preferably — the brooding, lowering men were on horseback, black horses with huge muscled haunches, glistening with sweat —

"Milly?"

"What?"

"You're not listening to me, I was saying that we could use some of the money from the house to take a really good holiday." Julia was laying a fire in the grate, folding and pleating sheets of newspaper into makeshift firelighters. Amelia frowned and turned the television on. At first, Amelia had suggested to Julia that they might watch the more cultural channels, Performance or Discovery or, at a pinch, TV5 to improve their rusty French (although unfortunately finding TV5 seemed to involve trawling through the porn and the sport), but this idea had been soundly squashed by Julia ("Get a life, Milly") and now they spent long fireside hours in front of reruns of seventies sitcoms and creaky dramas, *Bergerac,* followed by *Poldark,* and topped off by *Only Fools and Horses,* which seemed to run on a continual loop in the ether.

"I mean a really good holiday," Julia said. "An African safari or a Nepalese trek, visit the temples at Machu Picchu or take a boat to the Antarctic. What do you think, Milly?"

Amelia had never traveled because she'd never had anyone to travel with. Julia was the only person she had ever been on holiday with — once to Portugal (which had been pleasant) and once to Morocco (which had been a nightmare) so that Amelia felt her view of the world was through a small pane of glass, yet the idea of going *out there,* into the world, high up on some mountain, in the middle of an ocean, in some dangerous, foreign place, far from the safety of an English sitting room, made her instantly dizzy and sick with fear.

"And you could surprise Henry," Julia carried on blithely, "take him to New York or Paris for the weekend, stay somewhere gorgeous, the Georges Cinq or the Bristol —"

"Your fire's going out."

More often than not, "Henry" would come down to Oxford for the weekend, and if anyone asked her, Amelia would report back on Monday morning that they had spent a "lovely" weekend — a drive down to Cliveden, a "gorgeous" lunch in Bray. Not many people did ask, but there was a general agreement among her fellow workers that since she had met Henry, Amelia was a little less brittle and abrasive.

The version of Henry that was for her work colleagues was slightly less bald and paunchy than the one she had concocted for Julia. He was also more active and outgoing — all that fishing — and decidedly better off ("In finance, oh God, don't ask me what, it's all Greek to me"). She especially liked to flaunt the more dashing aspects of this Henry to Andrew Vardy, a fellow teacher in the "communications" department and the only man that Amelia had ever — in reality — had sex with.

Amelia had sex with Andrew Vardy ten years ago because she was afraid she would live and die an old maid. Because it had seemed ridiculous to be a virgin at thirty-five years old in the dying years of the twentieth century. Because she didn't understand how she was as good as dead without ever having lived. She supposed she must be in this virginal state because she was shy and easily embarrassed and sex seemed so downright daunting (and, let's face it, vaguely disgusting). At university, she'd had a reputation for being prim and proper, but she always expected that some boy (or some brooding, lowering man) would breach this defensive strategy and sweep away her inhibitions and admit sexual passion into her life. But no one, brooding, lowering, or otherwise, seemed to want her. Sometimes she wondered if perhaps she gave off the wrong scent, or no scent at all, because it was as primitive as that, wasn't it, like cats and queen bees and musk deer?

Perhaps more curious than the fact that there was no one who wanted Amelia was that she, in turn, wanted no one — apart from men in nineteenth-century novels, which put a whole new spin on the idea of "unattainable." Even Sylvia wasn't a virgin. She slept with dozens of boys before her "conversion." And if Sylvia could find boyfriends — Sylvia, who had grown into an ugly duck, not a swan — then why couldn't Amelia? For the longest time Amelia waited for someone to appear who would make her heart race and her brain fog and her intellect crumble and when it didn't happen she thought perhaps she had been intended by nature to be celibate, that she should rejoice (privately anyway) in this vestal state and rather than fretting about her unbroken hymen she should see it as a trophy unattainable to mere mortal men. (A dubious kind of prize, admittedly.)

She would die a noble virgin queen, a new Gloriana. This was during a period when she was having a kind of breakdown — mostly to do with the impossibility of "communicating" with the brickies and slaters and hairdressers and partly to do with the utter futility of life (although anyone with half a brain must surely be mired in existential gloom all the time) — and then, just when she was at her weakest and most vulnerable, Andrew Vardy said to her, "You know, Amelia, if you ever want to have sex, I'd be happy to oblige." Just like that — as if she were a cow that needed servicing, or a virgin who needed deflowering. Could he tell she was intact by looking at her, that her maidenhead was unbroken? How much nicer all those old terms were. What would the slaters say? "Popping your cherry." They probably didn't even know any virgins. And they didn't have any decent terms for sex, all they did was "shag" (every hour God gave them, from the sound of it). And the girls just the same.

She had taken a maidenhead fern in to college, to brighten the godless gloom of the staff room, a cutting she had taken from a plant belonging to Philip, the downstairs neighbor with the Pekingese. Someone, some sleazy old duffer who behaved as if the staff room were the library of a London gentleman's club, said, "Ah, some of these old English terms for plants, wonderfully venereal, maidenhead fern, a virgin's pubes — what could be more delicious?" which elicited sniggering from several people (including women, for heaven's sake, didn't they know any better?). Amelia would have liked to break the plant pot over his head. "And the cuckoopint," he persisted, "sounds innocent, doesn't it, but 'pint' is short for 'pintle' or 'penis'!" How would he feel if she chopped his off? That would shut him up. She busied herself with books as if she had a class to teach, which she didn't, and tried to pretend that her face wasn't the deep crimson shade of shame and humiliation. Thankfully, the plant soon withered and died and Amelia refused to see that as metaphorical in any way but when Andrew Vardy made his overture a few weeks later she surprised herself with her response.

Nowadays, when she viewed Andrew Vardy across the jaded, Cup-A-Soup scented air of the staff room, she felt completely baffled as to why she would ever have — vile to remember — got naked with him, let alone conjoin intimate, delicate parts of her anatomy with his ugly, goosefleshed ones. The only man she'd ever had and he wasn't even remotely good looking. His skin was pitted and pinched by ancient acne and he had a little gay mustache that his wife should have told him to get rid of. He wasn't gay, not at all, he was a Catholic and had five children and he was on the short side, in fact he was slightly shorter than Amelia, but he could be funny, and, dear God, that was something, and for two years they had shared cynical little exchanges over coffee and the occasional longer, more philosophical conversation during one of the college cafeteria's atrocious lunches. Andrew was a skinflint (he had five children, after all, he said) and only offered to pay for Amelia on the days when the first-year hotel management students had to cook and serve a three-course lunch at half the normal price (because the risk of dying from food poisoning was twice as high).

Amelia was flattered by the fact that Andrew Vardy enjoyed her company, because no one else seemed to, and so it was that when, at the fag end of a wearisome day, when they were the last two people left in the staff room, and he spoke his honeyed words of seduction (to recap — "You know, Amelia, if you ever want to have sex, I'd be happy to oblige"), she had thought, yes, why not?

Not right away of course, not there in the staff room — how awful would that have been, if he'd ravished her among the crumpled newspapers and the old mugs with their dregs of Nescafé while she wondered if the janitor was going to put his head round the door. But, no, he simply picked up his rucksack and said, "Good-bye, then, see you tomorrow," as if nothing of any significance had passed between them.

Before Andrew Vardy, Amelia imagined that sex would be (somehow, God knows how) an amalgam of the mystical and the coarsely animalistic, a warm and blurry experience that would transcend the mechanics. What she hadn't imagined was that it would be banal and rather tiresome. Although, unfortunately, still vaguely disgusting.

"Be bold," she thought and invited him round for "a cup of coffee, one evening," she was pretty sure that both of them knew what that meant but if it turned out to be just that — a cup of coffee — then she wouldn't look too stupid. She bought a woman's magazine that had a sealed book on the cover announcing that it contained "Sex Tips to Drive Him Wild" and tried (and failed) to learn some of them off by heart. She felt as if she were preparing for an exam that she was bound to fail. And why would anyone want hot candle wax dripped on their nipples anyway? Would he do that to her? Surely not. "Undress slowly," the book advised.

"All men appreciate a sexy striptease." Amelia had rather hoped that they might keep their clothes on throughout the whole process. Nonetheless, she shaved her legs and armpits, although for the life of her she couldn't see what was wrong with body hair, and painted (rather badly) her toenails, and showered and perfumed herself with something French that Julia had left behind after a visit. She felt as if she were preparing herself for a sacrifice. She kept ready a very good bottle of Bordeaux and bought stuffed olives and peanuts as if she were readying herself for a Tupperware party. She had been to a Tupperware party once, at the invitation of a woman who was a tutor in the beauty and hairdressing department, and had bought a very useful cereal dispenser. It was the only party of any description that she had been to in five years.

The olives and peanuts were not a sex tip, although the book did suggest doing something with popcorn that Amelia considered belonged in a blue movie, not a front-of-counter woman's magazine. You would never think that sex was meant for procreation of the species, that it was simply about male and female organs accommodating each other for a biological purpose. Certainly not according to the authors of "Sex Tips to Drive Him Wild," for whom it seemed to be a case of stuffing every orifice with anything that came to hand.

For five nights in a row, she waited. By the sixth night Amelia began to wonder if she had misheard him, if he had offered to "oblige" her with something else, the loan of a book or a computer program. In the staff room, no mention was made between them of coffee or sex, the only conversation of any kind they had was about how you had to pretend that the slaters had fulfilled all their criteria-based topics of learning in order to get them through the course and off your hands. She stopped preparing herself every night, her legs grew bristles, and she had forgotten all the sex tips, so, of course, Sod's Law, Andrew Vardy turned up at the door when she was in her oldest clothes, painting a little bedside table she had bought in an auction.

No flowers, no chocolates, no wooing — she had rather expected some wooing — and when she said, "Would you like a cup of coffee?" he actually smirked and she offered the good wine only because she knew she couldn't go through with the experience in a cold-stone-sober state. She emptied the peanuts and the olives into glass dishes and put them on the coffee table. Is this what other people did? Other women, preparing for a lover? Didn't they rub themselves with perfumed oils and unguents and comb out their hair, lie down on silken sheets, and present their pomegranate breasts for their lover's kisses? Not put out hors d'oeuvres, surely?

As soon as they sat on the sofa he started kissing her and she could feel how dry and chapped his lips were. He was wearing the same clothes he'd worn into college that day and he smelled stale. Then he was tugging at her paint-stained T-shirt and pawing at her breasts, kneading them as if they were lumps of plasticine, at the same time as he was undoing his trousers so that she wondered what had been the point of mugging up on all that foreplay. Squashed into the sofa cushions, she couldn't really see what he was doing and when she realized he was putting on a condom she felt incredibly embarrassed (which was ridiculous) although part of her wanted to tell him to stop right there so that they could have a discussion about Catholicism and the ethics of contraception — he had five children, after all, was it one rule for his wife and one for his mistress (there was definitely a certain frisson in applying that word to herself)? And, in general, did he really believe in papal infallibility because she had often wondered how an intelligent person (Sylvia, for example) could believe such nonsense, but the moment for an argument over dogma had already passed because he was fitting himself inside her (so much smoother and colder than she'd expected) and she had to stifle the instinct to push him off because it felt so uncomfortable and unnatural. Then they rolled about awkwardly for a bit, scattering the peanuts everywhere and knocking over the wine (which was incredibly careless of him) and then suddenly he let out a low animal sound like a cow giving birth and the next second, his limp thing had slid out of her and flopped like a small dead goldfish on her thigh.

Amelia looked at the ceiling and saw a crack she'd never noticed. Had it always been there or was the house subsiding? She looked at the floor where the peanuts had been broadcast and where the Bordeaux had made a huge stain on the pale carpet, like weak blood, and she wondered if even professional cleaning would be able to remove it.

Andrew Vardy pulled himself and his clothing together — there was a patch of curdled white foam on the shoulder of his jacket that Amelia suspected was baby sick. Her insides seemed to sag. "I'm sorry, I'm going to have to go, Amelia," he said, as if she'd been begging him to stay. "I promised Bernie I'd pick up a pint of milk." Amelia supposed she had been fitted in with the groceries. Pint of milk and a quick shag. So she'd seen him to the door and he'd kissed her on the cheek and said, "That was bloody fantastic," and then he tossed an olive into his mouth as if it were a party trick and then he was gone! Almost skipping down the stairs while Henry, the Pekingese, yapped furiously at him from somewhere down below. There was another darker stain on the sofa and it took Amelia a few seconds to realize that it was not the Bordeaux but her own blood. Her knees felt weak and she slumped down onto the floor. She felt damaged. She heard Andrew Vardy's child-soiled Passat drive away and started to cry.

She wanted Jackson. Desperately. And yes, she did lie in her bed and think about him and pleasure herself. Christ, what a stupid term. *Mr. Brodie would save you,* Julia had said when she declared he was a German shepherd. Amelia wanted to be saved by Jackson, she wanted that more than anything. Jackson, the idea of Jackson, was a hope and a promise and a comfort, it was a sun-warmed pebble in the hand, the scent of wet roses in the rain, it was the possibility of change. Maybe she should just say to him, "If you ever feel like sex, Jackson, I'd be happy to oblige."

She started to undress for bed. It was early, too early to go to bed really. There was still light in the sky outside and she remembered how when she was a child she used to like going to bed in summer when it was still light because she was afraid of the dark. That was before Olivia disappeared, after that there was no safety to be had in either the light or the dark.

She regarded her naked body in the foxed, silver-spotted mirror on Sylvia's small wardrobe. Her flesh looked like curd cheese, she had rolls of fat, like the Michelin Man, her belly folded over, her breasts swinging with their own weight, she looked as if she'd borne a dozen children, she looked like one of those ancient fertility symbols carved from stone. Yet there was nothing fertile about her, was there? She was passing the point of childbearing, her womb was shrinking unseen inside her. "I've still got time to push one out," Julia said to her yesterday in her usual disgusting way. Amelia no longer had time to push one out, soon the planet would have no further use for her. No one had ever found her attractive, no one had ever wanted her, even Victor hadn't wanted her, her own father had found her too ugly to seduce — a howl cut into her thoughts, a terrifying noise as though Julia was having her bowels ripped out, a noise that presaged absolute horror and Amelia grabbed her dressing gown and ran downstairs.

Julia was lying on the floor in a corner of the kitchen and at first Amelia thought something dreadful had happened to her, but then she realized that she had her arms clasped around Sammy's body. His eyes were dull, everything about him was dull as if he were fading, but when he heard Amelia's distressed voice his tail gave a weak little beat. "I'll call the vet, shall I?" Amelia said, and Julia, her voice muffled because her face was pressed into Sammy's neck, said, "I think it's too late. I think he's had a stroke."

"Then we have to call the vet,"

"No, really, Milly, he's on his way out, he's an old dog. Don't upset him." Julia held one of his paws and kissed it. She murmured soothing words into the dying dog's ear, she kissed his ears, his nose, his mouth, rubbed her face on the white hairs of his muzzle. Amelia hated her for being the one who thought she was doing the right thing. "Just stroke him," Julia said but Amelia was raking through the yellow pages looking for the number for an out-of-hours vet and so she missed the moment when the dog died and only realized he was gone when Julia got up from the floor, covered in dog hair and her face all creased. She looked as if she had been hanging onto the dog for a long time.

She couldn't bear it. She had phoned Jackson because she wanted him to stop the pain. She didn't want anyone else to stop the pain, just Jackson. She wanted him to take her in his arms and soothe her the way Julia had soothed the dog. (*"Please, Jackson, please come, I need you."* There had been something thrilling about speaking such passionate, desperate words. She had felt passionate. She had felt desperate.) What she hadn't wanted was for him to arrive on the doorstep looking pissed off (oh, God, slater language) and she certainly hadn't wanted him arriving on the doorstep with a small child in tow. *His* small child. She had never imagined him having a child, of course, she had never asked. Did he have a wife? She asked him that, when he was hardly over the threshold, accusing like a madwoman, she knew she looked like a madwoman, her hair all over the place, her face ravaged by crying, her breasts flapping around inside the oversize dressing gown. "I didn't know you were married, Mr. Brodie," spitting out the words as if he had betrayed her. The girl looked upset and Jackson was even more annoyed because she was upsetting the girl and it was Julia who calmed the situation, saying, "I'm sorry, Mr. Brodie, we're not ourselves tonight, I'm afraid poor Sammy passed away." After that it was all a little shadowy, Julia kept pouring from the brandy bottle, and the child had been almost unnaturally interested in the dead dog, stroking its lifeless fur, saying, "Poor dead dog," until Amelia wanted to slap her because the dog didn't belong to her, forgetting that it was actually Victor's dog. Jackson had explained to the girl that the dog was happy in dog heaven and then Julia had helped Amelia up to bed and that's where she'd been ever since, sobbing her heart out in a quiet but nonetheless ugly fashion, and it was a crying that wouldn't stop because it encompassed too much.

She was crying from a general sense of wretchedness (which everyone was allowed now and then, surely), and crying for herself and her dried-up meaningless little life. She couldn't bear it, she really couldn't. Crying for Victor and Olivia and Rosemary and for Rascal (who died two years after Olivia disappeared). And she was crying because she'd only ever had sex with Andrew Vardy and because Mozart had died young and Sammy had died old, and because she was fat and ugly and had to teach the slaters and was never going to be wrapped in the comfort of Jackson's arms.

And she was crying because she didn't believe in Jesus or dog heaven and no one was ever going to lie in bed with her on a Sunday morning and read the papers or rub her back and say, "Is there anything I can do for you?" And because there was no happiness, only emptiness. And because she wanted to be sixteen years old with long shiny hair (which she'd never had), and she wanted to be looking anxiously out of an upstairs window and hear her mother downstairs shouting, "He's here," and then she would run lightly down the stairs and climb into the car where at the wheel would be her good-looking boyfriend and they would drive away and have warm, blurry sex somewhere and then he would bring her back home and her family would be waiting. Victor would acknowledge her with a gruff paternal nod as she came in the door, contrary teenage Julia would ignore her while willowy first-year student Sylvia would smile in a superior manner. Somewhere, in the guest bedroom perhaps, the vague unformed shape of a five-year old Annabelle could be found sleeping. And Rosemary, her mother, would ask her, in a womanly, conspiratorial way, if she'd had a nice time and then would offer her hot milk and honey (which she was sure she had never done in real life) and perhaps before she dropped into the sweet untroubled sleep of a pretty sixteen-year-old, Amelia would look in on Olivia, eight years old and safely asleep in her own bed.

Sometime in the night, Julia came into her bedroom and lay down on the bed, putting her arms around her and holding her the way she had the dying Sammy. And Julia said, "Everything's all right, Milly, really it is," which was such a huge, wonderful lie that it wasn't even worth arguing about.

14

Jackson

"Jesus, Jackson, what happened to you?" The same note of reproach in Deborah Arnold's voice as in Josie's, Jackson noticed.

"Yes, thank you, I'm feeling much better," he said, making his way into the inner sanctum where Shirley Morrison was waiting for him. She visibly flinched when she saw him (and she was a nurse so he must look bad). He had a stunning black eye thanks to David Lastingham (the bastard) and he imagined that being hit over the head and lying unconscious all night in the open air had probably not improved his appearance.

"Not as bad as it looks," he said to Shirley Morrison although it probably was. Shirley Morrison was sitting in a neat lotus. She was straight backed and had a thin dancer's body. She was forty but could have passed for thirty until you looked in her eyes and saw that she'd lived enough for more than one lifetime. He knew who she was, she'd never changed her name, it was before Jackson's time in Cambridge but when he'd asked Deborah to find out about Shirley Morrison she said, "Shirley Morrison — wasn't she Michelle Fletcher's sister? The ax murderer?"

* * *

" . . . She was just sitting on the floor, still holding the ax. I don't know how long she'd been there. Keith had been dead about an hour, according to the pathologist's report." Shirley Morrison held her cup of coffee with two hands as if it were providing her with warmth, although it was as hot as hell inside Jackson's office and the coffee must have gone cold a long time ago. She stared off into the distance and Jackson got the impression that she was mentally reviewing Keith Fletcher's autopsy. "When I walked in," she continued, "she smiled at me and said, 'Oh, Shirley, I'm so glad you're here, I made you a chocolate cake.' So I knew straight away that she'd lost it."

"Her defense pleaded temporary insanity," Jackson offered. Deborah had done the research for him, as well as giving him the gossip. Michelle Rose Fletcher, née Morrison, eighteen years old, sent down for life for, in the esteemed judge's words, "the cold-blooded, calculated murder of your spouse. An entirely innocent man." Jackson didn't believe in the entire innocence of anyone apart from animals and children, and not all children, at that. He offered her more coffee but she just shook her head as if he were a distracting insect.

"Michelle was such a control freak, I mean I loved her to bits, she was my big sister, you know?" Jackson nodded, he knew what big sisters were like. His own big sister, Niamh.

"But everything had to be just so for Michelle, all the time. All the bloody time. I can see why, I mean the way we were brought up — it was . . ." Shirley Morrison shrugged, searching for a word. "Shambolic. Our mother couldn't control a dog, let alone a house and kids. Dad was a drinker and Mum was not exactly capable. And so it was really important to Michelle not to be like them. But the baby did her head in. You can't control babies."

"So do you think she was suffering from postnatal depression?" Jackson remembered Josie after Marlee's birth, crying all day with misery while Marlee cried all night with colic. Jackson had felt completely helpless because he didn't know what to do for either of them. And then suddenly it was over, like the sun coming out, and Josie looked at Marlee sleeping peacefully in her cradle and laughed and said to Jackson, "She's cute, let's keep her." Way back when they were happy.

Shirley Morrison gave him a look, as if she was wondering what he could know about postpartum misery, and then shrugged and said, "Maybe. Probably. She wasn't getting any sleep, people go crazy if they don't sleep. But they were out to get her, the press, Keith's family. He didn't do anything wrong, he didn't beat her or anything. He was a nice guy, very easygoing. I liked him. Everyone liked him. And he loved Tanya."

"Michelle had bruising to her face," Jackson said.

Shirley looked at him blankly. "Did she?"

"It was in the arresting officer's report, why wasn't it used in her defense?"

"I don't know."

Shirley's slender feet were very brown, as if she went around barefoot a lot outside. She was wearing Indian sandals, embossed leather, which made her feet look even better. Jackson liked women's feet, not in a fetishistic way (he hoped) and not ugly feet, and, for some mysterious reason, a lot of lovely women had ugly feet, he just thought nice feet were attractive. (Was he trying to justify something to himself here?) Nicola Spencer had big feet, he'd noticed. She was on an overnight to Málaga, doing God knows what.

"The smell was incredible, awful, that's what I remember most, just . . . revolting. Tanya was in her playpen and she was screaming, really screaming, I've never heard a baby cry like that before or since. I'm a pediatric nurse," she added, "in the ICU," but Jackson already knew that, he'd phoned up the hospital and asked, "Shirley Morrison, what ward is she on again?" and they'd told him. It was much easier to get information than most people thought. Ask a question and people give you the answer. Not the big questions, obviously, like who killed Laura Wyre and where were the remains of Olivia Land. Big questions like why the woman he had once promised to love and protect as long as there was breath in his body had decided to remove their only child to the opposite side of the world. Just like that. ("Yes, Jackson, 'just like that.'")

"The first thing I did was pick Tanya up but she still wouldn't stop screaming. She was filthy, God knows when she'd last been changed, and, there was blood spattered all over her." This image, and all it implied, tripped her up for a moment, breaking her composure. Shirley Morrison stared out the office window but she wasn't looking at anything to be found outside.

"She was wearing these new dungarees I'd bought her. OshKosh. I had a job working in a corner shop, after school, on Saturdays. Michelle and I had always worked, we'd never have had anything if we hadn't. I remember thinking how much those dungarees had cost and how the blood was never going to come out. My brother-in-law had just been killed by my sister and I was thinking about stain removal."

"The brain disassociates to stop us from going mad."

"You think I don't know that, Mr. Brodie?"

Shirley Morrison's toenails were painted with a pale polish and she was wearing a delicate gold chain around one ankle. Jackson remembered a time when only tarts and whores wore chains around their ankles. There used to be a prostitute who lived on the same street as Jackson when he was young. She wore emerald green eye shadow and red stilettos and had white, veiny legs. Did she wear an anklet? Did she have a name? Jackson used to run past her house in terror in case she came out and caught him because his mother told him that she was "a servant of Satan," which had confused him because "Satan" was the name of a dog — a big rottweiler — owned by a guy on the allotments.

Jackson hadn't thought about that street for a long time, a gloomy terrace with passages like tunnels that went through to a back alley. They'd moved to a better class of street when Jackson was nine. No whores hanging around on the doorstep, smoking their lungs out. Was Shirley Morrison married? She had a ring on her finger but it was neither a wedding ring nor an engagement ring, it was silver, Celtic or Scandinavian, what did that mean?

"When I picked Tanya up, Michelle laughed and said, 'She does go on, doesn't she?' Now *that's* disassociation."

"She must have had *some* reason for killing him," Jackson puzzled, "even if it wasn't premeditated. Something must have triggered it."

It felt as if all the air in the office had been used up. It wasn't midday yet but it was already sweltering. Shirley's light brown hair was screwed up carelessly on top of her head and the fine hairs at the nape of her neck were dark with sweat. He wondered what she'd do if he invited her to lunch, a nice pub with a garden, or buy a sandwich and go for a walk by the river. It wouldn't be unprofessional, it would just be moving this appointment outside. Who was he kidding? His motives were entirely unprofessional.

If Josie died Jackson would get sole custody. Marlee wouldn't go to the other side of the world (*"Lord of the Rings,"* she'd said to him, quite thrilled, as if Bilbo and Gandalf and the rest of their crew actually lived in New Zealand and were waiting for her to join their fellowship. She hadn't read the books, only seen the DVDs, which were far too scary for an eight-year-old in Jackson's opinion, but not in the opinion of David Lastingham apparently).

For her part, of course, Josie had failed to keep any of the promises she had made — to love and honor him, to be faithful to him — he could still hear that little flutter of emotion in her voice when she said, "Until death us do part." They had opted for the traditional wedding service. Now she was planning a tropical beach ceremony with a Maori gospel choir and homemade vows. She was going to marry that wanker and "start a new life."

Jackson wondered if he was capable of killing Josie. He was better placed than most people — he knew all kinds of ways to do it, it wasn't doing it that was the problem, not being found out, that was the thing. He wouldn't wait around for hours with an ax sitting in his lap. What was that Lizzie Borden rhyme? "Lizzie Borden took an ax, gave her mother forty whacks." If he killed Josie it would have to be done in a "calculated, cold-blooded killing" — fire, explosives, a gun. A gun for preference, an L96 A1 sniper with a Schmidt and Bender sight, so you could be as far away as possible — he couldn't do an intimate killing, something close-up and personal like strangling or a knife, he couldn't be there, watching the blood stop pumping round her cheating heart, couldn't watch the life fade from her eyes. And not poison. Poison was for psychopaths and deranged Victorian women. Had he really been mugged the other night? Nothing had been taken from him, his wallet, his watch, his car, were all left behind, but then he'd fought back before the guy could take anything. In Jackson's experience, muggers didn't usually try and smash your skull in. "There's a lot of bad people out there, sir," the DC ("DC Lowther, sir") who took his statement said. They'd sent a DC where they'd normally have sent a PC. Jackson supposed he should feel flattered. He remembered DC Lowther when he was an eager young recruit in uniform. "There's been a spate of muggings recently, Inspector," DC Lowther said, and Jackson said, "It's just plain 'Mr. Brodie' now." It was funny, he'd never really been Mr. Brodie, he'd joined the army at sixteen and until then he'd just been Jackson, sometimes "Brodie!" from the male teachers. Then it was "Private Brodie" and so on up the ranks until he left the army and then he'd started again as "PC Brodie." He wasn't sure how he felt about being "plain Mr. Brodie."

"Do you have any enemies, sir?" DC Lowther asked hopefully.

"Not really," Jackson said. Just about everyone he'd ever met.

Jackson's shirt was sticking to his skin, it was way too hot to be in an office.

"I don't know what triggered it," Shirley said. "She just went berserk."

There was always a trigger, there was a lot of things that the defense could have used — psychotic episodes, sleep deprivation, baby blues, shit childhood, self-defense (what about the bruise on her face?). "In court," Jackson said, "Michelle said that he woke the baby. *The baby was asleep and Keith woke her up,* that was the nearest she got to giving a motive." Jackson could imagine how that went down with the judge. She might as well have pleaded guilty. Michelle Fletcher hadn't run away or made up a story, she had simply waited to be found. By her sister.

If she had served two-thirds of her sentence Michelle Fletcher would have been back on the outside in 1989, at the age of twenty-eight. The same age Laura Wyre would be if she'd lived. Jackson would lay a bet that Michelle had been a model prisoner, trans-ferred to an open prison by '85, catching up with her exams prob-ably, so she could start her "new life" when she came out. Like Josie. A fresh start, wiping out the past. Just like that. What was Michelle doing now? Shirley Morrison didn't know, of course she didn't know. That was why she was here.

"I promised Michelle I would look after Tanya," Shirley said, "and I would have done, of course I would have done, but I was only fifteen and social services decided our parents were unfit — which they were — and gave custody to Keith's parents. But they weren't much better. The last time I ever saw my sister was in the court the day she was sentenced. She refused to see us, knocked back all our visitor's orders, refused to read letters, there was noth-ing we could do about it. I could have understood if she didn't want to see Mum or Dad, they both died without seeing her again. But not to see me . . . I mean I didn't care that she'd killed Keith, she was still my sister, I still loved her." She shrugged and added, "Anyone's capable of killing, given the right circumstances." She was looking at that faraway world again, the one that existed on the other side of the office window, and Jackson supposed he could have said, "Yeah, I've killed people," but that didn't seem like the kind of dialogue he wanted to enter into at half past eleven on a Monday morning in these temperatures, so he said nothing at all.

"They told us when she was released," Shirley continued, "but she never got in touch. I don't know where she went or what she's doing now. In the end she got a new life and we were stuck with her old one. 'Murder' — it's such a stigma, isn't it? It's so . . . trashy. I wanted to go to medical school, be a doctor, but that was never going to happen, not after everything we went through."

"And now you want me to look for your sister?"

Shirley laughed as if he'd said something absurd, "God, no. Why would I want to look for Michelle when she's made it so obvious she doesn't want to be found? She doesn't care about me anymore. I don't want to find Michelle. I want to find Tanya."

It was teatime in Binky's garden. Everything was so wildly over-grown that a machete would have been a more fitting accompani-ment at the tea table instead of the extensive array of tarnished butter knives and jam spoons that formed part of Binky's complex tea ceremony. "Darjeeling," Binky announced, but it was a gray washy brew that hadn't seen a tea plantation in years and which tasted like old socks. The cups didn't look as if they had been cleaned for a long time. "We are being joined today by a guest," she an-nounced like a rather grand chat-show hostess, "my great-nephew, Quintus." What kind of a name was that to get stuck with for life, for God's sake?

"Really?" Jackson said. Binky had never mentioned having fam-ily. "I hardly know the boy," she added, with a dismissive wave of her hand. "My nephew and I weren't close, but the boy's the only fam-ily I have." Had Binky Rain ever been close to anyone? Strange to imagine that there had once been a Dr. Rain who had shared bed and board with her. She couldn't always have been old, but it was hard to believe she had ever been a young nubile wife, compliant to "Julian's" sexual needs — ah, Jesus, Jackson, shoot that idea right out of your head. He was so alarmed by the unpalatable image he'd con-jured up that he knocked over his tea, not that one more stain could make any difference to a cloth that was a palimpsest of previous tea-related accidents. "Something wrong, Mr. Brodie?" Binky inquired, mopping up the tea with the hem of her skirt, but before he could reply a cry like a huntsman's tantivy from the top end of the garden announced the arrival of Quintus Rain.

Binky's use of the word "boy" had led Jackson to expect a teenager, so he was surprised when "Quintus" turned out to be a substantial forty-something with broad, bland features and floppy hair. He was built like a rugby forward but his muscle had turned to flab and he looked too soft to survive a scrum. He was wearing chinos and a blue-and-white-striped shirt with a white collar and a pink tie and had a navy blue blazer slung over his shoulder. Break him in two and you'd find "Tory" written right through him. "Brought up in Herefordshire," Binky murmured to Jackson as if this somehow explained everything about Quintus. The really interesting thing about Quintus, interesting to Jackson anyway, was that Quintus was sporting a considerable plaster across a nose that looked damaged in just the way you would expect a nose to be damaged if you'd been nutted by someone who was trying to stop you from pistol-whipping them.

But why on earth would someone he'd never met before, with whom he had no relationship whatsoever, want to attack him like that? Quintus seemed particularly put out to see Jackson in his great-aunt's garden. Binky herself blithely ignored the fact that she was taking tea with two hostile, beat-up men and kept wittering on about Frisky.

Quintus didn't give the impression that he had been a frequent visitor to his elderly great-aunt, but then the boy had led a busy life — shipped over from the daughterland at an early age to be made into an English gentleman — Clifton, Sandhurst, a commission in the Royal Lancers (Jackson thought he'd recognized the braying tones of the officer class), then "a stint down the mines," and now something vague that occupied his time in London.

"Down the mines?" Jackson repeated doubtfully, fishing cat hair out of his teacup.

"Efrican," Binky said.

"Efrican?"

"Sarth Efrican. Diamond mines. In charge of the blecks."

Binky went inside to make a fresh pot of tea, saying, "You two should have a lot to talk about, Mr. Brodie. You're both army men, after all."

Jackson hadn't thought of himself as an army man for a long time. He wasn't sure he'd ever thought of himself as an army man. "Which regiment?" Quintus asked gruffly.

"Infantry. Prince of Wales's Own," Jackson said laconically.

"What rank?"

What was this, Jackson wondered, a game of "Mine's bigger than yours?" He shrugged and said, "Private."

"Yeah, I could have guessed that," Quintus said. He pronounced all the vowels in "Yeah" and then a few extra for luck.

Jackson didn't bother saying that although he went in to the army as a private he came out as a warrant officer, class one, in the military police, because he had no intention of playing Billy Big-Dick with him. Jackson had been offered a commission before he left the army but he knew he'd never be comfortable on the other side, taking dinner in the mess with pricks like Quintus who thought of the Jacksons of this world as bottom-feeding thugs.

"I could show you my tattoos," Jackson offered. Quintus declined, which was just as well because Jackson didn't have any tattoos. Shirley Morrison had a tattoo, between the base of her neck and her shoulder blades, a black rose on the fifth vertebra. Did she have other tattoos on her body, in less visible places?

Quintus suddenly pulled his chair closer to Jackson as if he were going to tell him a secret and in a menacing voice said, "I know your game, Brodie." Jackson tried not to laugh, he had (with little enthusiasm) fitted two wars into his army career and it took more than guys like Quintus rattling their sabers to frighten him. By the look of him Quintus wouldn't last three rounds with a rabbit. "And what game would that be exactly, *Mr.* Rain?" Jackson asked but never got to find out because at that moment a particularly manky tom decided it needed to spray its territory and favored Quintus's leg as one of its outposts.

Jackson walked down to the river and found some shade on the bank. He had a squashed sandwich in his pocket that he had bought in Pret a Manger and now he shared it with a group of eager ducks. There was a continual traffic of punts along the river, most of them containing tourists being chauffeured by students, or student types, dressed in straw boaters and striped blazers, the boys in flannels, the girls in unflattering skirts. The tourists were a mixed bag — Japanese, Americans (fewer than before), a lot of Europeans, some unidentifiable (a kind of generic East European), and north-erners, who in the torpid air of Cambridge seemed more foreign than the Japs. They all appeared to be thrilled, as if they were hav-ing a genuine experience — as if this was how the natives spent their leisure hours — punting down the river and eating cream teas to the sound of the Grantchester clock chiming three. What a load of shite, to quote his father.

"Mr. Brodie! Yoo-hoo, Mr. Brodie!"

Oh, dear God, Jackson thought wearily, was there no escape from them? They were punting, for fuck's sake, or at least Julia was punting, while Amelia watched her from beneath a big floppy sun hat that looked as if it had last seen better days on her mother's head. She was also wearing sunglasses and gave the general impres-sion of someone who'd just been discharged from the hospital af-ter a particularly challenging face-lift.

"What a beautiful day!" Julia shouted to Jackson. "We're going to Grantchester for tea, hop in. You have to come with us, Mr. Brodie."

"No, I don't."

"Yes, you do," Julia said cheerfully. "Get in. Don't be so cur-mudgeonly." Jackson hauled himself up from the grass with a sigh and helped pull the punt into the bank. He climbed in awkwardly and Julia laughed and said, "Not a sailor, then, Mr. Brodie?" Why were they still in Cambridge? Were they ever going home? Amelia, at the other end of the vessel, gave him a vague acknowledgment without making eye contact. The last time he saw her she was dis-traught about the dog's death (*"Please, Jackson, please come, I need you"*). She'd looked rough, she'd looked like a dog actually, wear-ing an old dressing gown, and makeup — he'd never seen her in makeup before — it looked terrible, as if she'd applied it in the dark, and she hadn't put her hair up so that it hung in dry hanks around her face. All women come to an age when they're just too old to wear their hair down, even beautiful women with beautiful hair, and neither Amelia nor her hair had ever been beautiful.

Jackson thought it was best if he behaved as if nothing had hap-pened the other night. What *had* happened the other night? *"I didn't know you were married, Mr. Brodie?"* — what the hell was that all about? As if he was an adulterous lover who'd betrayed her. He had never given Amelia Land a single reason to think there was anything between them. Had she really developed a crush on him? (Please, God, no.) Stan Jessop had a crush on Laura Wyre. Were crushes dangerous things? They sounded so harmless.

"Crikey, what happened to you, Mr. Brodie?" Julia was peering at him in a shortsighted way. "You've been in a fight!" Amelia looked at him for the first time, but when he caught her eye she looked away. "How exciting," Julia said.

"It was nothing," Jackson said. (Just someone's trying to kill me.) "What day is it today?"

"Tuesday," Julia said promptly.

Amelia grunted something that sounded like "Wednesday."

"Really?" Julia said to her. "Cor lummy, how the days fly, don't they?" (Cor lummy? Who said things like that? Apart from Julia?) "I always think," Julia said, "that Wednesdays are violet." Julia seemed in an exceptionally merry mood. "And Tuesdays are yellow, of course."

"No, they're not," Amelia said. "They're green."

"Don't be silly," Julia said. "Anyway, today's violet and it's a jolly good day for the Orchard Tea Rooms. We used to go there a lot when we were children. Before Olivia. Didn't we, Milly?"

Amelia had lapsed back into silence and waved a hand vaguely in answer. For the first time since he'd met them they were dressed suitably for the weather. Amelia was wearing a baggy cotton dress and ugly hiking sandals. If she got a good haircut and some decent clothes she'd improve 100 percent. At least Julia wasn't hard on the eye, and she was pretty competent at the punting thing. She was wearing a skimpy top that belonged on a teenager but it revealed her neat, hard biceps (she definitely worked out) and at least she had triceps, unlike Amelia, who had the kind of swinging under-arm flesh that would have made it easy for her to glide among the treetops. Despite the sunshine Amelia had remained pale and uninteresting, whereas Julia had turned the color of toasted cashews. He looked at her, hauling on the pole, fag hanging out the corner of her lipsticked mouth, and thought that she was a good sport and was surprised to realize that he was growing genuinely fond of Julia. And that "good sport" was her language, not his.

"You're looking at my tits, Mr. Brodie."

"I am not."

"You are so." Julia gave a sudden little yelp of surprise and Jackson swiveled round to see what she was looking at. A middle-aged man was climbing out of the river onto the bank — bollock-naked and skinny and tanned all over. A nudist? They called themselves naturalists now, didn't they? The man toweled himself off and then lay down on the riverbank, completely unselfconsciously, and started reading a book.

"Golly gosh," Julia laughed. "Did you *see* that? Did you see that, Milly? Is that legal, Mr. Brodie?"

"Not really."

"Wouldn't that be lovely," Julia said, "just to take off all your clothes and plunge into the water? The neo-pagans used to swim naked in Byron's Pool, couldn't you just do that, Mr. Brodie, strip off and dive in?" Julia licked her top lip with her pink cat's tongue and Amelia made an unattractive snorting sound. Jackson suddenly remembered Binky Rain saying that the Lands were "wild girls." It was hard to believe Amelia had ever been wild, but Julia, definitely Julia. He thought he might quite like to swim naked with Julia.

"What was he reading?" Julia asked, and Amelia, who had given no sign of having even looked at the naked man, said, *"Principia Mathematica,"* and glared at Jackson.

"More tea, Mr. Brodie?" Julia asked, pouring the tea without waiting for an answer, "And is there honey still for tea? Yes, there most certainly is and we shall have it on our scones. Milly, do you want honey on your scones?"

At least the tea in the Orchard Tea Rooms was decent, unlike Binky's. Julia's little finger had a scar, like a thin silver ring, that ran all the way round it. She had it crooked, in a very ladylike way, as she drank her tea. She caught Jackson looking at it. "Chopped it off," she said breezily. Amelia snorted. "Accidentally," Julia added. Amelia snorted again. "You'll turn into a pig if you carry on like that, Milly," Julia said.

It struck Jackson that he'd asked Binky Rain about the Land girls but he'd never asked the Land girls about Binky Rain. "Binky Rain," Jackson said, "your neighbor, Victor's neighbor?" Julia looked vague. "Cats," Jackson said.

"I was a tabby in the chorus," Julia said, "but I only lasted a few weeks, I got bronchitis, it was a shame, it was a number-one tour."

"No," Jackson said patiently. "Binky Rain, she keeps cats."

"The old witch," Amelia said suddenly, and Julia said, "Oh, *her.* We never went anywhere near her."

"We used to," Amelia said. "And then we didn't."

"Why not?" Jackson asked, but Amelia seemed to have lapsed back into her catatonic state.

"Sylvia told us not to," Julia said. She frowned with the effort of remembering. "That was after Olivia, I think. She said the garden was cursed and if we went in there we'd be turned into cats. That all her cats were people who'd gone into her garden. Sylvia was always a bit strange, of course. Mrs. Rain isn't still alive, is she? She must be three hundred years old by now."

"Almost," Jackson said.

There was something undeniably pleasant about being sprawled in a deck chair beneath the trees. The hum of insects and tourists was soporific and Jackson could think of nothing he wanted to do more than close his eyes and drift off, but Julia kept prattling on about neo-pagans and Wittgenstein and Russell.

"Weren't they all right-wing snobs?" Jackson asked.

"Oh don't spoil it by being all northern and socialist," Julia said.

Amelia remained a brooding presence, communicating in monosyllables. "Brooke used to run around with no clothes on," Julia said. "Maybe nudism is some kind of Cambridge thing."

"Rupert Brooke was just a protofascist," Amelia said suddenly, from somewhere beneath her sun hat, and Julia said, "Well, he's dead and he was a terrible poet, so he's had his comeuppance," and Amelia said, "That's a specious argument if ever I heard one," and Julia said — but Jackson was asleep by then.

Jackson retrieved his car from where it was still parked, in front of Binky's house. A gold Lexus, not a vehicle (nor a color) that Jackson had any time for, was parked right up against the Alfa's bumper and Jackson felt pretty sure it belonged to Quintus. He had no idea what was going on between them. Surely Quintus hadn't attacked him?

He drove down Silver Street, listening to Gillian Welch's *Hell Among the Yearlings* album. His taste in music was getting more depressive by the minute, if that was possible. He was on his way to a meeting in The Eagle with Steve Spencer, not that he had anything to report about Nicola, but his mind was still on Quintus when all of a sudden he found himself driving straight into the back of a Ford Galaxie that was stationary at traffic lights by Fitzbillies on Trumpington Street.

The front of the Alfa Romeo came off a lot worse than the back of the Ford Galaxie, but things would have been more serious if Jackson hadn't already been easing up for the red light. That wasn't a fact that impressed the driver of the Galaxie, who leaped out and started yelling at Jackson that he had intentionally endangered the life of her children. Three small, inquisitive faces peered out the rear window of the Galaxie. When the traffic police rolled up, the woman was standing in the middle of the road, jabbing her finger at the CHILD ON BOARD sticker on her rear window.

"The brakes failed," Jackson said to the older of the two traffic policemen.

"Liar! Bloody liar!" the woman shouted.

"Jeez, Jackson," the policeman said, "you really know how to pick them."

The crash had jolted something loose in Jackson's head. His tooth felt less like a tooth and more like a knife being pushed through his gum. He didn't think his body could take much more punishment.

The traffic cops breathalyzed Jackson, took down details of the accident, and sent the Galaxie and its furious driver on their way. Then they called a police tow truck and had Jackson's car taken to the police garage, where a mechanic looked it over. The older traffic cop owed Jackson a tenner from a derby sweep three years ago and Jackson reckoned it was a debt paid in full now.

"The brakes failed," Jackson said for the umpteenth time. The accident had unnerved him. He'd been in accidents before, skids and shunts, but he'd never been the one doing the shunting. He could still see himself gliding helplessly into the back of the Galaxie, magnetically drawn on by the CHILD ON BOARD sign. "I think the brake fluid must have leaked," he said to the mechanic.

"It leaked alright," the mechanic said, "leaked through the bloody great hole that was drilled in the reservoir. I think there's someone out there who doesn't like you."

"Christ," one of the traffic policeman said cheerfully, "that'll make it hard to narrow down."

"Thanks." Perhaps he should mention Quintus Rain's name to the eager young DC Lowther who had taken his statement in the hospital.

A police car dropped him off outside his front door. He sensed he was beginning to lower the tone of the neighborhood. It was nine o'clock and the smell of barbecue was everywhere on the air. He knew without looking at his mobile that it was full of messages from Steve Spencer wondering what had happened to him. He avoided thinking that the day couldn't get any worse and was rewarded with a sight that suddenly made everything better. Shirley Morrison was sitting on his doorstep, two bottles of cold beer in her hand. "I thought maybe you could do with some nursing," she said.

Later, much later, when there was already light in the sky and the dawn chorus had struck up and it was Thursday (which was blue according to Julia and orange according to Amelia), Jackson turned and looked at Shirley's sleeping face and tried to remember why he wasn't supposed to sleep with her? Oh yes, because she was a client. Ethics. Nice one, Jackson. He wondered if he had crossed a line he was going to regret. It wasn't so much that she was a client, or that he thought there was going to be anything between them, they'd swerved out of their orbits and collided, that was all.

(Although it was nice to think there might be more.) It had been cataclysmic, extraordinary, but he didn't see a future in it. It wasn't *that* that was worrying Jackson, it was the fact that when Shirley was telling her awful story to him yesterday, she had spent most of her time looking up to the right.

15

Theo

It was very hot in the churchyard. His face was dripping with sweat, he imagined all the fat on his body was melting. Even though Little St. Mary's on Mill Lane was in the middle of everywhere, Theo had never encountered another soul, living or dead, among its gravestones and wildflowers. Laura told him that she used to come here and revise, sitting on the grass with her books scattered around her, and so he had placed a bench here with a plaque: FOR LAURA, WHO LOVED THIS PLACE, and he felt closer to her — in some indefinable way — when he sat here. It was one of the stations of the cross for Theo, one of the places that was connected with Laura. Her bones rested in the City Cemetery on Newmarket Road, but the whole of Cambridge acted as a reliquary for her memory.

People scattered the ashes of their cremated relatives in the churchyard, and a chamomile lawn had been planted on the gray, gritty soil of the dead. On Laura's grave, in the characterless municipal cemetery, Theo had planted snowdrops, her favorite flower. There were trees in the cemetery and Theo wondered if their roots had found Laura yet, whether they had twined their way through her rib cage, curled around her ankles, and braceleted her wrists. Jackson had been to London to see Emma. Theo's memories of Emma were indistinct, he seemed to remember that she had been involved with a man and the whole thing had turned out badly in some way. Emma was working for the BBC, Jackson said. Theo never speculated about what Laura would be doing if she had lived. There was no future to imagine, her life was self-contained, February 15, 1976, to July 19, 1994. Her A Level results had arrived three weeks after she died, like an odd postscript. Theo had opened the big brown envelope addressed to "Laura Wyre" and seen that she had four "A" grades. He'd never thought to cancel her university place and a week into the autumn term someone rang up from the university administration office in Aberdeen and said, "Can I speak to Laura Wyre, please?" and Theo said, "No, I'm sorry, you can't," and then burst into tears.

Theo was too hot, Laura's bench stood in a sun trap against the wall of the church. He could feel the sweat pooling in the fatty concave of his lower back. It wasn't a good day to be here. Theo was allergic to almost every living thing that grew in the churchyard, but he had prearmed himself with sunglasses and Zyrtec and had hoped to battle it out a little longer with the abundant flora of Little St. Mary's, but his eyes and nose had begun to stream with water and he knew he was going to have to make a move. He struggled to his feet. "Bye, bye, sweetheart," he said, because she was everywhere. And nowhere.

On Christ's Pieces a man was cutting the grass, sitting on one of those little tractor mowers. Theo could hardly see for the tears rolling down his face. The handkerchief he was holding up to his nose was already sodden. People were giving him odd looks but he lumbered on regardless. The buses at the Drummond Street Bus Station roared their engines like mechanical beasts, Theo swore he could taste exhaust fumes in his mouth. Who would build a bus station next to a green space? He could hear the breath in his chest, it sounded as loud as the lawn mower. To be allergic to summer seemed wrong somehow. His wife, Valerie, had never been sympathetic, she'd seen his allergies and asthma as another kind of character weakness. There'd been no pets in the house until Laura was fourteen and she'd wanted a dog so badly that he had finally given in and they drove to the dog's home and came back with Poppy. She was still only a few months old, someone had thrown her out of a moving car. How could anyone do that? What kind of person could inflict suffering like that? Laura said she was going to "smother" Poppy with love to make it up to her. And Theo had gradually grown accustomed to the dog hair, until he could even let her sit on his knee while he stroked her. He loved that dog too, it had been terrible when she was run over, a tiny premonition of what was to come.

Theo could feel his chest tightening. He began to wheeze and reached in his pocket for his Ventolin inhaler. It wasn't in the usual pocket. He tried all his pockets and then had a sudden, clear picture of his inhaler sitting on the hall table, waiting to be transferred from one jacket to another. The panic was like a punch to the heart. His legs almost went from under him and he stumbled to a bench in the Princess Diana Memorial Rose Garden, trying to keep calm, trying to keep the terror at bay. The sunny day had already grown black round the edges and spots were dancing before Theo's eyes. He could feel a knotty pain in his chest and wondered if he was having a heart attack.

He was fighting for breath. He should try and signal to someone that he needed help, that he wasn't just some fat bloke sweating on a park bench, that he was a fat bloke who was dying. The panic was screwing up his chest, wringing it hard. He could hear the terrible noises he was making as he fought to find a breath, surely someone could hear him?

This too shall pass, he thought to himself, but it didn't. He would have expected that by now he would be feeling peace and acceptance, that the oxygen deprivation would have made him ready for death, but his body was still struggling with every nerve and fiber. Whether he liked it or not he was going down fighting.

There was a dark silhouette in front of him, a person, blocking out the sunlight, and he thought it must be Laura, come to take him home. He wanted to say her name but he couldn't speak, couldn't see, couldn't breathe. She was saying something to him but the words sounded as if they were coming from underwater. She touched his arm and her fingers felt icy. He heard her say, "Can I help you?" the words booming and crashing in his ear like the surf, and part of him wanted to say, "No, I'm fine," because he didn't want to worry her, but another part, a stronger insistent part over which he had no control, was clawing at the air, trying to convey his desperation. Now he could hear voices, there were other people there and someone thrust something toward his mouth and it took him a second to realize it was an inhaler.

Then blackness. Then the ambulance, where he felt nauseous and weak, but the oxygen mask on his face was extraordinarily re-assuring. The paramedic lifted it slightly so he could speak and he asked if he'd had a heart attack and the paramedic shook his head and said, "No, I don't think so." And then he slept.

And woke in a bed in a side ward. There was an old man in the other bed, hooked up to a lot of tubes. Theo realized that he was hooked up to a lot of tubes as well. When he woke the next time the old man had gone and when he woke the time after that he was in a different ward and it was visiting time, people flooding into the ward with magazines and fruit and plastic carrier bags of clothes. Theo turned his head to follow the visitors' progress and saw a girl sitting on a chair next to his bed. He realized two things at the same time: first, it was the beggar girl with the custard-yellow hair, and second, it had been this girl who had helped him on Christ's Pieces. Not Laura.

* * *

She was there the next afternoon, perched cautiously on the edge of the chair as if she didn't trust it to hold her weight although she was as thin as a stick. She hadn't brought magazines or fruit or any of the things that the other visitors brought, but instead she pressed something into his closed hand, and when he opened it he saw a pebble, smooth and still warm from her own dry, grubby hand, so that it seemed like a curiously intimate gift. Theo wondered if she was simple. He was sure there was a more politically correct term but he couldn't remember what it was. His brain felt foggy and he supposed it was the drugs.

She wasn't inclined to talk but that was alright because neither was he. She did tell him though that her name was Lily-Rose, and he said, "That's a pretty name," and she smiled a small, shy smile and said, "Thank you, it's my own," which seemed an odd thing to say.

A nurse came by to take his temperature. She stuck the thermometer in Theo's mouth and, smiling at Lily-Rose, said, "I think your Dad'll be discharged tomorrow," and Lily-Rose said, "That's good," and Theo said nothing because he still had the thermometer in his mouth.

Jackson came in the evening and Theo was touched because he seemed genuinely concerned about him. "You're going to have to look after yourself, big man," he said, and he patted his hand and Theo felt tears prick his eyes because no one ever touched him except for probing medical fingers. And the cold touch of the yellow-haired girl. Lily-Rose. Jackson looked as if someone had beaten him up again and Theo said, "Are you okay, Jackson?" and Jackson looked pained and said, "That would very much depend on your definition of 'okay,' Theo."

*   *   *

She walked him to the taxi, holding his elbow as if she would prop him up if he fell, although she didn't look strong enough to support a lupin.

The taxi driver and a nurse helped Theo inside the taxi. The nurse held the door open for Lily-Rose. Lily-Rose's dog jumped in but jumped out again when it realized she wasn't following. Theo wanted to write down his address and telephone number for her, but he didn't have any paper. Lily-Rose said, "Here, use this," and gave him a small white card, and it was only when he'd written down his address and phone number that he turned the card over and realized it was one of Jackson's. He gave her a puzzled look and said, "You know Jackson?" and she said, "Who?" but the nurse shut the taxi door and the driver pulled away. Both the nurse and Lily-Rose stood on the pavement and waved at him. Theo waved back and thought how absurd it was that when he thought she was going to climb in the taxi with him his heart had given an extra little beat of joy.

He'd only been away for two days and yet his house had already begun to grow strange to him. His inhaler was still sitting on the hall table. The rooms smelled stale so Theo opened all the windows and thought he might buy a perfumed candle, an expensive one, not the ones that smelled of cheap vanilla and air freshener. He went upstairs to the spare bedroom, "the incident room," Jackson had called it, and saw it through the eyes of a stranger for the first time, saw how macabre and frightening it might seem.

He sat down at the computer and went online to the Stationery Store and ordered storage boxes, pretty ones that had flowers printed on them, and thought he would box up everything and label it properly and then perhaps he would ask Jackson to give him a hand putting them up in the loft. Then he went to Tesco.com and ordered groceries, but he didn't go to "My Favorites" because he knew his favorites were killers — frozen cheesecakes and ice cream, Danish pastries and full-fat yogurts, and instead he started a new list of skim milk and oatmeal, vegetables and fruit and wholemeal bread and large bottles of Evian and thought it looked like a miserable shopping list. It wasn't that Theo was feeling better or more cheerful or that he could see a positive future for himself, it was just that he kept thinking about the way he had clung onto life when it was being taken away from him, how he had fought to stay alive on Christ's Pieces. Laura hadn't been given the chance to fight but he had and maybe that meant something, although exactly what, he wasn't sure.

He was about to go to the online checkout when he thought twice about it and went into the pet-food section instead and ordered six cans of "premium dog food." Just in case. He paid and signed out and turned the computer off.

Then he waited.

16

Caroline

She hadn't told anyone yet. She was four months' gone but she wasn't showing. Good abdominal muscles. She'd had a scan and everything was "normal" — she wasn't carrying twins or an alien. The midwife was a tight-lipped, superior cow and Caroline had considered lying when it came to the "Any previous pregnancies" question but she would be easily found out so she just said, "Yes, twenty-five years ago, the baby was adopted" (which was true). She could see the midwife doing the maths in her head, twenty-five years ago "Caroline Edith Edwards" would have been twelve. The midwife raised an eyebrow and Caroline felt like saying, "Fuck off, bitch," but she didn't because that would have been Michelle speaking, not Caroline Edith Edwards.

Caroline would have liked to talk about the increased risks of having a baby at forty-three, but she could hardly say, "Actually I'm six years older than you think," could she? And anyway, this baby felt anchored in, it felt whole and healthy, it felt like it had intentions.

She tried to imagine announcing to Hannah and James that they were going to have a baby sister (or brother, but she was sure it was a girl), she could imagine their expressions of disgust and jealousy, then the sly little conspiratorial smiles as they planned the horrors they could perpetrate on it. Caroline put a protective hand on her stomach and felt the cold jelly that the midwife cow hadn't bothered to wipe off. And Jonathan — how could she tell Jonathan? "Darling, guess what, you're going to be a daddy again," and he would puff up with pride at having his seed proved good, because it wouldn't be a *baby*, a person, it would be another *thing*, like the new John Deere, or Hannah's bay gelding, a dressage pony that was much too big for her, so with any luck she'd fall off and break her neck. (She really mustn't think things like that, it might be bad for the baby.) Dressage, that was Rowena's new plan for Hannah, "Never too early to start learning *control*," she'd said over a "luncheon" that she'd invited Caroline to in "my cosy little cottage," i.e., not the bloody great house you've taken away from me. Dressage. It was so English, so anal. Jemima, needless to say, was an expert.

"You don't mind me asking you this, dear, do you?" Rowena said, leaning closer to her over the remains of a poached salmon that someone else must have cooked because Rowena could barely find the bread knife. "But, how shall I put this . . ." Her pale blue eyes were distant, almost visionary, and Caroline thought, I can't stand this. "Am I knocked up?" she intervened helpfully, and Rowena gave a little twitch of unease at Caroline's vernacular. "No, I'm not." Caroline was very, very good at lying.

"Are you sure?"

"Yes." And she watched Rowena struggle to suppress a smile of relief as she said, "Shall we take coffee in the garden?"

It was the first time she'd been to a service at St. Anne's, the first time she'd heard him preach a sermon. He looked less like himself in his starched white Sunday surplice and she wondered who made it so white and starched, was it some "lady" he paid? He didn't mention God very much, which Caroline was grateful for, and he rambled a bit, but the general tenor of the piece was that people should all be nicer to one another and Caroline thought, Fair enough, and the ten people in the congregation, including Caroline, all nodded genially at this message and when the service ended everyone shook hands, which struck Caroline as quite Quakerly. She had gone to religious services all the time when she was in prison, just because they provided a break in the routine and the chaplains were always particularly pleasant to her, which was probably because of what she'd done. The worse the crime, the more the chaplains tended to like you if you turned up in the chapel. One lost lamb and all that.

He stood at the door and shook everyone's hands again as they left and he had a kind word for everyone, of course. She made sure she was the last person to leave the church and half expected him to invite her for a cup of coffee, or even lunch, but he didn't, he just said, "It's nice to see you here, Caroline," as if she were a new convert, and she felt absurdly disappointed but she smiled and said something inconsequential before wandering off round the churchyard, hoping that maybe he would follow, but he went back inside St. Anne's.

She'd never been in love with anyone since Keith and that had just been some crazy teenage thing that, in the normal way of things, should have petered out into an indifferent divorce. It felt good to be in love again, she felt it gave her back some of the personality she'd lost. She loved the bug, of course. Tanya. But that was a different kind of love, an elemental kind. She hadn't loved her *then*, not in a way she understood anyway, it was something she'd learned *since*, in the intervening years of absence. And even though it had come to her too late it still helped to fill all those missing years. Retroactive love. It wouldn't feel like that for Tanya, of course. She didn't know about all the love her mother had for her, not unless Shirley told her ("Your Mummy loved you so much, but she just couldn't be with you"). She had made Shirley promise to treat her as if she were dead and to look after the bug. She'd loved Shirley in that elemental way too or she wouldn't have done what she did. A fresh start. That's what she'd said to Shirley, "Take Tanya away, give her a fresh start, be the mother to her that I can't be." Although obviously not as articulate as that because of the circumstances —

"I thought you had a very lovely home to go to." He looked amused. He'd removed his surplice and put on his old gray cardigan again. It was very womanish garb, a cardigan over what was basically, let's face it, a dress, and she couldn't help but idly wonder what he would look like underneath those black skirts, but was pleasantly surprised to realize that, although she would have quite liked to drop onto her knees on the grass and suck him off right then and there in the graveyard, what she really wanted to do was to look after him, do something good for him, make scrambled eggs and toast and tea, rub his back, read out loud to him from an English classic. She was definitely insane. "I'm pregnant," she said.

"Oh, congratulations. That's wonderful." He scanned her features for clues. "Isn't it?"

"Yes." She laughed. "It is wonderful. Please don't tell anyone yet."

"Oh gosh, of course not."

How could she be in love with a man who said "gosh"? Quite easily, it seemed.

She had him in her sights. She followed him along the ridge of the hill and then down to the empty lambing pens at the bottom, where he rested with his elbows on a wooden gate, his own gun crooked over his arm. He was such a cliché in his green Wellingtons and blue Barbour, the dogs running around at his feet. He referred to Meg and Bruce as "gundogs," but they were useless. He must have been out looking for rabbits. What right did he have to kill a rabbit? What made his life more valuable than a rabbit's? Who decided these things? She cocked the trigger. His head really was the perfect target. From here she could take a shot that would smash right into the back of it — bull's-eye. Like a pumpkin, or a melon or a turnip. Bang, bang. Of course, she wouldn't do it, she'd never killed anything in her life, not even an insect, not intentionally anyway. He set off again, left the field and rounded the wood and disappeared out of sight. Caroline looked at her watch — time for tea.

17

Jackson

Jackson washed down a couple of Co-codamol with a cup of foul-tasting coffee. He was waiting in the terminal for Nicola and the rest of her flight crew to disembark from their aircraft. It was seven in the morning, which seemed a particularly hellish time to be in an airport. If an unknown assassin didn't kill him he supposed his tooth would.

The plane had already emptied its bedraggled, disoriented passengers. Jackson had never been to Málaga. When they were married Josie had insisted that they take an expensive holiday every year, villa holidays, "villas with private pools" in "lovely" places, Corsica, Sardinia, Crete, Tuscany. All he could do now was conjure up a kind of generic Mediterranean memory — Marlee slippery with suntan cream and buoyant with armbands, splashing in the shallow end of the pool; Josie lying on a recliner, reading a novel, while Jackson himself lapped the pool, his body a dark shape under the blue water, like a restless, obsessive shark.

Watching Nicola was just displacement activity, trying to keep his mind off the fact that someone was trying to kill him (although, let's face it, it was quite hard to forget something like that).

And now he had Tanya to think about as well. What was it that

Shirley hadn't been telling the truth about? Walter and Doreen Fletcher, Keith's parents, moved to Lowestoft after the murder and seemed to have done a pretty poor job of parenting their only son's only child. Shirley had tried, she said, to stay in touch with her niece, but the Fletchers told her to keep away from them. "The sister of the woman who murdered their only child," she said. "You can't entirely blame them." When she was twelve, Tanya started running away from home. When she was fifteen, she stopped coming back. "I've looked for her everywhere," Shirley said, "but she seems to have slipped through the cracks."

Jackson added Tanya to the grim table of calculations that he carried in his head these days. Presuming she was alive, Tanya Fletcher would be twenty-five now. Olivia Land would be thirty-seven. Laura Wyre would be twenty-eight, Kerry-Anne Brockley, twenty-six. He hoped Tanya was living her future, that she really was twenty-five and that her days rolled by unstopped, unlike the holy girls, the Kerry-Annes, Olivias, and Lauras. And Niamh. Jackson's big sister, who would have been fifty years old this week.

The crew appeared in the terminal, wheeling their neat little flight bags behind them, going at a cracking pace across the tarmac, focused entirely on getting home, being off duty. If any passenger had intercepted them, looking for a miniature of whiskey or a second bread roll, they would probably have knocked them down and barreled right over them with their flight bags. All the flight attendants were women, no men — not that it seemed likely that Nicola would have an affair with a male flight attendant, Jackson had yet to spot a heterosexual one. The women were wearing hats that looked as if they belonged on the heads of girls from St. Trinians. Nicola was bringing up the rear with the copilot. He looked as if he was in his thirties, good-looking (in a pilot kind of way), but not much taller than Nicola. Was he touching her? The pilot — older, more gravitas than the copilot — turned and said something that made Nicola laugh. This was more promising. Jackson couldn't recall seeing her laugh before.

Jackson followed them outside the terminal and into the car park. Nicola and the pilot had parked their cars next to each other and Jackson thought that maybe this was a sign of something, but they said good-bye nonchalantly with no kissing, no touching, no meaningful looks. No hint of adultery. Nicola got in her car, revved up, and was off in her usual grand-prix style. Jackson followed at a less suicidal pace. He had a Fiat Punto rental in place of the Alfa. The Punto was an orange color that made him feel conspicuous. It was definitely a woman's car. His own car was still in the police garage, where forensics was doing more tests on it. "The police take sabotage like this very seriously, Mr. Brodie," a new DS (new to Jackson anyway) had said to him, and Jackson said, "Right." He hadn't mentioned Quintus's name, Jackson didn't see how the police were going to do much that he couldn't do himself.

He'd been round to Binky's house the previous evening to see if Quintus was there, but there'd been no answer when he rang the bell. The Lexus was gone and Jackson wondered if Quintus had taken Binky for a drive or out for dinner. Did that seem likely?

He lost Nicola within minutes and when he pulled up, a discreet distance from her front lawn, she had already changed into jeans and a sweatshirt and was aggressively cutting the front grass with a push-and-pull mower in a way that reminded Jackson of Deborah's combative attitude toward her computer keyboard. Or of Josie's combative attitude toward everything — before David Lastingham gave her the Stepford lobotomy. Nicola was still wearing the full protective camouflage of her makeup, incongruous against her casual clothes. Her body language may have been belligerent but her face was a mask.

He should have brought Theo something, flowers, fruit, a good book, but he hadn't thought and now it was too late. Theo seemed smaller in the hospital bed. Less of a mountain man and more of a little, motherless boy. Jackson wished there was a way of making him happy. He told him about going to London to see Emma, but he seemed too zoned out to be really interested, although he had asked Jackson if he was okay (which was ironic given Theo's circumstances), and Jackson said, "That would very much depend on your definition of 'okay,' Theo."

The real worry for Jackson was that he might actually find the man in the yellow golfing sweater (although it hardly seemed likely) and it wouldn't do a damn thing to help Theo's pain. In fact it would make things worse because then he would have the "closure" he was looking for. And Laura would still be dead.

Jackson made his way through the overheated corridors of the hospital, from the medical admissions ward to the pediatric ICU. He walked into the unit unchallenged; the nurse at the desk recognized him and didn't question him. He would have preferred it if she had. It shouldn't be this easy to walk into places.

Jackson observed Shirley through a glass wall that felt like a one-way mirror for all the attention anyone paid to him. Shirley was wearing blue surgical scrubs. Jackson didn't think there was anything much sexier than the sight of a woman in surgical scrubs and wondered if he was alone in thinking that or if most guys did. There should be opinion polls on these things. Shirley was standing over an ICU cot, delicately lifting a small waxy baby. It still had an array of tubes and monitors attached to its body so that it seemed like some odd, fragile creature from outer space.

"Give me a sec and I'll let her know you're here," a young male Australian nurse said to him. (Who was running Australia? They were all over here. God knows why.)

Jackson watched a doctor walk over to Shirley and touch her on the shoulder and say something to her. There was something indefinably intimate about the gesture, and from the way she turned to him and smiled Jackson instantly knew that they'd slept with each other. They both gazed down at the baby. Jackson felt even more like a voyeur than usual. The nurse who had recognized him (What was her name? Elaine? Eileen?) came and stood by his side and said, "Ah, sweet."

"Sweet?" Jackson said, wondering what could be sweet about this little tableau. A woman he'd recently spent a night of unfettered lust with cooing over a sick baby with another lover.

"Well, sad, really, I suppose," Elaine/Eileen said. "They can't have children of their own."

"They? They're *married?* Shirley Morrison and the doctor guy?"

"Doctor Welch, head of pediatrics." Elaine/Eileen frowned at him.

"They're *married?*"

"Yes, Inspector Brodie. Are you investigating Shirley?"

"It's Mr. Brodie. I left the force two years ago, Eileen."

"Elaine."

"Why would I be investigating her?"

Elaine shrugged. "The way you're interrogating me, maybe."

"Sorry."

Elaine moved closer to him, her tone more confidential. "You know, don't you, that she's the sister of —"

"Yes," Jackson interrupted her. "I know." Shirley Morrison hadn't changed her name after her sister's conviction, she hadn't changed it when she got married. He had asked her, somewhere in the druglike haze of their morning after, "You never changed your identity?" and she said, "It was the only thing I had left." Her husband moved on to inspect another alien baby and Shirley put the one she was holding back into its little spaceship cot.

The Australian nurse entered the ICU and said something to Shirley Morrison, who looked up and frowned when she saw Jackson. He shrugged at her and made a helpless face. He pointed at his own naked ring finger and then pointed at her. She raised her eyes heavenward as if she couldn't believe he was communicating in this

230 ~ KATE ATKINSON

ridiculous way. She signaled to him to go to the entrance of the unit. She opened the door a fraction, as if Jackson posed a threat.

"Why didn't you tell me you were married?" he asked her.

"Would it have made a difference?"

"Yes."

"Christ, Jackson, what are you, the last good man standing? It was just sex, get over it." She closed the door on him. He'd had a bad feeling about her, he should have gone with it. Was she a good liar or was she just good at avoiding the truth? Was there a difference? He liked to think truth was an absolute, but maybe that made him into a tight-arsed moral fascist.

On his way out of the ward, Jackson almost bumped into the yellow-haired homeless girl who was lurking in the corridor. She was muttering under her breath, as if she were saying the rosary, and Jackson wanted to say hello to her because he'd seen her around so much recently that he felt he knew her, but of course he didn't, so he said nothing and was surprised when she spoke.

"You know him, don't you?"

"Who?"

"The old fat geezer."

"Theo?" he guessed.

"Yeah, is he going to be alright?"

"He's okay," Jackson said. The girl started walking away from the ICU and Jackson said, "Visiting time isn't over, you can go in and see him, he's in medical admissions."

"No, I saw him this afternoon, I came to find someone else."

Jackson accompanied her out of the hospital. She shivered even though it was a balmy evening and lit up a cigarette and then said, "Sorry," and offered one to Jackson. He lit up and said, "You're too young to smoke," and she said, "And you're too old. And anyway I'm twenty-five, old enough for anything." Jackson thought she looked about seventeen, eighteen tops. She retrieved her dog from where it was tied to a bench outside. "Are you a friend of his?" she asked him.

"Theo? Sort of." Was he a friend of Theo's? Maybe he was. Was he a friend of Amelia and Julia? God forbid. (Was he?) And he wasn't a friend of Shirley Morrison no matter what they'd done under the cloak of darkness the other night. "Yes," he said finally, "I'm a friend of Theo's. My name's Jackson."

"Jackson," she repeated as if she were trying to lodge it in her memory. He took a handful of his cards out of his pocket — JACKSON BRODIE: PRIVATE INVESTIGATOR — and gave one to her.

"This is the bit when you tell me your name," he said, and she said, "Lily-Rose." Close-up, she didn't look so much like a druggie, more a victim of neglect and malnutrition. She seemed insubstantial enough to blow away on the wind, and Jackson wanted to take her to the nearest PizzaExpress and watch her eat. She had a little bowl of a belly like the starving African children you saw on television. Jackson wondered if she was pregnant.

"I found him," she said, "in the park. Christ's whatever."

"Pieces."

"Stupid name."

"Very stupid," Jackson agreed.

"He was having an attack."

"He said someone gave him an inhaler."

"That wasn't me," Lily-Rose said. "It was some woman. He's going to be alright?" she persisted.

"Absolutely fine," Jackson said and then realized he was talking to her as if she were Marlee's age. He couldn't believe she was twenty-five. "No, he's not really alright," Jackson said. "His daughter was murdered ten years ago and he can't get over it."

"Why should he?"

Stan Jessop taught at a different school now but lived in the same small thirties semi-detached that he had ten years ago. "Stan" made him sound like an old allotment guy, but he was only thirty-six. When Laura died Stan Jessop was only twenty-six. Twenty-six sounded incredibly young to Jackson — just a year older than Lily-Rose, two years younger than Emma Drake (he had to stop doing this). There was a well-worn Vauxhall Vectra in the driveway with a baby seat in the back, the floor littered with toys and sweet wrappers and general domestic grunge. Stan Jessop had one child, Nina, ten years ago, according to Emma Drake. Now he seemed to have a zoo of them — the front garden looked like a battleground for a war being fought with the contents of Toys "R" Us. "Kids." Stan Jessop shrugged. "What can you do?" And Jackson thought, Well, tidy up for a start, but he shrugged in return and accepted the mug of weak instant coffee that Stan made him and took a seat in the living room. The mug had drip marks down the side as if it hadn't been washed properly. Jackson put it down on the coffee table and didn't drink from it.

Emma Drake said Stan Jessop was "really cute" ten years ago, and he still had a handsome, boyish air about him. "I'm looking into some aspects of the Laura Wyre case," Jackson said, and Stan said, "Oh, yeah?" in an offhand way that didn't convince Jackson somehow.

From upstairs came the thunderous noise of small children resisting bedtime and the increasingly frustrated voice of a woman. It sounded like an old routine. "Three boys," Stan said, as if that explained everything. "It's like trying to put the barbarian hordes to bed. I should help really," he added and slumped down on the sofa. He looked like the barbarian hordes had defeated him long ago. "What about her?" he asked irritably.

"Who?"

"Laura — what about her? Is the case being reopened?"

"It was never closed, Mr. Jessop. I've been speaking to some of her friends. They think you had a crush on her."

"A crush?" Jackson thought he saw a shadow cross Stan Jessop's face. "Is that why you're here, because I had a 'crush' on Laura Wyre?"

"Did you?"

"You know" — he sighed, as if whatever it was he was about to explain wasn't really worth the effort — "when you're a young guy and you're put in that position, sometimes things can get out of hand." He grew sullen. "All those girls, intelligent, pretty girls, their hormones are off the scale, they come on to you all the time."

"You're supposed to be the grown-up."

"They're all little prick teasers, they're screwing all the time, they open their legs for anyone at that age. Don't tell me you'd act differently. If it was offered to you on a plate, what would you do?"

"I'd refuse."

"Oh, don't give me that holier-than-thou crap. At the end of the day you're just a man." (What had Shirley said, *What are you, Jackson, the last good man standing?* Was he? He hoped not.) "Put any man in that position and they'd be tempted. You would."

"I would refuse," Jackson said, "because I've got a daughter. As you do."

Stan Jessop got up from the sofa as if he were about to punch Jackson (Why not? Everyone else did), but his wife came into the room at that moment and glared at both of them suspiciously. She didn't conform to Emma Drake's description of "blond and tarty" *("common")*. She was wearing jeans and a T-shirt and had short dark hair. Emma said that she and Laura got on well together, yet no one had ever interviewed Kim Jessop. (Why not?) Jackson held out his hand and said, "How d'you do, Mrs. Jessop, my name's Jackson Brodie. I'm looking into some aspects of the death of Laura Wyre," and she looked at him blankly and said, "Who?"

From the car Jackson phoned Deborah Arnold at home and said, "Can you write a standard kind of letter to Miss Morrison and tell her that we're unable to act for her anymore?"

"Have you ever heard of office hours?"

"Have you?"

Was he being petty? Okay, so she was married, and she'd slept with him, adultery happened all the time (look at his own wife). Did that explain the bad feeling he'd had about her? Did that explain why there was something wrong with her story about Michelle? Perhaps if Tanya wanted to find Shirley she would already have done so? Jackson didn't want to help Shirley. He didn't want to *see* Shirley. He rooted around in the glove compartment for a Lee Ann Womack CD and jumped to the "Little Past Little Rock" track. Every other country song was about women leaving — leaving town, leaving the past, but mostly leaving men. After his own woman left Jackson made a compilation tape of all the women in pain, the Lucindas and Emmylous and Trishas, singing their sad songs about departing on trains and planes and buses, but mainly driving off in cars, of course. Another *hejira*.

When he got home Jackson heated up something tasteless in the microwave. It was only nine o'clock but he was dog tired. There was only one message on his answering machine; it was from Binky. He'd meant to swing by her house to check on her, but now he didn't think he had the energy. He played the message. "Mr. Brodie, Mr. Brodie, I really need to see you. It's urgent," and then nothing, not even good-bye. He phoned her back but there was no answer. The second he replaced the receiver the phone rang and he snatched it up.

It was Amelia. A hysterical Amelia. Again.

"Who's dead now, Amelia?" he asked when she paused for breath. "Because if it's anything smaller than a large horse I'd appreciate it if you took care of it yourself." Unfortunately, this response had the effect of making her twice as hysterical. Jackson cut her off, counted to ten, and then hit the "caller redial" button and watched as Binky Rain's number came up. He had a bad feeling. (Did he ever have good ones?) "What is it?" he said when Amelia answered, and she managed to calm herself long enough to say, "She's dead. The old witch is dead."

It was one in the morning when Jackson got home. He felt like he'd gone beyond sleep into some other place, a gray, foggy place where all his energy was being used to keep his autonomic nervous system ticking over and the rest of his brain and body had shut down long ago. He actually went up the stairs on his hands and knees. His bed hadn't been made since the night he'd spent with Shirley Morrison. He wasn't sure whether he'd actually slept since that night. She'd been wearing that Celtic ring on her wedding finger. It was his own fault for not asking. "Are you married?" — it would have been a straightforward enough question. Would she have lied? Probably. The woman who loved babies who couldn't have any of her own, is that why she'd slept with him, to get pregnant? God forbid. Did her husband know? The woman who loved babies who'd lost touch with the one baby above all others that she was supposed to look after. Tanya. Something scratched at the edge of his memory, but he was so tired he could hardly remember his own name.

He opened a window. There was no air in the bedroom. Heavy weather. If a thunderstorm didn't break the heat soon, people would start to go mad. The weather had broken after Olivia disappeared. Amelia reported that Sylvia had said it was "God crying for his little lost lamb." Amelia had been behaving even more oddly than usual, blethering about Olivia even though it was Binky's body she had found. Blethering. That was one of his father's words. It was nearly a year now since the old man had died. Lonely and alone in his hospital bed. He was seventy-five and had everything possible, silicosis, emphysema, cirrhosis of the liver. Jackson didn't want to become the man his father had been.

What had Binky wanted to tell him? He was never going to find out now, was he? He thought of Binky's small featherweight body lying in the remains of her orchard, the long grass damp with dew, although not the grass beneath her body, which had remained as dry as her old bones. "She's been lying here for hours," the pathologist said, and Jackson felt his heart lurch. He had driven by her house. Maybe he could have helped her. He should have broken in, he should have climbed the wall. He should have helped her.

He was about to close the curtains when something caught his eye. Walking along the wall on the other side of the lane, weaving its way in and out of the hollyhocks that grew like weeds. A black cat. If Binky Rain were reincarnated, would she come back as a cat? A black one? How many black cats were there in Cambridge? Hundreds. Jackson opened the window wider and leaned out and shouted, "Mrs. Chippy?" into the warm night air.

The cat stopped in its tracks and looked around. Jackson ran down the stairs and out of the house and then slowed himself down to a cartoon kind of tiptoe so that he wouldn't frighten the animal. "Mrs. Chippy?" he whispered again, and the cat meowed and jumped off the wall. Jackson picked it up and felt its skinny weight in his arms. He experienced an odd sense of comradeship with the bedraggled animal and said, "It's okay, old boy, do you want to come in my house?" He didn't have any cat food in the house — he didn't have any food in the house — but he had some milk. He was surprised by an unexpected surge of affection for the cat. Of course, it probably wasn't Mrs. Chippy. The cat would probably have responded to anything, but the coincidence seemed too much for Jackson in his exhausted state. He turned to go back into the house. And the house exploded. Just like that.

What was it Hank Williams had sung? Something about never getting out of this world alive?

18

Amelia

Amelia was the only one who had seen that there were more of them. Julia was too busy flirting — *Mr. Brodie this, Mr. Brodie that,* and Jackson was too busy looking at Julia's breasts. Of course, it was difficult for a man not to look at Julia's breasts when they were on display like that. She had actually licked her lips when she'd suggested swimming naked to him! They had swum in the river when they were children, even though Rosemary always told them not to. Julia was the best swimmer out of the three of them. The four of them. Could Olivia swim? Amelia thought she could see Olivia's little frog body, in a blue shirred swimming costume, moving through the water, but she didn't know whether it was a real memory or not. Sometimes Amelia felt as if she had spent her whole life waiting for Olivia to come back, while Sylvia was talking to God and Julia was *fucking.* And she felt so unbearably sad when she thought of all the things Olivia had never done, never ridden a bike or climbed a tree or read a book on her own, she'd never been to school, or a theater or a concert. Never listened to Mozart or fallen in love. She had never even written her own name. Olivia would have lived her life; Amelia had merely endured hers.

You're looking at my tits, Mr. Brodie. Julia was such a tart some-

2 3 8   *KATE ATKINSON*

times. Amelia could remember Victor once, hauling a teenage Julia back into the house when she was trying to sneak out to see some boy and yelling at her that she looked like "a common tart." (How many men had Julia slept with? Too many to keep count of undoubtedly.) Victor made her scrub her makeup off with a nailbrush. Sometimes he ignored them for days, only coming out of his study for meals. Other times he was on their case continually like some kind of religious patriarch.

After Rosemary died Victor employed a woman to cook and clean every day. She was called Mrs. Gordon and no one ever knew her first name. It was typical of Victor to employ someone who didn't like children and was a terrible cook. Sometimes Mrs. Gordon would make them the same tea every day for days on end — burned sausages, baked beans, and watery boiled potatoes were a particular favorite with her. Victor never seemed to notice. "Food is just fuel," he used to say. "It doesn't matter what it is." What an appalling childhood they'd had.

And really Jackson had been the last person she had wanted to see. Why was he sitting on the riverbank? Why him of all people? It wasn't fair. (Nothing was fair.) The gods were *taunting* her with him. She hadn't wanted to go to Grantchester, not at all, it was Julia who had persuaded her to go punting on the river, coaxing her as if she were a frail invalid or an agoraphobic. "Come on, Milly, you can't sit moping in front of the television all day." She wasn't moping. She was *depressed,* for God's sake. And she could be depressed if she wanted to be, she could sit and watch *Dogs with Jobs* on the National Geographic Channel and eat her way through a packet of chocolate bourbon biscuits if she felt like it because nobody cared about her. In fact, she could sit there all day, from *Barney and Friends* to *Porn Babes Laid Bare,* with hours of the Landscape Channel in between, and eat the contents of an entire biscuit factory until she was an obese, earthbound balloon whose dead and bloated body would have to be hydraulically lifted from the house by a fire crew *because nobody cared.* "I care, Milly." Yeah, right, as the slaters would say.

If Julia cared so much she wouldn't flirt with Jackson in front of her. She imagined them in the water together, Julia swimming like an otter around Jackson's naked body, her red lips closing around his — no! Don't think that, don't think that, don't think that.

One evening Amelia found the God Channel between Discovery Health and the Fashion Channel and discovered that there was a program called *A Word from God* that went on at midnight and she had actually watched it! To see if God had anything to say to her. But he didn't. Obviously.

Milly, do you want honey on your scones? And now she was talking about Rupert Brooke being naked. Couldn't she just shut up about naked people? Because actually it was quite nice being here, sitting in a deck chair in the orchard, soaking in the warmth of summer — why couldn't she be here on her own with Jackson, without Julia, why couldn't *he* be pouring her tea and buttering her scones, why did Julia have to be here with her breasts almost popping out of her bra when she leaned over him, *drooling* honey onto his scones. And it was such a pretty bra, all white and lacy. Why had Amelia never had underwear like that? It wasn't fair.

She had made an utter fool of herself the other night *("Are you married, Mr. Brodie?")*, like some ruined girl in a sentimental Victorian novel. She could tell by the way he looked at her that he thought she was delusional. (Was she?) She was so embarrassed that she couldn't look at him. Thank goodness she was wearing sunglasses and a hat. (Did they make her look even the slightest bit mysterious and enigmatic?) And his lovely face was all beaten up (because, of course, she *had* looked at him), and she would have liked to comfort him, to take his face and hold it between her own breasts (which were just as big as Julia's, even if they didn't occupy the same horizontal plane). But that was never going to happen, was it?

✳   ✳   ✳

She had seen them though. The others. Jackson and Julia thought it was just the man who was reading *Principia Mathematica* but she had seen the others, seven or eight of them, all as equally naked as the *Principia Mathematica* man. A couple of them dived into the water, but the rest chatted to one another, reclining on the bank in various positions of repose as if they were enacting an ideal pastoral scene. Were they naturalists? Amelia had a sudden, unexpected memory of swimming in the river, her sun-warmed body moving smoothly through the cool, lucent water. She felt a sudden physical craving, like hunger. Why was she trapped in her clumsy, baggy body? Why couldn't she have the body of her childhood back? Why couldn't she have her childhood back?

Maybe they were situationists, creating their own bizarre piece of art, indifferent as to whether anyone viewed it or not. Or some kind of cult? A nudist coven? Most of them looked as if they were more than forty, and they had imperfect bodies — jodhpur thighs and drooping bottoms, gray pubic hair and moles and freckles and old operation scars and some of them were as wrinkled as a Neapolitan mastiff. They were tanned all over, so whatever it was they were doing they must be doing it frequently. And then they were gone, beyond a bend in the river, vanishing like a dream.

Amelia stomped off ahead of Julia because she was annoyed with her about everything but particularly for flirting so much with Jackson yesterday on the river. Julia ran to keep up but then they heard the chimes of an ice-cream van and Julia said, "Hark the chimes of midnight," and Amelia said, "Hardly an appropriate analogy," but Julia had responded as obediently as a Pavlovian dog to the sound and had trotted off to find ice cream.

Amelia strode on, across Christ's Pieces, past the Princess Diana Memorial Rose Garden, in whose direction she threw a contemptuous glance. What nonsense (dead or alive) the whole Princess Diana thing was. There was no memorial to Olivia anywhere on earth, neither a rose garden nor a bench, not even a headstone on an empty grave. And then, suddenly, out of the blue, Amelia was accosted by the homeless girl with the canary-colored hair. She grabbed Amelia by one arm and started pulling her back along the path and Amelia thought, I'm being mugged, how ludicrous, and tried to cry out but found she'd fallen into the voiceless state of nightmares. She struggled to look around, to see where Julia was — Julia would save her from the yellow-haired girl, Julia had always been a scrapper when they were children — but the girl was dragging her along the path as if she were a recalcitrant child. It was absurd because Amelia was at least twice the size of her captor, but the yellow-haired girl was unnervingly and uncharacteristically animated, besides which she was filthy and homeless and addicted to drugs and possibly retarded in some way and Amelia was frightened of her.

The yellow-haired girl's dog ran along beside them, jumping up and down like an excitable accomplice. If the girl would just loosen her grip on Amelia for a second she would give over her purse or her handbag, or whatever it was she wanted. The words "stand and deliver" suddenly came into Amelia's mind (the brain really did do the oddest things under stress). Highwayman girl — highwaygirl — you never heard of "highwaywomen," did you? Did they exist? Were highwaymen like pirates and robber barons — more myth than fact? What *was* a robber baron? The highwaygirl wasn't saying, "Stand and deliver." She was saying what she usually said — "Help me."

No, she wasn't. She was saying, "Help him, help him," pointing at a fat man on a bench who was wheezing the same death wheeze as Victor except that Victor had suffocated passively and the fat man on the bench was fighting the air around him, as if he could scoop up oxygen with his hands. "Help him," the yellow-haired girl said again, but Amelia stood paralyzed, staring at the dying fat man. For the life of her she couldn't think of a single thing she could do that would be of any help to him.

Fortunately for the fat man, Julia appeared at that moment, tri-umphantly bearing aloft two cones like someone (an actress per-haps) carrying flaming torches. When she saw what was happening she dropped the ice cream and ran toward the bench, pulling her Ventolin inhaler from her handbag and holding it to the fat man's gaping fish mouth. Then she produced her mobile and thrust it at Amelia, shouting, "Phone an ambulance!" as if she were back in *Casualty,* but Amelia couldn't even put out a hand to take the phone from her. "For fuck's sake, Milly," Julia snapped and gave the phone instead to the yellow-haired girl, who might be retarded and stupid and filthy and homeless and addicted to drugs, but at least, unlike Amelia, she was capable of dialing 999 and saving someone's life.

Julia scrambled eggs for their supper, and after they had eaten she phoned the hospital and reported back to Amelia, "He's alright ap-parently," and Amelia said, "Really?" and Julia said, "Don't you care?" and Amelia said, "No." Because she didn't, not really, maybe in theory but not in her heart because why should she care for someone else (how could she care for someone else) when nobody cared about her? And Julia said, "Oh, for Christ's sake, Amelia, pull yourself together" (which, everyone knew, was something you weren't supposed to say to depressed people), and Amelia ran into the back garden in tears and flung herself down on the grass and sobbed.

The ground was hard and uncomfortable beneath her body, al-though it was still warm from the day's heat, and she suddenly re-membered what it had felt like sleeping in the tent. In fact this was almost the exact spot where the tent had been pitched that fateful night. Amelia sat up and looked around. Here was where Olivia had slept. She ran her hand over the grass, as if Olivia's shape might have flattened it. Here Olivia had said, "Night-night, Milly," full of sleep and happiness, clutching Blue Mouse in her arms. Amelia had watched her fall asleep and had felt wise and grown-up and re-sponsible because she was the one who had been put in charge by Rosemary, the only one who was allowed to sleep outside in the tent. With Olivia. Was "Milly" the last word Olivia had ever said? Or were there other words before the silence — dreadful words of fear and mortal terror that Amelia could never, would never, bring herself to imagine? Her heart started beating fast at the thought of the terror Olivia must have endured. No, don't think.

Olivia was close, she was palpable. Where was she? Amelia stood up too quickly and felt dizzy as she stumbled around in the grass trying to sense a direction, as if her body were a divining rod. No, she had to stop and listen. If she listened she would hear her. And then very faintly she did hear something, a tiny mewling from the other side of the wall, a cat, not Olivia, but a sign surely. She tried opening the wooden door in the wall, tugging off the ivy that was binding it shut. She pulled hard on its rusty old hinges until she managed to squeeze through an opening and found herself in the lane.

The cat, tiny, half cat, half kitten, looked cowed when it saw her but it didn't run away, and Amelia bent down and tried to make herself smaller and friendlier (fat chance) and held out her hand to it and said, "Here, kitty, kitty. Good kitty," until it ad-vanced cautiously toward her and she was able to stroke its small, bony body. Eventually, after much cajoling, it allowed her to pick it up and she pressed her face into its fur and wondered if maybe she could keep it.

The door opposite, the one that led into Mrs. Rain's garden, was open. They used to climb over a broken-down part of the wall and hide in that garden when they were small. Amelia never thought of Mrs. Rain as still being alive. Sylvia had fallen out of her beech tree and broken her arm.

"Shall we take a little look?" Amelia whispered to the cat.

Yes, this had been an orchard. They used to steal the apples and plums. And they knocked on the door and shouted, "Is the witch at home?" and then ran away, terrified. Sylvia, Sylvia was always the ringleader, of course. Sylvia the tormentor. Sylvia had just been Sylvia then, but looking back Amelia thought what an odd, *powerful* child Sylvia was, always leading them into trouble.

It was a huge garden, out of proportion to the size of the house. The garden had been overgrown when they were children, and now it had reverted to nature. How wonderful if she could get her hands on all that untamed wilderness. She could replant the orchard, put in a wildlife pond, an arch of roses, perhaps a herbaceous border to rival Newnham's.

The sense of Olivia was even stronger in here. Amelia imagined her hiding behind a tree, like a sprite, leading her on. Amelia's feet caught on the couch grass and sticky willow, she was stung by nettles and scratched by briars, but she was being drawn onward by an invisible hand until she almost stumbled over the dark shape on the ground, a bundle of rags and twigs dropped beneath a tree —

"Frisky," Jackson said, nodding at the kitten in Amelia's arms. Amelia couldn't let go of the kitten. A policewoman had walked Amelia home and made her a cup of tea. (Why was it always the women? Still?) There were a lot of police in Victor's kitchen — they seemed to be using it as a makeshift command center (Was that the word?). Woken by the commotion, a sleepy Julia wandered into the kitchen and looked astonished. She was half naked, of course, wearing just her knickers and a T-shirt and completely unbothered by the fact. *Oh, Mr. Brodie, we can't keep meeting like this.*

When Amelia had touched old Mrs. Rain's dead body she had felt as fragile and bony as the cat in her arms. The police had put a little marquee over her body and had erected arc lights and you wouldn't do that for an old woman that died of natural causes, which meant that Amelia had not just discovered a dead body, she had discovered a murdered body. A shiver spasmed her body and woke the cat. It jumped out of her arms and Julia went into full *Kitty, kitty, kitty* mode, picking it up and holding it against her obvious breasts, and Amelia said, "For God's sake, Julia, put some clothes on," and Julia made a face at her and sauntered out of the kitchen, the cat still in her arms, while all the policemen watched her bottom. Thank God she wasn't wearing a thong — which was surely the most ridiculous piece of underwear ever invented, apart from crotchless knickers, of course, because it was all about sex —

"Amelia, do you want more tea?" Jackson was regarding her with concern, as if she were a mental patient.

It was almost morning and they had only just gone to bed. She could still hear the police, cars departing and arriving, the sound of their radios. At least Sylvia's room was at the front of the house, away from the arc lights. She didn't even have the cat now because it had followed Julia to her room. She was never going to sleep, not unless she took something. Julia kept her sleeping tablets in the bathroom. Julia always had prescription drugs of one kind or another, it was part of the drama of her life. Amelia couldn't read the bottle without her glasses, but then what did it matter? Did two send you to sleep, four into a deeper sleep? How about ten, where would they send you? They were so tiny! Like children's pills. Rosemary used to give them a junior aspirin every day, even when there was nothing wrong with them. That must be where Julia got it from. Rosemary had always had a medicine chest of drugs, even before she was dying. How about twenty? That would be a long sleep. Nothing had saved Rosemary, of course, but then nothing would save any of them, would it? Thirty? What if they just made you groggy? Jackson thought she was ridiculous and she was never going to find Olivia and now Julia had a cat and nothing was fair. No one wanted her, even her own father didn't find her attractive enough to want her. Not fair. Not one little bit. Not fair, not fair, not fair. The whole bottle? Because it wasn't fair. Not fair, not fair, not fair. Can you help me? No.

Notfairnotfairnotfairnotfairnotfairnotfairnotfairnotfairnotfairnot fairnotfairnotfairnotfairnotfairnotfairnotfairnotfairnotfairnotfair —

"Milly, are you alright? Milly? Milly?"

19

Jackson

You forgot it was colder up north. Britain was such a small country you wouldn't think you'd notice a climate change over a couple hundred miles. It was still warm enough to sit in the beer garden though, warm enough for northerners anyway. Jackson got the drinks in. They were at an old coaching inn, in the middle of nowhere in Northumberland. There was a lot of nowhere in Northumberland. Jackson wondered about buying a cottage there. It would be cheaper than Cambridge, where he no longer had a home. His house was still standing but he had lost more or less everything in it — clothes and CDs and books, all of Theo's files on Laura — if not to the explosion then to the water in the fire hoses. Well, it was one way of getting a fresh start, a new life: just blow up the old one.

"Gas?" he'd said hopefully to the fire investigation officer.

"Dynamite," the fire officer said. (A short, manly kind of exchange.) Who had access to dynamite? People who worked in mines, obviously. Jackson fished in his wallet for DC Lowther's card and phoned him. "The plot thickens," he said, and wished he hadn't said that because it sounded like something from a bad detective novel. "I think we have a suspect." That didn't sound much better. "My house has just exploded, by the way." At least that was novel.

("Quintus Rain," DC Lowther ruminated, "what kind of a name is that?"

"A bloody stupid one," Jackson said.)

He carried the drinks outside, an orange juice for himself, a Coke for Marlee, and a gin and tonic for Kim Jessop, except she was called Kim Strachan now because at some point in the last ten years she had married and then divorced a "mad Scottish head case" called George Strachan. Now she owned a bar in Sitges and a restaurant in Barcelona and was partnered up with a Russian "businessman." She was still blond and sported the deep leathery tan of someone who thought skin cancer happened to other people, although, judging by her smoker's cough, it was going to be a race with lung cancer. As befitted a mafia mistress, she was wearing enough gold to furnish an Indian wedding. She hadn't lost any of the Geordie in her — Kim Strachan, née Jessop, didn't have a single drop of soft southern DNA in her body. Jackson warmed to her immediately.

"It was lucky you got hold of me," she said, taking a deep drag on a Marlboro. "I'm only in the country for a couple of weeks, seeing Mum, she's bad on her legs these days, I'm trying to persuade her to move out to Spain."

Stan Jessop had reluctantly given Jackson his first wife's mobile number, complaining sullenly that he hardly ever saw his daughter, Nina, because "the bitch" had put her in a Quaker boarding school in York, and Jackson thought to himself that a Quaker boarding school in York sounded pretty accessible compared to a school of any denomination in New Zealand.

Kim Strachan and her family were taking a "farmhouse holiday" somewhere in the vicinity. "A sheep farm," she said. "Bloody noisy things, sheep. The silence of the lambs, my arse." Her "family" seemed to include not only Nina and the mother who was bad on her legs but also "Vladimir" and any number of Vladimir's "associates," one of whom was driving Kim and was currently sipping a Fanta two tables away and scrutinizing every passerby as if he or she might be a potential assassin. "Oh, he's a teddy bear, really." Kim laughed. She'd come a long way since her days in the little thirties semi she had once shared with Stan Jessop.

It turned out that Kim had left Stan the week before Laura Wyre's murder. She had already "taken up" with George Strachan and was behind the bar of a British expatriate pub in Alicante when Laura was killed. Kim had never returned to Cambridge, hadn't even spoken to Stan for two years after she left, "because he was such a bloody wanker," so that when Jackson phoned her and said he was "investigating certain aspects of Laura Wyre's death," she said, "Jesus. Laura Wyre's dead? How?" Jackson felt his heart sink because talking about a girl who was ten years' dead was a very different thing to breaking fresh news of that death. "She's only twenty-eight," Kim said.

Jackson sighed, thinking, No, she was only eighteen, and said, "Actually she died ten years ago. I'm afraid she was murdered." There was a silence at the other end of the phone, disturbed only by a surly rumble of Russian in the background. Jackson remembered Emma Drake saying that it was worse hearing about Laura's death when "it was already consigned to history for everyone else." It seemed like the whole world had been out of the country when Laura died.

"Murdered?"

"I'm really, really sorry," Kim said, fishing the slice of lemon out of her gin and putting it in the ashtray.

"Her killer was never found," Jackson said. "Laura might not even have been the intended victim." Jackson cast a doubtful glimpse at Marlee. He probably sounded like he was talking about an episode of *Law and Order* or *CSI* rather than real life. He hoped he did, he hoped she didn't actually watch *Law and Order* and *CSI,* he hoped she watched *Blue Peter* and reruns of *Little House on the Prairie*. He had told Marlee about Laura, that she had been killed by a "bad person" because "sometimes bad things happened to good people," and Marlee frowned and said, "Theo said she was called Jennifer," and Jackson said, "That's his other daughter." How did Jennifer feel, always being the other daughter, the one that got less attention than a dead sister?

"Laura was a nice girl," Kim Strachan said. "She was stuck-up when I first met her, but she was just middle class, you know. You can't hold that against a person, can you? Aye, well, you can, but not Laura. She had a good heart."

"I'm just following up on a few things, people who weren't interviewed at the time," Jackson said. "I'm working for her father."

"Fat bloke?"

"Yeah, fat bloke."

"Theo," Marlee said. "He's nice."

"Yes, he is," Jackson said. He looked at Marlee and said, "Do you want to go and get yourself a packet of crisps, sweetheart?" He reached into his pocket for change but Kim Strachan had already opened her purse and produced a new five-pound note that she gave to Marlee, saying, "Here you go, pet, get what you want. Bloody stupid Brits," she added to Jackson. "Why can't they just get with the euro? Every other bloody country in Europe's managed it."

Kim Strachan lit another cigarette, shaking one out for Jackson, and when he refused she said, "For God's sake, you're gagging for one, man, I can tell."

Jackson took a cigarette. "I was off them for fifteen years," he said.

"What started you again?"

Jackson shrugged. "An anniversary."

"Must have been a big one," Kim Strachan said.

Jackson laughed humorlessly. "No, it wasn't. A thirty-third, that's not a significant one, is it? Thirty-three years since my sister died."

"I'm sorry."

"I think it was just one too many. She would have been fifty this year. This week. Tomorrow."

"There you go, then," Kim Strachan said, as if that explained everything. She lit his cigarette with a heavy gold lighter that had something in Cyrillic engraved on it.

"Don't tell me," Jackson said. "From Russia with love."

Kim Strachan laughed and said, "Much filthier than that."

"You wouldn't have any idea who might have wanted to kill Laura, would you?" Jackson asked her. "Any idea, however unlikely."

"Like I said, she was a nice middle-class girl. They don't usually have many enemies."

Jackson produced the photograph of the yellow golfing jumper and held it out to her. She took it from him and studied it carefully. Then her face sort of fell apart. "Jesus Christ," she said.

"You recognize it?" Jackson asked.

Kim downed the rest of her gin and took a long drag on her cigarette before stubbing it out. She had tears in her eyes but her voice was raw with anger. "I should have known," she said. "I should have fucking known it would be him."

They drove to Bamburgh and he took Marlee for a long walk on the beach. He kept his shoes and socks on (like an old man, like his father), but Marlee rolled up her gingham pedal pushers and ran in and out of the waves. They didn't bother going to look round the castle, even though he thought it had some kind of Harry Potter link that Marlee had been excited about initially. Jackson tended to close his ears to her incessant Harry Potter chatter (he had a wizard-free childhood himself and failed to see the attraction), in the same way he closed his ears to Christina and Justin and the cloned pubescent boy bands that she had brought with her and insisted on alternating with his own CDs.

She was more interested in playing with the mobile phone he'd bought for her. It was a kind of Barbie pink and she spent her whole time texting her friends. He couldn't imagine what they said to each other. Instead of going in the castle, they ate vinegary fish-and-chips in front seats of the car, looking at the sea (like pensioners), and Marlee said, "This is nice, Daddy," and Jackson said, "Isn't it just?"

He was supposed to have taken Marlee for the last two weeks of the school holiday, but Josie had phoned him and said, "Look, we've been offered this *gite* in the Ardèche for a week by friends of David, and we thought it would be nice if just the two of us went."

"So you can fuck each other without your child being present?" Jackson asked and Josie put the phone down on him. It took them another two phone calls before they managed a semicivilized exchange on the subject. Of course, David would have "friends who had a *gite* in the Ardèche," wouldn't he? He was sure it wasn't coincidence that "git" and *"gite"* were almost the same word.

Jackson shook their chip papers out for the gulls, instantly recreating a scene from *The Birds,* and then drove away as quickly as possible before the Punto got covered in gull shit.

"Are we going home now?" Marlee was eating a Cornetto that was melting faster than she could eat it. It dripped on the upholstery of the Punto. There was something to be said for hired cars after all.

"Daddy?"

"What?"

"I said are we going home now?"

"Yes. No."

"Which, Daddy?"

Jackson found them a ropy-looking B and B, which nonetheless seemed to be the best one available in his old hometown. It had a red neon VACANCIES sign in the window that made him feel he was checking into a brothel. The drive had taken longer than he expected and had brought them through a series of depressing post-industrial wastelands that made Cambridge seem positively paradisial in comparison. "Never forget this is what Margaret Thatcher did to your birthright," Jackson said to Marlee, and she said, "Okay, I won't," and popped the top on a tube of Smarties. Kim Strachan's five-pound note had been fully utilized in the last Shell Shop they visited.

The B and B was run by a sharp-faced woman called Mrs. Brind who looked dubiously at Marlee before glaring at Jackson and informing him that she had "no twins left, only doubles." Jackson half expected her to call the vice squad the minute he was inside the gloomy room, with its years of nicotine impregnated into the wallpaper and curtains. It was like smoking-aversion therapy. He would give up smoking, he would give up tomorrow. Or the next day.

The next morning Mrs. Brind scrutinized Marlee for signs of distress or abuse, but she cheerfully scrunched her way through a bowl of Frosties, a cereal outlawed in David Lastingham's muesli-inclined household. Marlee followed the Frosties with a slippery fried egg that was served up with a stiff strip of streaky bacon and a single obscene-looking sausage. Jackson imagined getting up in the morning in France, wandering down to a village bakery for a warm baguette, making one of those little espresso pots of freshly ground coffee. For now he had to make do with a cup of acrid instant coffee and a couple of Nurofen because he'd run out of Co-codamol. He wasn't really sure what hurt anymore, whether it was his tooth, his head, the punch David Lastingham had surprisingly landed on him. It was just pain, generic pain. "You shouldn't take those on an empty stomach," Mrs. Brind said to him unexpectedly and pushed a plate of toast in front of him.

It was raining when they got back in the Punto and drove across town. Jackson noticed a leaden feeling growing in his bowels that owed nothing to the miserable weather or the cheap, acidic coffee.

"Okay, sweetheart?"

"Yes, Daddy."

He pulled up on a garage forecourt and filled up the Punto, breathing in the comforting smell of petrol. There were buckets of flowers arranged outside the shop, but there wasn't much in the way of choice. There were big pink daisies that looked artificial, some brightly colored dahlias, and lots of carnations. He recalled the heartfelt testimonial of one of Theo's divorce clients. *He buys me carnations, carnations are crap, every woman knows that, so why doesn't he?* Jackson beckoned Marlee out of the car and asked her to choose, and without any hesitation she picked the dahlias. Dahlias always reminded Jackson of the allotments where his father had spent most of his spare time. Jackson's mother used to say that his shed was kitted out better than their house. They'd passed the allotments a couple of streets back and if they took the next left at the crossroads they would come to the street where Jackson lived between the ages of nine and sixteen, but they didn't take a left and Jackson didn't mention it to Marlee.

Jackson hadn't visited the cemetery for ten years, but he knew exactly where to go, there was a map that had been burned into his memory a long time ago. There had been a time when he came here nearly every day, long ago when the dead were the only people who loved him. "This is where my mother's buried," he said to Marlee. "My grandma?" she checked, and he said, "Yes, your grandma." She stood respectfully in front of a headstone that looked more weather-beaten than it should have been after thirty-three years and he wondered if his father had ordered a cheap sandstone for his wife's memorial. Jackson didn't feel much when he looked at it. He found it hard to conjure up many memories of his mother. They walked on and Marlee worried that he hadn't left the flowers on his mother's grave and Jackson said, "They're not for her, sweetheart."

20

Holy Girls

Jackson never thought much about anything before his mother started to die. He was just a boy, he did things boys did. He was in a gang that had a den in a disused warehouse, they played on the banks of the canal, they pilfered sweets from Woolworth's, they cycled out to the country and swung on branches across the river and rolled down hills, they bribed older boys to buy them cigarettes and they smoked and drank themselves sick on cider in their den or in the town cemetery, to which they gained entry at night via a hole in the wall that only they and a pack of feral dogs knew about. He did things his mother (and probably his father) would have been horrified by, but when he looked back on it in later life it seemed a healthy, harmless sort of boyhood.

He was the baby of the family. His sister, Niamh, was seventeen and his brother, Francis, was eighteen and had just finished serving his time as an apprentice welder with the Coal Board. His father always told both his sons not to follow him down the pit, but it was hard to get away from mining when it was the only industry in town. Jackson never considered the future but he thought being a miner looked okay, the comradeship, the drinking — like being in a grown-up gang really, but his father said it was a job that you wouldn't make a dog do, and this was a man who hated dogs. Everyone voted Labour, men and women, but they weren't socialists. They "craved the fruits of capitalism" more than anyone, that's what his father said. His father was a socialist, the bitter, chip-on-the-shoulder Scottish kind that attributed everything that had gone wrong with his life to someone else but particularly "capitalist bosses."

Jackson had no idea what capitalism was and no desire to know. Francis said it was driving a Ford Consul and buying a Servis twin tub for his mother and Jackson was the only person who knew that when Francis had become part of the first generation of eighteen-year-olds to vote last year he had put his cross next to the name of the Tory candidate even though "he hadn't a fart in hell's chance" of winning. Their father would have disowned Francis (possibly killed him) because the Tories wanted to wipe the miners off the face of the earth, and Francis said who gives a fuck because he planned to save enough money to drive a Cadillac across the States, only pausing to pay his respects at the gates of Graceland and otherwise not stopping until he hit the Pacific Highway. Their mother died the week after the election, so politics weren't on anyone's mind for a while, although their father tried hard to find a way of blaming the government for the cancer that ate Fidelma up and then spat her out as a shriveled, yellowed husk to die on a morphine drip in a side ward of the Wakefield General.

Their father was a good-looking man but their mother was a big plain woman who always seemed to have just come in from milking the cows or cutting peat. Their father said, "You can take the woman out of Mayo, but you can't take Mayo out of the woman." He said it as a joke but no one ever thought it was funny. He never bought his wife flowers or took her out for a meal, but then no one else did that for their wives either, and if Fidelma felt badly done by it was no more than any other woman she knew. Niamh expected something different from her life. She left school at fifteen and went to college, where she did shorthand and typing and left with her RSA certificates and a box of Dairy Milk from her teacher for being top of her class. Now she caught the bus every day to Wakefield, where she had a job as "personal secretary" to the manager of a car dealership. She gave a third of her six pounds a week to her mother, a third went into a savings account, and the remainder she spent on clothes. She liked clothes that made her look the role, pencil skirts and angora cardigans, lambswool twinsets and pleated skirts, all worn with fifteen deniers and black court shoes with a three-inch heel, so that she looked strangely old-fashioned even when she was sixteen. To complete her look she wore her hair up in a neat plait and bought a string of fake pearls with matching earrings. For winter, she invested in a good herringbone tweed coat with a buttoned half belt, and when summer came she bought a belted mac in a thick cream gabardine that her father said made her look like a French film star. Jackson had never seen a French film, so he didn't know if this was true. Luckily for Niamh she had inherited none of her mother's peasant genes and was, everyone agreed, "a lovely girl" in all ways.

She took Fidelma's death worse than anyone. It wasn't so much her death, it was the time she took dying, so that when their mother did finally expire her last, sickly breath, it was welcomed by everyone. By that time Niamh was already doing all the cooking and cleaning as well as going to Wakefield every day in her nice clothes, and one day, a few weeks before their mother died, she had come into the room that Jackson shared with Francis — Francis was out on the town, as usual — and she sat down on the old, small single bed that there wasn't really room for and said, "Jackson, I can't do this." Jackson was reading a *Commando* comic and wondering if Francis had any cigarettes hidden anywhere and didn't know what to make of his sister's trembling mouth and her big dark eyes brimming with tears. "You have to help me," she said. "Promise me?" And he said, "Okay," without having any idea

what he was signing up to. And that was how he found himself
spending all his spare time vacuuming and dusting, peeling potatoes, hauling in coal and hanging up sheets and going down to the
Co-op all the time so that his friends laughed their heads off at
him and said he'd turned into a girl. They were already at the secondary school by then and Jackson knew life was changing and if
he had to choose between his sister and a gang of morons it had to
be his sister, even if he'd rather be with the morons, because no
matter how you felt, blood always came first, and that wasn't even
something you learned, it was just something that was. And anyway she paid him ten bob a week.

It was just a normal day. It was January, a few months after Fidelma
died and a week after Jackson's twelfth birthday. Francis bought
him a secondhand bike and restored it so that it looked better than
new. His father gave him five quid and Niamh bought him a
watch, a grown-up watch with an expanding bracelet that hung
heavily on his wrist. They were all good presents and he supposed
they were trying to make up to him for not having a mother.

Their father was on a night shift and came home as they were all
having their make-do breakfasts before rushing off into their day.
At that time of year it was dark when they left the house and it was
dark when they came home and that day seemed darker than ever
because of the rain, a cold, wet, winter rain that made you want to
cry. Francis was hungover from the night before and in a foul mood,
but he gave Niamh a lift to her bus stop. Niamh kissed Jackson
good-bye, even though he tried to duck out of it. Fidelma used to
kiss him as he went off to school and now Niamh had taken over.
Jackson wished she wouldn't because she always left the mark of
her lipstick on his cheek and the other boys laughed at him if he
didn't manage to wipe it all away.

Jackson cycled to school on his brand-new bike and was so wet when he arrived that he left puddles of water all the way along the corridor leading to his classroom.

Jackson came home from school and shoved a wash into the Servis twin tub that their mother hadn't lived long enough to appreciate, then he peeled potatoes and chopped onions and took out the soft, dead-smelling packet of mince from the fridge where Francis kept his fishing maggots in a Tupperware container, now that his mother wasn't there to stop him. Jackson wouldn't have minded cooking so much if it had got him out of homework, but Niamh stood over him every night and watched him, slapping him round the ear when he got anything wrong.

Once the mince and potatoes were on he crept upstairs to his room. His father was still in bed and he didn't want to wake him for all kinds of reasons but mainly because he wanted to sneak one of Francis's fags from a cache he'd discovered in his wardrobe. He had to open the window to smoke so Francis wouldn't smell it when he came in, and the wind blew the rain onto his face, freezing him half to death and making the cigarette too soggy to smoke. He put it under his pillow and hoped it would dry out overnight.

If Francis was home before Niamh and it was bad weather, he would usually drive to the bus stop and pick her up, but today, despite the relentless rain, he collapsed in the chair by the fire, still in his overalls, and lit a cigarette. He smelled of metal and coal and he looked liverish and even more irritable than he had this morning. It must have been some bender he was on the night before, and Jackson said to him, "You shouldn't drink so much," and Francis said, "When did you turn into a fucking woman, Jackson?"

"She must have missed the bus," their father said. The plates were on the table and there was a momentary hesitation about whether they should start without her, but Jackson said, "I'll put her plate in the oven." Of course, Niamh never missed the bus, but as their father said, "There's always a first time," and Francis said, "She's grown-up. She can do what the fuck she likes." Francis swore a lot more now that Fidelma was dead.

Her mince and potatoes were all dried up now. Jackson took her plate out of the oven and put it at her place at the table as if that might make her hurry up. Their father had gone to work, he had been on the night shift since Fidelma died. Niamh said it was because he didn't want to sleep alone, and Francis said, "He still sleeps alone," and Niamh said, "It's different sleeping alone in the daytime to sleeping alone at night." Francis had gone to meet the next bus. "She's probably gone out for a drink with her friends," he said to Jackson, and Jackson said, "Yeah, probably," even though Niamh only ever went out on Fridays and Saturdays. When Francis came back he got soaked to the bone just running from the car to the house. It was only half past seven and they both felt stupid for feeling worried. They watched *Coronation Street,* which both of them hated, so that they could tell Niamh what had happened when she came in.

At ten o'clock, Francis said he was going "to drive around a bit" and see if he could spot her, as if she might be wandering around the streets in a downpour. Jackson went with him, he didn't think he could sit and wait any longer without going mad. They ended up back at the bus stop, waiting for the last bus. Francis gave Jackson a cigarette and lit it with his new lighter, which was a present from a girlfriend. Francis had lots of girlfriends. When the bus came into view, its bright yellow lights shining through the rain, Jackson was absolutely sure she would be on it, he didn't doubt the fact for a second, and when she wasn't, he jumped out of the car and ran after the bus because he thought she must have fallen asleep and missed her stop. He walked back to the car, shoulders hunched uselessly against the rain. He could see the windshield wipers of Francis's Ford Consul moving relentlessly back and forth against the curtain of rain and Francis's face pale behind the glass.

"Best go to the police," Francis said when Jackson climbed back in.

Forty-eight hours later they took her body out of the canal. She was still wearing her skirt, knee-length green bouclé that she'd bought with the Christmas money her father had given her. Her umbrella was found near the bus stop. Her shoes, and some of her clothes, including her good herringbone tweed coat, were found on the bank of the canal, and her handbag was found a week later by the side of the A636. Her blouse was never found, nor was the little gold crucifix that her mother had bought her for her first confirmation. The police thought the chain must have broken and perhaps her killer had taken it as a "souvenir." The only souvenir Jackson had was a little pottery wishing well that Niamh had brought back for him from a trip to Scarborough two years ago. It had WISHING YOU WELL FROM SCARBOROUGH painted on the side.

What was known was that Niamh had caught her bus home from work as she did every day, and she had got off the bus at her usual stop, and then somewhere along the ten-minute walk from the bus stop to her front door someone must have persuaded (or forced) her into a car and taken her down to the canal, where they had raped her and strangled her, although not necessarily in that order. Jackson moved into her room that night and didn't move out of it until he left home to join the army. He didn't change the sheets on her bed for two months. Even then he was sure he could still smell the old-fashioned violet cologne that she liked to sprinkle on her sheets when she ironed them. For a long time he kept the teacup she had drunk from at breakfast that last day. She was always complaining that no one washed the pots after breakfast. The cup still carried the pink lipstick outline of her mouth, like the ghost of a kiss, and Jackson treasured it for weeks until one morning Francis caught sight of it and threw it out the window onto the concrete of the backyard. Jackson knew that Francis felt guilty that he hadn't picked her up from the bus stop that night. Some dark part of Jackson felt that he was right to feel guilty. After all, if he had picked her up she wouldn't now be under six feet of heavy, wet soil. She would be warm and living flesh, she would be complaining that no one did the washing up, she would be going off to work in the miserable winter mornings and her pink mouth would still be talking and laughing and eating, and kissing Jackson's reluctant cheek.

One day, six months after the funeral, Francis gave Jackson a lift to school. It was raining, a summer monsoon downpour, and Francis said, "Hop in, our kid." He parked the car at the school gates and took a pack of cigarettes out of the glove compartment and handed the whole pack to Jackson. Jackson said a surprised, "Thanks," and opened the car door, but Francis pulled him back and gave him a rough punch on the shoulder that made him yell with pain and then Francis said, "I should have picked her up, you know that, don't you?" and Jackson said, "Yes," which in retrospect was the wrong answer. "You know I love you, tyke, don't you?" Francis said and Jackson said, "Yes," embarrassed for Francis, who never used words like "love." Then Jackson scrambled out of the car because he was late and he could hear the bell ringing. In the middle of the most boring maths lesson that had ever been taught in the history of the school, Jackson remembered it was Niamh's nineteenth birthday, and he was so shocked at the realization that he leaped up from his desk. The maths teacher said, "Where are you going, Brodie?" and

Jackson sat down and muttered, "Nowhere, sir," because she was dead and she was never coming back and she was never going to be nineteen. Ever.

When he came home from school and walked in the house it felt as if there were something missing, but it was only after he'd changed out of his school uniform and made himself a sandwich that he went into the living room to watch television, and that was where he found Francis's body hanging from the fake chandelier light fitting that had once been Fidelma's pride and joy.

His sister's killer was never found.

21

Jackson

They stopped in at the Catholic church and Jackson lit two candles, one each for his brother and sister. Marlee asked to light one for Fidelma. *Passio Christi, conforta me.* Both Fidelma's sisters were now dead of cancer — Jackson prayed that Marlee had missed that particular gene. Jackson's father was an only child, so Marlee was the only blood relative that Jackson had in the world now that his father was dead. It seemed unlikely that Jackson would have more children. This was it — one girl in pink jeans and a T-shirt that was emblazoned with the message, SO MANY BOYS, SO LITTLE TIME. Did the people who designed these T-shirts, did the people who *made* these T-shirts in size "8–10 yrs" ever stop to think that what they were doing might actually be immoral? Of course the people who made the T-shirts were probably themselves "8–10 yrs" in a sweatshop in the Philippines somewhere.

"Daddy?"

"Yep?"

"Can we light a candle for my hamster?"

"You should get a T-shirt," Jackson said. "So many hamsters, so little time."

"Not funny. Now are we going home?"

"No. We're going to take a quick detour. I have to go and see a woman called Marian Foster."

"Why?"

"Just because."

They were on the bypass when Jackson realized something was wrong. The swiftness of the feeling took him by surprise, one minute he felt okay — cracked, bruised, sore, and aching but okay — the next minute he felt himself spiking an incredible temperature and only a few seconds later he was seeing the world very much how he imagined a fly would see it and the next he was slipping into unconsciousness. Every last bit of his remaining energy was concentrated on bringing the car to a stop on the hard shoulder, after that — nothing.

The next thing he was waking up in a hospital and looking into Howell's eyes.

"Why are you here?" Jackson noticed that he seemed to be using someone else's voice.

"I'm your next of kin, apparently."

"Oh, yeah," Jackson said weakly. "Josie didn't want the job anymore."

"You never used to be the kind of guy that carried an organ-donor card."

"Well, I guess I'm that kind of guy now." Jackson struggled to sit up. "Someone's trying to kill me, Howell."

Howell seemed to think this was incredibly funny. When he stopped laughing he said, "Don't be so paranoid, Jackson. You've got blood poisoning. Apparently you had a tooth you were supposed to get seen to."

Jackson panicked suddenly. What was he thinking? "Where is she, where's Marlee? Is she okay?"

"She's fine. Keep your hair on your chest."

"But where *is* she, Howell?"

"On a sheep farm," Howell said.

Jackson didn't know why Marlee had given the police Kim Strachan's number — he supposed she'd scrolled through the address book in his phone and thought Kim was a trustworthy person. Maybe it was because Kim had given her five pounds (Marlee was that kind of girl). Was it Marlee who called the police and the ambulance? Was the first call she made on her Barbie pink phone to the emergency services? What if he hadn't managed to stop the car? Or an articulated lorry had plowed into them as they were stuck on the hard shoulder? He supposed his daughter would be pretty safe on a sheep farm in the middle of nowhere, surrounded by Russian gangsters.

"How long have I been here?" he asked Howell.

"Three days."

"Three days. Jesus, Josie's back tomorrow. I need to get Marlee home to Cambridge."

"Didn't know you were pussy whipped, Jackson."

Jackson ignored this comment. "Josie's taking Marlee to New Zealand."

"Well, it's only for a year," Howell said. "It'll pass in no time."

"No, it's for good," Jackson said.

"No, it's not, Jackson," Howell insisted. "It's just a year, ask Marlee."

"You fucking bitch!" Jackson shouted. "Your wanker boyfriend's only going on a year's exchange to New Zealand. You told me you were going for good." Josie said something indistinct on the other end of the phone, her voice had a throaty, lazy timber that it took on straight after she'd had an orgasm. If she hadn't been in the Ardèche and he hadn't been in a hospital somewhere south of Doncaster he would definitely have killed her. He was sitting on a bench outside the hospital, still tied to his drip. A lot of people were giving him odd looks and he dropped his voice a little.

"Why, Josie? Why did you lie to me like that?"

"Because you were out of order, Jackson. Get over it," she added. "Get over me."

Jackson wanted a cigarette, very badly. His tongue found the empty socket of his tooth, both tooth and root had been removed by the emergency dentist on call while Jackson was blissfully unconscious. Sharon was going to be very annoyed when she discovered she had been denied the pleasure of torturing him. He caught sight of himself in the plate glass of the hospital, he looked like the walking wounded you saw in war documentaries.

He punched another number into his phone. "Theo?"

"Jackson!" Theo sounded almost happy. "Where are you?"

"In the hospital," Jackson said.

"Again?"

"Yeah, again."

Jackson discharged himself against the hospital's advice. The only way they could be mollified was by Howell promising to drive him to Northumberland to pick up Marlee and then home to Cambridge.

"Christ, Jackson," Howell said as he eased his huge frame into the driver's seat of the Punto. "What happened, have you turned into a woman?"

"Worse things could happen," Jackson said. "I can drive."

"No, you can't." Howell raked through Jackson's CDs. "You still listening to this shit, Jackson?"

"Yes."

Howell tossed Trisha and Lucinda and Emmylou and the rest of the women in pain onto the backseat and put on one of Marlee's Christina Aguilera CDs. By the time he'd played it three times they were up the A1 and almost back in the middle of nowhere again.

"You don't have to do this," Jackson said.

"Yes, I do, I'm your friend. Anyway I could do with a break, bit of culture, city of dreaming spires and all that."

"I think that's Oxford."

"Same difference," Howell said. "Who's trying to kill you?"

"Guy in a gold Lexus."

"That would be the one that's following us, then?" Howell said, glancing in the rearview mirror.

Jackson tried to turn round to see but his neck didn't really turn anymore. Howell read out the number plate.

"Yeah, that's the one." Jackson reached for his phone and said, "Don't turn off the main road," just as Howell swung a sudden violent left onto the slip road.

"Why not?" Howell said. "We'll lead the Lexus somewhere quiet, a nice country lane, and then we'll deal with him."

"Deal with him?" Jackson said. "As in what, take him out?"

"Well, I wasn't thinking anything that drastic, but if you want, yeah, why not?" Howell said.

"No, I *don't* want. I want everything done by the book. I'm going to call it in. There's a warrant out for the guy's arrest."

"You're such a policeman, Jackson."

"Yeah, I know. I'm a policeman, I've turned into a woman, I'm pussy whipped, and I carry an organ-donor card. It's called middle age."

The Lexus was glued to their tail. Jackson turned the rearview mirror so that he could catch a glimpse of Quintus. His posh moon face was choleric. Jackson couldn't imagine what it was he'd done that had enraged the guy so much.

They could hear sirens in the distance. Jackson stayed on the phone with the dispatcher, although he was having a hard time giving her an idea of their position. They were on a narrow road now, made narrower by the overgrown hedgerows. Howell was driving as if he were playing Grand Theft Auto. They turned a sharp bend and found themselves almost bonnet to bonnet with a silver Mercedes SL 500 sports car being driven at equal speed. Jackson closed his eyes and braced himself, but somehow or other the driver of the Mercedes went to her left and Howell went to his left — it felt to Jackson as if they were on the Wall of Death — and they missed each other by a feather. "Fucking hell," Howell said admiringly, "what a babe, what a driver, what a car." "Jesus," Jackson said. He looked at his hands — they were actually shaking.

The Lexus seemed to have disappeared off the radar. Howell stopped the Punto and reversed cautiously back up the road and round the bend. The sound of police sirens was growing progressively nearer. The Lexus had managed to avoid the Mercedes but not the bend and had plowed relatively harmlessly into the overgrown hedge, where it was caught like an insect in a net. Quintus could just be seen inside, pushing helplessly at the door.

A couple of traffic cars appeared, followed by a plainclothes patrol car, all of them slewing to a stop in an overexcited way. An approaching police helicopter added to the sense of adrenalin-filled drama. Jackson knew how much they'd be loving this, anything that was out of the routine of speeding tickets and the misery of road accidents.

Howell and Jackson got out of the car and walked over to the Lexus. "Why does he want to kill you, anyway?" Howell asked.

"I've got no idea," Jackson said. "Let's ask him."

"And when you see your mother," Jackson said to Marlee, "it might be a good idea not to show off your Russian to her."

"Why not?"

"Because . . ." Jackson frowned, thinking of all the things he really didn't want Josie to know. "Just because. Okay, sweetheart?"

She looked doubtful. Jackson gave her a ten-pound note.

"Spaseeba," Marlee said.

When Jackson had phoned Theo from the hospital Theo told him that Lily-Rose, the yellow-haired girl, was staying with him. Jackson didn't know what to make of that, but as it wasn't anything to do with him he decided not to think much about it at all. He was trying not to think too much because thinking did actually physically hurt his brain. He said to Theo, "That's good," and hoped it was.

Jackson told Theo on the phone that he was going to send him a name, *the* name, the one he had been looking for for ten years, the name that Kim Strachan had given him. Of course, it might *not* be the name of the man who killed Laura (Innocent until proved guilty — did he believe that? No), and Jackson knew that, even if he suspected it for a moment, he should tell the police, but this was Theo's quest and it was up to Theo to decide where to take it from here.

He wrote the name and address on the back of a postcard that he picked up in a service station near the Angel of the North. The picture on the postcard was of one of the artificial-looking pink daisies that he'd passed over for Niamh's grave. Maybe it was a new kind of flower. He put a stamp on the postcard and Marlee ran to the postbox with it because she was still young enough to find posting a letter quite an exciting thing to do. When she came back in a year perhaps she would be blasé about it. She wouldn't be the same Marlee in twelve months' time: she would have different skin and different hair, she would have outgrown the shoes and the clothes she was wearing, she would have new buzzwords (New Zealand words), and she might not like Harry Potter anymore. But she would still be Marlee. She just wouldn't be the same.

* * *

Jackson dropped Marlee off at David Lastingham's house. Josie looked him over dispassionately. "You look terrible, Jackson."

"Thanks."

He turned to leave but Marlee ran down the path and caught him at the gate. She threw her arms round him and hugged him. "*Dasvedanya,* Daddy," she whispered.

Jackson went back to what remained of his own house. The building smelled sour and sooty, as though the dormant spores of ancient diseases had been released into the air. He raked with his foot through the clinker and slag that now carpeted his living room. He wondered what had happened to Victor's ashes — there was no sign of his urn. Ashes to ashes. He found a broken shard of pottery, a piece of wishing well, the letters G . . . FROM SCAR still legible. He let it fall back into the debris. Just as he was turning to leave something caught his eye. He squatted on his haunches to get a better look. One blue arm, covered in ash, was sticking up in the air, like an earthquake survivor signaling for help.

Jackson tugged at the arm and pulled Blue Mouse out of the ruins.

Superintendent Marian Foster had moved to Filey on her retirement from the force and was still doggedly unpacking cardboard boxes in her kitchen when Jackson and Marlee arrived on her doorstep. Jackson had phoned her from the car to tell her he was coming, and she seemed pleased to be interrupted, as if she already realized that burying herself in a small seaside town might not be the best way to spend her nonworking life. "I expect I'll find a committee or two that needs a firm hand." She laughed. "Finally do that OU degree, join an evening class." She sighed and added, "It's going to be fucking awful, isn't it, Inspector?"

"Oh, I don't know, ma'am," Jackson said. "I'm sure you'll get used to it." Try as he might, Jackson couldn't think of anything more positive to say. He could see his own future reflected only too clearly back at him.

Marian Foster could obviously recognize a sugar junkie when she saw one, and she sat Marlee down in front of the television with a can of Coke and a plate of chocolate biscuits. She made a mug of achingly strong tea for herself and Jackson. "Gone soft?" she said when she saw him flinch at the taste. "You're back in Yorkshire now, boy."

"Don't I know it."

"So," Marian Foster said, suddenly businesslike, "Olivia Land? What can I tell you? I was a lowly PC, and a woman to boot. I interviewed the Land girls, but I doubt whether there's anything I can add to what you know."

"I'm not so sure," Jackson said. "Feelings, impressions, instincts, anything. Tell me what you would have done differently if you'd been in charge."

"Knowing everything I know now about the world?" She sighed, a weighty sigh. "I would have looked at the father more closely. I would have suspected abuse."

"Really? Why?"

"There was something wrong with Sylvia, the eldest. There were things she was hiding, things she wasn't saying. She would start to disassociate if you questioned her too closely. And she was . . . I don't know — strange." *Strange* — the same word Binky Rain had used about Sylvia.

"And the father was a cold fish," Marian Foster continued. "Controlled and controlling. The rest of them were a mess — the mother, the other girls. I've forgotten their names."

"Amelia and Julia."

"Of course. Amelia and Julia. You want my honest opinion?"

"More than anything," Jackson said.

"I think the father did it. I think Victor Land killed Olivia."

Jackson removed the crucial evidence from his pocket and laid it down on Marian Foster's kitchen table. Tears welled in her eyes, and for a moment she couldn't speak. "Blue Mouse," she said finally. "After all this time. Where did you find him?"

The thing about Sylvia was that she hadn't really been surprised to see Blue Mouse. It was as if she'd been waiting for him to turn up eventually. And she hadn't been curious as to where Jackson had found it — Jackson had told her, but she hadn't asked. Wouldn't that be your first question? It was Marian Foster's first question. "Where did you find him?"

Jester wagged his tail when he saw Jackson, but Sylvia looked less pleased to see him on the other side of the grille in the visiting room. She frowned and said, "What do you want?" and Jackson thought he caught a glance of a different Sylvia, a less spiritual one.

Jackson's painkillers were wearing off. He would have liked to have taken his head off and given it a rest. How was he going to go about this? He took a deep breath and looked into Sylvia's mud-colored eyes.

"Sister Mary Luke," he said. "Sylvia." Her eyes narrowed when he spoke her real name but her gaze didn't waver. "Sylvia, think of me as a priest in the confessional. Whatever you say to me will never go beyond me. Tell me the truth, Sylvia. That's all I want." Because in the end that was what it came down to, didn't it? "Tell me the truth about what happened to Olivia."

He had to push hard on the gate to open it. He felt like an intruder. He *was* an intruder. There was a piece of crime tape caught on one of the branches of Binky's apple trees. It wasn't a crime scene anymore. Binky had died of natural causes — "old age really," the pathologist said to Jackson. Jackson supposed it was pretty much a triumph if you went that way. He hoped Marlee died of old age, under an apple tree somewhere, long after Jackson himself had gone.

The place was like some kind of nature conservation area. There were bats flitting in and out of the eaves of the house, and a frog lolloped lazily away from him as he approached, and, despite sweeping the path with his big police-issue Maglite, he almost stood on a baby hedgehog as he worked his way round the thorns and weeds to the corner of the garden. The brambles were almost impenetrable and Jackson could see how something could get overlooked here. Something precious. It wasn't going to be as easy as simply raking through grass and dead leaves. In fact, Jackson didn't actually expect to find anything. It wasn't just that there was so much wildlife around — you could hardly walk into one of these gardens without encountering a fox — it was just that it was so rare when you went searching for something precious that had been lost that you actually found it.

In the corner, Sylvia said, beyond the apple trees, beyond the big beech. Jackson couldn't tell a beech from a birch, couldn't do tree identification at all, so he followed the wall round until it turned into another wall and reckoned that must be the corner.

He dug with his hands, an inefficient, filthy way of doing it, but a spade seemed too brutal. He didn't dig, he *excavated*. Delicately. The ground was hard and dry and he had to scrape at the soil. It was pitch black by the time he uncovered the first sign of her. His face and forearms were prickling with dirt and sweat. He kept thinking about Niamh, about the two days he and Francis had searched for her, in every stinking bin and rubbish heap, every corner of every piece of waste ground until Jackson felt like a feral animal, a creature that had moved far beyond the normal bonds and bounds of society. He had watched the police dragging the canal and had seen them lifting out his sister's body, sluicy with mud and water. He remembered that the first feeling he had, before all the other more complex feelings flooded in, was one of relief that they had found her, that she wouldn't be out there, lost forever.

Sylvia said Olivia had simply been left, more or less, where she died, covered up with some branches and grass. Every square inch of this garden should have been searched on hands and knees, that was how Jackson would have done it, a fingertip search of the immediate vicinity. He remembered Binky saying something about seeing the officers off her property, giving them "short shrift." Was that all it took, one domineering old Tory to tell you to get lost and you did? And all this time Olivia had simply been lying here, patiently waiting for someone to come and find her. Jackson thought about Victor, covering his smallest child up with weeds and garden rubbish as if she wasn't worth anything, leaving her behind in a strange place while her body was still warm. Not taking her home. Victor, who then went back to his bed, locking the back door, leaving Amelia outside alone to discover her sister gone. Victor, who for thirty-four years had kept Blue Mouse locked up like the truth. The Land girls used to play in Binky's garden and then Sylvia told them to keep out. Because she knew Olivia was here.

The first thing he found was a clavicle and then what looked like an ulna. He stopped his excavating and moved the Maglite around until it caught the small, pale moon of the skull. Jackson took out his phone and called the station at Parkside.

He sat back on his heels and examined the clavicle, brushing the soil off it with the tenderness of an archaeologist finding something rare, something unique, which it was, of course. The clavicle was tiny and fragile, like an animal's, a rabbit or a hare, the broken wishbone of a bird. Jackson kissed it reverently because he knew it was the holiest relic he would ever find. It started to rain, Jackson couldn't remember when it had last rained. *Aqua lateris Christi, lava me.* Jackson wept. Not for Niamh, or Laura Wyre or Kerry-Anne Brockley or any of the other lost girls — he wept for the little girl with gingham ribbons in her hair, the little girl who had once held Blue Mouse in her arms and told him to smile for the camera.

* * *

Jackson settled into his economy seat, row twenty, a window seat. He could have afforded to fly business class, but he wasn't going to start throwing the money around. He was still his father's son, it seemed.

He was rich. Unexpectedly, absurdly rich. Binky had made him the sole beneficiary of her estate — two million pounds, in bonds and stocks, all of which had been sitting in a safe-deposit box all these years while she hadn't spent a bean on anything but her cats. "To my friend, Mr. Jackson Brodie, for being kind." He had cried when her solicitor had read that out to him. Cried, because he hadn't been particularly kind to her, cried because she didn't have a better friend, that she had died alone, without a hand to hold. Cried because he was turning into a woman.

Two million on condition that the cats were looked after. Did that mean their offspring as well? Would he have to look after Binky's cats forever and ever, until he died, and then would Marlee and her descendants have to look after them? The first thing he would do would be to have them all neutered. He knew he didn't deserve it, of course he didn't deserve it, it was like winning the lottery without buying a ticket. But then, who did deserve it? Not Quintus, her only blood relative, that was for sure. Quintus, who had found his aunt's will made out in favor of Jackson and then had tried to kill Jackson to stop him from inheriting. Quintus, who would probably have killed his aunt if she hadn't preempted him by dying quietly of old age.

At first Jackson had worried that the money was tainted, that it had originated in the diamond mines, made out of the blood and sweat and slave labor of "bleck" miners. Filthy lucre. He had wondered about just handing it all over to Howell. "Because I'm black?" Howell said, looking at him as if he'd just grown an extra head. "You stupid fucker." Jackson supposed it was a bit much to make Howell the token representative of the whole sordid history of imperial exploitation. Howell and Julia were playing cribbage, sitting at Victor's dining-room table, drinking gin, Julia slamming her empty glass down, saying, "Hit me again," to Howell. Jackson would never have taken either of them on in a drinking competition.

Howell and Jackson were staying in the Garden House Hotel now that Jackson no longer had a home in Cambridge. Julia had offered to put them up but Jackson couldn't bear the idea of staying in Victor's old, cold house, sleeping in a room last occupied by one of the lost Land girls.

He was the one who had told Julia. He had taken her to see the delicate leveret bones laid out in the police mortuary ("Against the rules, Jackson," the forensic pathologist rebuked him mildly). Julia was strong, he knew that, she could look at what was left of Olivia's tiny skeleton without growing hysterical. She reached out a hand to her sister, and the pathologist said, "Don't touch, dear. Later, later you can touch her," and Julia had retracted her hand and held it over her heart as if her heart hurt and said, "Oh," very softly and Jackson hadn't realized that such a small word could be so unbearably sad.

Jackson's story went like this — he had been out walking a dog when the dog had nosed its way into Binky's garden, where it had rooted around in the undergrowth, barking its head off until Jackson had come and investigated, at which point he had discovered Olivia's body. "And where's the dog now, Inspector?" the first detective on the scene asked. "Ran off." Jackson shrugged and didn't bother to add, "It's plain Mr. Brodie now." He didn't mention his visit to the convent, neither to the police nor to Julia. He felt, rightly or wrongly, that if Sylvia wanted to tell the truth then it was up to her. He had offered her the shelter of the confessional, he had given his word. "Looks like a tragic accident," he said to the investigating DS. "Poor police procedure. Thirty-four years ago, what can you do?"

Howell poured more gin for himself and Julia. "Why don't you join us, Mr. B.?" she said. "We can play three-handed Gladstone. I'll teach you."

"We can try and win some of your excessive and undeserved wealth off you," Howell said. Jackson declined.

"Miserable bugger," Howell said.

Perhaps Jackson could set Howell up in business. He would put some of the money in trust for Marlee. And he could give some to Lily-Rose. He had been to see Theo, had seen the postcard with the picture of the pink flower propped up on the mantelpiece. Neither of them mentioned it. Lily-Rose had made them a pot of tea and they sat and drank it in the garden and ate slices of a Victoria sponge sandwich that Theo had made. "Good, in't it?" Lily-Rose said appreciatively.

And he would have to give some of the money to charity, to salve his conscience if nothing else. It turned out that the money hadn't come from diamonds. A long time ago one of Binky Rain's forebears had invested in the building of the American railroads, so the money had been made from the blood and sweat of whoever built the Union and Central Pacific lines (Chinese? Irish?), which wasn't particularly ethical either, Jackson supposed, but what could you do?

Which charities? There were so many. He thought about asking Amelia, it might be good to give her something to get her teeth into. She had become "a little overwrought," Julia had explained to him, and had taken too many pills and was now "resting" in the hospital.

"You mean she tried to kill herself?" Jackson interpreted.

Julia frowned. "Sort of."

"Sort of?"

He had volunteered to bring Amelia home from the hospital. She was doped up and untalkative, but when they reached the house on Owlstone Road Julia was waiting at the door with Mrs. Chippy, who she pressed into Amelia's arms as a welcoming gift, and when Jackson observed Amelia burrowing her face into the black fur ("He's called Lucky," Julia said), he realized that he might have found the perfect custodian of Binky's legacy.

"What do you think?" he asked Julia later. "Binky's place would have to be done up, obviously, but then Amelia could live there and look after the cats."

"Oh, and she could rescue the garden as well," Julia said excitedly. "She would love that. Oh, what a splendid idea, Mr. Brodie!"

Jackson hadn't thought about the garden. "Do you think that would be alright though," he said. "I mean with Olivia being there all that time — it wouldn't freak Amelia out?" Amelia hadn't been told about Olivia yet, Julia was still trying to find the "right time," and Jackson had said, "There never will be a right time," and Julia said, "I know."

"I think," Julia said, "that it would be a very good thing. It would be somehow *appropriate.*" She turned her head on the pillow to look at him — because they were conducting this conversation about Amelia's future in bed — and gave him one of her big lazy smiles. She stretched extravagantly and one of her warm feet rubbed up and down his calf.

"Oh, Mr. Brodie," she said, "who would have imagined this would be so delicious?"

Who indeed, Jackson thought. "You might try calling me Jackson now," he said.

"Oh no," she said, "I much prefer 'Mr. Brodie.'"

As the plane went through its preflight routine Jackson perused the estate agents' details. There was a nice château, not too showy, in the Minervois (châteaus seemed to be ten-a-penny in France) and a thirteenth-century presbytery in a small village south of Toulouse, a *maison de maître* in a village near Narbonne. Not that he'd decided which area to live in, but you had to start somewhere. He imagined he could motor his way round France, viewing houses, take his time. He'd sold his business to Deborah Arnold. If she'd been only a slightly nicer person he might have knocked something off the price. He closed his eyes and thought about France.

"Can I get you a drink, sir?" He opened his eyes and looked into Nicola Spencer's bland, indifferent face. She smiled at him without warmth and repeated her question. He asked for an orange juice in order to prolong the encounter a little. In some ways he knew everything about Nicola Spencer, and in other ways he knew absolutely nothing. She gave him a small packet of pretzels with his orange juice and moved on to the next passenger. He watched as she pushed her trolley past him, her muscular buttocks straining against her uniform skirt. He thought about following her when they landed — out of curiosity and because she was unfinished business — but by the time he'd gone through the rigmarole of picking up a rental car at Toulouse Airport, he'd lost interest.

22

Caroline

Jonathan said, "What do you want for your birthday?" and she said, "A Mercedes SL 500," joking, obviously, and he said, "Any particular color?" and she said, "Silver," and fuck me (she thought) if it wasn't sitting there in the driveway, seventy thousand quid's worth, tied with a big, pink ribbon. He must be even richer than she thought. She had no idea how much money he had, she didn't want any of his money, she hadn't even wanted the car, not really, although now that she had it she loved it. Two seats, no room in the back for dogs or kids.

"Goodness," Rowena said when she saw it. It was amazing how much meaning you could pack into one two-syllable word.

Maybe the car was a farewell gift. Maybe he was getting ready for his next wife. She was pretty sure he had someone in London. She'd be surprised if he didn't, men like Jonathan always had mistresses. They never married them though. She should have been a mistress — temperamentally she was much better suited to being a mistress than a wife.

They still didn't know about the baby, safe inside her. She was getting ready to shed her skin again, grow another new one. She had to leave before she got stuck in inertia, before someone dis-

covered her. Before they stopped her when they found out about
the baby. They would want to get their hands on the baby. And it
was a shame because she really loved the school and the job, but
there were other schools and other jobs, everything was possible
when you turned your mind to it. And she was taking the baby
with her (obviously) out of this place because it wouldn't be a
good environment for it — it might grow up speaking French on
Wednesdays and not understanding about love. She *ached* with love
for this baby. That was something that no one in this house was capable of understanding. There was a time when she hadn't been
capable of understanding love, and what a mess that had made of
everything. She'd said to Shirley, "Treat me as if I'm dead," but
she hadn't expected her to actually do as she said. But there'd been
nothing: no visits, no cards, no birthday gifts, no word at all. For
months she waited for Shirley to turn up on visiting day, with
Tanya in her arms *(Look, here's Mummy),* or chaperone their useless
parents *(Come on, you have to visit Michelle),* but no. All her letters
went unanswered, all her hopes were knocked back until she came
to think maybe it really was for the best. Let them get on with their
lives, let them be free of her, because what good had she ever done
them? She hadn't loved the people that she'd had a duty to love,
and you had to pay the price for that, sooner or later.

When you left you didn't leave any traces. You packed minimally,
you walked out as if you were going to Leeds for the day (but you
took the beautiful car). You didn't leave evidence, you didn't place
your fingerprints all over the handle of the bloody ax to protect
other people. This time she was taking the bug, the new bug, and
she would love this baby so much that it would wake up every day
in a state of bliss and she herself would be in a state of grace, at last.

   She would have to stop living her life as one variation after another on a pastoral theme, she would have to think of something
absolutely different to do next time. She should probably move

abroad — Italy or France. Of course you could never move far enough — Patagonia, China — nowhere was far enough, but the trick was to keep moving. The trick was not to leave the bug behind. And one thing was certain: you could never go back.

She was going to give him a chance to come with her, just one chance: He was going to be shocked and he wouldn't come, but he was going to get that chance.

He was on his bicycle (with bicycle clips — for heaven's sake — around the ankles of his cheap, black trousers), and he looked round when he heard the car approaching. She had the top down, and when she drew level she stopped and he dismounted and laughed and said, "That's one snazzy set of wheels, Mrs. Weaver," as if he were a secondhand car dealer, and she said, "Sure is, Vicar," and she patted the seat beside her and said, "Do you want to come for a ride?" and he made some kind of helpless gesture toward the bike but then said, "Oh, what the . . ." and lay the bike down in the long grass of the verge. But when he put his hand on the door handle, she reached over as if to stop him and said, "But I have to tell you, I'm going to drive off and I'm not coming back, not here, not ever, and when I leave I'm going *fast*," and he said, "You're not joking, are you?" and she thought how she loved the way he looked like a solemn little boy when he was trying to think of the right answer to something. She revved the engine and said, "I'm going to count to ten . . ."

23

Everything from Duty,
Nothing from Love

Michelle thought that she'd been angry before, but never like this. It was like being a volcano, plugged and stoppered and unable to get rid of the boiling stuff inside. Which was called — what? Magma? Lava, for fuck's sake. She couldn't even remember the simplest words anymore. "Maternal amnesia," the books said, but if it was amnesia then it was very selective; it didn't allow her to forget how completely miserable and unhappy she was, did it? And today had been going really well up until this moment — she'd been on top of everything, everything under control, and then he'd barged into the house without a second thought and woken the baby up.

Michelle tugged at the ax, but it was stuck like bloody Excalibur in the log, and she was so lost in her fury that she didn't hear Shirley and when she turned round and saw her she nearly jumped out of her skin and said, "Jesus, you frightened me," and just for a nanosecond in time she forgot how angry she was but then she heard the baby screaming inside the house — half of East Anglia must be able to hear the bloody baby — and it all came boiling up again and she knew this time it was going to blow and it was going to be a mess. Krakatau. You see, she could still remember some things. "You look like you're going to kill someone with that ax," Shirley said, laughing, and Michelle said, "I am."

She charged through the back door like a Viking berserker and when Keith saw her he laughed as well. They were all fucking laughing at her as if nothing she said was important, as if she didn't mean what she said, and she lifted up the ax, although it was awkward because she didn't really understand where its center of gravity was, and she flung it at Keith, but it was a girly throw and the ax bounced heavily and landed harmlessly on the floor.

He was furious, he was even more angry than she was, and at first she thought it was just because of the ax, although it was *miles* away from him, but then she realized he was shouting about Tanya. "You might have hit her, you might have really hurt her," and she said, "Don't be ridiculous. It was nowhere near her," and he yelled, "You crazy fucking bitch, that's not the point," and she felt suddenly frightened because she could see that Keith had lost it now — he didn't even look like himself and he made a move to pick up the ax but the next moment it was in Shirley's hands and she didn't do any girly tossing. She just lifted the whole weight of the ax up and brought the blade down on Keith's head and then everyone was quiet, even the bug.

Shirley was a member of the St. John Ambulance, but it didn't take medical training to see that there was nothing anyone could do for him. Michelle was on the floor, hugging herself as if she were in a straitjacket, rocking backward and forward, and she could hear a weird keening noise that she realized was coming from her, and Shirley said, "Don't do that," her voice cold, but she couldn't stop the noise so Shirley grabbed her and pulled her to her feet and shouted, "Shut up, Michelle, shut up!" but she couldn't so Shirley punched her in the face.

The shock was so great she thought she might have actually stopped breathing for a second, and all she wanted to do was curl up in a ball and find oblivion. Shirley said, "You've just ruined both our fucking lives, not to mention Tanya's," and Michelle thought, Not to mention Keith's, but she knew Shirley was right because when it came right down to it, it was her fault.

So she got up from the floor — she felt as stiff as an old woman — and picked up the ax, which at least wasn't actually embedded in his head, which was something to be grateful for, and then she wiped the handle of the ax on her jeans and grasped it herself and said to Shirley, "You go."

Tanya was standing up, hanging on to the edges of her playpen, and she started screaming again, just as if she'd been stuck with a pin. Shirley picked her up and tried to quiet her, but that child didn't look like she would ever be quiet again. "Just go," Michelle said. "Please just go, Shirley." Shirley put the baby back on the floor and said, "I promise I'll look after her for you," and Michelle said, "I know you will. Take her away, give her a fresh start, be the mother to her that I can't be," because if there was one person in the world she could trust it was Shirley.

"Right," Shirley said, and you would think she'd done this before, she was so in control. "Right, I'm going to phone the police and I'm going to tell them that this was how I found you? Right? *Right,* Michelle?"

"Right."

And then Shirley picked up the receiver and dialed 999 and when the operator answered she started screaming hysterically, you would think she was the best actress in the world, and then finally she stopped and replaced the receiver and they waited in silence for the police to come. The bug had fallen asleep on the floor. It was very cold and Michelle would have liked to clean up a bit for the police coming, but she didn't have the energy. Finally, they heard the sound of a siren, and then another, and the noise of the police cars bumping their way along the farm track, and Michelle said to Shirley, "You never had any chocolate cake."

24

Theo

She had dyed her hair a startling pink color that made him think of flamingos. It suited her much better than the custard yellow. It made her look healthier, although she *was* healthier — she must have put on half a stone in a week, although that was hardly surprising, as Theo had been feeding her with the single-mindedness of a parent feeding a chick: beans on toast, Horlicks, macaroni and cheese, bacon rolls, sausages and mashed potatoes, bananas and cherries and peaches. She didn't like apples; neither did Theo. Laura had liked apples. Lily-Rose wasn't Laura, Theo was very clear about that in his own mind. Theo was sticking to his donkey food — he got more satisfaction from watching Lily-Rose eat. You would never think to look at her that she would have such an appetite. It was as if she were making up for years of starvation.

She slept in Laura's room, and her dog slept at the foot of the bed. Theo couldn't go near the dog and Lily-Rose worried that it would trigger another asthma attack in Theo. Theo worried too but he told her about Poppy and how he had got used to her and that he believed you could get used to anything in time, and she said, "Yeah, I think that too." They looked at photographs of Poppy, and of Laura, and Lily-Rose said, "She's lovely," and Theo was glad that she didn't use the past tense because it always hurt. He hadn't told Jenny about the girl living with him, he could just imagine what she would say.

He had Jackson's postcard, a picture of a pink flower, the same pink as Lily-Rose's hair. The postcard was propped up on the mantel-piece, next to a photograph of Poppy when she was a puppy. In some odd way Theo identified Poppy with Lily-Rose — little abandoned, mistreated creatures with their new, flowery names. Lily-Rose said she had given herself a new name so she could be a new person. A "fresh start," she said.

She was the product of a profoundly dysfunctional background and she almost certainly needed professional help. She had a history of running away from home, of drug abuse, petty theft, prostitution, although she seemed clean of everything for now. Her mother had murdered her father and she was brought up by her grandparents, who sounded just as bad as her own parents (he suspected abuse). Her life was unreal, like a television program — a documentary or a bad soap opera. Yet she seemed remarkably happy, playing with the dog in the garden, eating an ice cream, reading a magazine. She loved being woken in the morning by a cup of sugary tea and a slice of buttered toast. In the evenings they'd started (bizarrely) doing a jigsaw puzzle together.

"We're like a pair of fucking old-age pensioners," she said, but not unkindly. He didn't want to save her or keep her or change her, although he was doing all of those things and would continue to do them if she wanted. The one thing he didn't do was worry about her. So many bad things had happened to her that she was damage proofed. He was happy just to give her back a childhood. And when she was ready she would move on and he'd deal with that when it happened.

25

CASE HISTORY NO. 2 1994

Just a Normal Day

The thing that happened with Mr. Jessop was stupid. (He was always saying, "Call me Stan," but she just couldn't. It sounded wrong, he was a *teacher*.) It was funny because she hadn't felt particularly singled out or anything, he'd had Christina over a couple times, and Josh as well, and last year the whole biology A Level class went to his house for an end-of-term barbecue. That was the first time she was in his house, in fact. The barbecue was rained off and he'd rushed to the supermarket and bought stuff for sandwiches, which she had helped Kim to make. She always called her Kim, never Mrs. Jessop. Kim had seemed really pissed off at having them all in the house. She'd just had a baby a few weeks before, so maybe you couldn't blame her. Kim was the same age as Jenny and yet you couldn't have found two people on the whole planet who were more different from each other.

They made ham sandwiches with that cheap, shiny ham — Kraft processed slices for the vegetarians — Kim slapping margarine onto doughy white Sunblest bread, and Laura thought, Yuck, and then berated herself for being such a snob. Dad had always been obsessed with feeding them well — home-cooked meals, whole-meal bread, and loads of fruit and veg (although God knows what crap he ate himself when he got the chance). Of course, poor people couldn't afford all that good stuff, but then the Jessops weren't poor. Teachers moaned all the time about their pay but they weren't exactly paupers. Although, to be honest, Josh was right when he said Kim was white trash, and it did make you wonder how Mr. Jessop had ended up with her in that horrible little house that smelled of sour milk and baby shit.

She was wearing red high heels that somehow weren't what you expected new mothers (or teachers' wives) to wear. Her hair was dyed almost white, very *Blonde Ambition,* and made her skin look unhealthy. Mr. Jessop was completely in thrall to her, it was like she controlled him with one eyebrow, and he seemed quite a different person than the classroom Mr. Jessop (although not so different that you would want to call him Stan). When he was in the classroom he was funny and cynical and always saying mutinous things about the school. He was nothing like any of the other science teachers, more like an English teacher. When he was at home he was less interesting somehow, and you would have thought it would be the other way round really.

All the girls cooed over the baby — Nina — when Kim brought her downstairs. Even the boys were interested in her, as if she were a novel science project ("Can she focus yet?" "Does she recognize you?"), but Laura felt completely disinterested. She knew it would be different when she had her own, but other people's babies left her cold. Kim wasn't breast-feeding. One of the girls — Andi — had asked her and she said, "God, no," as if she couldn't imagine anything more unnatural, and Josh and Laura exchanged a look and both of them tried not to laugh.

"Of course, I'm not educated like you lot," Kim said later, when they were washing up together, by which time they'd formed a kind of alliance — Mr. Jessop had bought a crate of beer and boxes of wine and everyone was in the living room completely pissed, in that stupid loud way, and neither Kim nor Laura was drinking, Laura because she was on antibiotics for an ear infection and Kim because of the baby — "I need my wits about me," she said, and Josh whispered to Laura, "If she can find any," and Laura pretended to ignore him because Mr. Jessop was looking at them as if he knew they were saying things about his wife.

Kim was from Newcastle and her accent seemed totally foreign. The fact that she was Geordie made her a little frightening. Laura imagined the North was populated with hard, no-nonsense women that you wouldn't want to take on in a fight. "I left school at sixteen," Kim told her, "and did a year at college. Secretarial, since you ask," and Laura said, "Oh?" although she wasn't really listening because she was wiping down the kitchen surfaces, which were already spotless because Kim might be trashy and stupid but she kept a very clean house, which was something Dad would have approved of. It would be good if, when she left to go to university (and definitely not before that), Dad were to meet a *really* nice woman (not a Kim), someone mature, even a little dowdy and a real homemaker, someone who would appreciate all his good qualities and would want to make him very, very happy. He deserved happiness, and when she went to university he was going to be heartbroken, even though he pretended he wouldn't be. Maybe not heartbroken, not the way she felt when Poppy died, but he was going to be very sad because it had been just the two of them for so long and he *lived* for her. That was why she was going to Aberdeen, because it wasn't on the doorstep. She had to get away, to be herself, to become herself. As long as she stayed with Dad she'd be a child.

She wouldn't be like Jenny. Jenny was really bad, she never phoned or wrote — all the effort was always on Dad's side. It was almost like she didn't care about him at all. When Laura left she was going to phone a lot and she'd already bought a little stock of postcards, funny ones and ones with cute animals on them that she was going to send to him regularly. She loved him more than anything. That was why she'd agreed to work in his office, even though it was much more fun in the bar, but it was only for a few weeks and then she'd be off, like an arrow into the future. And she couldn't wait.

After that day, the day the barbecue didn't happen, she started babysitting for them — apparently Kim suggested her to Mr. Jessop, so she must have liked her in some way (although you would never have guessed). Mr. Jessop asked her at the end of class one day and she said, "Well, okay, but I don't know anything about babies," and he said, "God, Laura, neither do we."

She usually got Emma to come over and sit with her because Emma was good with babies. She really loved them in fact, which was ironic and pretty sad really because she'd had that abortion, and for a while she seemed to really lose it, but she was the sort who always pretended to be bright and cheerful, which was why Laura liked her. And they'd usually just sit and do their homework together, although sometimes they looked through Kim's wardrobe, which was always an education in itself, although it didn't feel right being in their bedroom because, unlike with most other adults, you could actually imagine Kim and Mr. Jessop having sex, which was kind of embarrassing.

She'd told Dad that she was a virgin, because she knew that was what he wanted to hear, and as lies went it was pretty harmless. In fact it was charitable. And it wasn't that far from the truth because she'd only had sex with four boys, and one of them was Josh so that hardly counted because they'd been to primary school together and had known each other since they were four years old and they'd decided it would be a good idea to get over the whole "losing virginity" thing to each other because that would be safe and friendly, if a bit weird. And better than Emma, for example, who lost it to a married man (in his car, for heaven's sake), or poor Christina, who was raped by a guy who put something in her drink.

They did it in Josh's bedroom, which his parents never went into. They were those arty, liberal types who'd let him do whatever he wanted since the age of twelve (so it was amazing really that the boy had turned out as well as he had). His parents were downstairs watching some nature documentary about whales.

At first it had been funny and they couldn't stop laughing and then they'd grown quite formal, examining each other's bodies like anatomy students and having foreplay by the book, but then they'd got completely into it and were down on the floor like dogs and it was just as well that the television was turned up loud because she could hear herself yelling like someone she didn't know at all and afterward, when they were lying there on the floor, stunned by the way it had taken them over, all they could hear was whale song and they'd both started laughing again because his parents must have heard them, but if they did they never said anything. Josh said, "Well, we surprised ourselves there, did we not, Miss Wyre?" and she said, "Can we do it again, please?" and he said, "God, woman, give me a minute, will you."

When Dad picked her up he said, "Are you alright, you look flushed," and she said, "I think I'm coming down with something," and he made her hot lemon and honey and she sat up in bed, in her Winnie-the-Pooh pajamas, and hugged him and said, "Thank you, Best Dad in the World," and hoped he couldn't smell Josh's spunk. That was when they were fourteen and they'd done it a few times since and she knew Josh was in love with her, but was grateful that he was careful never to say so.

She'd been round to the Jessops' quite a few times without any babysitting being involved. She'd grown to like Kim. Being Kim's friend made her feel more like a woman and less like a girl. Once, after a supper of (tough) steak and chips, Kim had plucked Laura's eyebrows and given her a manicure, although usually she visited on a Saturday afternoon when Stan wasn't there and they just sat in the garden while Nina crawled around on the grass. Stan played on an amateur football team on Saturdays. "You've got to let them off the leash sometimes," Kim said, as if she were giving tips on how to keep a difficult pet. That was when Laura'd encountered Stuart Lappin the first time. He was mowing his lawn next door. When he finished, he looked over the fence and offered to do the Jessops' lawn, and Kim kept on filing her nails and said loudly to him, "No, thank you, Stuart," without making eye contact with him. It seemed a bit rude to Laura and she gave "Stuart" an encouraging smile to compensate.

"I can't stand him," Kim hissed when he had disappeared, "he's always trying to be friendly. He gives me the creeps. He's in his thirties and he still lives with his mother, it's pathetic," and Laura said, "He looks harmless," and Kim said, "Those are the ones you've got to look out for."

The last time was just before her final exam. Mr. Jessop had suggested some extra tuition, and she didn't think anything of it because he'd offered it to some of the others. She was disappointed that Kim wasn't at home. Stan said, "Oh, she's taken Nina to her mother's," very offhand, as if he couldn't care less what his wife was doing. He had a pad of paper and a couple of textbooks out on the dining-room table, but she didn't even get to sit down before he started, coming at her from behind, arms round her waist, trying to kiss the back of her neck, and she could smell alcohol on his breath, which was absolutely disgusting. She was furious, how could he, it was so *unethical*. She jabbed him with her elbows and yelled at him to get off her, and he said, "Oh, come on, Laura, you've done it with half the boys in your class. It's time you had a real man, you know you want it." The bastard, the fucking bastard! She stamped hard on his foot, the way they taught you in self-defense, but it was difficult because he was still holding her really tightly round the waist and she started to get panicky when she realized she couldn't get away from him. He was twisting her round so that he could get his lips on hers and then he put his hand on her crotch, thank God she was wearing jeans, and it meant he had less of a grip on her and she managed to get far away enough from him to be able to jab a finger into one of his eyes. And then she ran.

She'd been revising with Josh in the churchyard of Little St. Mary's. It was hot and they'd started fooling around a bit, no one ever went in that place, but then there was a rustling of leaves as if an animal were making its way through the summer vegetation, and then a man's face suddenly popped up from behind a gravestone and she'd shrieked in a really girly way, and Josh had got all manly despite having his jeans round his ankles and shouted at the guy to fuck off and then they had collapsed with laughter. She thought the man looked vaguely familiar but it was only when he ordered half a lager shandy from her in the bar a couple weeks later that she realized he was the Jessops' lawn-mowing neighbor, but she couldn't remember his name. Luckily he didn't seem to recognize her at all.

By then everyone had gone: Christina had gone to teach in Tanzania for a year, Ayshea was spending the summer in France, Joanna was Euro-railing with Pansy, Emma was in Peru (Emma, for God's sake!), and Josh was a camp counselor in the middle of nowhere in Michigan. She felt like she'd been deserted. They all agreed to meet up in front of the Hobbs Pavilion on Parker's Piece in ten years' time, but how likely was that really? Mr. Jessop had tried to organize a "farewell get-together" for his class but everyone had been busy — not that she would have gone. She hadn't seen him since he'd tried it on with her. Dad, bless his heart, said, "Don't you want to go traveling then, Laura?" even though it

would have been his idea of living hell for her to be abroad somewhere, somewhere he couldn't pick her up from in the car at the
end of an evening.

Then she bumped into him coming out of Heffers Bookshop and
she said, "Hello," in a neutral kind of way because it wasn't as if
she was looking to get into a conversation with the guy or anything, and then the next day there was this teddy bear left on the
doorstep, not that really she connected the two things, not con-
sciously anyway, it was just this stupid-looking bear, an ugly, pink
thing with eyes that were all wrong, not like the cute old-fashioned
ones Laura had piled on her bed. The bear on the doorstep was the
kind of thing that someone with no taste would buy if they thought
you liked teddy bears.

She went up to London for the day (she was beginning to hate
everyone for having left Cambridge for the summer). She visited
the British Museum and then went and bought some new clothes,
but it wasn't much fun on her own. She didn't see him getting on
at King's Cross but she saw him walking into her carriage about
ten minutes after the train had pulled out of the station — she was
sure he was looking for her, even though when he spotted her he
tried to look surprised. Luckily, there were no empty seats round
about her, but when she got up at Cambridge he followed her
down the carriage and stood at the door with her and spoke for
the first time, saying, "Are you getting off here?" which was a
bloody stupid question as it was obvious she was, but she just said,
"Yes," and then when they were on the platform he said, "Can I
give you a lift home? My car's in the car park," and she said, "No
thanks, my Dad's meeting me," and hurried away from him. And
she remembered his name was Stuart. Kim was right, he was pathetic. She couldn't go and see Kim anymore because that would
probably mean seeing Mr. Jessop. She phoned the house a couple
times and he always answered and she put the phone down and

said nothing. The last time, he'd shouted into the phone, "Kim —
is that you? Where the fuck are you?" so she figured things couldn't
be too good between them.

Her last night in the bar and he came in and sat in the corner and
made his one half-pint of lager shandy last an hour. When he got
up to leave he said to her, "I don't know why you're ignoring me,"
and she said, "I don't know what you're talking about," and he said,
"You know there's an incredible bond between us, you shouldn't
deny it," and she was suddenly furious (the guy was a fucking nut-
ter, for God's sake) because she'd been feeling sorry for the guy but
really he was just *intruding* into her life uninvited — just like Mr.
Jessop — and she said, "Look, just leave me alone, will you? My
dad's a solicitor and he could make real trouble for you if you keep
turning up like this," and he said, "Your father can't stop our love,"
and then he slunk away, and the bar manager said, "Everything
okay?" and she said, "Yeah, just some guy who can't hold his drink."
Of course, she would never have told her father. He would have
worried himself to death. And anyway Stuart Lappin was harmless.
He was a total freak, but he was harmless.

The good thing about working in the bar was that she only
worked the evening shift and had the day to herself. It was going
to be a real drag being stuck in an office all day for the rest of the
summer. Dad was so happy and he was upset that he had to go to
Peterborough instead of being there for her first day.

She made him promise to walk to the station because he was
(supposedly) on a new, healthy regime after he'd been to the doctor.

"Don't forget your inhaler, Dad," she'd said to him as he was
leaving the house, and he patted his jacket pocket to prove it was
in there and said, "Cheryl will show you the ropes. I'll be back in
the office before lunch, maybe we can go out?" and she said,

"That would be nice, Dad." And then she saw him off at the front door, kissing him on the cheek, saying, "I love you, Dad," and he said, "Love you too, sweetheart," and she'd watched him walk down the street because she suddenly had a horrible feeling that she wasn't going to see him again, but when he got to the corner and turned back to look at her she gave him a cheerful wave because she didn't want him to know that she worried about him because he worried enough for the two of them.

She watched him disappear round the corner and felt her heart fill up and she wondered if she'd ever meet anyone she loved as much as her father. And then she cleared the breakfast table and loaded the dishwasher and made sure the house was clean and tidy for them both to come home to later.

26

Amelia

No more slaters, no more Garys and Craigs and Darryls. No more Philip and his yapping Pekingese. No more Oxford. No more old Amelia. A fresh start, a new person.

She had thought it might be an orgy, but it really was just the barbecue they had promised ("Oh, *do* come.") and the conversation was about the difficulty of finding a good plumber and how to keep snails off delphiniums ("Copper tape," Amelia offered and they all said, "Really? How fascinating!"). The only difference was that they were all naked.

When she arrived on the riverbank (feeling overdressed and terrified), Cooper ("Cooper Lock, erstwhile history professor at St. Cat's, now a ne'er-do-well,") strode toward her, his balls swinging, and said, "Amelia, you came, how wonderful," and Jean ("Jean Stanton, lawyer, amateur rock climber, local Conservative Party secretary") rushed up, all smiles and small bouncing breasts and said, "Good show. Everyone, this is Amelia Land. She's *so* interesting."

And then she had swum naked in the river with them and it had been just as she remembered it except that there was no swimming costume between her body and the water and she could feel the plants and weeds streaming over her body like thick wet ribbons.

And then they ate grilled sausages and steaks and drank South African Chardonnay as the twilight deepened and then later she had lain next to Jean, in Jean's pine sleigh bed in an attic room painted white and scented by Diptyque candles, the cost of one of which would probably have kept a family in Bangladesh for a year. But Amelia managed to ignore this fact, as she managed to ignore the fact that Jean was the secretary of the local Conservative Party (although obviously Jean's politics couldn't remain off the conversational agenda forever), and Amelia could ignore these things and many other things because even though Jean was in her fifties she had a hard, lithe, brown body that she slid along Amelia's own pale, soft body (she felt like a sea creature that had been shelled), and Jean said, "You're luscious, Amelia, like a big ripe melon," and the old Amelia would have snorted with derision at this point but the new Amelia cried out like a startled bird because Jean was lapping at her labia like a cat ("Oh, call it a cunt, Amelia, don't be shy,") and giving her her first-ever orgasm.

And it was funny because she really had wanted to die, and now she really wanted to live. Just like that. Really and truly there wasn't much more she could ask for. She had a huge garden to look after, as many cats as she could handle, and she had experienced an orgasm. Was she really a lesbian? She still wanted Jackson. "Everyone's bi these days," Jean said nonchalantly. Amelia thought she might introduce Jean to Julia. She would have liked just once to see Julia look shocked ("Jean, this is Julia, my sister. Julia, this is Jean, my lover. Henry? Oh, everyone's bi, Julia, these days, didn't you *know* that?" Ha!) She must try to be nicer to Julia — she was her sister, after all.

They had been unsure what to do with Olivia. Neither of them wanted to cremate her, to lose what little they had, so hard-won after all this time. On the other hand, she had been buried in the dark alone for so long that it seemed wrong to put her back in the ground. If it hadn't been against all social practice (and probably illegal) Amelia would have kept her bones on display, made a kind of reliquary, a shrine. In the end they buried her, in a tiny white coffin, that was laid alongside Annabelle, the afterthought baby, on top of Rosemary's coffin in the family plot. Amelia and Julia both sobbed throughout the funeral. The local press had tried to take photographs ("Lost local tot finally laid to rest") and Jackson's big black friend had got very demonstrative with them. Amelia found Howell both terrifying and ravishing at the same time (thereby testifying to her bisexual nature, she supposed) and much more politically correct than Jean, of course. Jackson — utterly bizarre — was accompanied by the yellow-haired homeless girl, who was now pink haired and no longer homeless. "Why?" Amelia said to Jackson and Jackson said, "Why not?" and Amelia said, "Because —" but Julia came along and dragged her away.

Did it feel better to have found Olivia? To know that she had wandered off, wandered off while she was in *her* care? Amelia had been fast asleep and her sister had wandered off and died. Didn't that make it her fault? Then Jackson had taken her aside at the funeral and said, "I'm going to break the sanctity of the confessional," as if he were a priest. He would have made a very good priest. The thought of Jackson as a priest was very alluring, in a perverted kind of way. "I'm going to tell you what happened," he said, "and then you have to decide what you want to do about it." He didn't tell Julia, he told *her*. She finally became the keeper of a secret.

So Olivia would have a shrine, she would have a garden. And Amelia would fill Binky Rain's garden with roses, with *Duchesse d'Angoulême* and *Félicité Parmentier,* Eglantines and Gertrude Jekylls, the pale rosettes of the *Boule de Neige* and the fragrant peachy Perdita, for their own lost girl.

27

CASE HISTORY NO. I 1970

Family Plot

It was so hot. Too hot to sleep. The streetlight shone through the thin summer curtains like a secondary, sickly sun. She still had a headache, like a rope tied tightly round her skull. Perhaps this was what a crown of thorns felt like. God must be making her suffer for a reason. Was it a punishment? Had she done something bad? Something worse than usual? She'd slapped Julia earlier today, but she was always slapping Julia, and she'd put nettles in Amelia's bed yesterday but Amelia was being a prig and deserved it. And she'd been horrible to Mummy, but Mummy had been horrible to her.

Sylvia took three junior aspirins from a bottle in the bathroom cabinet. There were always a lot of bottles of medicine in the cabinet — some had been there forever. Their mother liked medicine. She liked medicine more than she liked them.

It said two o'clock on the illuminated dial of the big alarm clock beside her mother's bed. Sylvia swept her little Eveready torch over the bed. Their father was snoring like a pig. He *was* a pig, a big mathematical pig. He was wearing striped pajamas and her mother was wearing a cotton nightdress with a tired frill around the neck. Their parents had flung the covers off and were lying with their limbs askew, as if they had been dropped from a height onto the bed. If she was a murderer she could have killed them right there in their beds without them ever knowing what had happened to them — she could stab them or shoot them or chop them with an ax and there would be nothing they could do about it.

Sylvia liked wandering the house at night — it was her own secret life that no one else knew about. It made her powerful, as if she could see their secrets too. She wandered into Julia's room, no chance of disturbing *her* sleep. You could have pushed her out of bed onto the floor and jumped on Julia and she wouldn't have woken up. You could have put a pillow over her face and suffocated her and she would have known nothing about it. She was drenched in sweat, you couldn't even put your hand near her she was so hot, and you could hear her breath being squeezed in and out of her lungs.

Sylvia suddenly realized that Amelia's bed was empty. Where was she? Did she have a secret, wandering nightlife too? Not Amelia — she didn't have the initiative (Sylvia's new word) for a secret life. Was she sleeping with Olivia? Sylvia hurried to Olivia's room and found Olivia was gone from her bed too. Half of them missing — not taken by aliens, surely? If aliens existed — and Sylvia suspected they did — God must have created them, because God created everything, didn't he? Or had he not actually created everything, only the matter in our own galaxy? And if there were other worlds then they must have been created by other gods, alien gods. Was that a blasphemous thought?

There wasn't really anyone she could consult with over these knotty theological problems. She wasn't allowed to go to church, Daddy didn't believe in God (or aliens) and the religious education teacher at school had told her that she had to stop "bothering" her so much. Imagine Jesus saying, "Go away, don't bother me so much." God would probably send the religious education teacher straight to hell. It was very difficult when you had been brought up by an atheist who was a mathematical pig and a mother who couldn't care less and then you heard the voice of God. There was so much she didn't know — but then look at Joan of Arc: she was an ignorant French peasant and she'd managed, and Sylvia was neither ignorant nor a peasant. After God spoke to her Sylvia began to read the Bible, at night under the bedcovers by the light of her trusty Eveready torch. The Bible bore no relation to Sylvia's life in any way. That alone made it very attractive.

Sylvia tried to recollect bedtime the previous evening but she could only form a hazy memory. She had felt sick with the heat and the sun and had gone to bed before anyone else. The minute her back was turned had Mummy allowed Amelia and Olivia to sleep in the tent? Would she? Mummy had been so adamant all summer (for no good reason whatsoever) that they couldn't sleep outside.

Sylvia crept downstairs, avoiding the two steps that creaked. The back door was unlocked so that anyone could have walked right in and done the aforementioned murdering in the beds. It was unlocked, of course, because Amelia and Olivia were sleeping in the tent. It would be dawn soon, she could already hear a solitary bird greeting the morning. The grass on the lawn was wet. Where did all the dew come from when it was so hot and dry during the day? She must look it up in a book. She trod carefully across the lawn in case she stood on the soft, sluggy body of some other nocturnal creature leading its own secret life.

She lifted the flap of the tent. Yes, they were both there! What a cheek. Why should Amelia get the prize of sleeping all night in the tent, and not just sleeping in the tent but sleeping with Olivia and Rascal? It wasn't fair. Sylvia was the eldest, she should be in the tent. Rascal climbed out from beside Olivia and wagged his tail and licked Sylvia's nose.

They were both sleeping on their backs, dead to the world, like corpses. Sylvia shook Amelia's feet but she wouldn't wake up. She squeezed herself into the tent, between the two of them. It was incredibly hot in the tent — it was probably hot enough to kill them. The hottest place on earth — was it the Atacama Desert? Death Valley in America? Somewhere in Mongolia? They weren't dead, were they? She pinched Amelia's nose and Amelia muttered something and rolled over. She should wake Olivia up and take her out of this hothouse. The Black Hole of Calcutta, the people who died in there died from the heat, not the lack of air — a common *misconception*. "Misconception" was an excellent word. The *afterthought* — there was a misconception if ever there was one. Ha. Their mother really should stop breeding, it was very *base*. Perhaps she was a secret Catholic. That would be wonderful, then they could have long, clandestine conversations about mystery and ritual and the Virgin Mary. Neither the Virgin Mary nor Jesus had spoken to Sylvia. She didn't think that Jesus actually spoke to people. Joan of Arc was another matter — Joan of Arc was downright chatty.

Sylvia rubbed Olivia's earlobe because Rosemary had once said that was how they roused sleeping patients when she was a nurse. Olivia stirred and then fell helplessly back into sleep. Sylvia whispered her name and she struggled to open her eyes. She was bewildered with sleep, but when Sylvia whispered, "Get up, come on," she followed Sylvia out of the tent, carrying her little pink rabbit slippers in her hand. Sylvia said, "Don't bother about your slippers, feel how wet the grass is between your toes," but Olivia shook her head and put her slippers on. Sylvia said, "You have to learn to be *rebellious*. You mustn't do everything Mummy and Daddy tell you. Especially Daddy." And then she added, "Except me, you should obey me." She wanted to say, "Because I have heard the word of God," but Olivia wouldn't understand. Nobody understood, except for God, of course, and Joan of Arc.

The first time God spoke to her she was sitting on the sidelines during a hockey match. Sylvia, an inventive right wing, had been sent off for hitting her opponent around the ankles with her stick (the whole point to win, surely?) and she was sulking furiously when a voice close by said, "Sylvia," but when she looked round there was no one there, only a girl called Sandra Lees who spoke with a squeaky Cambridge accent, so unless Sandra Lees was practicing ventriloquism or had changed into a man, it couldn't have

306 ～ KATE ATKINSON

been her. Sylvia decided she had imagined it, but then the voice said her name again — a deep, mellifluous voice, a voice that bathed her in warmth, and this time Sylvia whispered, very quietly on account of the proximity of Sandra Lees, "Yes?" and the voice said, "Sylvia, you have been chosen," and Sylvia said, "Are you God?" and the voice said, "Yes." You couldn't get a much clearer message than that, could you? And sometimes she felt so transformed by the holy light that she simply *swooned* away. She loved it when that happened, loved the feeling of losing control, of not being responsible for her body or her mind. Once (perhaps more than once), she had swooned in Daddy's study — blacking out and crumpling to the floor like a tortured saint. Daddy threw a glass of water in her face and told her to pull herself together.

Sylvia whispered to an almost sleepwalking Olivia, "Come on, let's go and play a game," and Olivia said, "No," and sounded whiny and not at all like her usual pliant self. "S'night," she objected, and Sylvia said, "So what?" and took her hand and they were halfway across the lawn when Olivia exclaimed, "Blue Mouse!" and Sylvia said, "Hurry up and fetch him then," and Olivia crawled back into the tent and reemerged, clutching Blue Mouse by one arm, Rascal bouncing happily at her heels.

Joan of Arc had spoken to her when she was sitting high up in the branches of Mrs. Rain's beech tree. Joan of Arc talked into her ear, for all the world as if she were sitting companionably on the branch next to her. The funny thing was that after these conversations Sylvia could never really remember anything that Joan of Arc had actually *said* and she had the impression that she hadn't spoken at all, she had *sung,* like a great bird perched in the tree.

God had chosen her, he had *noticed* her, but for what purpose? To lead a great army into battle and then burn in the fires of purification like Joan of Arc herself? To be sacrificed? From the Latin *sacer,* which meant "sacred," and *facere,* "to make." To make sacred.

She was holy, like a saint. She was special. She knew no one would believe her, of course. She told Amelia and Amelia said, "Don't be silly." Amelia had no imagination, she was so *dull*. She had tried to tell Mummy but she was baking a cake, watching the paddle of her Kenwood mixer going round and round as if she were hypnotized by it, and when Sylvia said, "I think God has spoken to me," she said, "That's nice," and Sylvia said, "A tiger's just eaten Julia," and her mother said, "Really?" in that same dreamy, abstracted way and Sylvia had stalked out of the room.

God continued to speak to her. He spoke to her from the clouds, from the bushes, he spoke to her as she was dropping off to sleep at night and he woke her in the morning. He spoke to her when she was on the bus and in the bath (her nakedness was nothing to be ashamed of in front of God), he spoke to her when she was sitting in the classroom or sitting at the dinner table. And he always spoke to her when she was in Victor's study. That was when he said to her, "Suffer the little children," because she was still, after all, a child.

"No," Olivia said loudly and started tugging on Sylvia's hand. "Shh, it's alright," Sylvia said, pushing open the wooden gate in the wall of Mrs. Rain's garden. "No," Olivia said, dragging her feet, but she had the strength of a kitten compared to Sylvia. "The witch," Olivia whispered. "Don't be silly," Sylvia said. "Mrs. Rain isn't really a witch, that's just a game we play." Sylvia wasn't actually sure if she believed that. But did God create a world that contained witches? And what about ghosts? Were there ghosts in the Bible? She was having to drag Olivia along now. She wanted to take her into the beech tree, she wanted to show her to Joan of Arc, show her how pure Olivia was, what a holy child she was, just like the baby Jesus. She wasn't sure how she was going to get Olivia up in the tree. There didn't seem much chance that she would actually climb it. Olivia started to cry. Sylvia began to get annoyed with her. The old witch would hear. "Be quiet, Olivia," she said sternly, and she yanked on her arm to pull her along. She hadn't meant to hurt her, she really hadn't, but Olivia started to cry and make a fuss (which wasn't like her, really it wasn't) and Sylvia hissed, "Don't," but Olivia just *wouldn't* stop it so Sylvia had to put her hand over her mouth. And then she had to keep it there for the longest time until Olivia was finally quiet.

Suffer the little children to come unto me. A sacrifice. Sylvia had thought that she was going to be the sacrifice, martyred because God had chosen her. But it turned out that it was Olivia who was meant to be given up to God. Like Isaac, only, of course, he hadn't actually died, had he? Olivia was sacred now. Pure and holy. She was pure and holy and safe. She couldn't be touched. She would never have to go into Daddy's study, she would never have to choke on Daddy's stinky thing in her mouth, never feel his huge hands on her body making her impure and unholy. Sylvia looked at the small body lying in the long grass and didn't know what to do. She would have to get someone to help her. The only person she could think of was Daddy. She would have to fetch Daddy. He would know what to do.

28

And Julia Said

*A*u *revoir tristesse.* Jackson drove with the top down, the Dixie Chicks playing loudly on the car stereo. He picked them up at Montpellier Airport. They were dressed ready for the convertible, in chiffon head scarves and sunglasses, so that Julia looked like a fifties movie star and Amelia didn't. Julia had said on the phone that Amelia was a lot more cheerful these days, but if she was then she was keeping it to herself, sitting in the backseat of his new BMW M3, harrumphing and grunting at everything that Julia said. Jackson suddenly regretted not buying the two-seater BMW Z8 instead — then they could have put Amelia in the boot.

"Cigarette?" Julia offered, and Jackson said, "No, I've given them up," and Julia said, "Well done you."

They drove into Montpellier, where it was very hot, and where they ate little silver dishes of ice-cream — *glaces artisanales* — in a café in the town square. Julia ordered and Jackson was impressed by her proficient French.

"She used to be a poodle," Amelia said (unfathomably), and Julia said, "Don't be such a crosspatch, Milly, we're *en vacances,*" and Amelia said, "You're always on holiday," and Julia said, "Well, I can think of worse ways to live your life," and Jackson wondered if he was in love with Julia and then the sky suddenly darkened to the color of ripe Agen plums, thunder growled in the distance, and the first drops of heavy rain thudded onto the café's canvas awning and Julia shrugged (in a commendably French way) at Jackson and said, "*C'est la vie,* Mr. Brodie, *c'est la vie.*"

ACKNOWLEDGMENTS

With thanks to:

My agent, Peter Straus

My editor, Marianne Velmans

Maureen Allan, Helen Clyne, Umar Salam,
Ali Smith, and Sarah Wood
for Cambridge in July, with special gratitude to Ali Smith

Reagan Arthur, Eve Atkinson-Worden, Helen Clyne,
and Marianne Velmans for being enthusiastic manuscript readers

My cousin, Major Michael Keech

Stephen Cotton, he knows why

David Lindgren for the sheep story

And last, but not least, Russell Equi,
god of all things vehicular

Reading Group Guide

Case Histories

A

Novel by

KATE ATKINSON

A GOOD MAN IS HARD TO FIND

Kate Atkinson talks with
Sally Stanton for *Publishers Weekly*

Do you see your new novel, Case Histories, *as a cross-genre book?*
I'm not sure I even know what that means. I don't think of myself
as writing in a particular genre. I don't know what genre you
would say my first three novels belong to. I know people talk about
Case Histories being "a literary crime novel," but I think of it as a
novel that contains several crimes and mysteries. There is always a
mystery to be solved at the heart of everything I write.

Did any true-life crimes inspire the events in Case Histories?
I didn't go looking for particular cases, or information about what
happens if you put an axe in someone's head. If I come across
something and need to know more about it, I run immediately to
the Internet, so all my research is ad hoc. The sister of a close
friend was murdered a couple of years ago — in quite banal circumstances (if such a thing can be called banal) — and that set me
thinking a lot about what it's like when something dreadful and ir-
reparable happens out of the blue.

*You've written a screenplay — did any contemporary actors pop into
your head as you were imagining Jackson Brodie, the private detective
in* Case Histories?
A screenplay exists in limbo for *Behind the Scenes at the Museum.*
There's an actor over here [in Britain] called Ken Stott who's very
Jacksonlike, although it's only since people have pointed that out
to me that I realize it.

Were you very surprised to receive the Whitbread Book of the Year Award for Behind the Scenes at the Museum? *How did it affect your writing?*

Well, I had a one-in-five chance, so not that surprised. I doubt that I started writing differently because of the prize.

The protagonists in your past novels have mostly been women (and girls). What prompted you to create Jackson Brodie?

I thought it was time to try and write a man who wasn't a wimp or dead. I wanted to write a good man but with a darkness at his core, a world-weary kind of hero. I think it's difficult for writers to get into the psyche of the opposite gender.

You endow the lives of your characters with a rich variety of family dysfunction. Is there any resemblance to your own history?

Hah! Novelists write fiction, by definition. All families are "dysfunctional" in that there is no standard or norm of "functional." Parenting is like writing, most people just make it up as they go along.

There is such a wonderful undercurrent of cynical humor in Case Histories, *yet the finale has an upbeat, hopeful feel. Do you consider yourself an optimist?*

Some days an optimist, some days a pessimist. Pretty much like everyone, I should think!

Are you a fan of any crime writers?

I love Lee Child and Harlen Coben. I like to read dynamic, page-turning books.

Can readers look forward to seeing more of Jackson Brodie in the future?

I have a lot more plans for Jackson. A good man is hard to find.

This interview originally appeared in Publishers Weekly, *October 25, 2004. Reprinted by permission.*

1. It's quite clear to the three eldest Land girls that their baby sister Olivia is their parents' favorite child. Do all parents have a special affection for a particular son or daughter? How does Victor and Rosemary's fondness for Olivia affect the personalities and lives of her sisters?

2. Theo idealizes Laura and he is protective of her to a fault — it's as if he is amazed that such a perfect woman could be the product of a man as imperfect as he. How do Theo's insecurities about himself distort his perception of Laura? How is her untimely death more devastating to Theo and the reader because of her apparent flawlessness? How would Theo's tragedy be different if Laura were different?

3. Michelle derives very little pleasure or joy from motherhood. For her, playing wife and mommy is an almost unbearable burden. Is Michelle a bad mother? Is her attitude toward parenthood any different from Victor and Rosemary's, or does she only manage it more poorly?

4. When we first meet Jackson, he's sitting in a used sports car, smoking a cigarette, listening to a ladies' radio program, thinking about his beloved daughter and his selfish ex-wife, all while spying on a woman. What kind of first impression does he make on the reader? Is the complexity of his personality endearing, perplexing, or off-putting? How does this first encounter make more sense as the novel progresses?

5. While Amelia and Julia think Olivia might still be alive, poor Theo knows for certain that Laura is dead. At one point, Jackson

admires Theo, thinking: "Just carrying on living required a kind of strength and courage that most people didn't have." Do you agree? Is not knowing the fate of a loved one preferable to being aware of his or her death simply because it allows room for hope? Or does not knowing present a new kind of grief that precludes any opportunity for closure and healing?

6. Amelia can't bring herself to tell Julia about the night she caught Victor molesting Sylvia. How might sharing this knowledge change their pursuit of Olivia? How might it change their relationship?

7. At times, *Case Histories* can be quite gruesome, the tragedies its characters face quite devastating — and yet Kate Atkinson maintains a sense of humor throughout the book. Is this humor inappropriate, or is there an element of the comic in even the most traumatic of human experiences? How does the humor affect the suspense and mystery?

8. In many ways *Case Histories* follows the rules of the mystery genre, but it also subverts them. How does the novel differ from other mysteries you've read? How would you classify it: mystery or family drama? Why?

9. *Case Histories* deftly weaves three plot lines into one narrative. Which of the three, if any, do you think could have been its own novel? Which characters would you like to know more about? Why?

10. Jackson Brodie will return in Kate Atkinson's next novel. Can you predict how his life might have changed after the events of *Case Histories?* What would you like to see him doing? With whom?

Kate Atkinson is the author of three previous novels —
Behind the Scenes at the Museum, which won the Whit-
bread Award for Book of the Year; *Human Croquet;* and
Emotionally Weird — and a collection of short fiction,
Not the End of the World. She lives in Scotland.

. . . AND HER MOST
RECENT NOVEL

Kate Atkinson's next novel, featuring Jackson Brody, the
detective hero of *Case Histories,* will be published by
Little, Brown and Company in fall 2006. Following is an
excerpt from the novel's opening pages.

He was lost. He wasn't used to being lost. He was the kind of man who drew up plans and then executed them efficiently, but now everything was conspiring against him in ways he decided he couldn't have foreseen. He had been stuck in a jam on the A1 for two mind-numbing hours so that it was already past the middle of the morning when he arrived in Edinburgh. Then he'd gone adrift on a one-way system and been thwarted by a road that had been closed because of a burst water main. It had been raining, steadily and unforgivingly, on the drive north and had only begun to ease off as he hit the outskirts of town. The rain had in no way deterred the crowds—it had never occurred to him that Edinburgh was in the middle of the Festival and that there would be carnival hordes of people milling around as if the end of a war had just been declared. The closest he had previously got to the Edinburgh Festival was accidentally turning on *Late Night Review* and seeing a bunch of middle-class wankers discussing some pretentious piece of theater.

He ended up in the dirty heart of the city, on a street that somehow seemed to be on a lower level than the rest of the town, a blackened urban ravine. The rain had left the cobbles slick and greasy and he had to drive cautiously because the street was teeming with people haphazardly crossing over or standing in little knots in the middle of the road, as if no one had told them that roads were for cars and sidewalks were for pedestrians. A queue snaked the length of the street—people waiting to get into what looked like a bomb hole in the wall but which announced itself as FRINGE VENUE 164 on a large placard outside the door.

The name on the driver's license in his wallet was Paul Bradley. "Paul Bradley" was a nicely forgettable name. He was several degrees of separation away from his real name now, a name that no longer felt as if it had ever belonged to him. When he wasn't working he often (but not always) went by the name Ray. Nice and simple. Ray of light, Ray of darkness. Ray of sunshine, Ray of night. He liked slipping between identities, sliding through the cracks. The rental Peugeot he was driving felt just right, not a flashy macho machine but the kind of car an ordinary guy would drive. An ordinary guy like Paul Bradley. If anyone asked him what he did, what Paul Bradley did, he would say, "Boring stuff. I'm just a desk jockey, pushing papers around in an accounts department."

He was trying to drive and at the same time decipher his *A–Z of Edinburgh* to work out how to escape this hellish street, when someone stepped in front of the car. It was a type he loathed—a young dark-haired guy with thick, black-framed spectacles, two days of stubble, and a cigarette hanging out of his mouth. There were hundreds of them in London, all trying to look like French existentialists from the sixties. He'd bet that not one of them had ever opened a book on philosophy. He'd read the lot—Plato, Kant, Hegel—even thought about one day doing a degree.

He braked hard and didn't hit the spectacled guy, just made him give a little jump, like a bullfighter avoiding a bull. The guy was furious, waving his cigarette around, shouting, raising a finger to him. Charmless, devoid of manners—were his parents proud of the job they'd done? He hated smoking, it was a disgusting habit, hated guys who gave you the finger and screamed, *"Spin on it,"* saliva flying out of their filthy, nicotine-stained mouths.

He felt the bump, about the same force as hitting a badger or a fox on a dark night, except it came from behind, pushing him forward. It was just as well the spectacled guy had performed his little *paso doble* and got out of the way or he would have been pancaked. He looked in the rearview mirror. A blue Honda Civic, the driver climbing out—big guy, slabs of weight-lifter muscle, gym-fit rather than survival-fit, he wouldn't have been able to last three months in the jungle or the desert the way that Ray could have done. He wouldn't have lasted a day. He was wearing driving gloves, ugly black leather ones with knuckle holes. He had a dog in the back of the car, a beefy rottweiler, exactly the dog you would have guessed a guy like that would have. The guy was a walking cliché. The dog was having a seizure in the back, spraying saliva all over the window, its claws scrabbling on the glass. The dog didn't worry him too much. He knew how to kill dogs.

Ray got out of the car and walked round to the back bumper to inspect the damage. The Honda driver started yelling at him, "You stupid fucking *twat,* what did you think you were *doing?*" English. Ray tried to think of something to say that would be nonconfrontational, that would calm the guy down—you could see he was a pressure cooker waiting to blow, *wanting* to blow, bouncing on his feet like an out-of-condition heavyweight. Ray adopted a neutral stance, a neutral expression, but then he heard the crowd give a little collective "Aah" of horror and he registered the baseball bat that had suddenly appeared in the guy's hand out of nowhere and thought, *Shit.*

. . .Gloria hadn't really seen what had happened. By the time the rumor of it had rippled down the spine of the queue she suspected it had become a Chinese whisper. *Someone had been murdered.* "Queue jumping, probably," she said matter-of-factly to a twittery Pam standing next to her. Gloria was stoical in queues, irritated by people who complained and shuffled as if their impatience was in some way a mark of strong character. Queuing was like life: you just got on with it. Gloria was born to queue. She wondered if she could have made a living from it. *I'll queue for you.* It seemed a shame she had been born just too late for the Second World War; she possessed exactly the kind of long-suffering spirit that wartime relied on. Stoicism was, in Gloria's opinion, a much underrated virtue in the modern world.

She could understand why someone might want to kill a queue jumper. If it had been up to her she would have summarily executed a great many people by now—people who dropped litter in the street, for example. They would certainly think twice about the discarded candy wrapper if it resulted in being strung up from the nearest lamppost. Gloria used to be opposed to capital punishment, she remembered, during her too-brief time at university, demonstrating against an execution in some faraway country that she couldn't have placed on the map, but now her feelings tended to run in quite the opposite direction.

Gloria liked rules, rules were Good Things. Gloria liked rules that said you couldn't speed or park on double yellow lines, rules that told you not to drop litter or deface buildings. She was sick and tired of hearing people complain about speed cameras and parking wardens as if there were some reason that they should be exempt from them. When she was younger she used to fantasize about sex and love, about keeping chickens and bees, being taller, running through fields with a black-and-white border collie. Now she daydreamed about being the keeper at the gates, of standing with the ultimate ledger and ticking off the names of the dead as they appeared before her, giving them the nod-through or the thumbs-down. All those people who parked in bus bays and ran the red light on pedestrian crossings were going to be very sorry when Gloria peered at them over the top of her spectacles and asked them to account for themselves.

Pam wasn't what Gloria would have called a friend, just someone she had known for so long that she had given up trying to get rid of her. Pam was married to Murdo Miller, Gloria's own husband's closest friend. Graham and Murdo had attended the same Edinburgh school, an expensive education that had put a civil polish on their basically loutish characters. They were now both much richer than their fellow alumni, a fact that Murdo said "just goes to show." Gloria thought that it didn't go to show anything except, possibly, that they were greedier and more ruthless than their former classmates. Graham was the son of a builder (Hatter Homes) and had started his career carrying hods of bricks on one of his father's small building sites. Now he was a multimillionaire property developer. Murdo was the son of a man who owned a small security firm (Haven Security) and had started off as a bouncer at a pub door. Now he ran a huge security operation—clubs, pubs, football matches, concerts. Graham and Murdo had many business interests in common, concerns that spread everywhere and had little to do with building or security and required meetings in Jersey, the Caymans, the Virgin Islands. Graham had his fingers in so many pies that he had run out of fingers long ago. "Business begets business," he explained to Gloria, "money makes money." The rich get richer and the poor get poorer.

Both Graham and Murdo lived with the trappings of respectability—houses that were too big for them, cars that they exchanged each year for a newer model, wives that they didn't. They wore blindingly white shirts and handmade shoes, they had bad livers and untroubled consciences, but beneath their aging hides they were barbarians.

"Did I tell you we've had the downstairs cloakroom done out?" Pam said. "Hand stenciling. I wasn't sure but I'm coming round to it."

"Mm," Gloria said. "Fascinating."

It was Pam who had wanted to come to this lunchtime radio recording (*Edinburgh Festival Comedy Showcase*) and Gloria had tagged along in the hope that at least one of the comics might be funny, although her expectations were not high. Unlike some Edinburgh residents who regarded the advent of the annual Festival as something akin to the arrival of the Black Death, Gloria quite enjoyed the atmosphere and liked to attend the odd play or a concert at the Queen's Hall. Comedy, she wasn't so sure about.

"How's Graham?" Pam asked.

"Oh, you know," Gloria said, "he's Graham." That was the truth of it, Graham was Graham, there was nothing more, nor less, that Gloria could say about her husband.

"There's a police car," Pam said, standing on tiptoe to get a better look. "I can see a man on the ground. He looks dead." She sounded thrilled. Gloria had fallen to dwelling a lot on death recently. Her elder sister had died at the beginning of the year and then a few weeks ago she had received a postcard from an old school friend informing her that one of their group had recently succumbed to cancer—the message "Jill passed last week. The first of us to go!" seemed unnecessarily jaunty. Gloria was fifty-nine and wondered who would be the last to go and whether it was a competition.

"Policewomen," Pam trilled happily.

An ambulance nosed its way cautiously through the crowd. The queue had shuffled on considerably so now they could see the police car. One of the policewomen shouted at the crowd not to go into the venue but to stay where they were because they would be collecting statements from them about the "incident."

Gloria had been brought up in a northern town. Larry, her father, a morose yet earnest man, sold insurance door-to-door to people who could barely afford it. Gloria didn't think people did that anymore. Gloria's past already seemed an antiquated curiosity—a virtual space re-created by the museum of the future. When he was at home and not lugging his ancient briefcase from one unfriendly doorstep to another, her father spent his time slumped in front of the fire, devouring detective novels and sipping conservatively from a half-pint glass mug of beer. Her mother, Thelma, worked part-time in a local chemist's shop. For work, she wore a knee-length white coat, the medical nature of which she offset with a large pair of pearl and gilt earrings. She claimed that working in a chemist made her privy to everyone's intimate secrets, but as far as the young Gloria could tell she spent her time selling insoles and cotton wool, and the most excitement she derived from the job was arranging the Christmas window with tinsel and Yardley gift boxes.

Gloria's parents led drab, listless lives that the wearing of pearl and gilt earrings and the reading of detective novels did little to enliven. Gloria presumed her life would be quite different—that glorious things would happen to her (as her name implied), that she would be illuminated within and without and her path would scorch like a comet's. This did not happen! Beryl and Jock, Graham's parents, weren't that different from Gloria's own parents. They had more money and were further up the social ladder, but they had the same basic low expectations of life. They lived in a pleasant "Edinburgh bungalow" in Corstorphine and Jock owned a relatively modest building firm from which he had made a decent living. Graham himself had done a year of civil engineering at Napier ("waste of fucking time") before joining his father in the business. Within a decade he was in the boardroom of his own large empire, *Hatter Homes, Real Homes for Real People*. Gloria had thought that slogan up many years ago and now really wished that she hadn't. Graham and Gloria had married in Edinburgh rather than in Gloria's hometown (Gloria had come to Edinburgh as a student), and her parents traveled up on a cheap day return and were away again as soon as the cake was cut. The cake was Graham's mother's Christmas cake, hastily converted for the wedding. Beryl always made her cake in September and left it swaddled in white cloths in the larder to mature, tenderly unwrapping it every week and adding a baptismal slug of brandy. By the time Christmas came around the white cloths were stained the color of mahogany. Beryl fretted over the cake for the wedding, as it was still far from its nativity (they were married at the end of October), but she put on a stalwart face and decked it out in marzipan and royal icing as usual. In place of the centerpiece snowman, a plastic bridal couple was caught in the act of an unconvincing waltz. Everyone presumed Gloria was pregnant (she wasn't), as if that would be the only reason Graham would have married her.

Perhaps their decision to marry in a register office had thrown the parents off balance, "But it's not as if we're Christians, Gloria," Graham had said, which was true. Graham was an aggressive atheist and Gloria—born one-quarter Leeds Jewish, one-quarter Irish Catholic, and raised a West Yorkshire Baptist—was a passive agnostic, although, for want of anything better, "Church of Scotland" was what she had put on her hospital admission form when she had to have a bunion removed two years ago, privately at the Murrayfield. If she imagined God at all it was as a vague entity that hung around behind her left shoulder, rather like a nagging parrot. Long ago, Gloria was sitting on a bar stool in a pub on the George IV Bridge in Edinburgh, wearing (unbelievable though it now seemed) a daringly short miniskirt, self-consciously smoking an Embassy and drinking a gin-and-orange and hoping she looked pretty while around her raged a heated student conversation about Marxism. Tim, her boyfriend at the time—a gangly youth with a white boy's Afro before Afros of any kind were fashionable—was one of the most vociferous of the group, waving his hands around every time he said *exchange of commodities* or *the rate of surplus value* while Gloria sipped her gin-and-orange and nodded sagely, hoping that no one would expect her to contribute because she hadn't the faintest idea what they were talking about. She was in the second year of her degree, studying history but in a lackadaisical manner that ignored the political (the Declaration of Arbroath and Tennis-Court Oaths) in favor of the romantic (Rob Roy, Marie Antoinette), which didn't endear her to the teaching staff.

She couldn't remember Tim's surname now—all she could remember about him was his great cloud of hair, like a dandelion clock. Tim declared to the group that they were all working class now. Gloria frowned because she didn't want to be working class, but everyone around her was murmuring in agreement—although there wasn't one of them who wasn't the offspring of a doctor or a lawyer or a businessman—when a loud voice announced, "That's shite. You'd be nothing without capitalism. Capitalism has saved mankind." And that was Graham.

He was wearing a sheepskin coat, a secondhand-car salesman's kind of coat, and drinking a pint on his own in the corner of the bar. He had seemed like a man, but he hadn't even reached his twenty-fifth birthday, which Gloria could see now was nothing. And then he downed his beer and turned to her and said, "Are you coming?" and she'd slipped off her bar stool and followed him like a little dog because he was so forceful and attractive compared to someone with dandelion-clock hair.

And now it was all coming to an end. Yesterday the Specialist Fraud Unit had made an unexpected but polite appearance at Hatter Homes' headquarters on Queensferry Road and now Graham feared that they were about to throw a light into every murky corner of his business dealings. He had arrived home late, the worse for wear, downed a double of Macallan without even tasting it, and then slumped on the sofa, staring at the television like a blind man. Gloria fried a lamb chop with leftover potatoes for him and said, "Did they find your secret books then?" and he laughed grimly and said, "They'll never find my secrets, Gloria," but for the first time in the thirty-nine years Gloria had known him, he didn't sound cocky. They were coming for him, and he knew it.

It was the field that had done it for him. He had bought a green-belt site that had no planning permission attached to it, and he had got the land cheaply—land without planning permission was just a field, after all—but then, hey presto, six months later the planning permission was granted and now a hideous estate of two-, three-, and four-bedroom "family homes" was under construction on the northeastern outskirts of town.

A tidy little sum to someone in the planning department was all it had taken, the kind of transaction Graham had done a hundred times before, *greasing the wheels,* he called it. For Graham it had been a little thing; his corruption was so much wider and deeper and far-reaching than a little green field on the edge of town. But it was the little things that often brought big men down.

Once the ambulance containing the Peugeot driver had disappeared, the policewomen started to take statements from the crowd. "Hopefully we'll get something on the CCTV," one of them said, indicating a camera that Gloria hadn't noticed, high up on a wall. Gloria liked the idea that there were cameras watching everyone everywhere. Last year Graham had installed a new state-of-the-art security system in the house—cameras and infrared sensors and panic buttons and goodness knows what else. Gloria was fond of the helpful little robots that patrolled her garden with their spying eyes.

Once the eye of God watched people; now it was the camera lens.

"There was a dog," Pam said, fluffing her apricot-tinted hair self-consciously.

"Everyone remembers the dog," the policewoman sighed. "I have several very accurate descriptions of the dog, but the Honda driver is variously described as 'dark, fair, tall, short, skinny, fat, midtwenties, fiftyish.' No one even took down his car's registration number. You would think someone would have managed that."

"You would," Gloria agreed. "You would think that." They were too late now for the BBC radio showcase. Pam was delighted that they had been entertained by drama rather than comedy.

"And I've got the Book Festival on Thursday," she said. "You're sure you don't want to come?" Pam was a fan of some crime writer who was reading at the Book Festival. Gloria was no fan of crime writing—it had sucked the life out of her father, and anyway there was enough crime in the world without adding to it, even if it was only fictional.

"It's just a bit of escapism," Pam said defensively. If you needed to escape, in Gloria's opinion, then you just got in a car and drove away. Gloria's favorite novel still resolutely remained *Anne of Green Gables,* which, when she was young, had represented a mode of being that, although ideal, hadn't yet become impossible.

"We could go for a nice cup of tea somewhere," Pam said, but Gloria excused herself, saying, "Things to do at home," and Pam said, "What things?"

"Just things," Gloria said. She was in an eBay auction that closed in two hours for a pair of Staffordshire greyhounds and she wanted to be in there at the finish.

"My, but you're a woman of secrets, Gloria."

"No, I'm not," Gloria said.